DEAD EYES

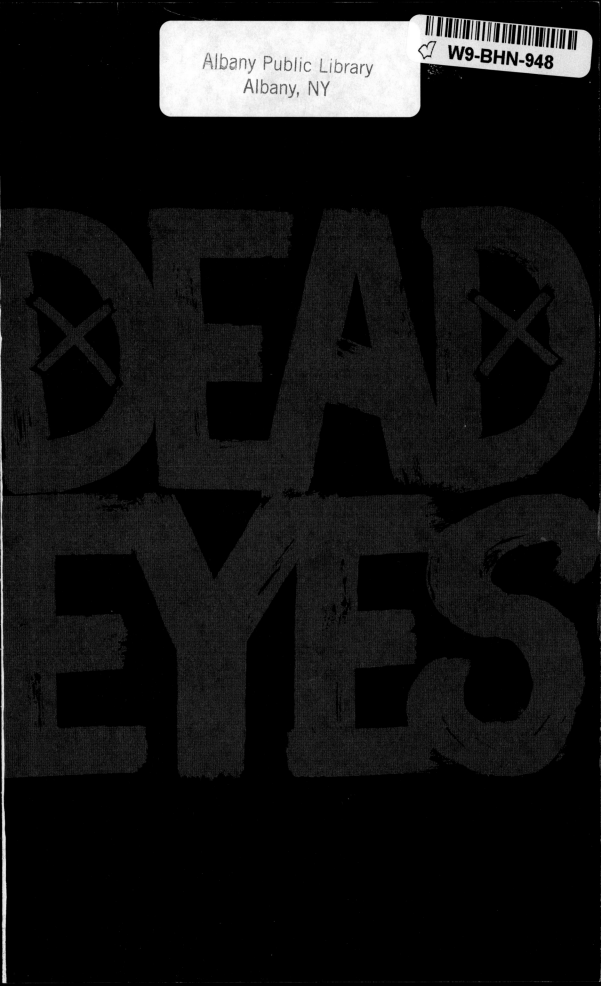

Writer: GERRY DUGGAN

Artist: JOHN McCREA

Colorist: MIKE SPICER

Letterer: JOE SABINO

Editor: WILL DENNIS

Cover: JOHN McCREA

LOGO & COVER DESIGN: DREW GILL

PRODUCTION & DESIGN: DEANNA PHELPS

IMAGE COMICS, INC. • Robert Kirkman: Chief Operating Officer • Erik Larsen: Chief Financial Officer • Todd McFarlane: President • Marc Silvestri: Chief Executive Officer • Jim Valentino: Vice President • Eric Stephenson: Publisher / Chief Creative Officer • Jeff Boison: Director of Publishing Planning & Book Trade Sales • Chris Ross: Director of Digital Services • Jeff Stang: Director of Direct Market Sales • Kat Salazar: Director of PR & Marketing • Drew Gill: Cover Editor • Heather Doornink: Production Director • Nicole Lapalme: Controller • IMAGECOMICS.COM

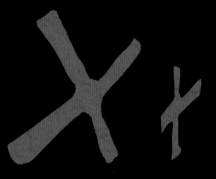

CHAPTER ONE

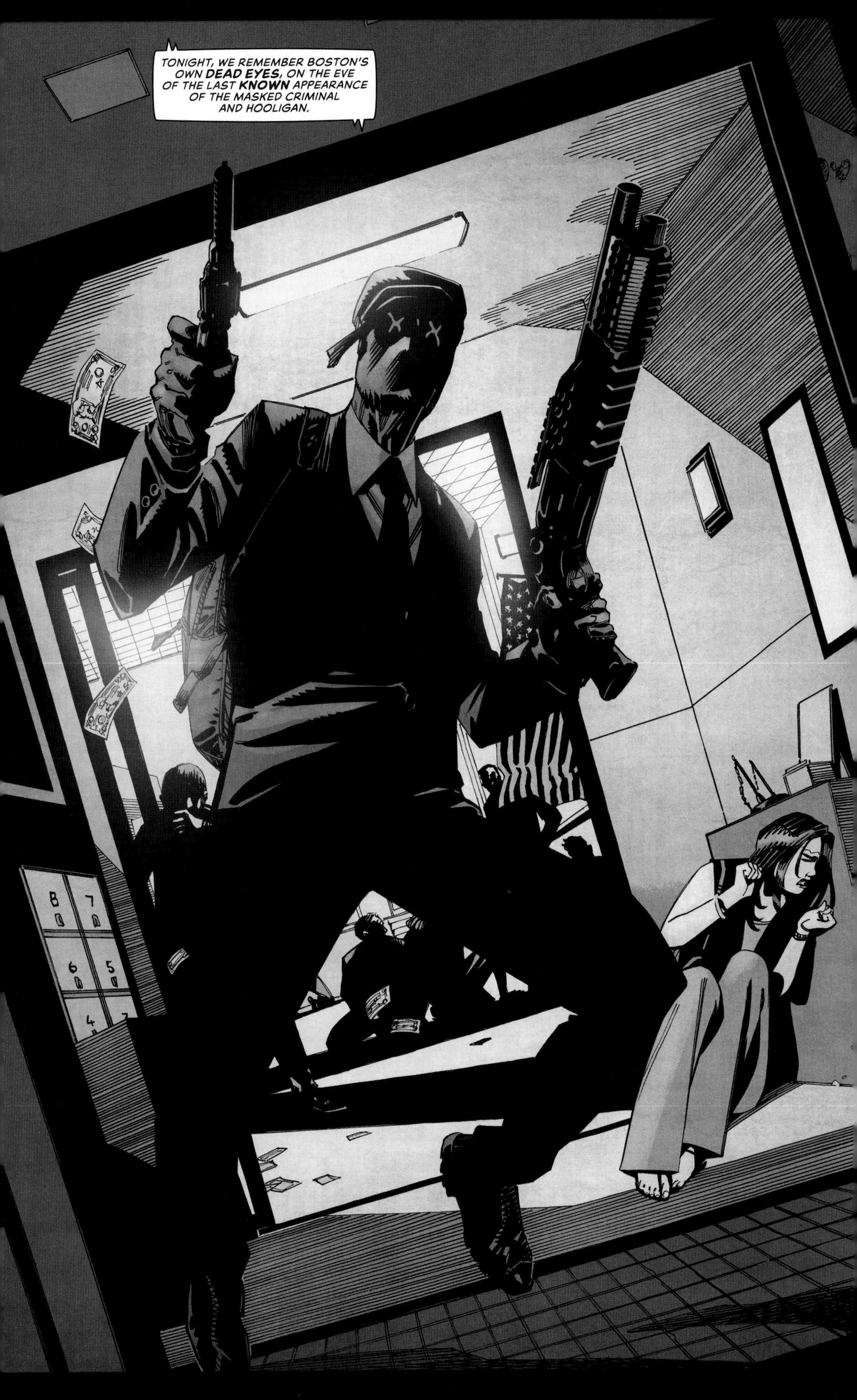
TONIGHT, WE REMEMBER BOSTON'S OWN **DEAD EYES**, ON THE EVE OF THE LAST **KNOWN** APPEARANCE OF THE MASKED CRIMINAL AND HOOLIGAN.

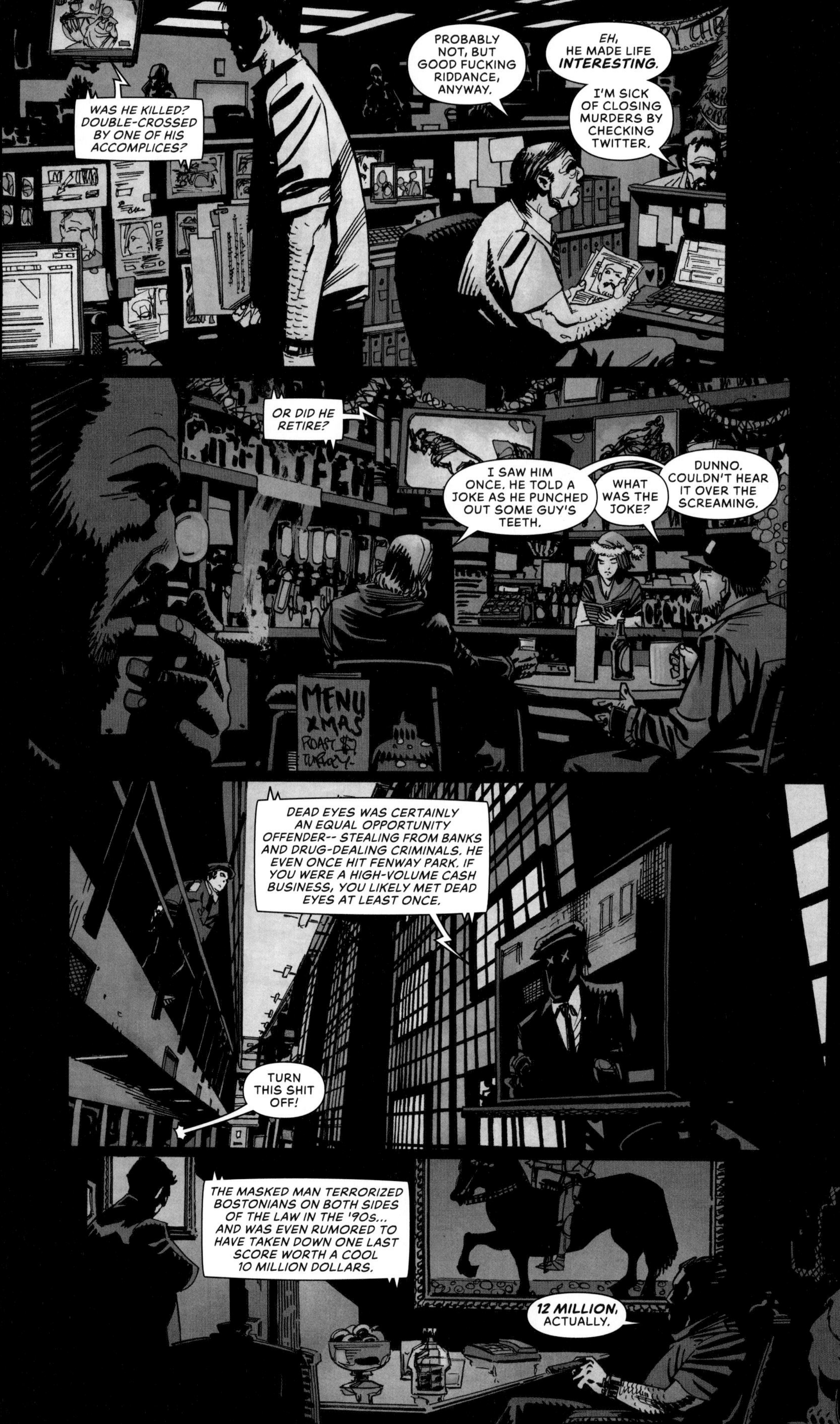
WAS HE KILLED? DOUBLE-CROSSED BY ONE OF HIS ACCOMPLICES?
PROBABLY NOT, BUT GOOD FUCKING RIDDANCE, ANYWAY.
EH, HE MADE LIFE **INTERESTING**.
I'M SICK OF CLOSING MURDERS BY CHECKING TWITTER.
OR DID HE RETIRE?
I SAW HIM ONCE. HE TOLD A JOKE AS HE PUNCHED OUT SOME GUY'S TEETH.
WHAT WAS THE JOKE?
DUNNO. COULDN'T HEAR IT OVER THE SCREAMING.
MENU
XMAS
DEAD EYES WAS CERTAINLY AN EQUAL OPPORTUNITY OFFENDER-- STEALING FROM BANKS AND DRUG-DEALING CRIMINALS. HE EVEN ONCE HIT FENWAY PARK. IF YOU WERE A HIGH-VOLUME CASH BUSINESS, YOU LIKELY MET DEAD EYES AT LEAST ONCE.
TURN THIS SHIT OFF!
THE MASKED MAN TERRORIZED BOSTONIANS ON BOTH SIDES OF THE LAW IN THE '90S... AND WAS EVEN RUMORED TO HAVE TAKEN DOWN ONE LAST SCORE WORTH A COOL 10 MILLION DOLLARS.
12 MILLION, ACTUALLY.

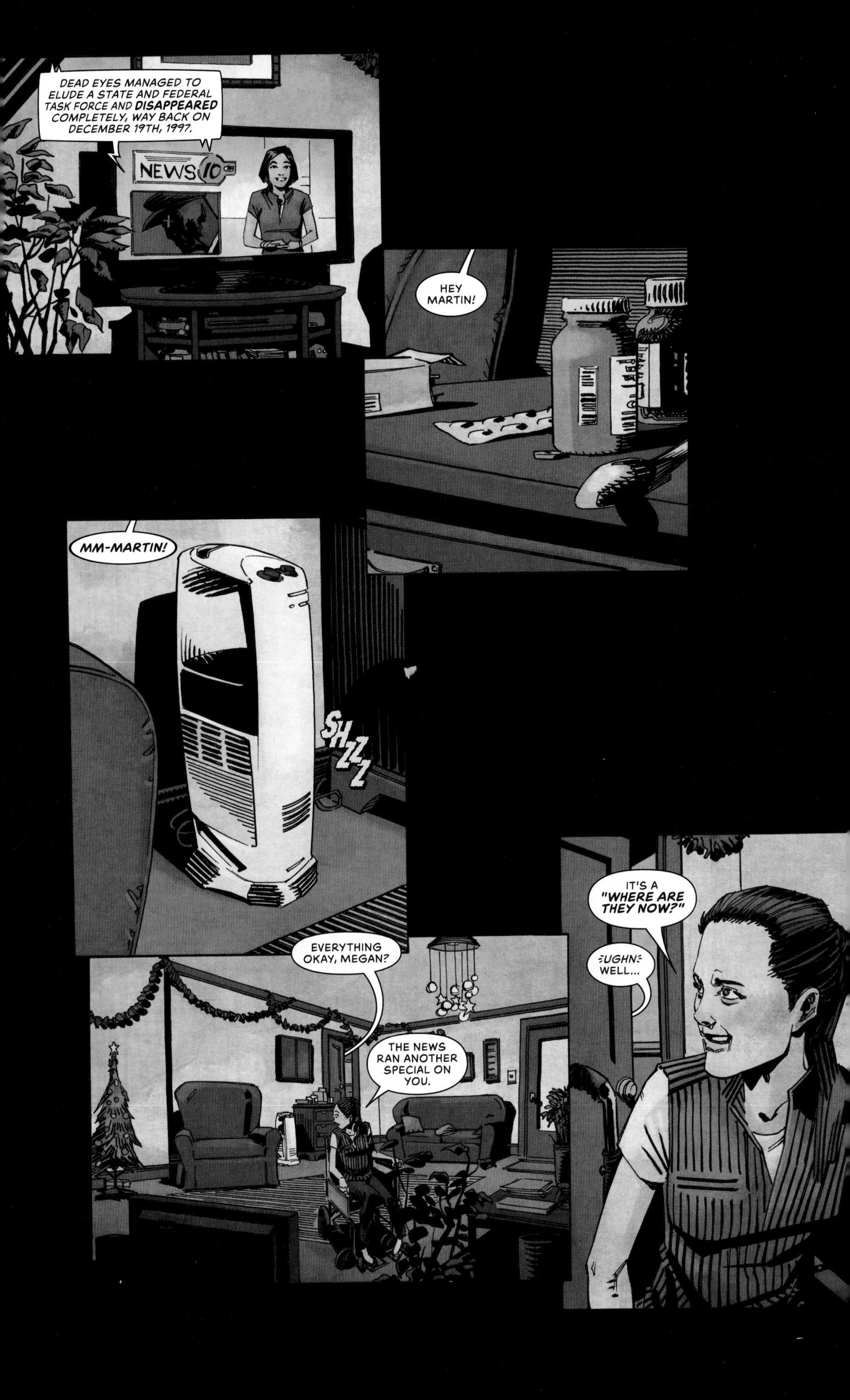
DEAD EYES MANAGED TO ELUDE A STATE AND FEDERAL TASK FORCE AND **DISAPPEARED** COMPLETELY, WAY BACK ON DECEMBER 19TH, 1997.
NEWS 10
HEY MARTIN!
MM-MARTIN!
SHZZZ
EVERYTHING OKAY, MEGAN?
THE NEWS RAN ANOTHER SPECIAL ON YOU.
IT'S A ***"WHERE ARE THEY NOW?"***
UGHN WELL...

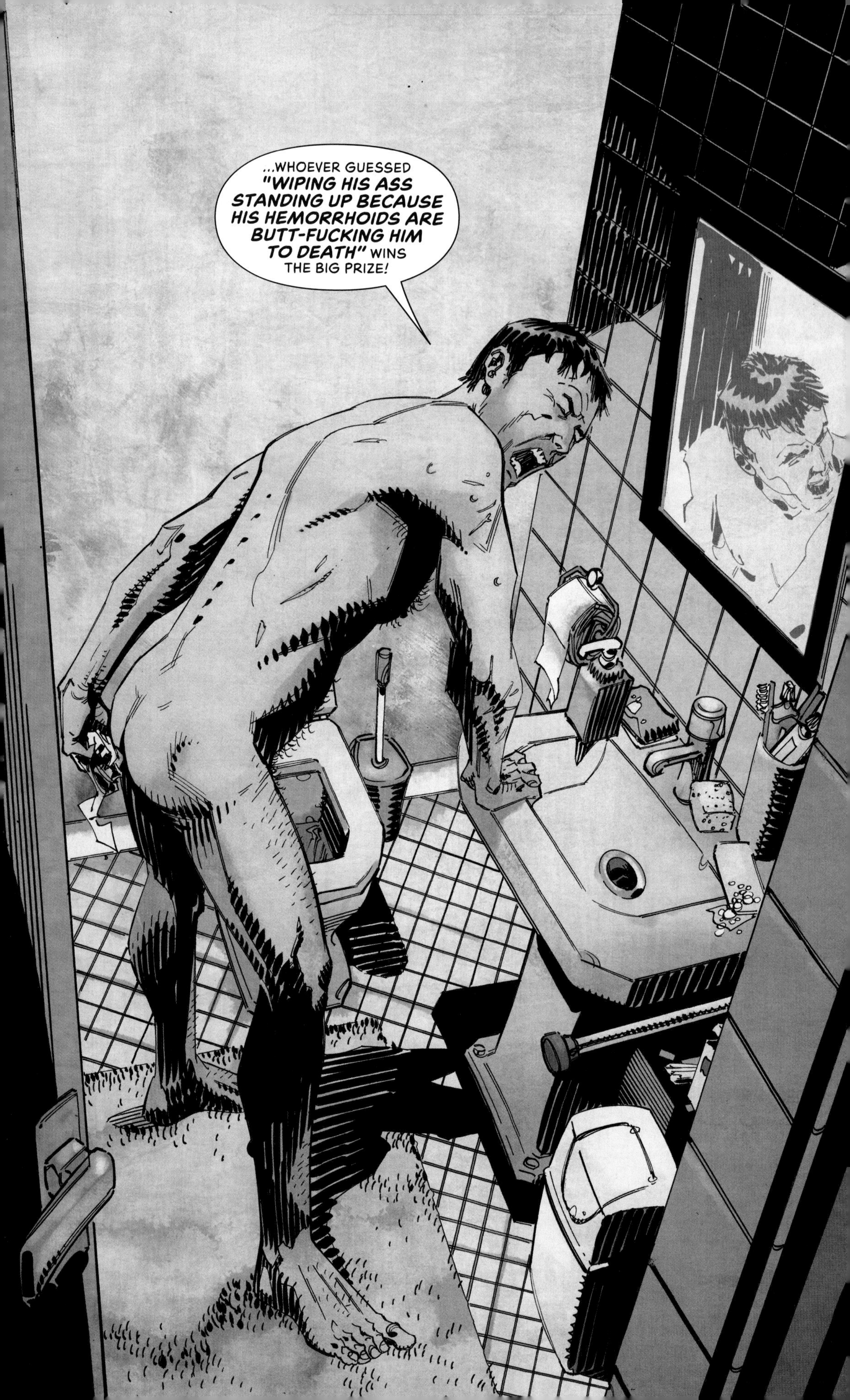
...WHOEVER GUESSED "WIPING HIS ASS STANDING UP BECAUSE HIS HEMORRHOIDS ARE BUTT-FUCKING HIM TO DEATH" WINS THE BIG PRIZE!

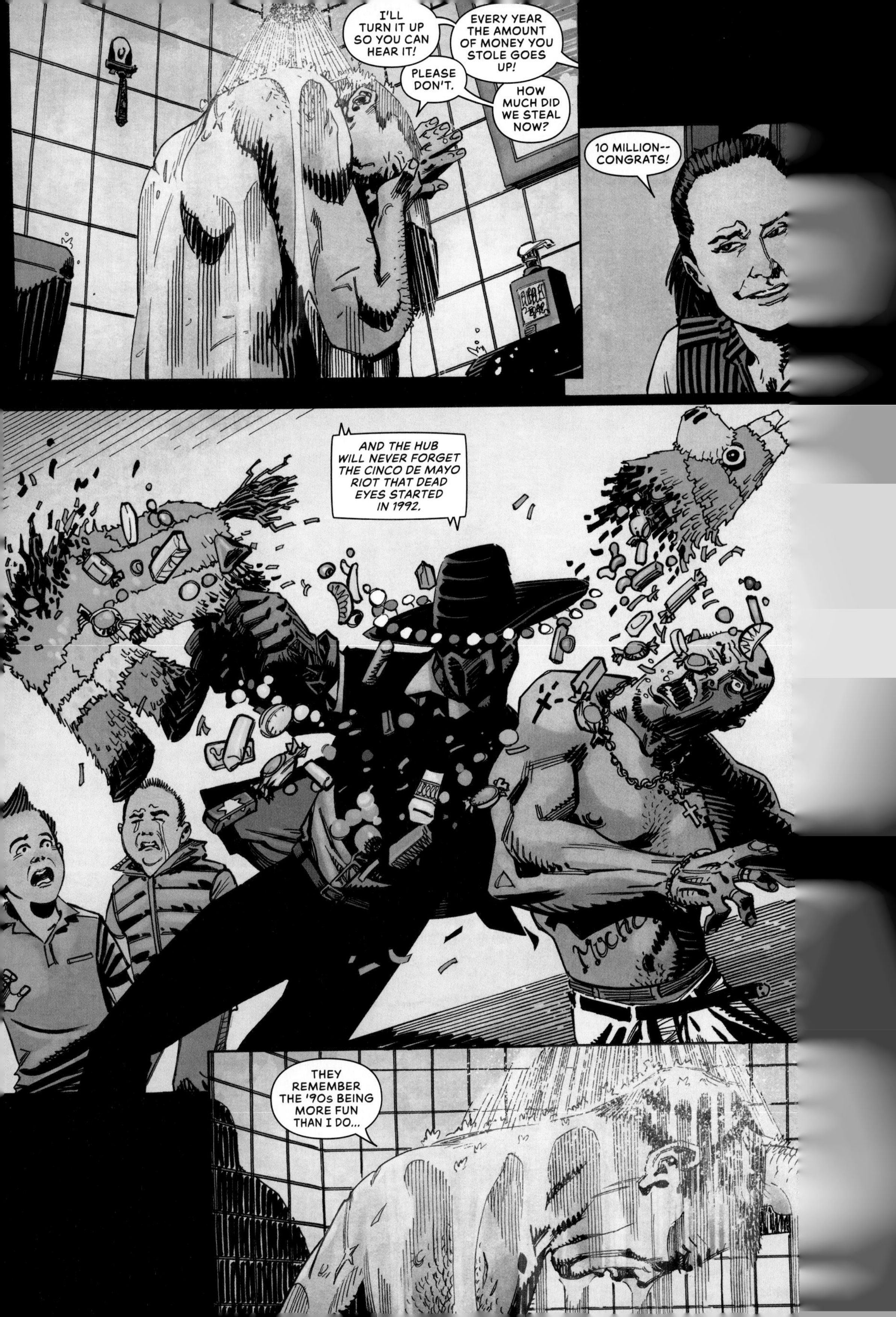

I'LL TURN IT UP SO YOU CAN HEAR IT!
EVERY YEAR THE AMOUNT OF MONEY YOU STOLE GOES UP!
PLEASE DON'T.
HOW MUCH DID WE STEAL NOW?
10 MILLION-- CONGRATS!
AND THE HUB WILL NEVER FORGET THE CINCO DE MAYO RIOT THAT DEAD EYES STARTED IN 1992.
THEY REMEMBER THE '90s BEING MORE FUN THAN I DO...

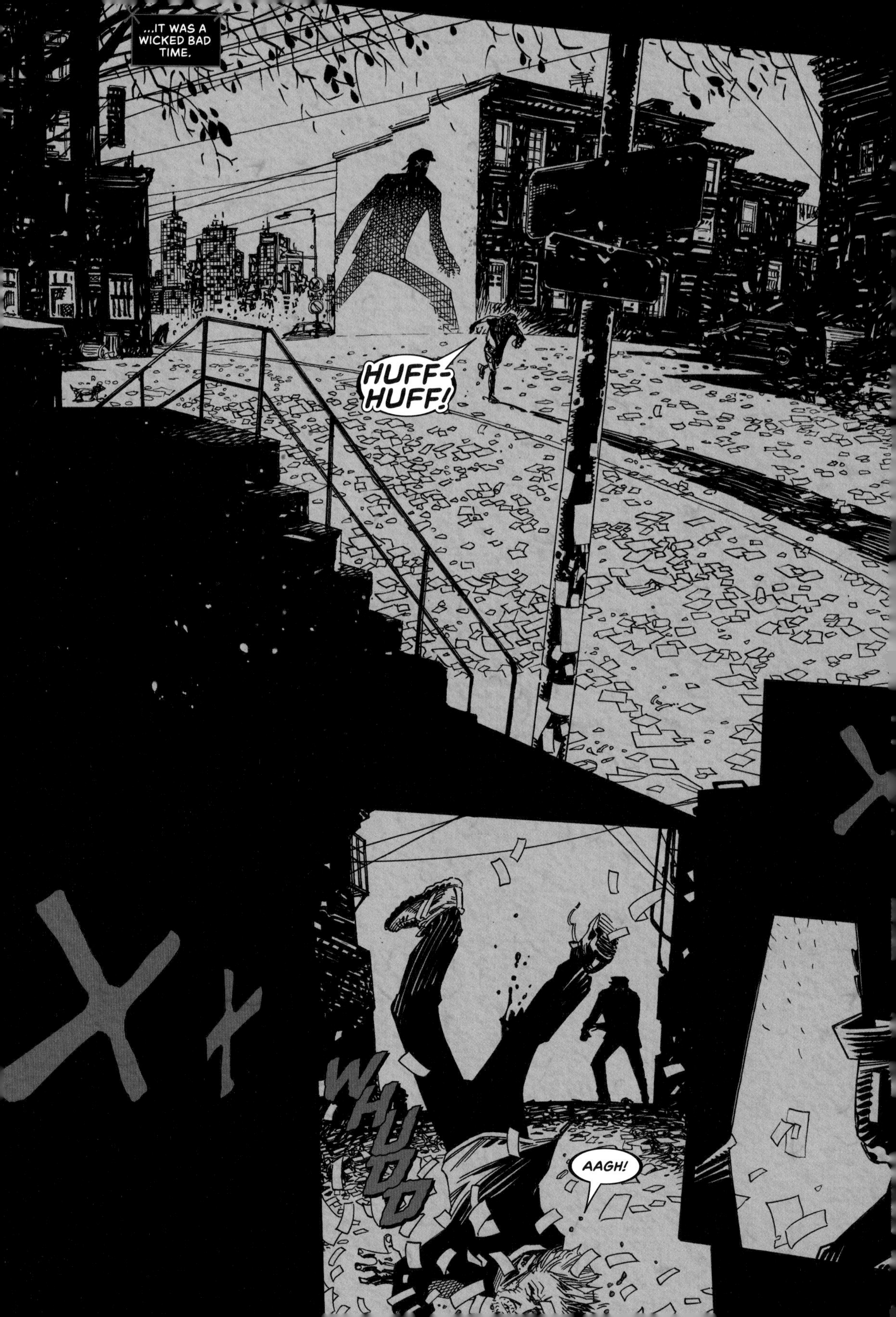
...IT WAS A WICKED BAD TIME.
HUFF-HUFF!
WHUDD
AAGH!

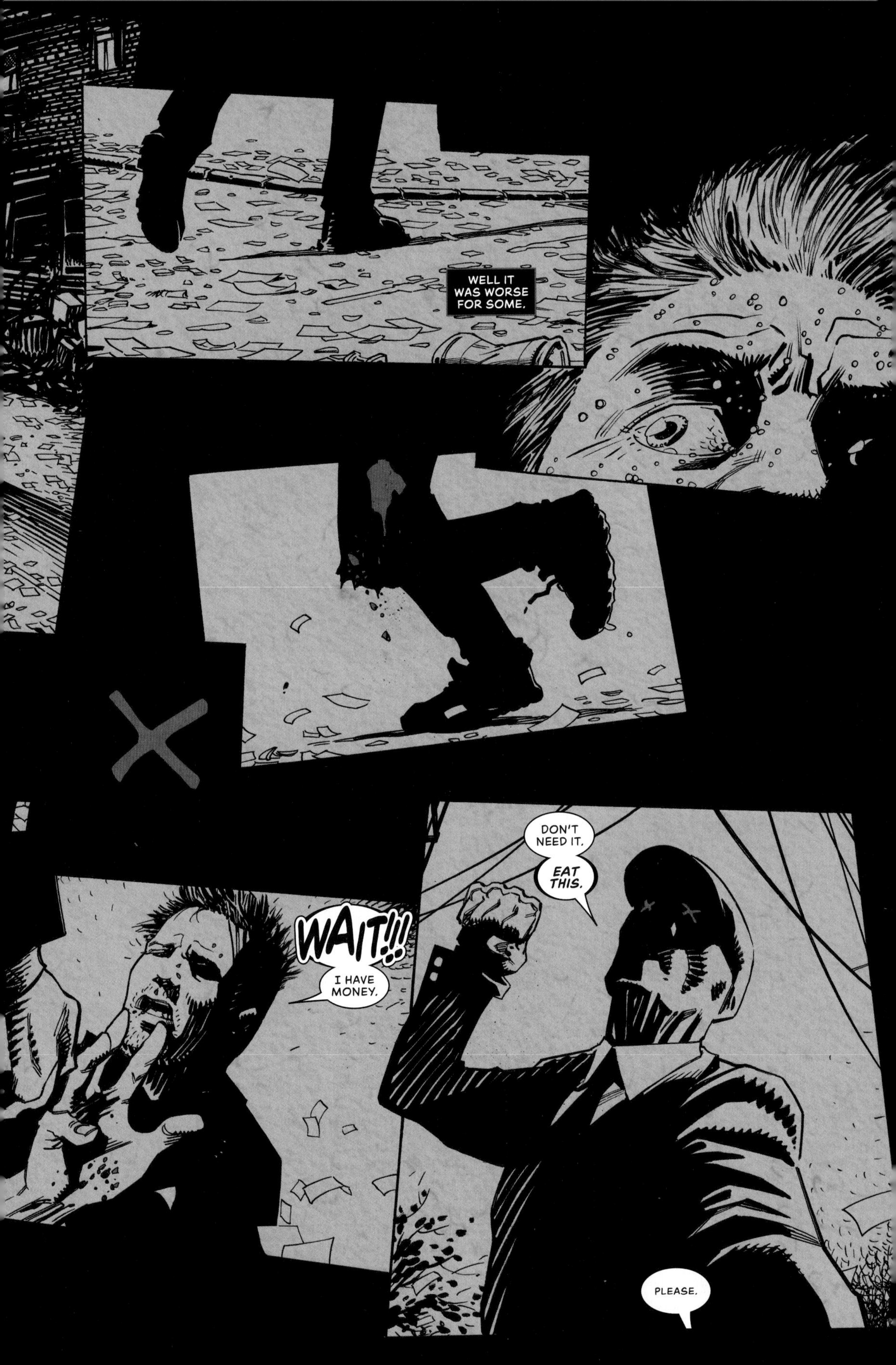
WELL IT WAS WORSE FOR SOME.
WAIT!!!
I HAVE MONEY.
DON'T NEED IT.
EAT THIS.
PLEASE.

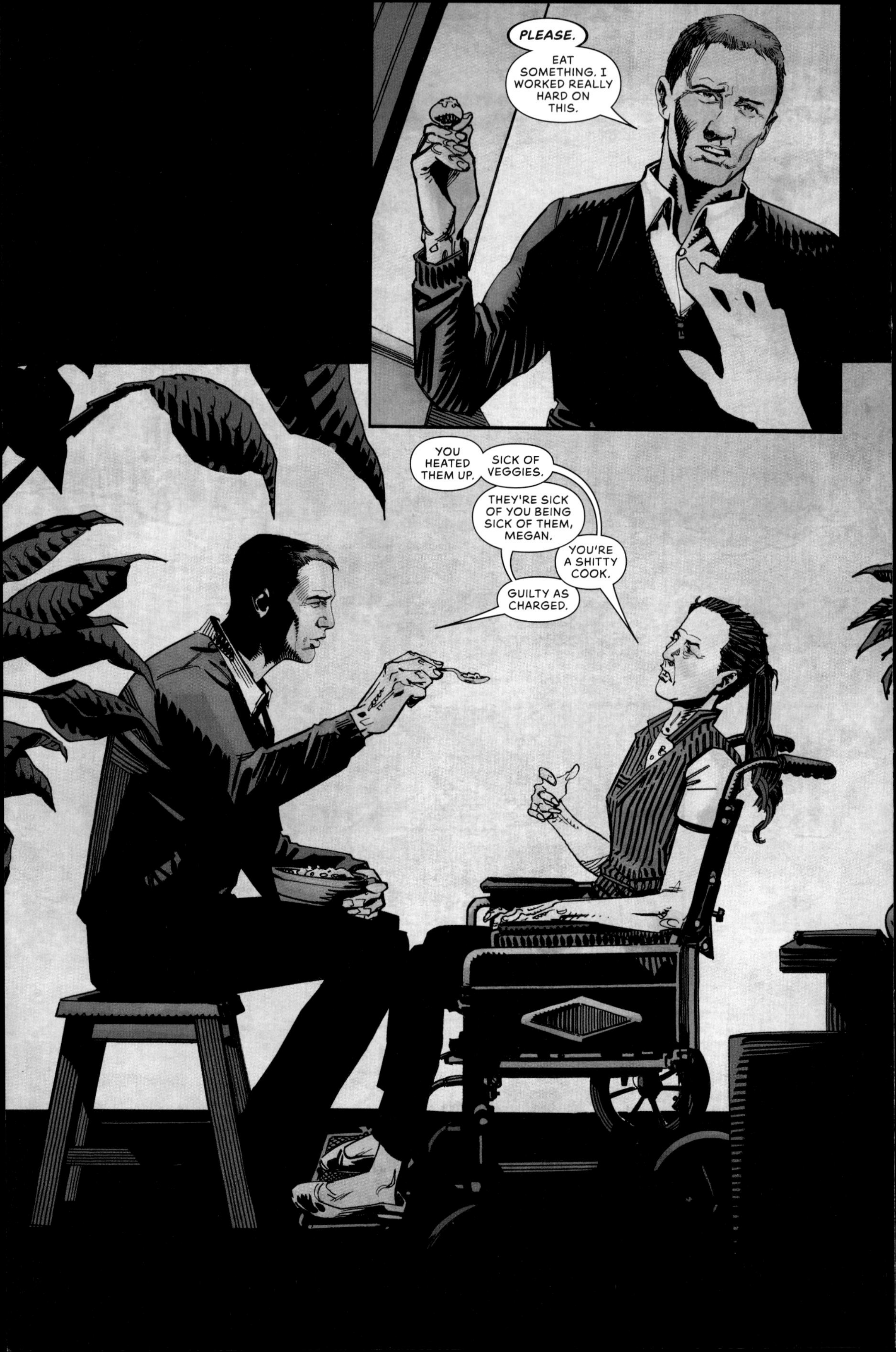
PLEASE.
EAT SOMETHING. I WORKED REALLY HARD ON THIS.
YOU HEATED THEM UP.
SICK OF VEGGIES.
THEY'RE SICK OF YOU BEING SICK OF THEM, MEGAN.
YOU'RE A SHITTY COOK.
GUILTY AS CHARGED.

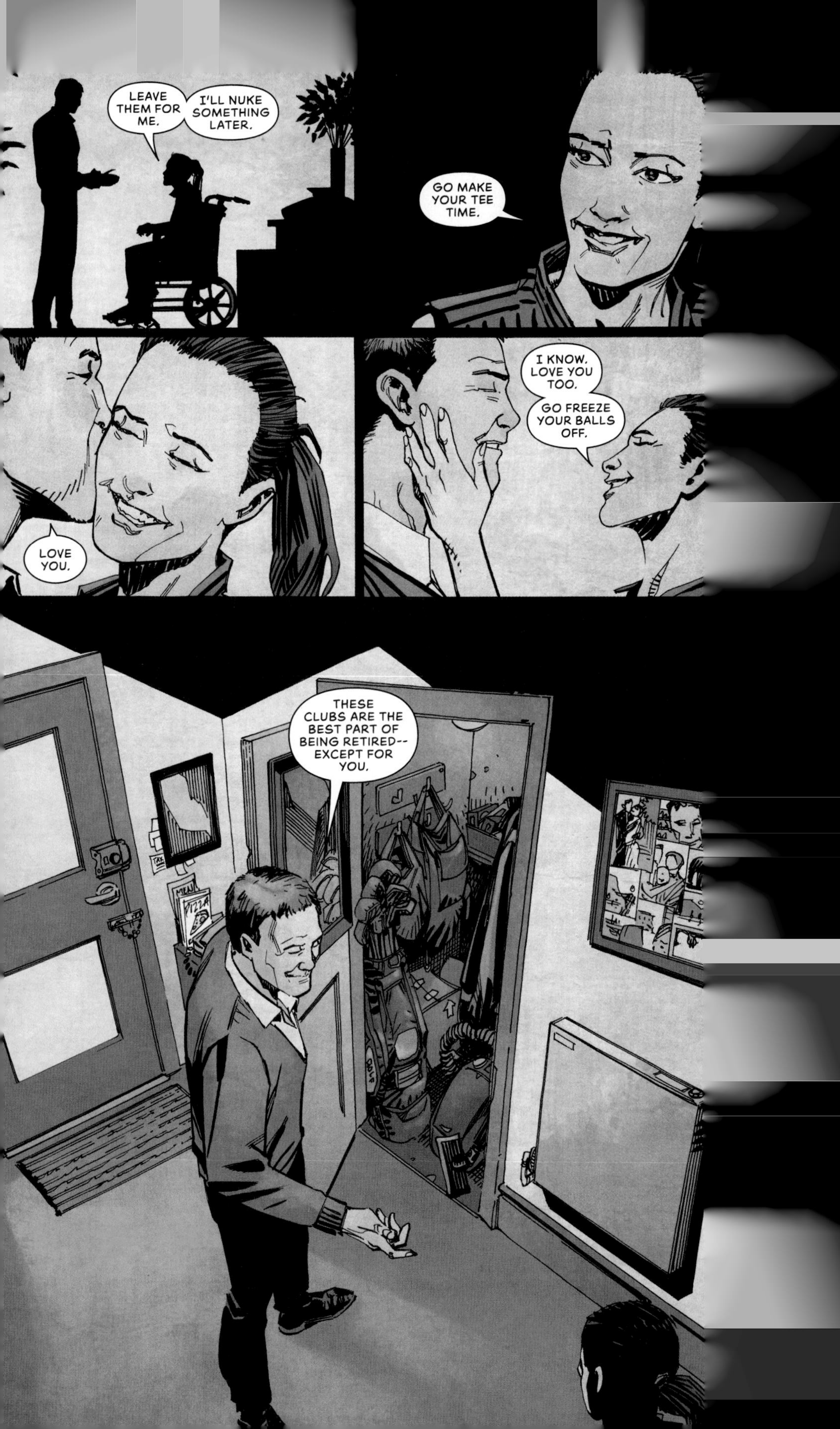
LEAVE THEM FOR ME.
I'LL NUKE SOMETHING LATER.
GO MAKE YOUR TEE TIME.
LOVE YOU.
I KNOW. LOVE YOU TOO.
GO FREEZE YOUR BALLS OFF.
THESE CLUBS ARE THE BEST PART OF BEING RETIRED--EXCEPT FOR YOU.

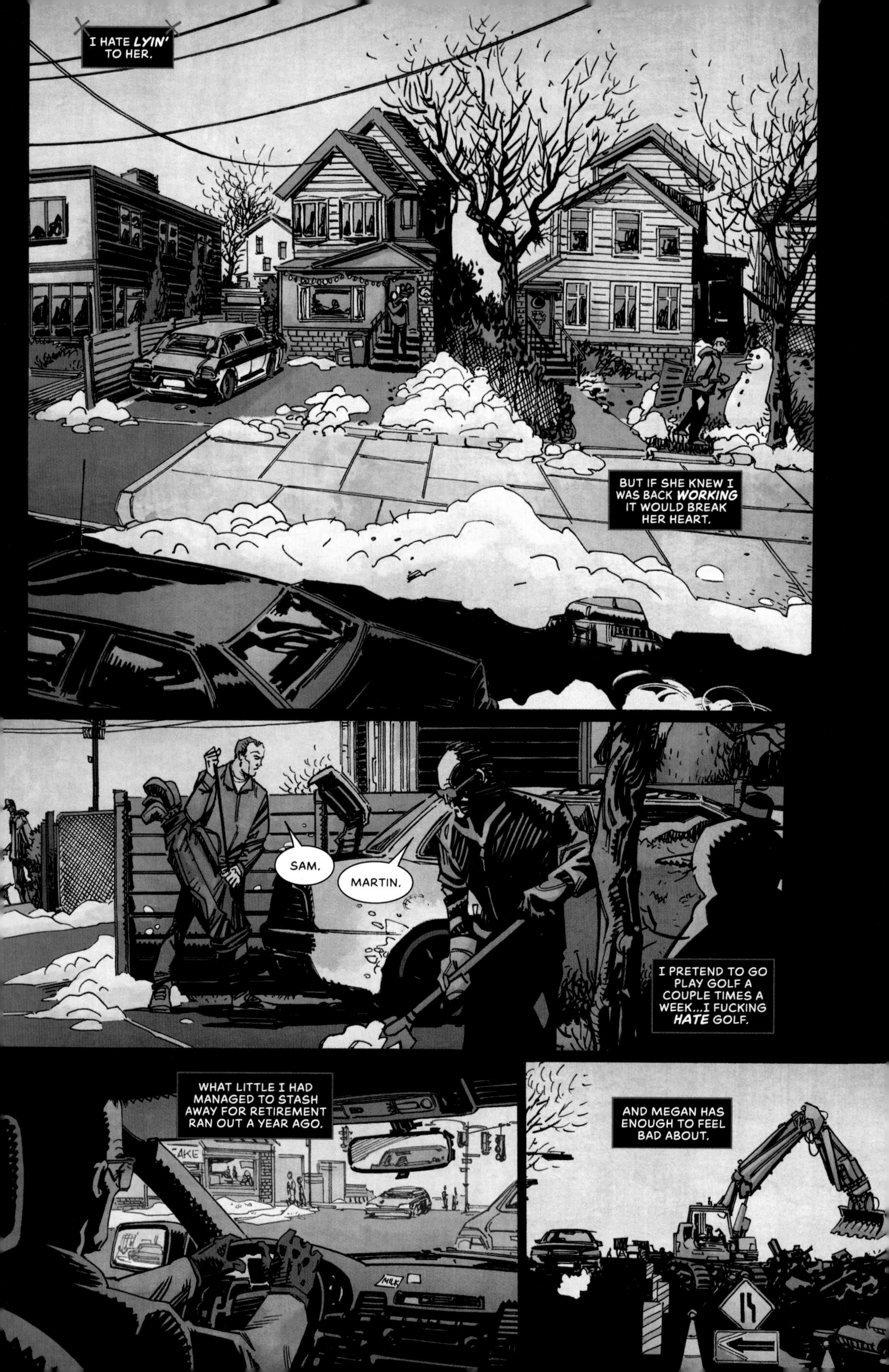
I HATE LYIN' TO HER.
BUT IF SHE KNEW I WAS BACK WORKING IT WOULD BREAK HER HEART.
SAM.
MARTIN.
I PRETEND TO GO PLAY GOLF A COUPLE TIMES A WEEK...I FUCKING HATE GOLF.
WHAT LITTLE I HAD MANAGED TO STASH AWAY FOR RETIREMENT RAN OUT A YEAR AGO.
MILK
AND MEGAN HAS ENOUGH TO FEEL BAD ABOUT.

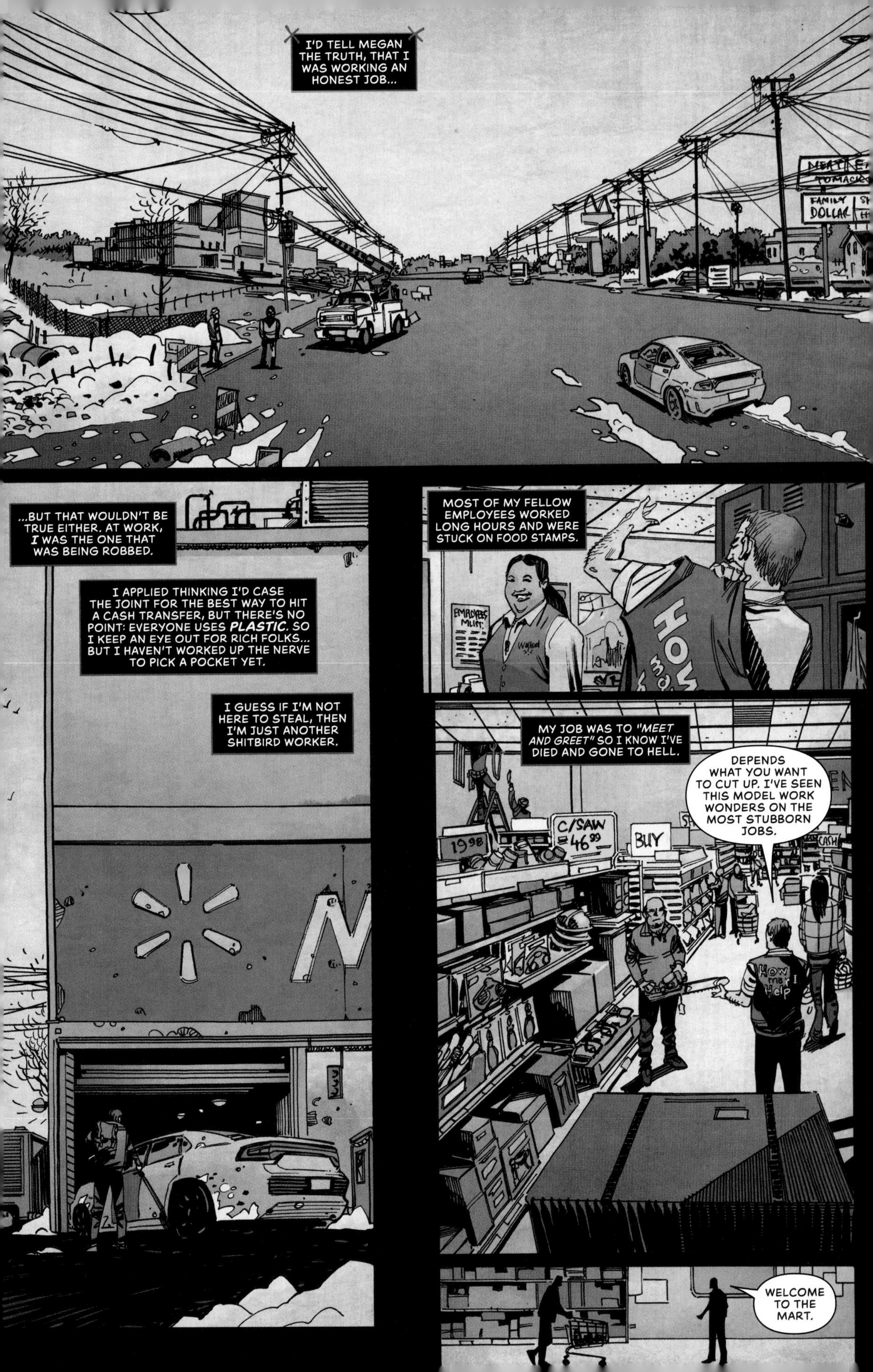
I'D TELL MEGAN THE TRUTH, THAT I WAS WORKING AN HONEST JOB...
FAMILY DOLLAR
...BUT THAT WOULDN'T BE TRUE EITHER. AT WORK, *I* WAS THE ONE THAT WAS BEING ROBBED.
I APPLIED THINKING I'D CASE THE JOINT FOR THE BEST WAY TO HIT A CASH TRANSFER, BUT THERE'S NO POINT: EVERYONE USES ***PLASTIC***. SO I KEEP AN EYE OUT FOR RICH FOLKS... BUT I HAVEN'T WORKED UP THE NERVE TO PICK A POCKET YET.
I GUESS IF I'M NOT HERE TO STEAL, THEN I'M JUST ANOTHER SHITBIRD WORKER.
MOST OF MY FELLOW EMPLOYEES WORKED LONG HOURS AND WERE STUCK ON FOOD STAMPS.
EMPLOYEES MUST:
MY JOB WAS TO *"MEET AND GREET"* SO I KNOW I'VE DIED AND GONE TO HELL.
DEPENDS WHAT YOU WANT TO CUT UP. I'VE SEEN THIS MODEL WORK WONDERS ON THE MOST STUBBORN JOBS.
C/SAW 46.99
19.98
BUY
How may I Help
WELCOME TO THE MART.

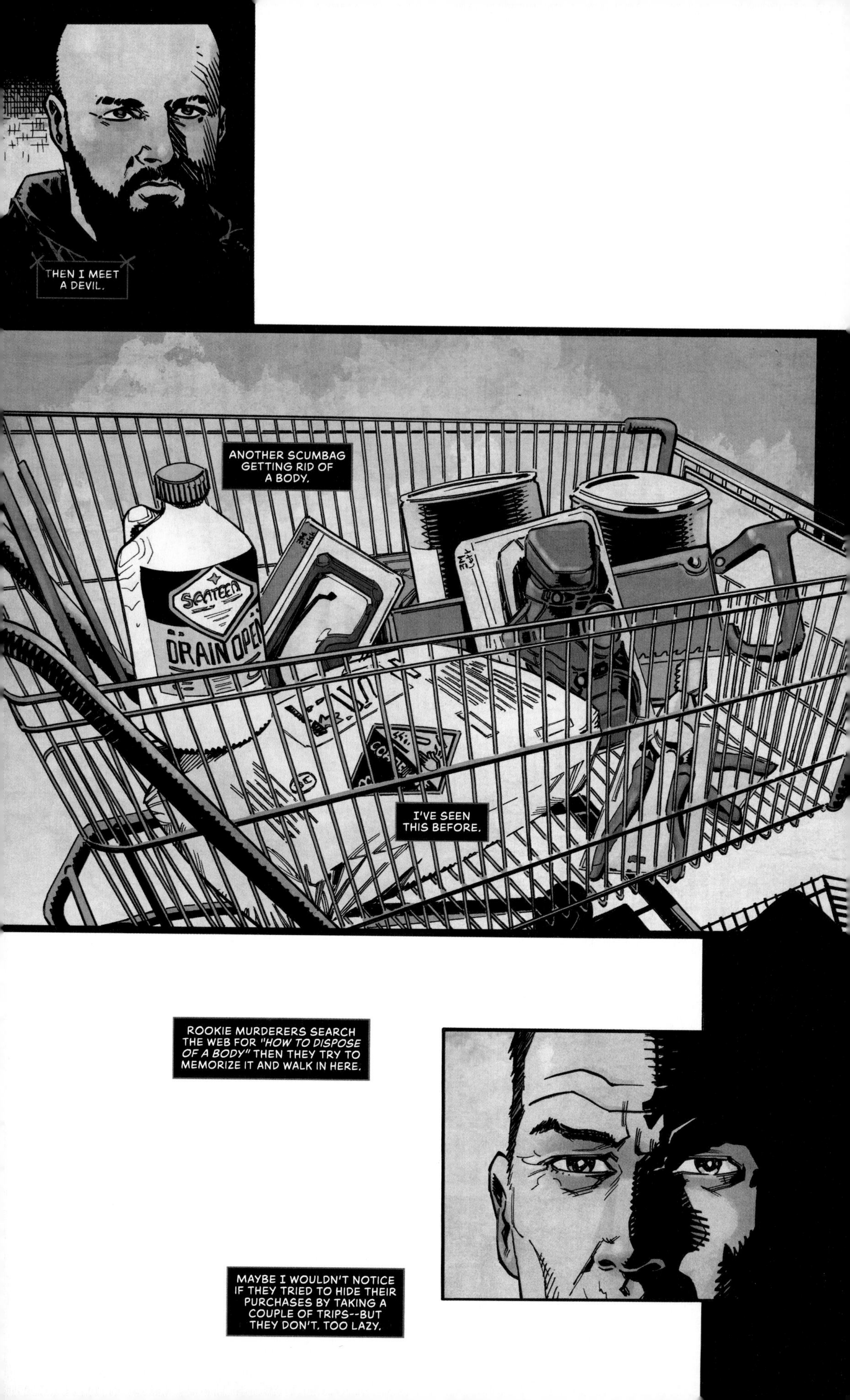
THEN I MEET A DEVIL.
ANOTHER SCUMBAG GETTING RID OF A BODY.
I'VE SEEN THIS BEFORE.
ROOKIE MURDERERS SEARCH THE WEB FOR *"HOW TO DISPOSE OF A BODY"* THEN THEY TRY TO MEMORIZE IT AND WALK IN HERE.
MAYBE I WOULDN'T NOTICE IF THEY TRIED TO HIDE THEIR PURCHASES BY TAKING A COUPLE OF TRIPS--BUT THEY DON'T. TOO LAZY.

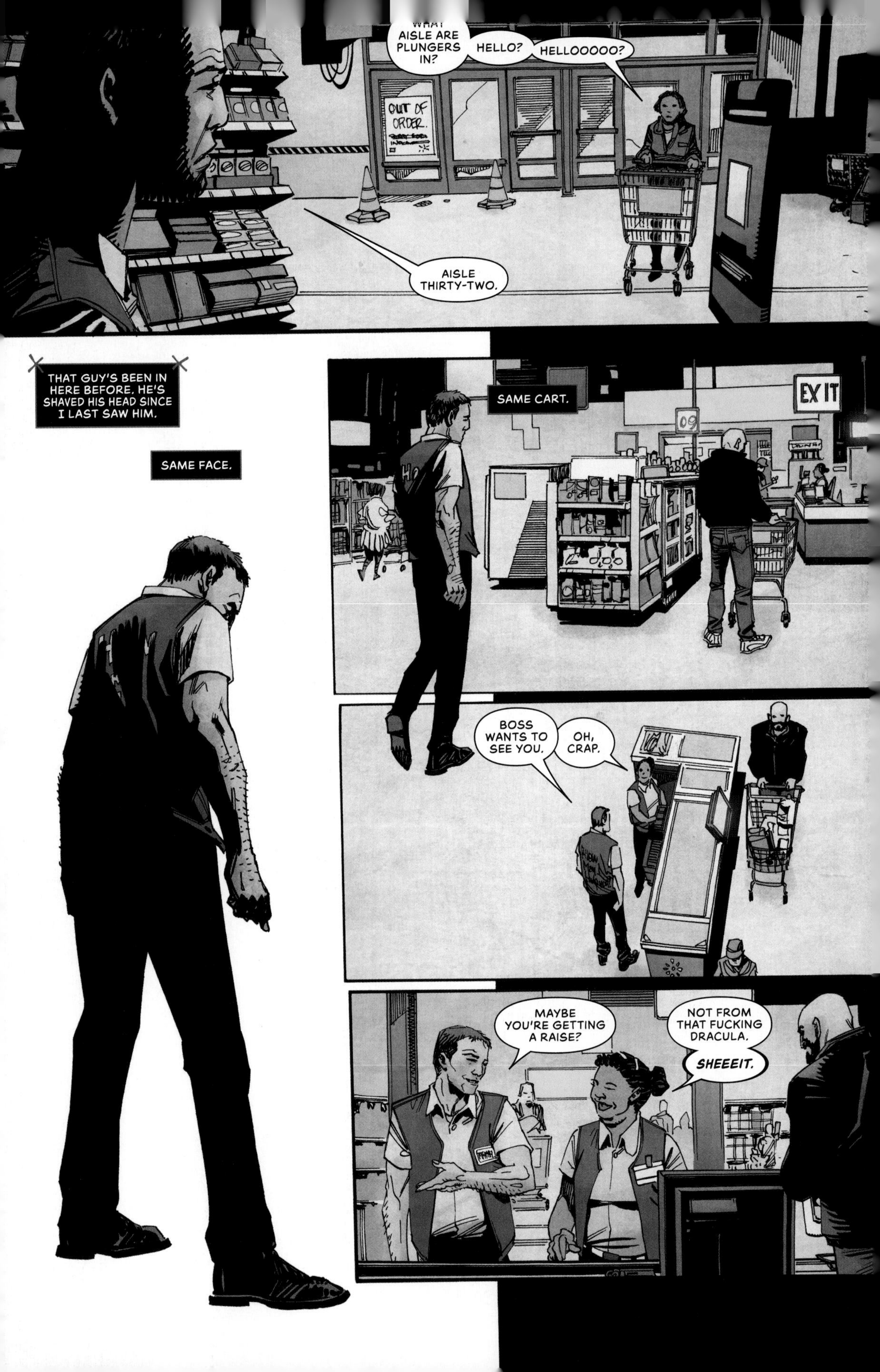
WHAT AISLE ARE PLUNGERS IN?
HELLO?
HELLOOOOO?
AISLE THIRTY-TWO.
OUT OF ORDER.
THAT GUY'S BEEN IN HERE BEFORE. HE'S SHAVED HIS HEAD SINCE I LAST SAW HIM.
SAME FACE.
SAME CART.
EXIT
09
BOSS WANTS TO SEE YOU.
OH, CRAP.
MAYBE YOU'RE GETTING A RAISE?
NOT FROM THAT FUCKING DRACULA.
SHEEEIT.

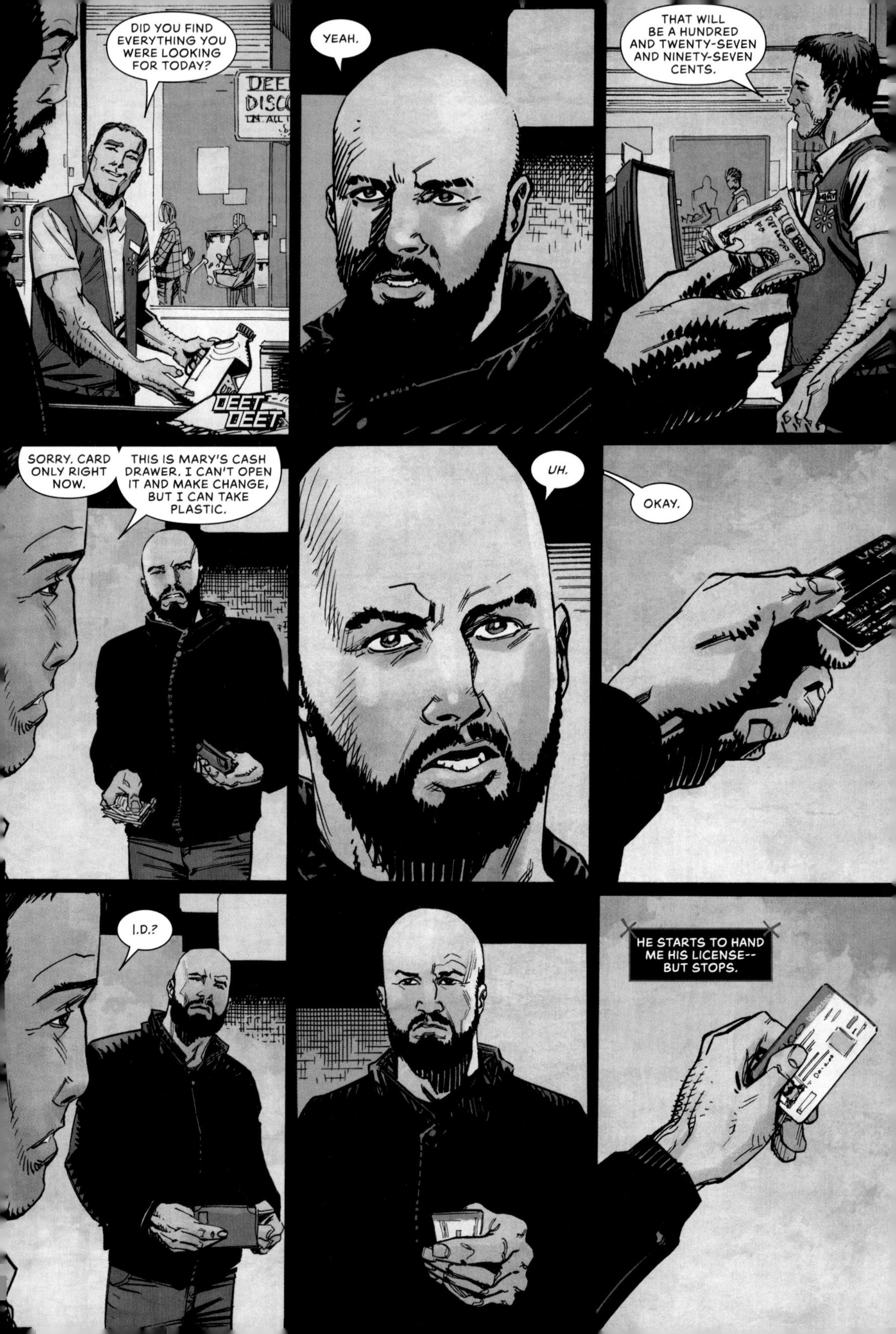
DID YOU FIND EVERYTHING YOU WERE LOOKING FOR TODAY?
DEET DEET
YEAH.
THAT WILL BE A HUNDRED AND TWENTY-SEVEN AND NINETY-SEVEN CENTS.
SORRY. CARD ONLY RIGHT NOW.
THIS IS MARY'S CASH DRAWER. I CAN'T OPEN IT AND MAKE CHANGE, BUT I CAN TAKE PLASTIC.
UH.
OKAY.
I.D.?
HE STARTS TO HAND ME HIS LICENSE-- BUT STOPS.

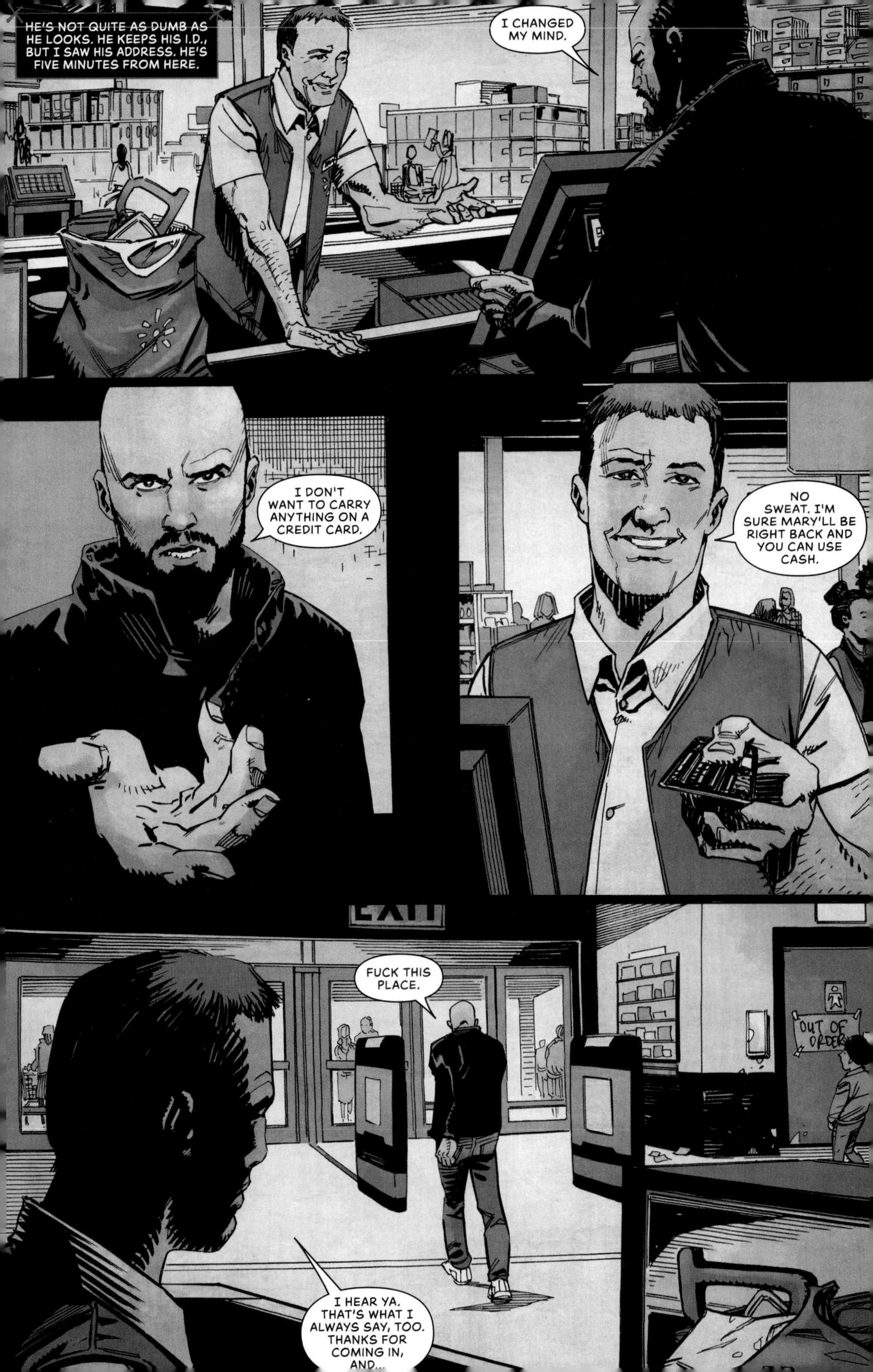
HE'S NOT QUITE AS DUMB AS HE LOOKS. HE KEEPS HIS I.D., BUT I SAW HIS ADDRESS. HE'S FIVE MINUTES FROM HERE.
I CHANGED MY MIND.
I DON'T WANT TO CARRY ANYTHING ON A CREDIT CARD.
NO SWEAT. I'M SURE MARY'LL BE RIGHT BACK AND YOU CAN USE CASH.
EXIT
FUCK THIS PLACE.
OUT OF ORDER
I HEAR YA. THAT'S WHAT I ALWAYS SAY, TOO. THANKS FOR COMING IN, AND...

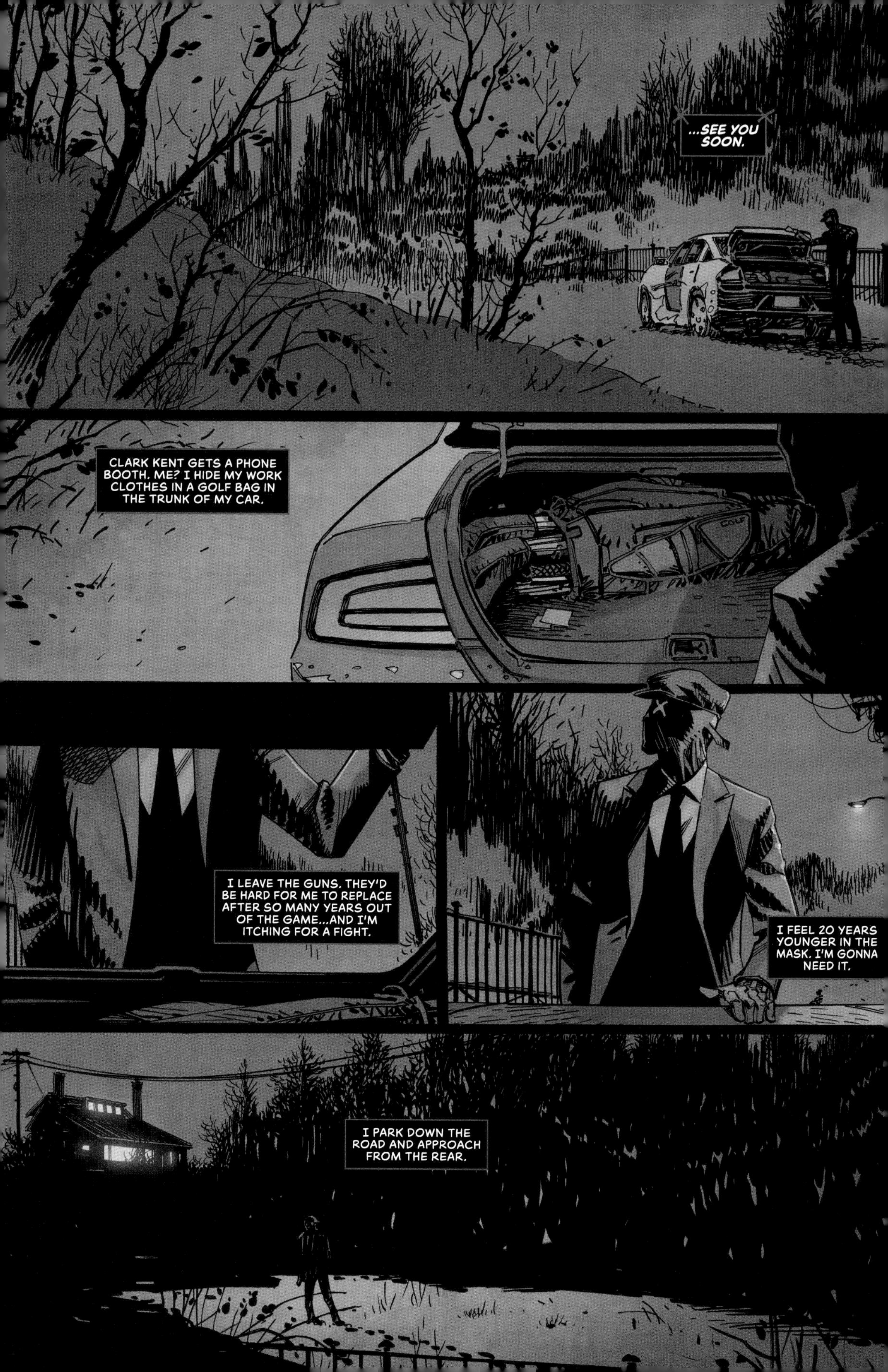

...SEE YOU SOON.
CLARK KENT GETS A PHONE BOOTH. ME? I HIDE MY WORK CLOTHES IN A GOLF BAG IN THE TRUNK OF MY CAR.
GOLF
I LEAVE THE GUNS. THEY'D BE HARD FOR ME TO REPLACE AFTER SO MANY YEARS OUT OF THE GAME...AND I'M ITCHING FOR A FIGHT.
I FEEL 20 YEARS YOUNGER IN THE MASK. I'M GONNA NEED IT.
I PARK DOWN THE ROAD AND APPROACH FROM THE REAR.

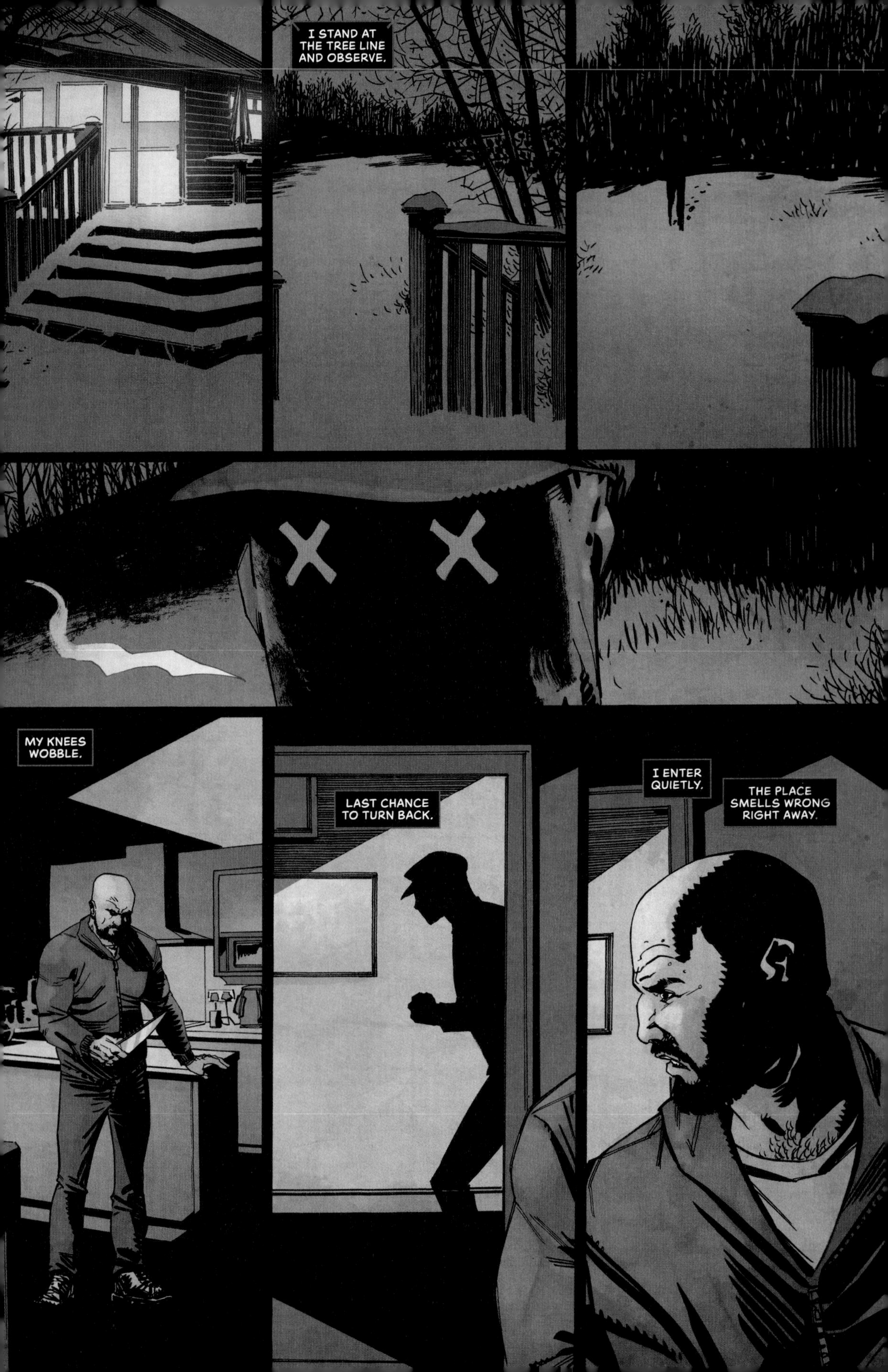
I STAND AT THE TREE LINE AND OBSERVE.
MY KNEES WOBBLE.
LAST CHANCE TO TURN BACK.
I ENTER QUIETLY.
THE PLACE SMELLS WRONG RIGHT AWAY.

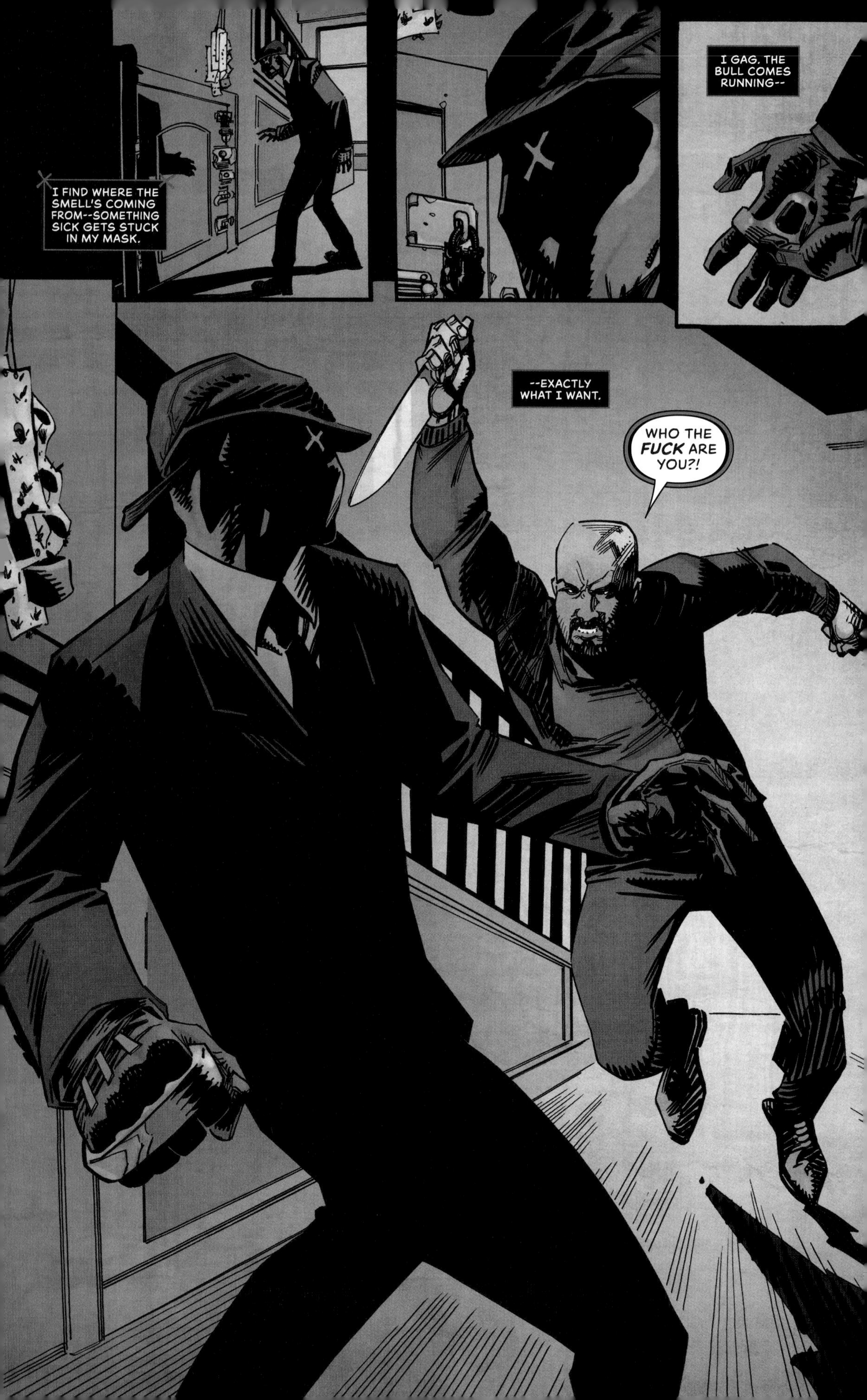
I FIND WHERE THE SMELL'S COMING FROM--SOMETHING SICK GETS STUCK IN MY MASK.
I GAG. THE BULL COMES RUNNING--
--EXACTLY WHAT I WANT.
WHO THE **FUCK** ARE YOU?!

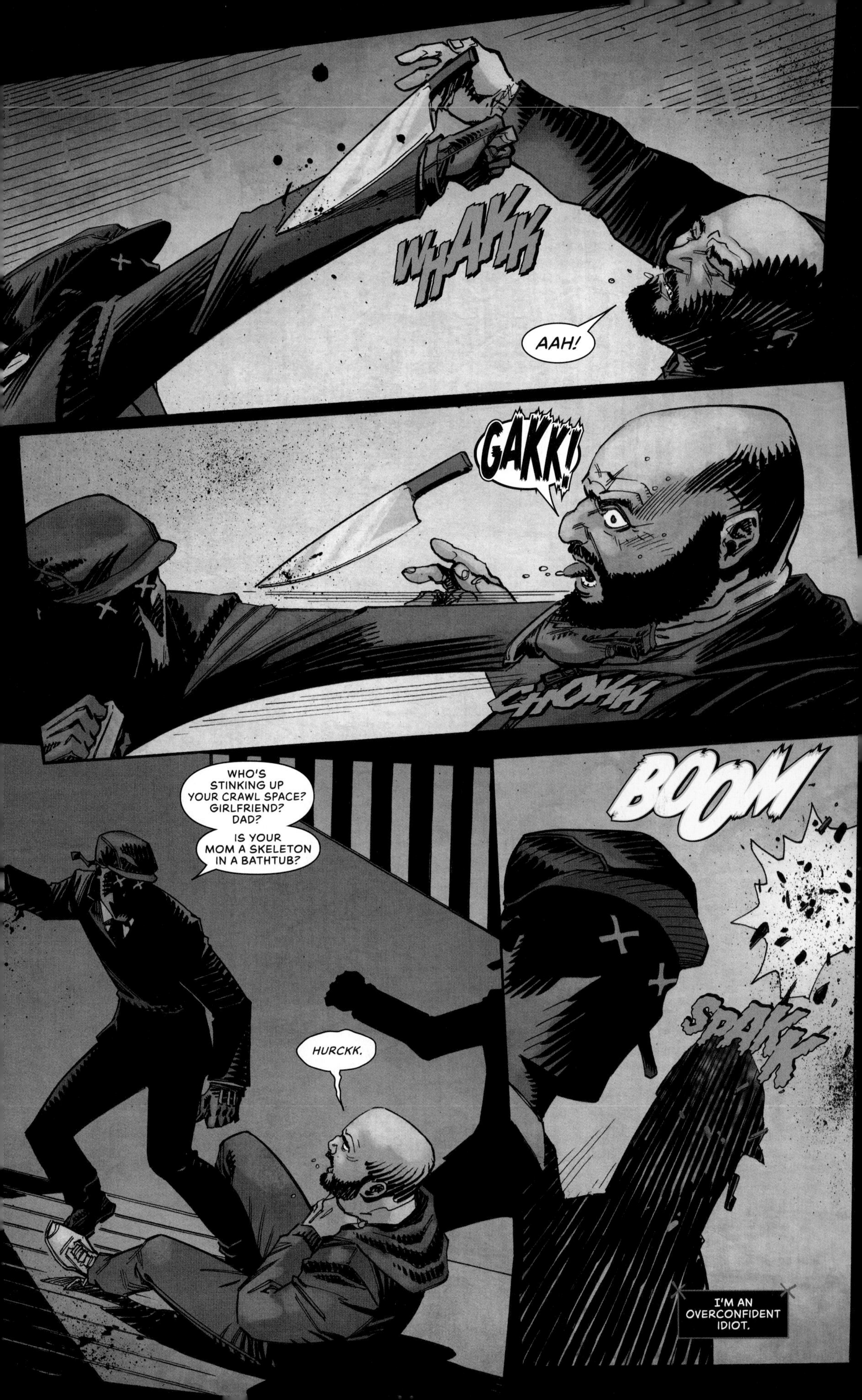
WHAKK
AAH!
GAKK!
CHOKK
WHO'S STINKING UP YOUR CRAWL SPACE? GIRLFRIEND? DAD?
IS YOUR MOM A SKELETON IN A BATHTUB?
HURCKK.
BOOM
SPAK
I'M AN OVERCONFIDENT IDIOT.

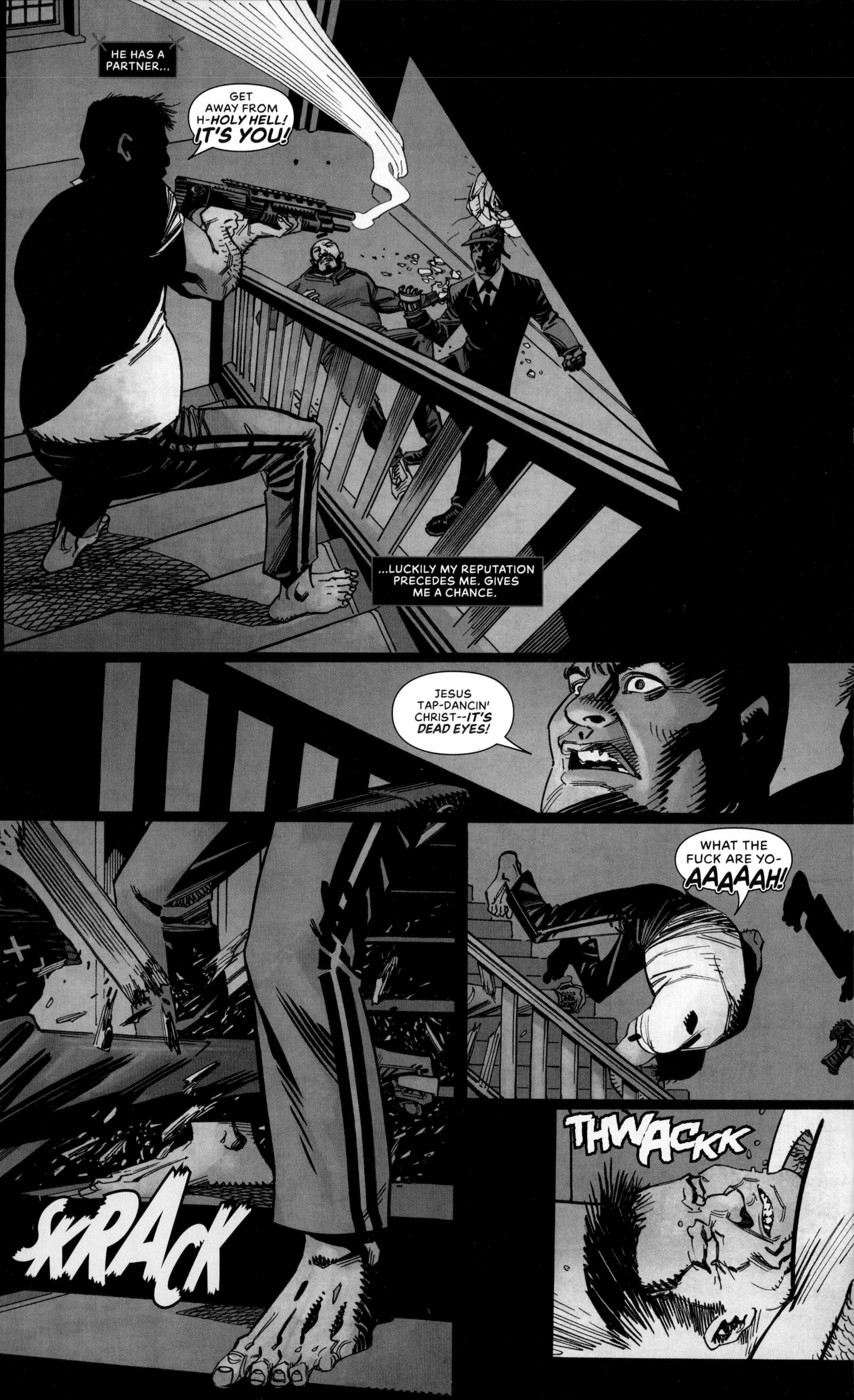
HE HAS A PARTNER...
GET AWAY FROM H-HOLY HELL! IT'S YOU!
...LUCKILY MY REPUTATION PRECEDES ME. GIVES ME A CHANCE.
JESUS TAP-DANCIN' CHRIST--IT'S DEAD EYES!
SKRACK
WHAT THE FUCK ARE YO-AAAAAH!
THWACKK

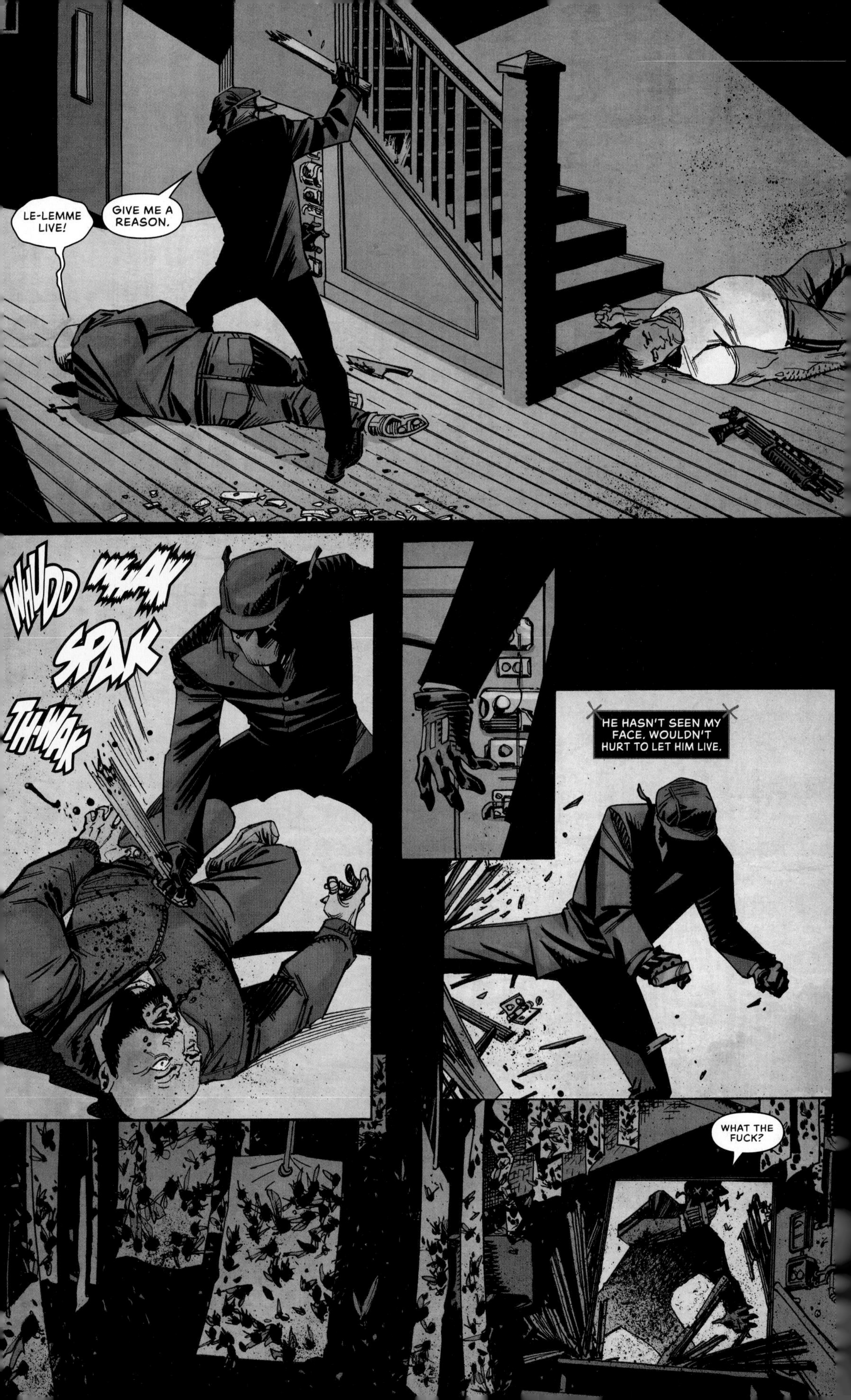
LE-LEMME LIVE!
GIVE ME A REASON.
WHUDD
WHAK
SPAK
TH-WAK
HE HASN'T SEEN MY FACE. WOULDN'T HURT TO LET HIM LIVE.
WHAT THE FUCK?

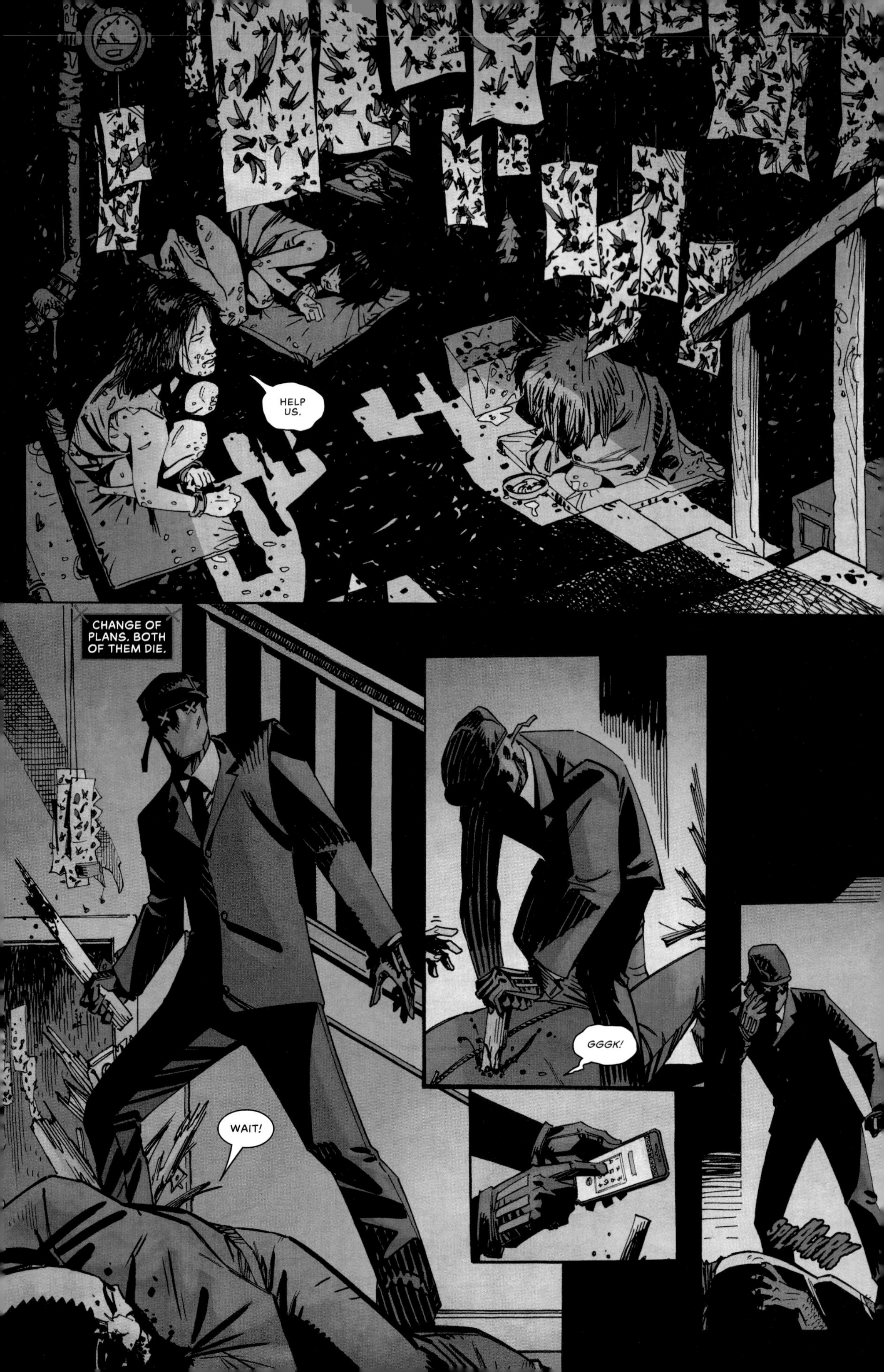
HELP US.
CHANGE OF PLANS. BOTH OF THEM DIE.
WAIT!
GGGK!

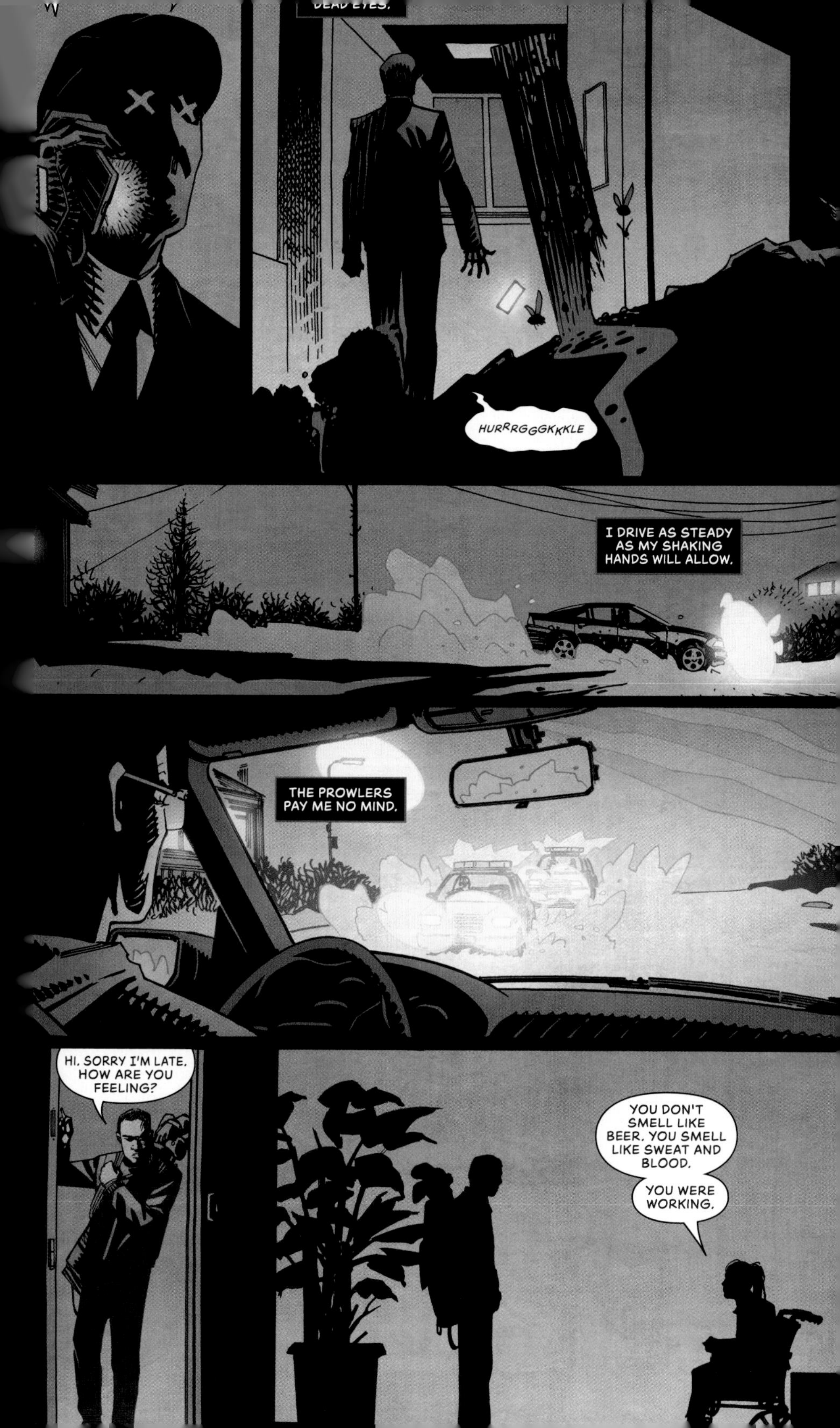

DEAD EYES.
HURRRGGGKKKLE
I DRIVE AS STEADY AS MY SHAKING HANDS WILL ALLOW.
THE PROWLERS PAY ME NO MIND.
HI. SORRY I'M LATE. HOW ARE YOU FEELING?
YOU DON'T SMELL LIKE BEER. YOU SMELL LIKE SWEAT AND BLOOD.
YOU WERE WORKING.

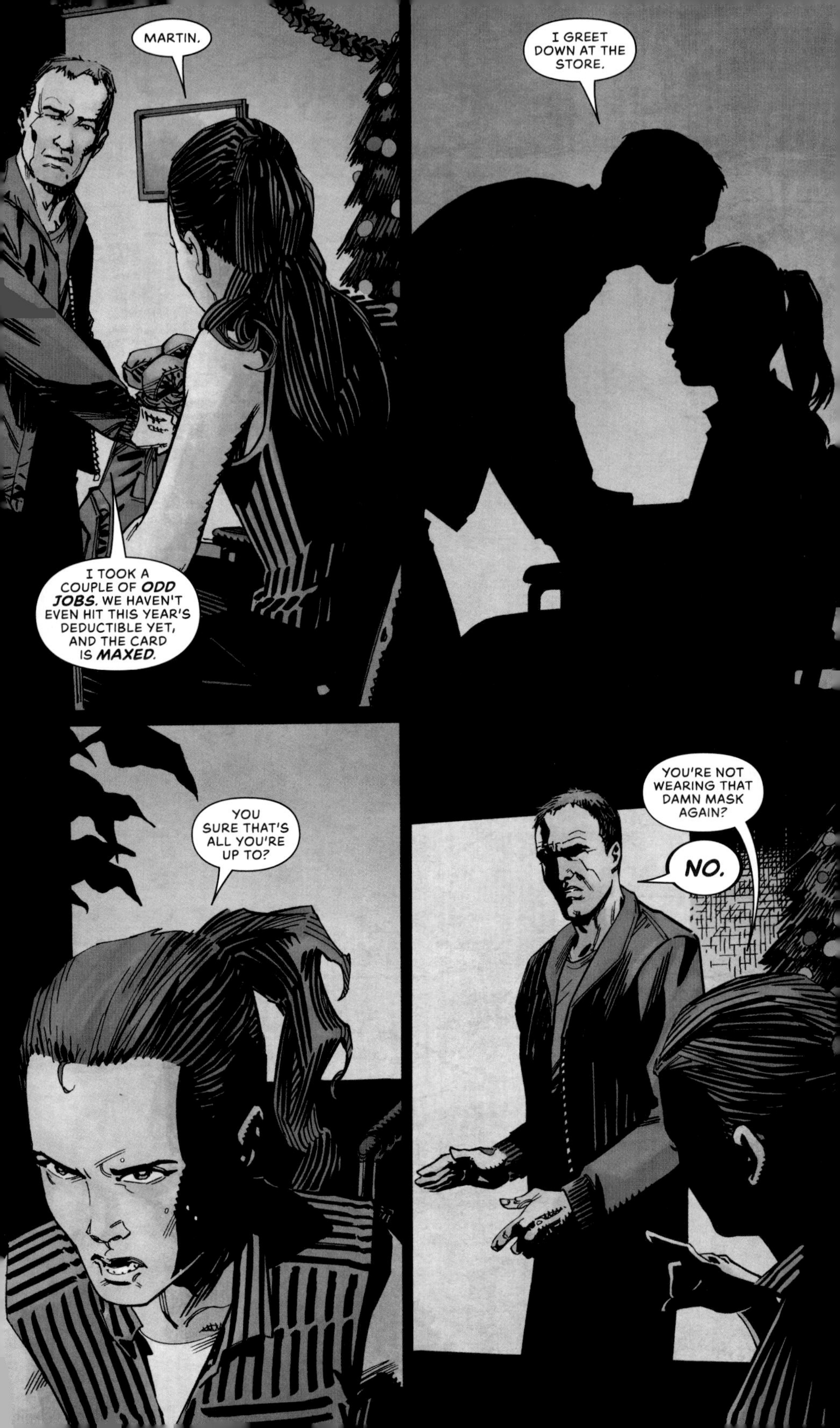
MARTIN.
I TOOK A COUPLE OF ODD JOBS. WE HAVEN'T EVEN HIT THIS YEAR'S DEDUCTIBLE YET, AND THE CARD IS MAXED.
I GREET DOWN AT THE STORE.
YOU SURE THAT'S ALL YOU'RE UP TO?
YOU'RE NOT WEARING THAT DAMN MASK AGAIN?
NO.

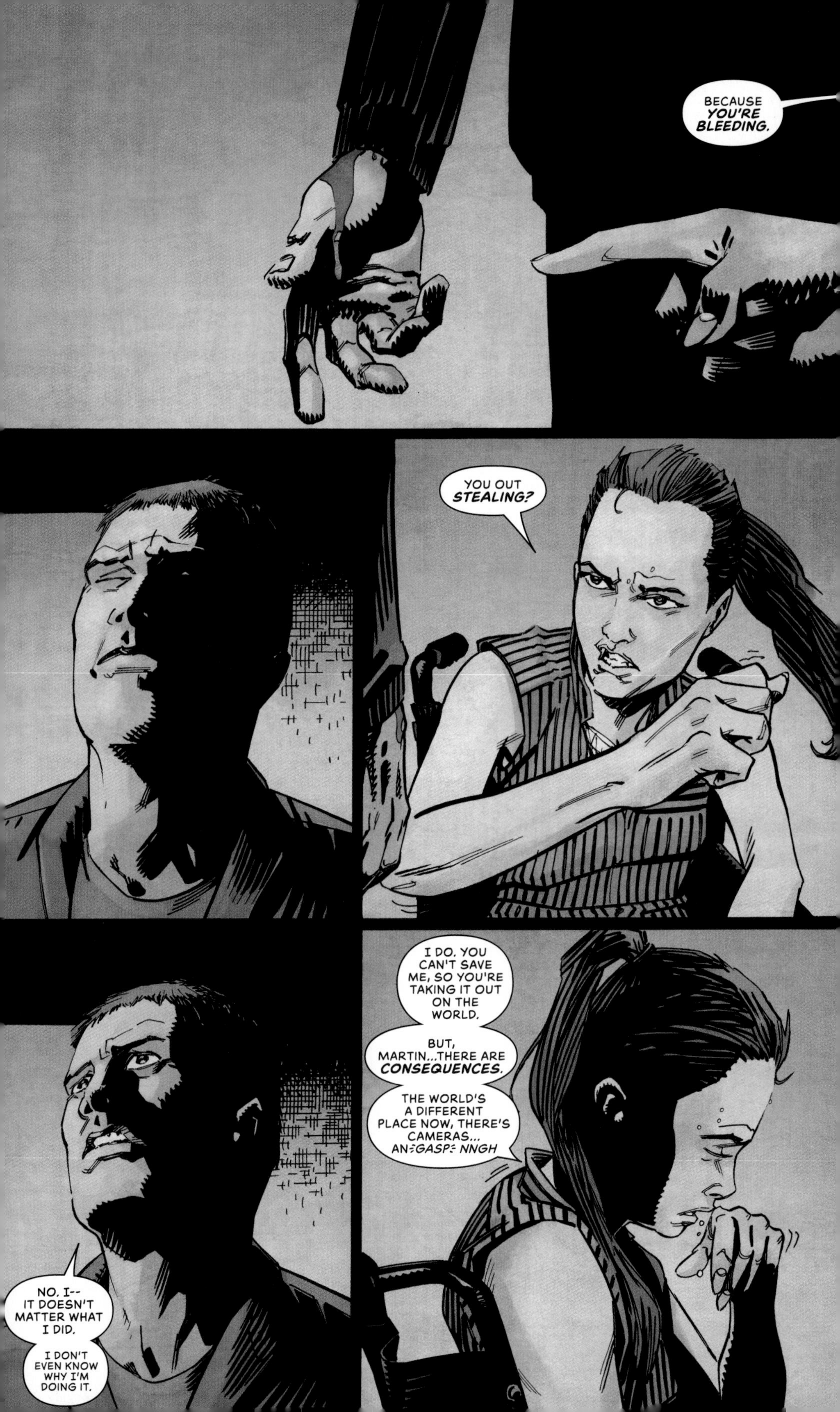

BECAUSE *YOU'RE BLEEDING.*
YOU OUT *STEALING?*
I DO. YOU CAN'T SAVE ME, SO YOU'RE TAKING IT OUT ON THE WORLD.
BUT, MARTIN...THERE ARE *CONSEQUENCES.*
THE WORLD'S A DIFFERENT PLACE NOW, THERE'S CAMERAS... AN=GASP= NNGH
NO, I-- IT DOESN'T MATTER WHAT I DID.
I DON'T EVEN KNOW WHY I'M DOING IT.

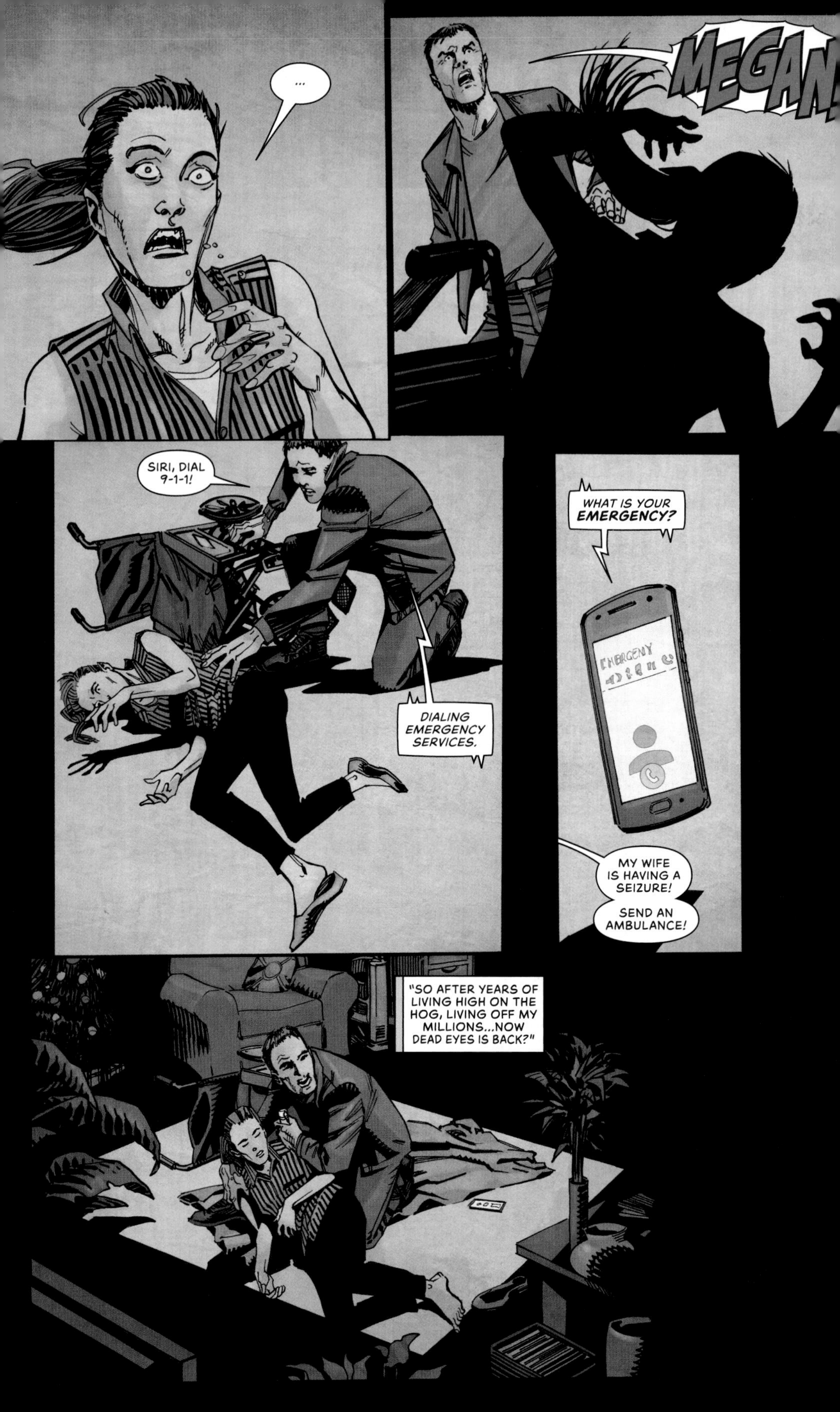
...
MEGAN
SIRI, DIAL 9-1-1!
DIALING EMERGENCY SERVICES.
WHAT IS YOUR EMERGENCY?
MY WIFE IS HAVING A SEIZURE!
SEND AN AMBULANCE!
"SO AFTER YEARS OF LIVING HIGH ON THE HOG, LIVING OFF MY MILLIONS...NOW DEAD EYES IS BACK?"

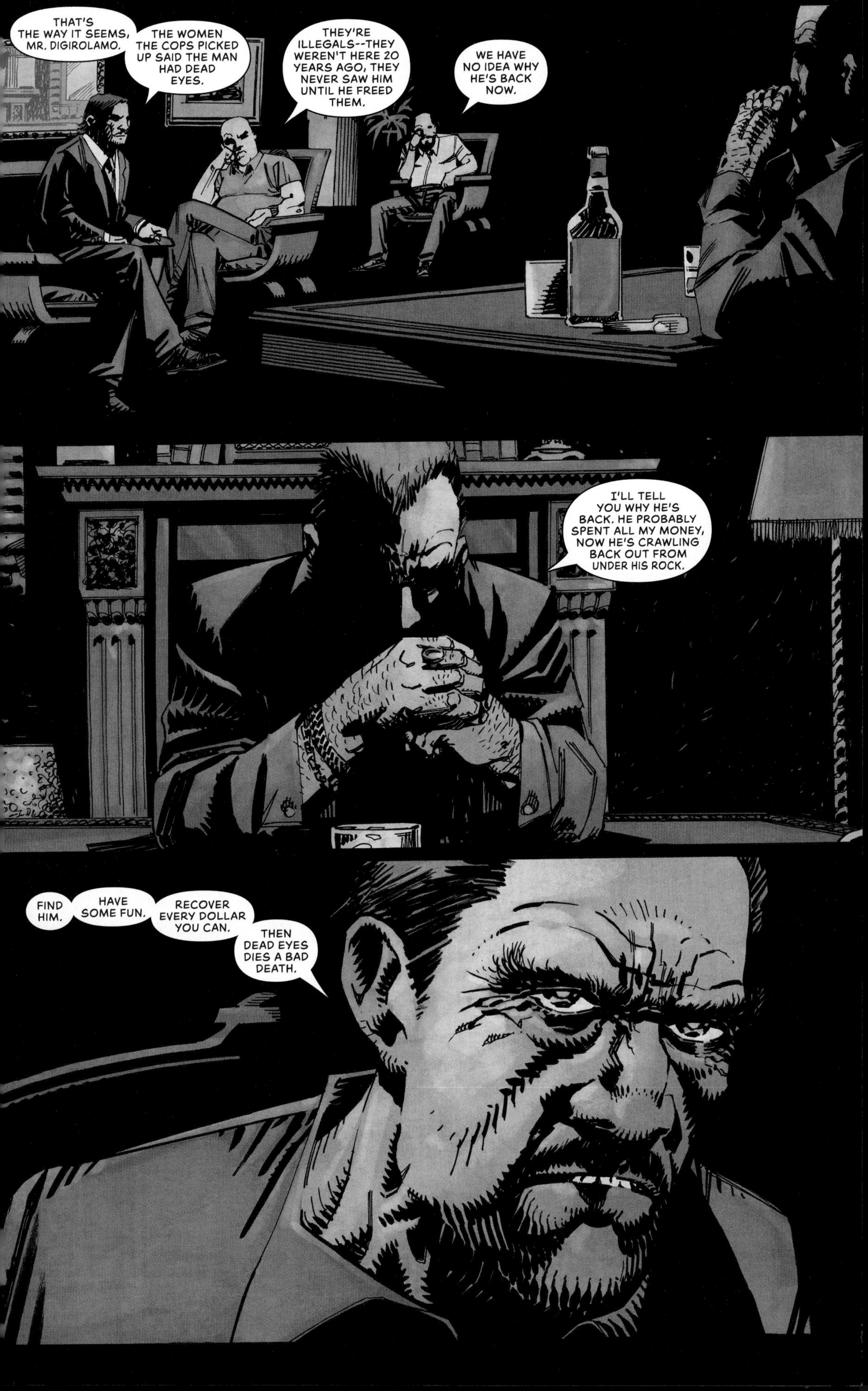
THAT'S THE WAY IT SEEMS, MR. DIGIROLAMO.
THE WOMEN THE COPS PICKED UP SAID THE MAN HAD DEAD EYES.
THEY'RE ILLEGALS--THEY WEREN'T HERE 20 YEARS AGO, THEY NEVER SAW HIM UNTIL HE FREED THEM.
WE HAVE NO IDEA WHY HE'S BACK NOW.
I'LL TELL YOU WHY HE'S BACK. HE PROBABLY SPENT ALL MY MONEY, NOW HE'S CRAWLING BACK OUT FROM UNDER HIS ROCK.
FIND HIM.
HAVE SOME FUN.
RECOVER EVERY DOLLAR YOU CAN.
THEN DEAD EYES DIES A BAD DEATH.

CHAPTER TWO

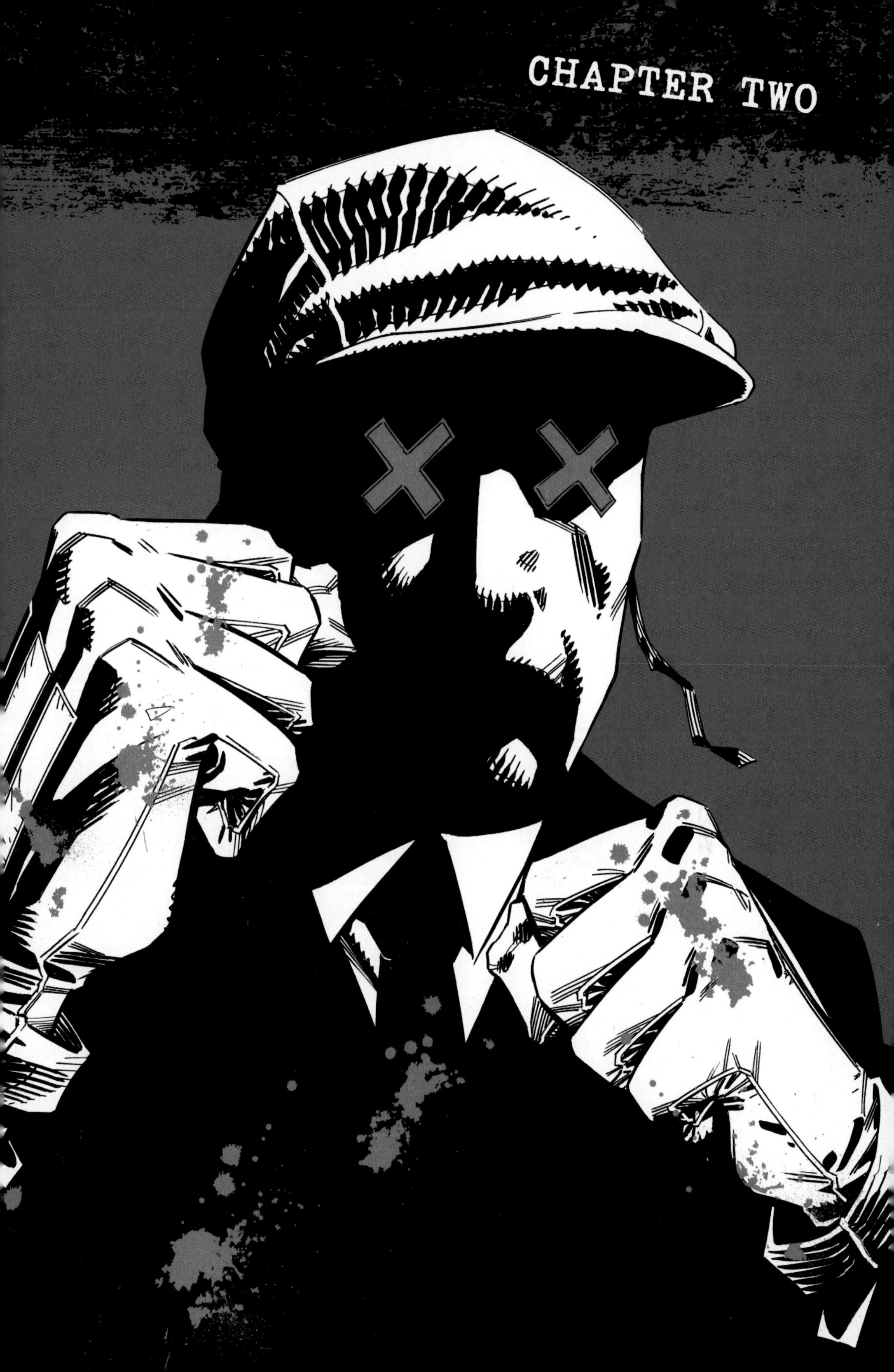

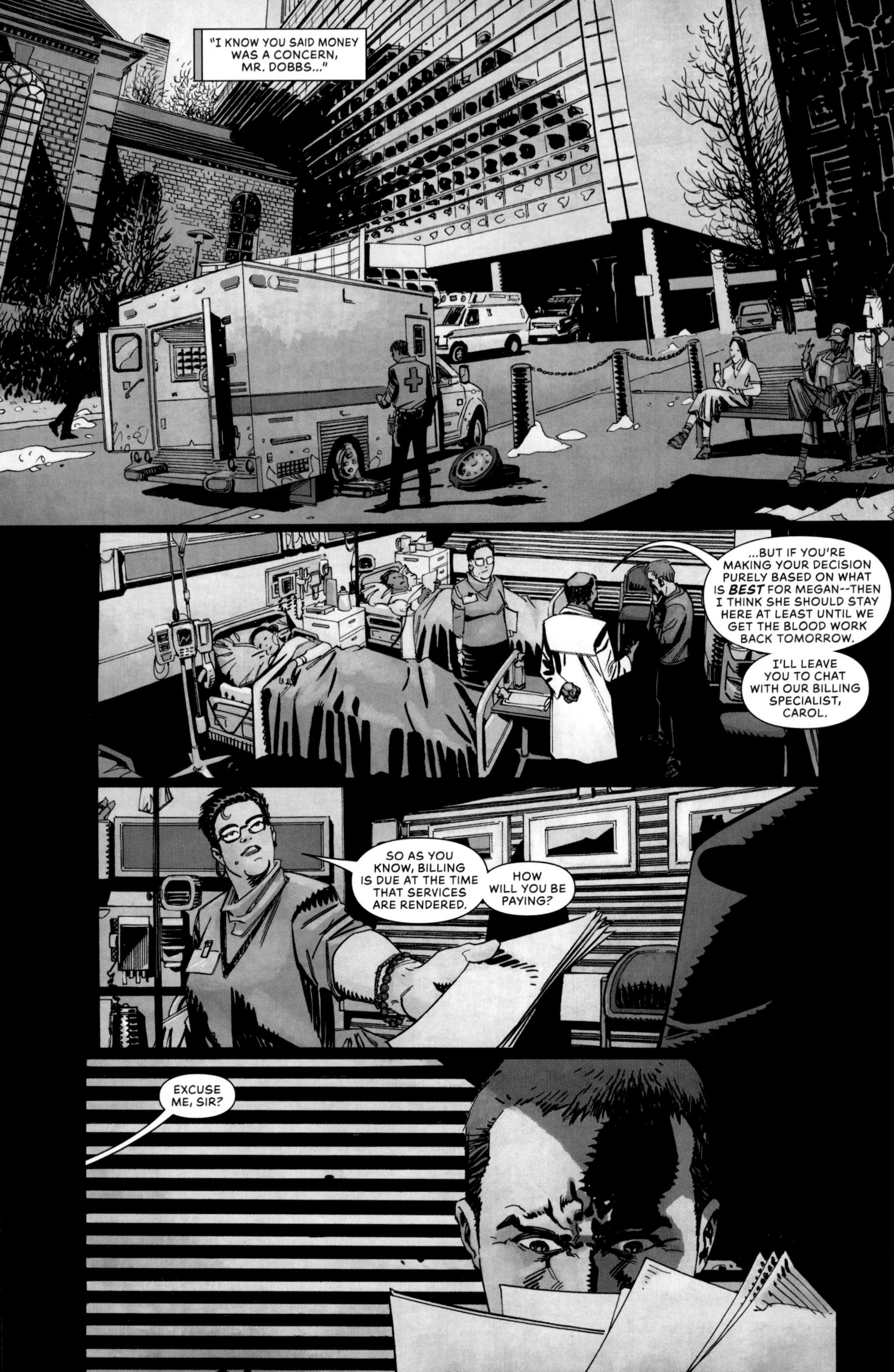
"I KNOW YOU SAID MONEY WAS A CONCERN, MR. DOBBS..."
...BUT IF YOU'RE MAKING YOUR DECISION PURELY BASED ON WHAT IS **BEST** FOR MEGAN--THEN I THINK SHE SHOULD STAY HERE AT LEAST UNTIL WE GET THE BLOOD WORK BACK TOMORROW.
I'LL LEAVE YOU TO CHAT WITH OUR BILLING SPECIALIST, CAROL.
SO AS YOU KNOW, BILLING IS DUE AT THE TIME THAT SERVICES ARE RENDERED.
HOW WILL YOU BE PAYING?
EXCUSE ME, SIR?

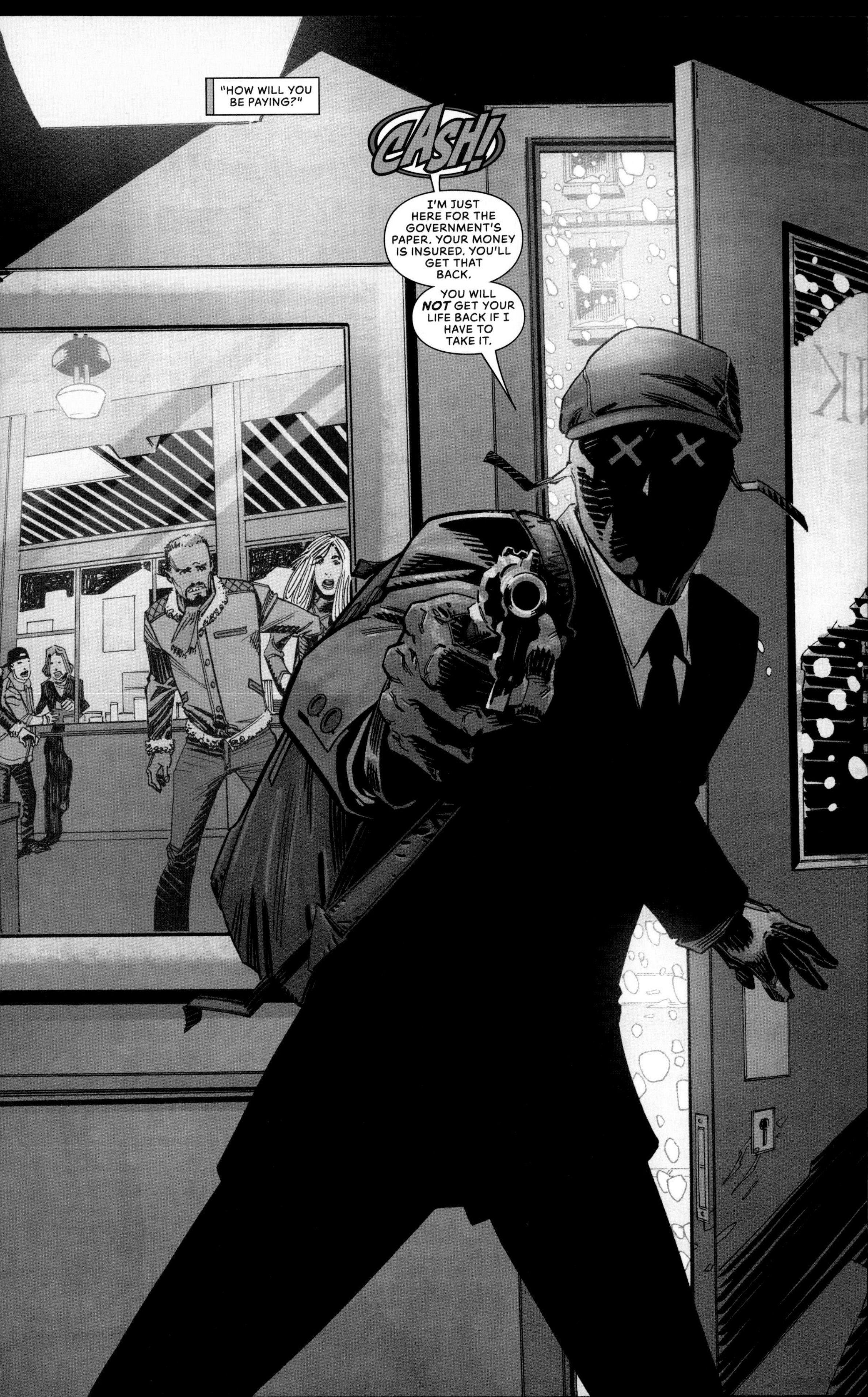
"HOW WILL YOU BE PAYING?"
CASH!
I'M JUST HERE FOR THE GOVERNMENT'S PAPER. YOUR MONEY IS INSURED. YOU'LL GET THAT BACK.
YOU WILL **NOT** GET YOUR LIFE BACK IF I HAVE TO TAKE IT.

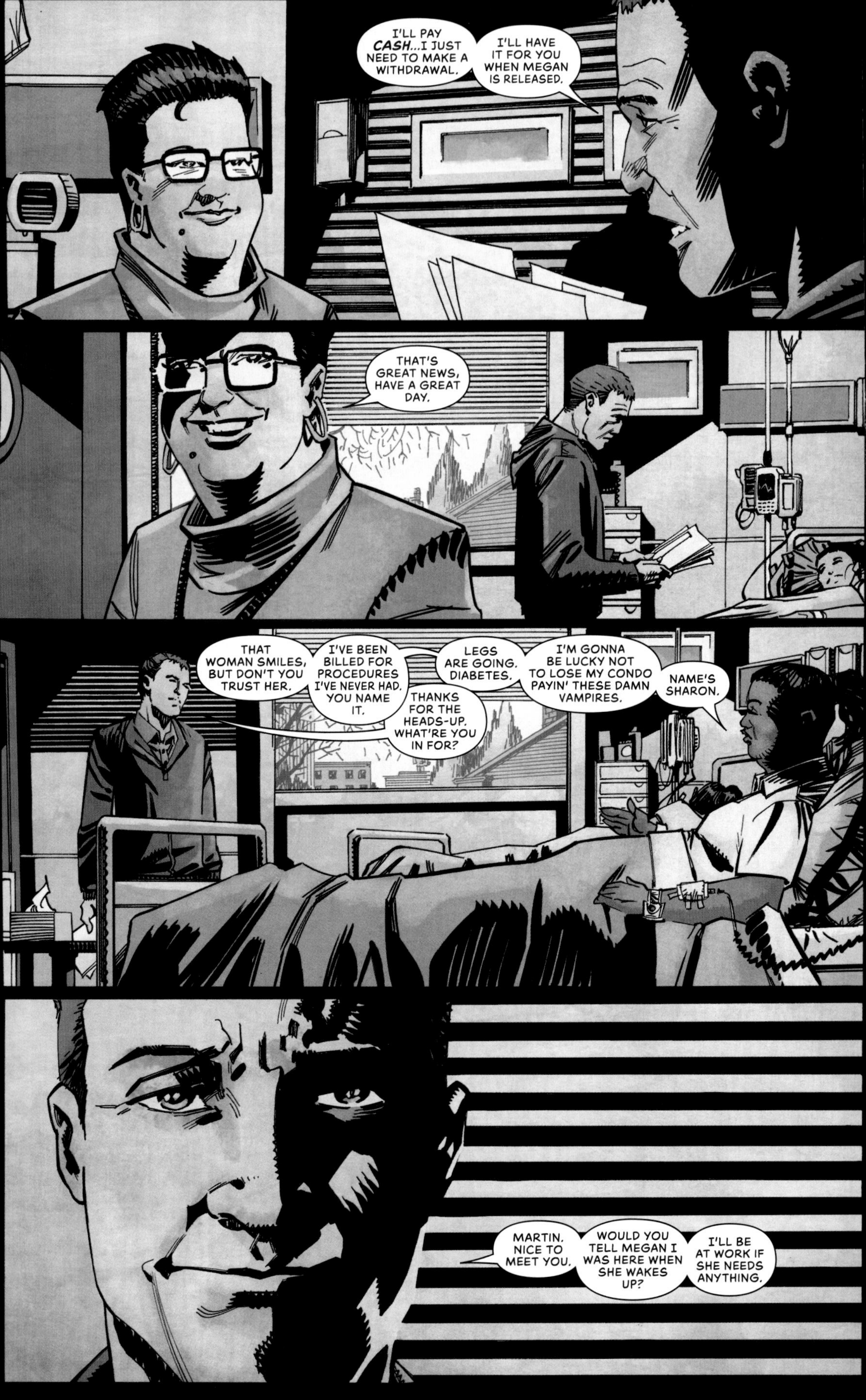
I'LL PAY CASH...I JUST NEED TO MAKE A WITHDRAWAL.
I'LL HAVE IT FOR YOU WHEN MEGAN IS RELEASED.
THAT'S GREAT NEWS, HAVE A GREAT DAY.
THAT WOMAN SMILES, BUT DON'T YOU TRUST HER.
I'VE BEEN BILLED FOR PROCEDURES I'VE NEVER HAD. YOU NAME IT.
THANKS FOR THE HEADS-UP. WHAT'RE YOU IN FOR?
LEGS ARE GOING. DIABETES.
I'M GONNA BE LUCKY NOT TO LOSE MY CONDO PAYIN' THESE DAMN VAMPIRES.
NAME'S SHARON.
MARTIN. NICE TO MEET YOU.
WOULD YOU TELL MEGAN I WAS HERE WHEN SHE WAKES UP?
I'LL BE AT WORK IF SHE NEEDS ANYTHING.

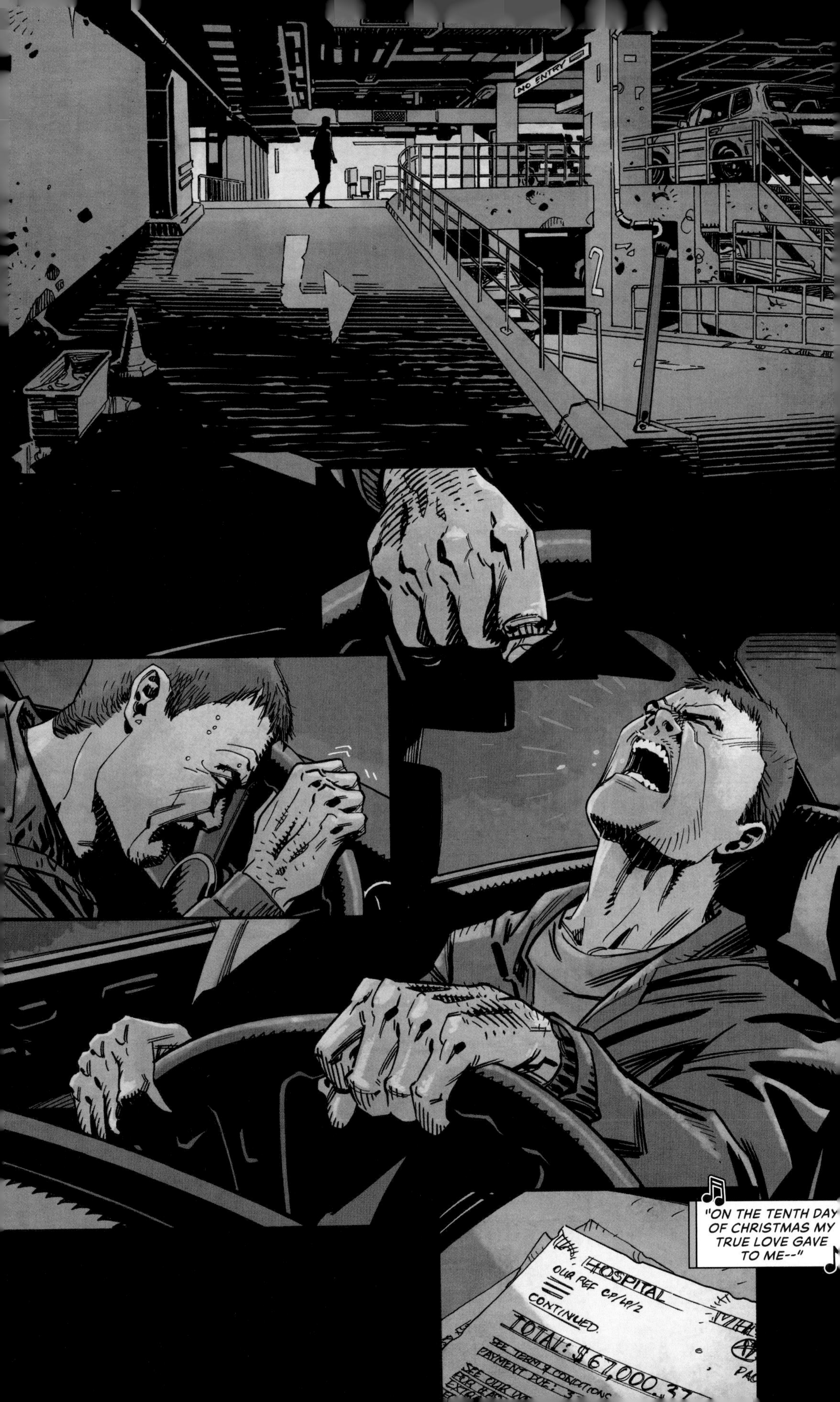
NO ENTRY
2
"ON THE TENTH DAY OF CHRISTMAS MY TRUE LOVE GAVE TO ME--"
HOSPITAL
CONTINUED.

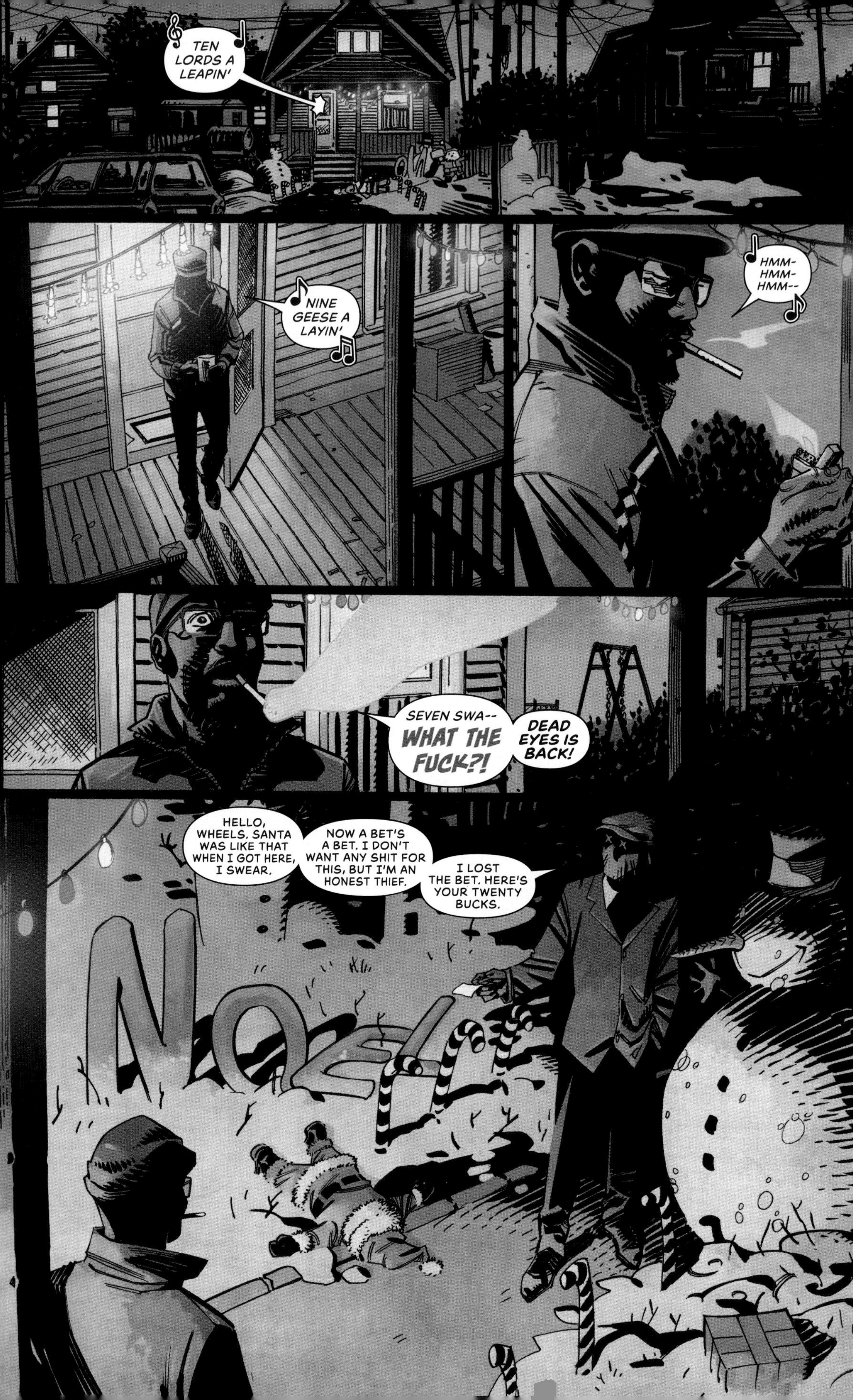
TEN LORDS A LEAPIN'
NINE GEESE A LAYIN'
HMM-HMM-HMM--
SEVEN SWA-- WHAT THE FUCK?!
DEAD EYES IS BACK!
HELLO, WHEELS. SANTA WAS LIKE THAT WHEN I GOT HERE, I SWEAR.
NOW A BET'S A BET. I DON'T WANT ANY SHIT FOR THIS, BUT I'M AN HONEST THIEF.
I LOST THE BET. HERE'S YOUR TWENTY BUCKS.

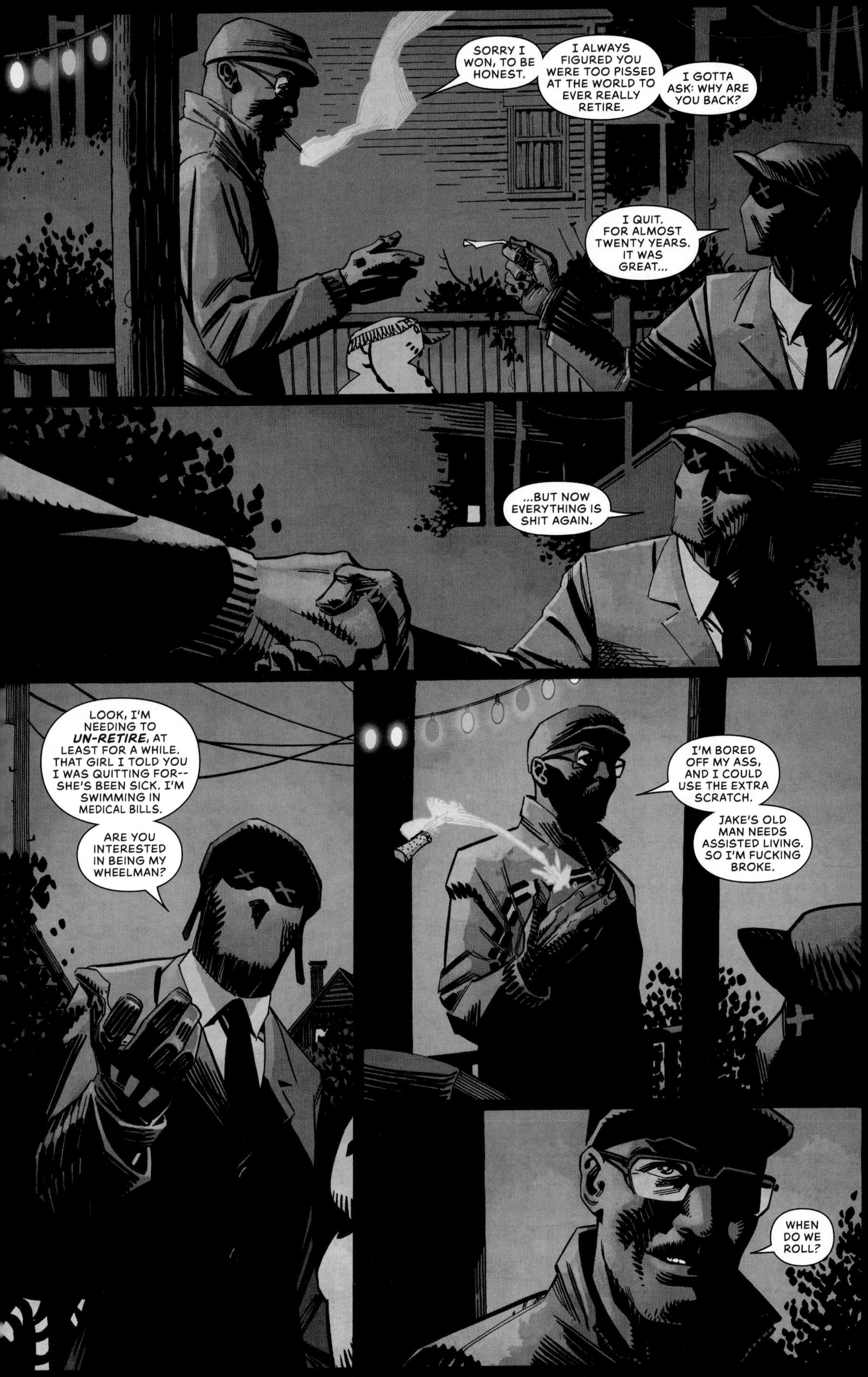
SORRY I WON, TO BE HONEST.
I ALWAYS FIGURED YOU WERE TOO PISSED AT THE WORLD TO EVER REALLY RETIRE.
I GOTTA ASK: WHY ARE YOU BACK?
I QUIT. FOR ALMOST TWENTY YEARS. IT WAS GREAT...
...BUT NOW EVERYTHING IS SHIT AGAIN.
LOOK, I'M NEEDING TO ***UN-RETIRE***, AT LEAST FOR A WHILE. THAT GIRL I TOLD YOU I WAS QUITTING FOR--SHE'S BEEN SICK. I'M SWIMMING IN MEDICAL BILLS.
ARE YOU INTERESTED IN BEING MY WHEELMAN?
I'M BORED OFF MY ASS, AND I COULD USE THE EXTRA SCRATCH.
JAKE'S OLD MAN NEEDS ASSISTED LIVING. SO I'M FUCKING BROKE.
WHEN DO WE ROLL?

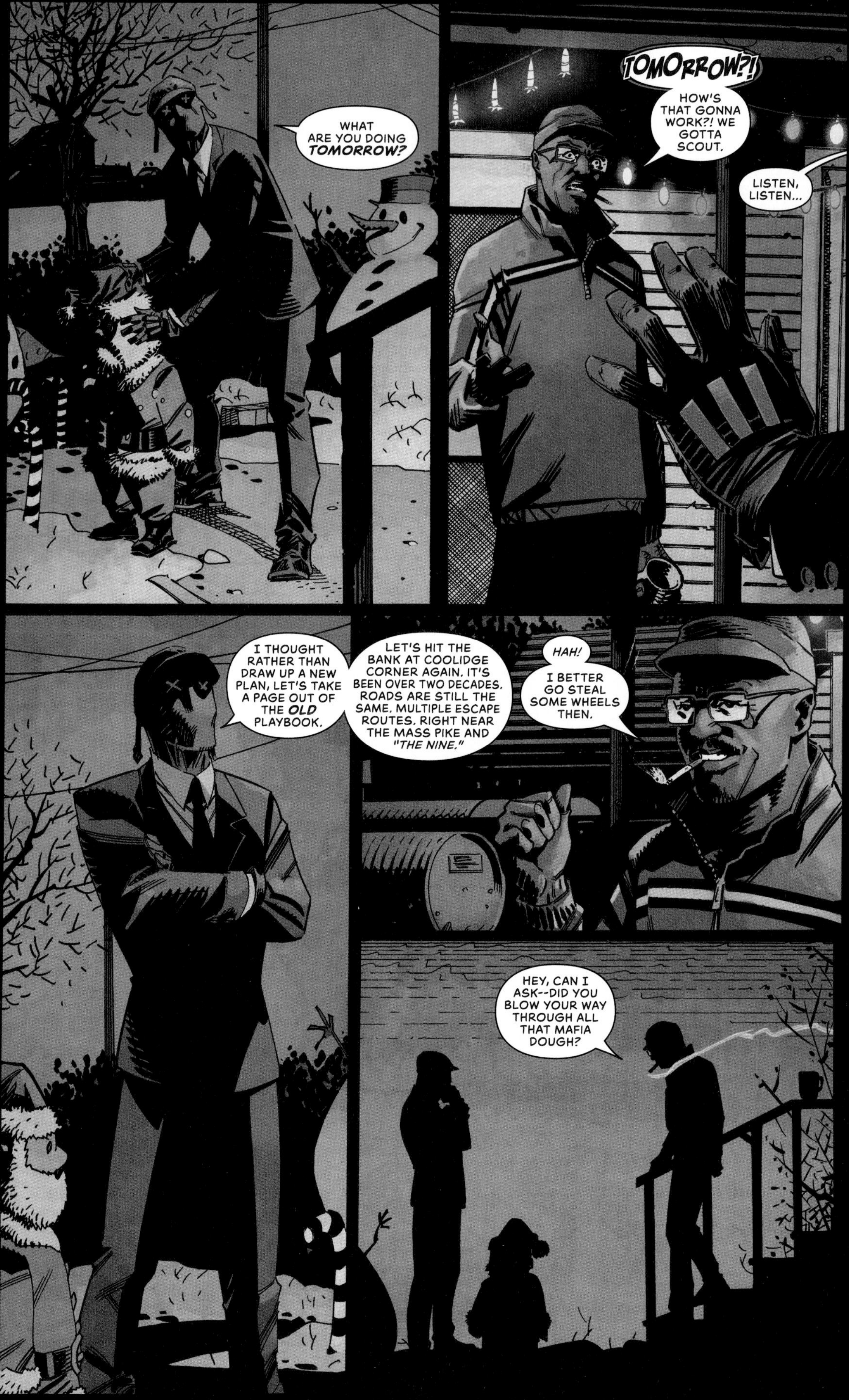
WHAT ARE YOU DOING TOMORROW?
TOMORROW?!
HOW'S THAT GONNA WORK?! WE GOTTA SCOUT.
LISTEN, LISTEN...
I THOUGHT RATHER THAN DRAW UP A NEW PLAN, LET'S TAKE A PAGE OUT OF THE OLD PLAYBOOK.
LET'S HIT THE BANK AT COOLIDGE CORNER AGAIN. IT'S BEEN OVER TWO DECADES. ROADS ARE STILL THE SAME. MULTIPLE ESCAPE ROUTES. RIGHT NEAR THE MASS PIKE AND "THE NINE."
HAH!
I BETTER GO STEAL SOME WHEELS THEN.
HEY, CAN I ASK--DID YOU BLOW YOUR WAY THROUGH ALL THAT MAFIA DOUGH?

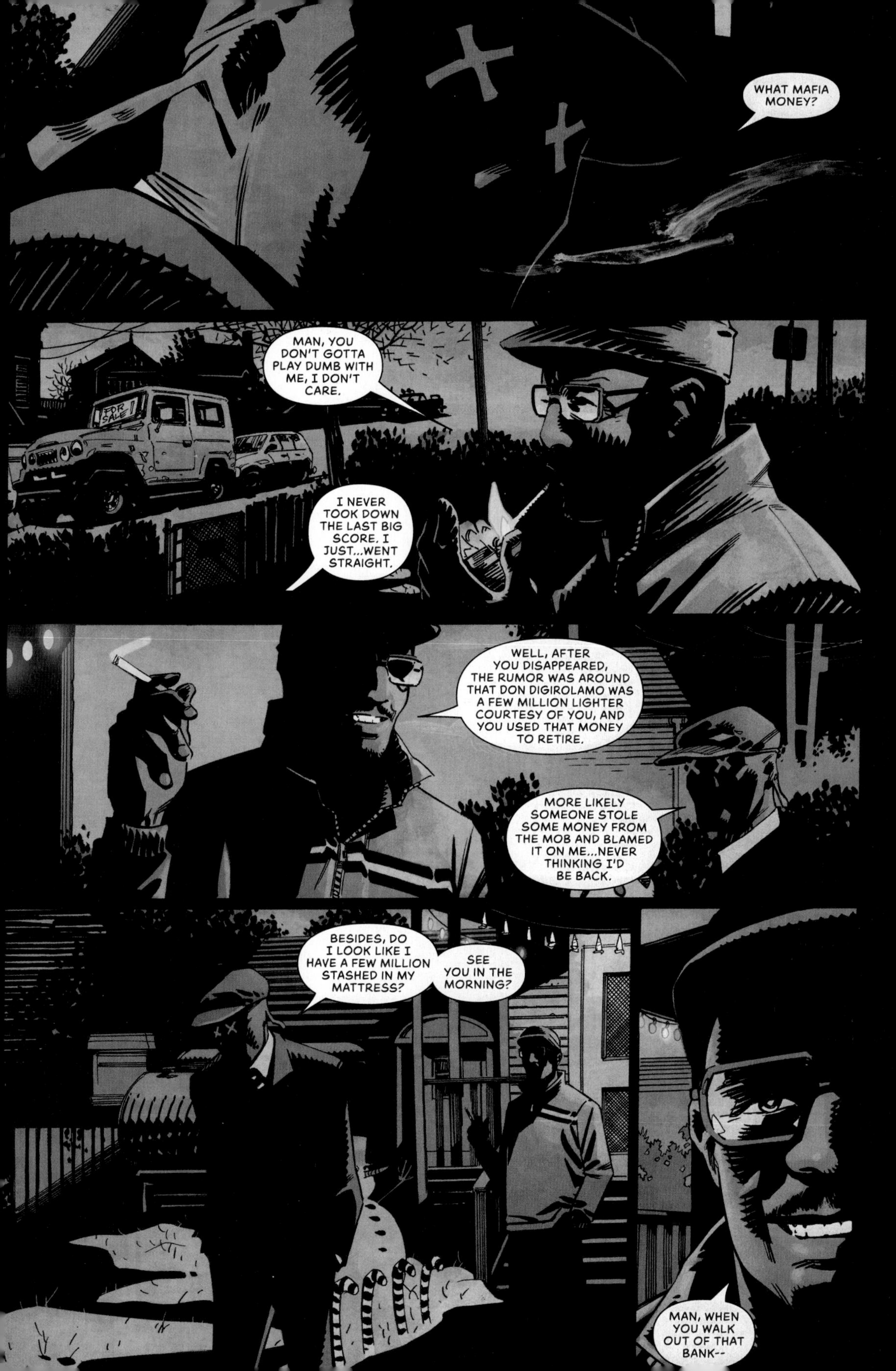
WHAT MAFIA MONEY?
MAN, YOU DON'T GOTTA PLAY DUMB WITH ME, I DON'T CARE.
I NEVER TOOK DOWN THE LAST BIG SCORE. I JUST...WENT STRAIGHT.
WELL, AFTER YOU DISAPPEARED, THE RUMOR WAS AROUND THAT DON DIGIROLAMO WAS A FEW MILLION LIGHTER COURTESY OF YOU, AND YOU USED THAT MONEY TO RETIRE.
MORE LIKELY SOMEONE STOLE SOME MONEY FROM THE MOB AND BLAMED IT ON ME...NEVER THINKING I'D BE BACK.
BESIDES, DO I LOOK LIKE I HAVE A FEW MILLION STASHED IN MY MATTRESS?
SEE YOU IN THE MORNING?
MAN, WHEN YOU WALK OUT OF THAT BANK--

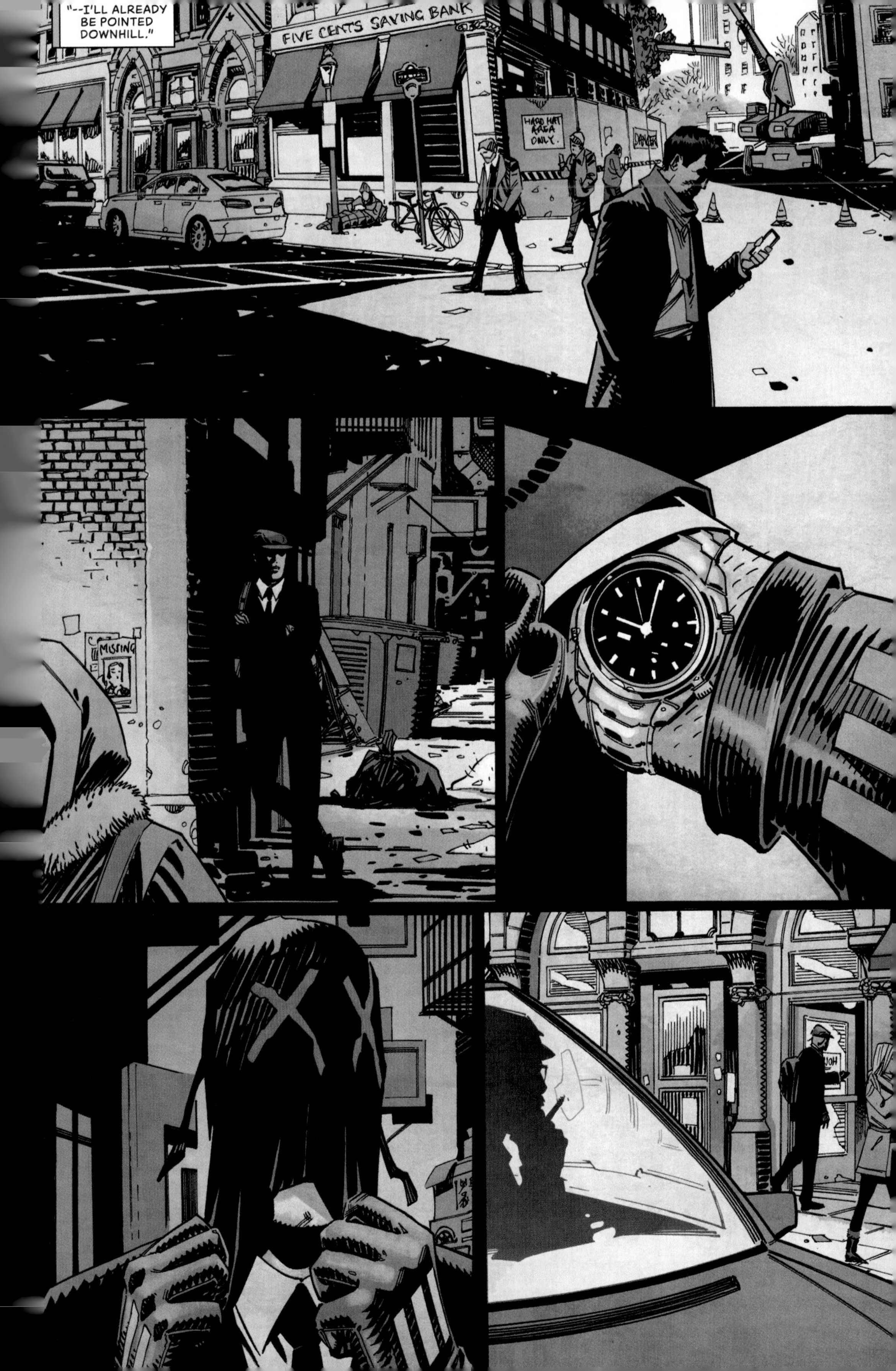
"--I'LL ALREADY BE POINTED DOWNHILL."
FIVE CENTS SAVING BANK
HARD HAT AREA ONLY.
DANGER
MISSING

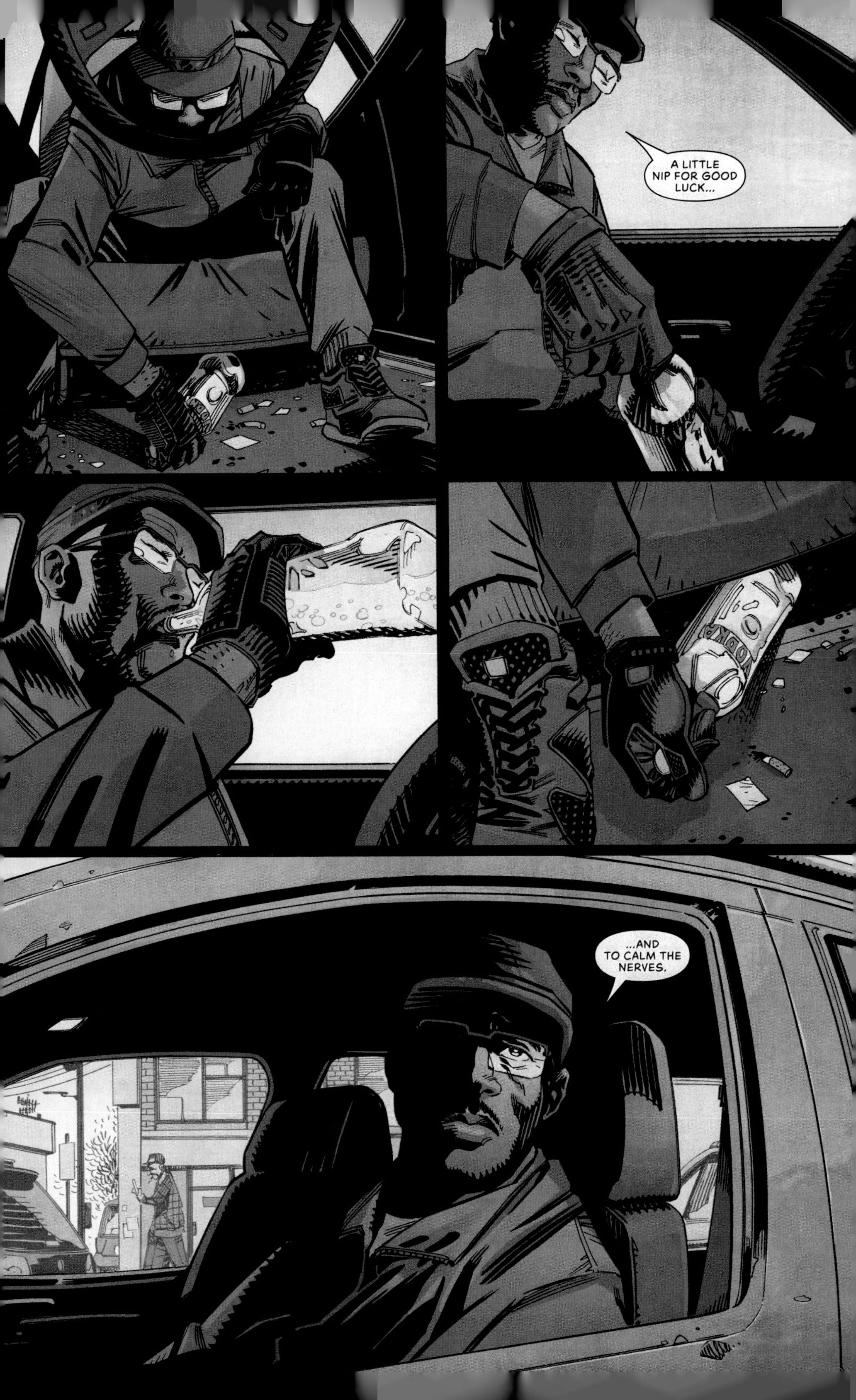
A LITTLE NIP FOR GOOD LUCK...
VODKA
...AND TO CALM THE NERVES.

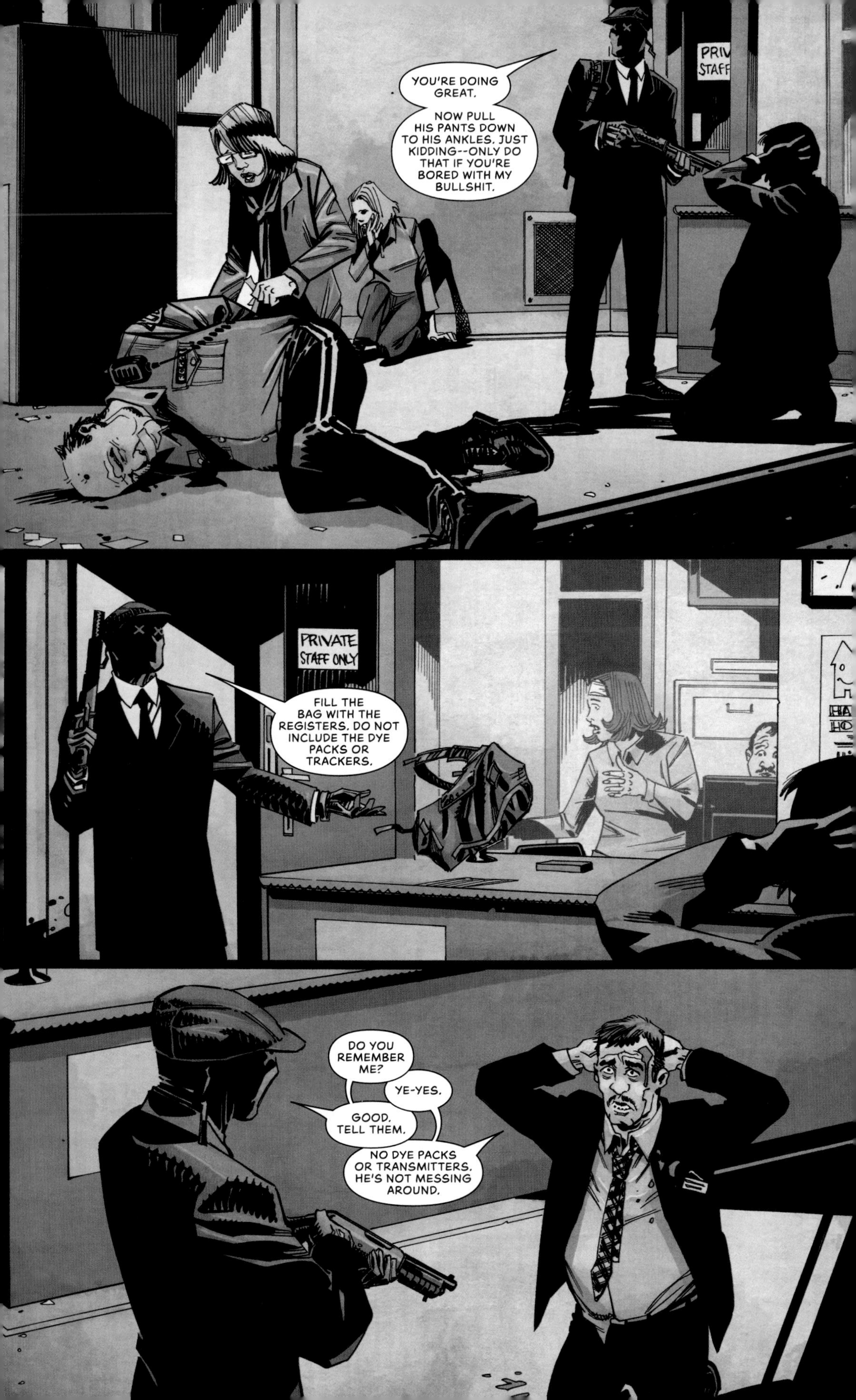
YOU'RE DOING GREAT.
NOW PULL HIS PANTS DOWN TO HIS ANKLES. JUST KIDDING--ONLY DO THAT IF YOU'RE BORED WITH MY BULLSHIT.
PRIVATE STAFF ONLY
FILL THE BAG WITH THE REGISTERS. DO NOT INCLUDE THE DYE PACKS OR TRACKERS.
DO YOU REMEMBER ME?
YE-YES.
GOOD. TELL THEM.
NO DYE PACKS OR TRANSMITTERS. HE'S NOT MESSING AROUND.

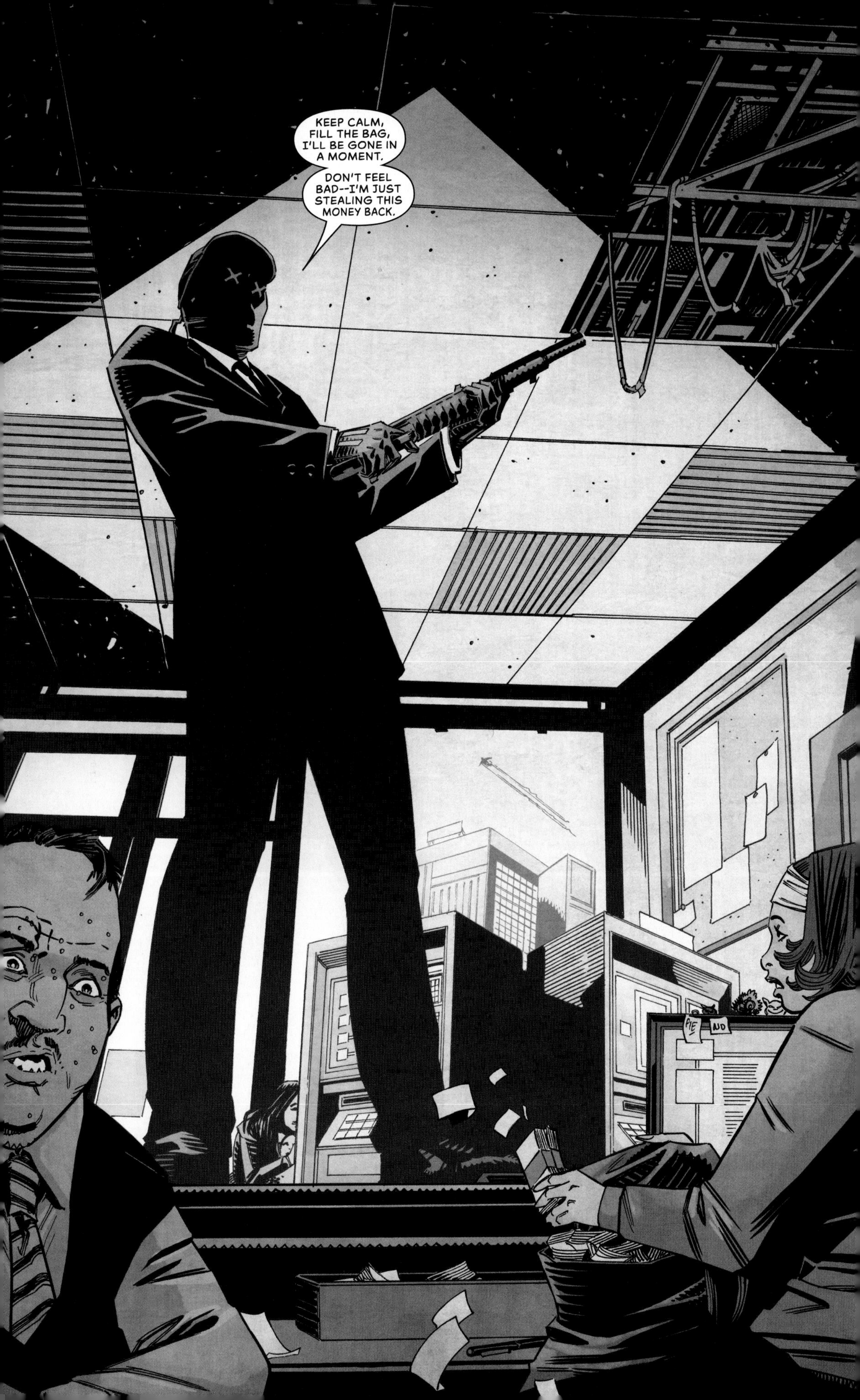
KEEP CALM, FILL THE BAG, I'LL BE GONE IN A MOMENT.
DON'T FEEL BAD--I'M JUST STEALING THIS MONEY BACK.
PIE
AND

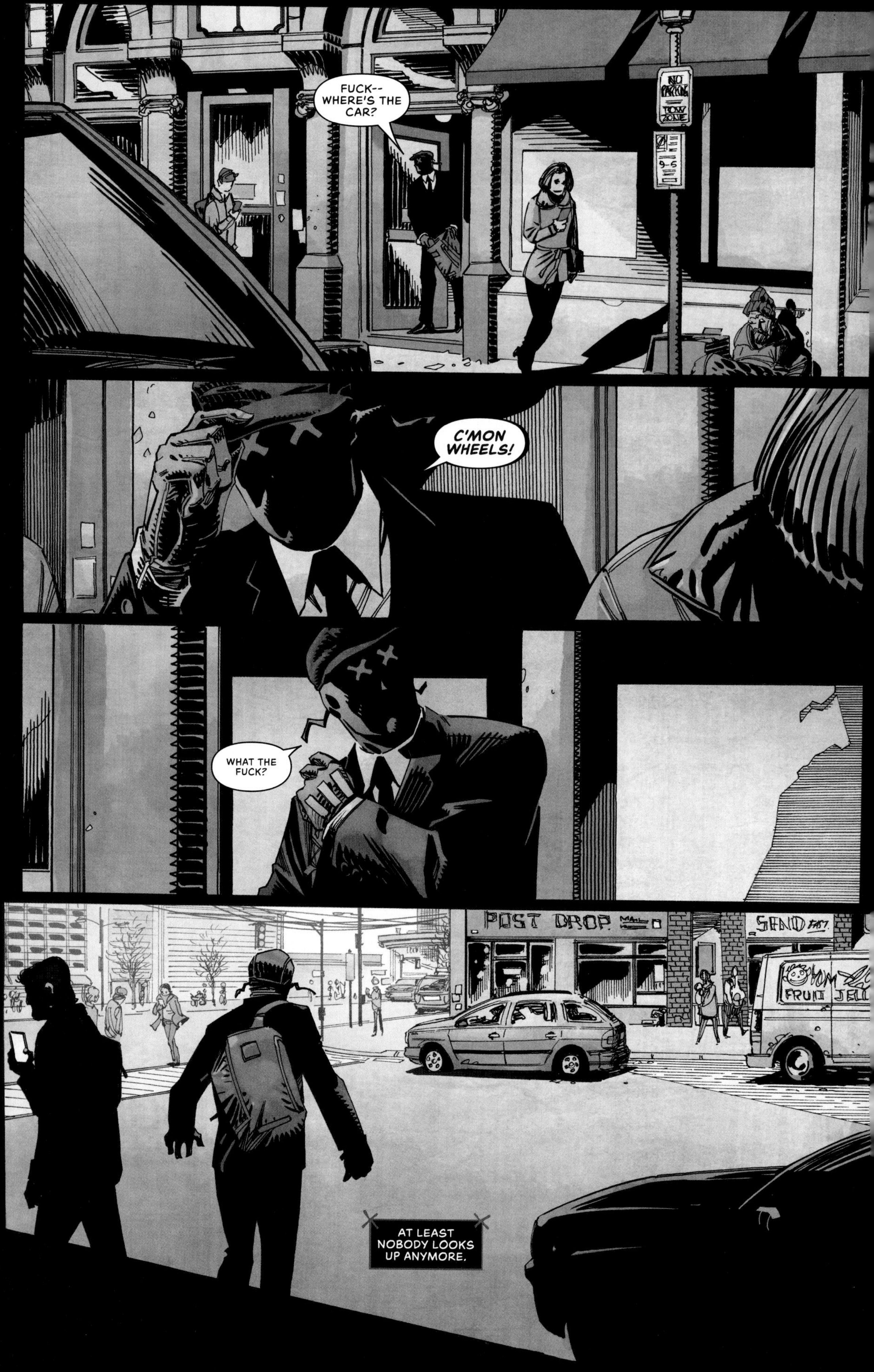
FUCK-- WHERE'S THE CAR?
NO PARKING TOW ZONE
9-5
C'MON WHEELS!
WHAT THE FUCK?
POST DROP
SEND
FRUIT JELL
AT LEAST NOBODY LOOKS UP ANYMORE.

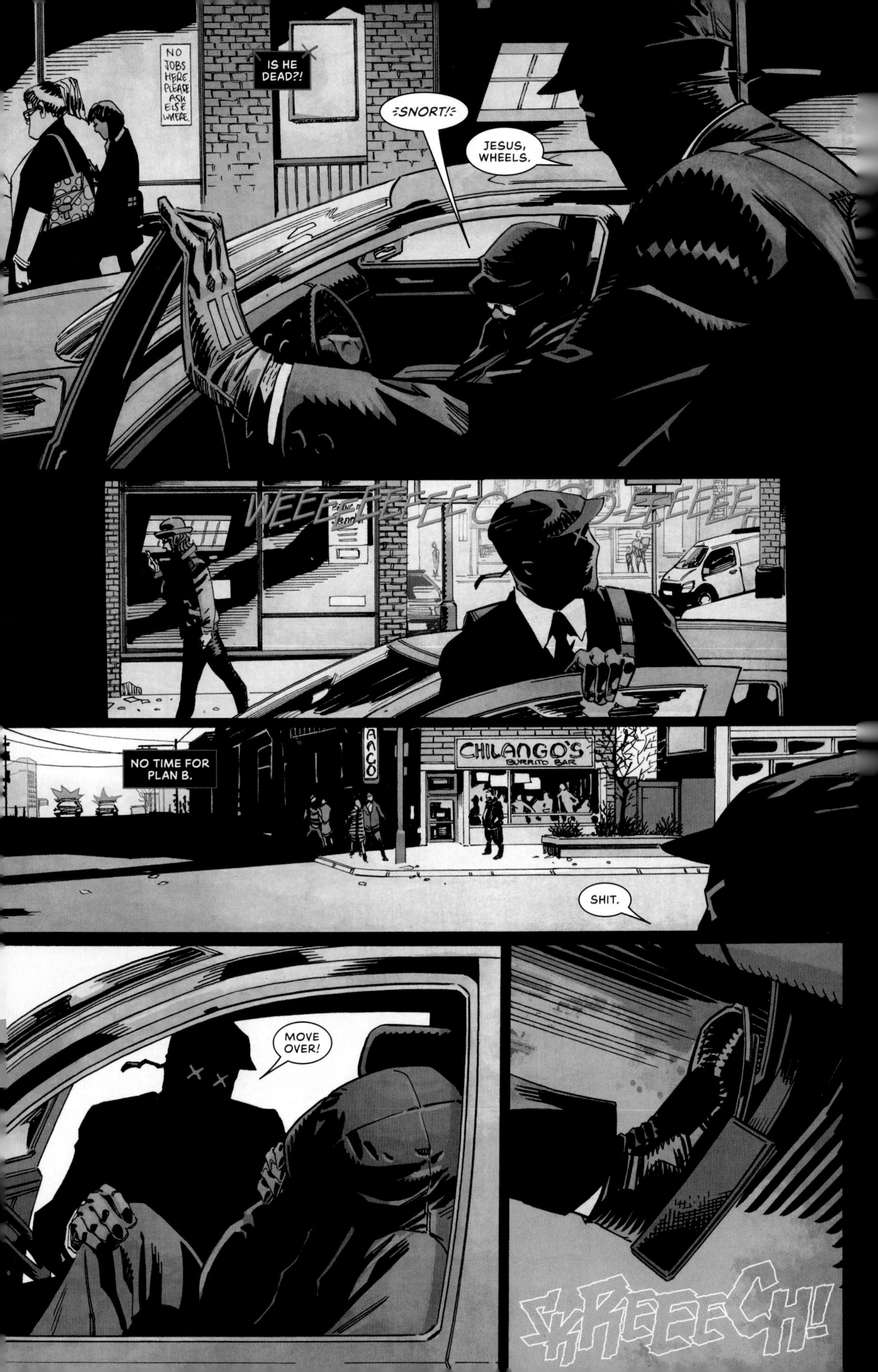
NO JOBS HERE PLEASE ASK ELSE WHERE.
IS HE DEAD?!
SNORT!
JESUS, WHEELS.
WEEEEEEEEEEEO-OO-EEEEEE
NO TIME FOR PLAN B.
CHILANGO'S BURRITO BAR
SHIT.
MOVE OVER!
SKREEEECH!

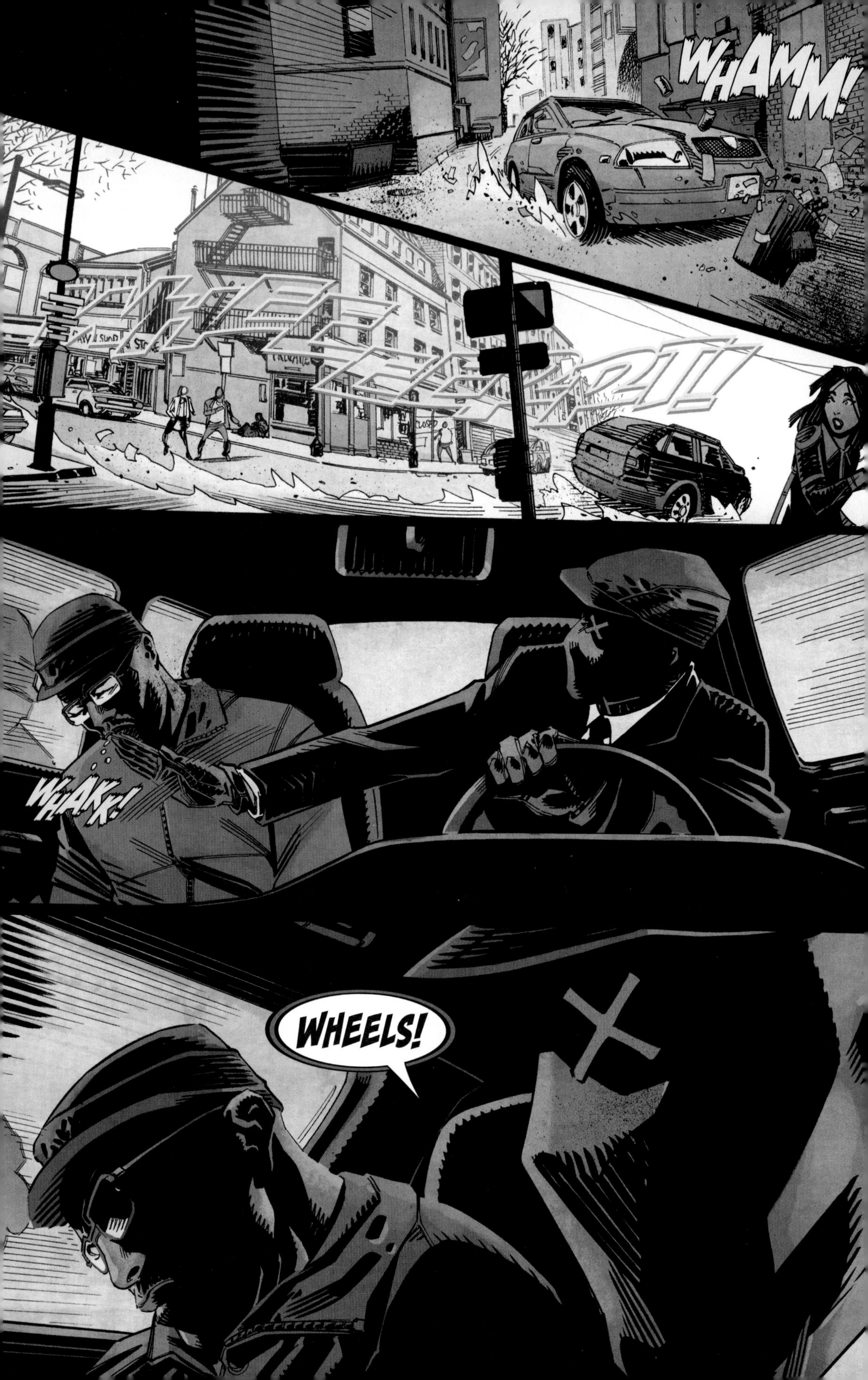
WHAMM!
CLOSED
WHAKK!
WHEELS!

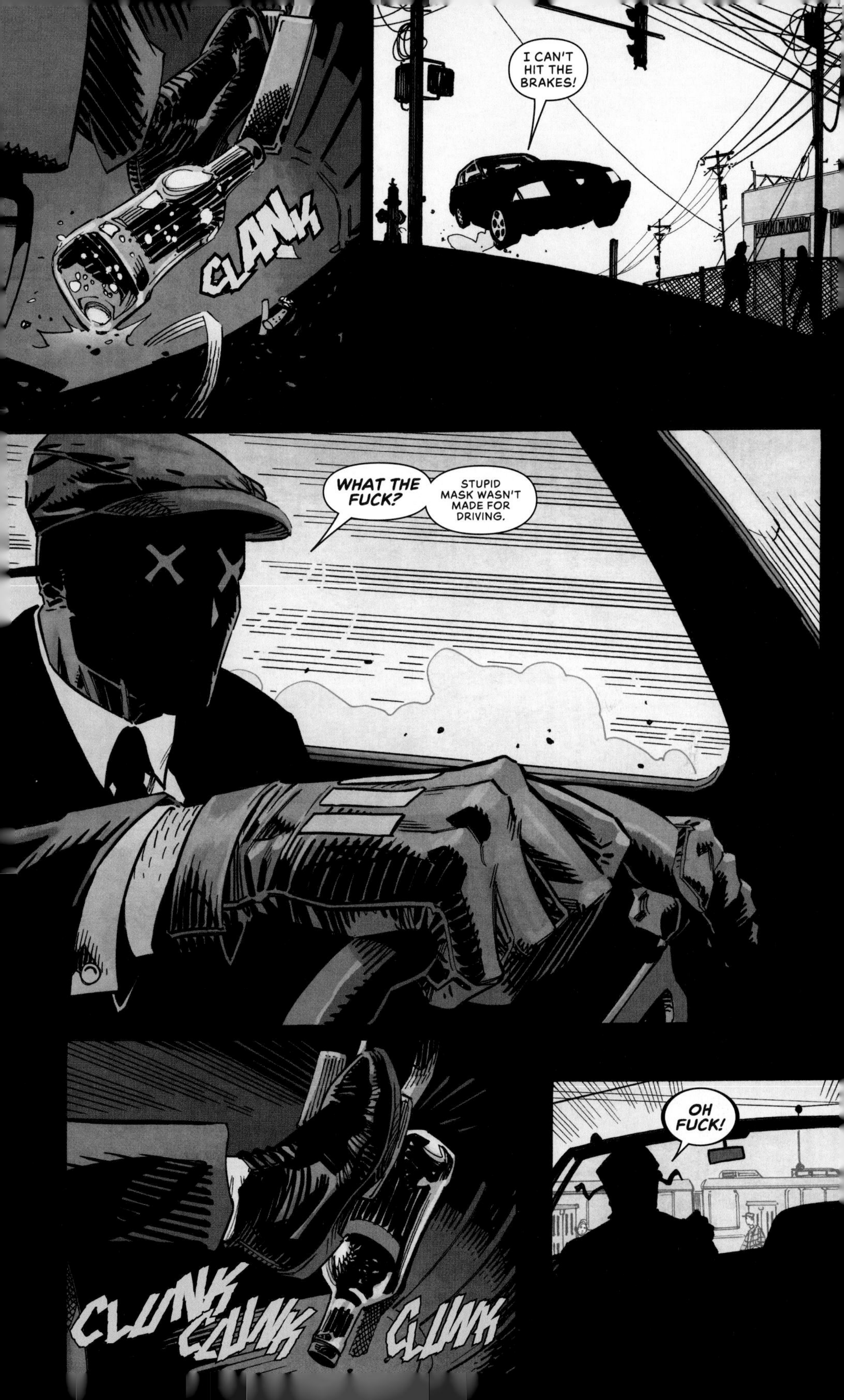
CLANK
I CAN'T HIT THE BRAKES!
WHAT THE FUCK?
STUPID MASK WASN'T MADE FOR DRIVING.
CLUNK CLUNK CLUNK
OH FUCK!

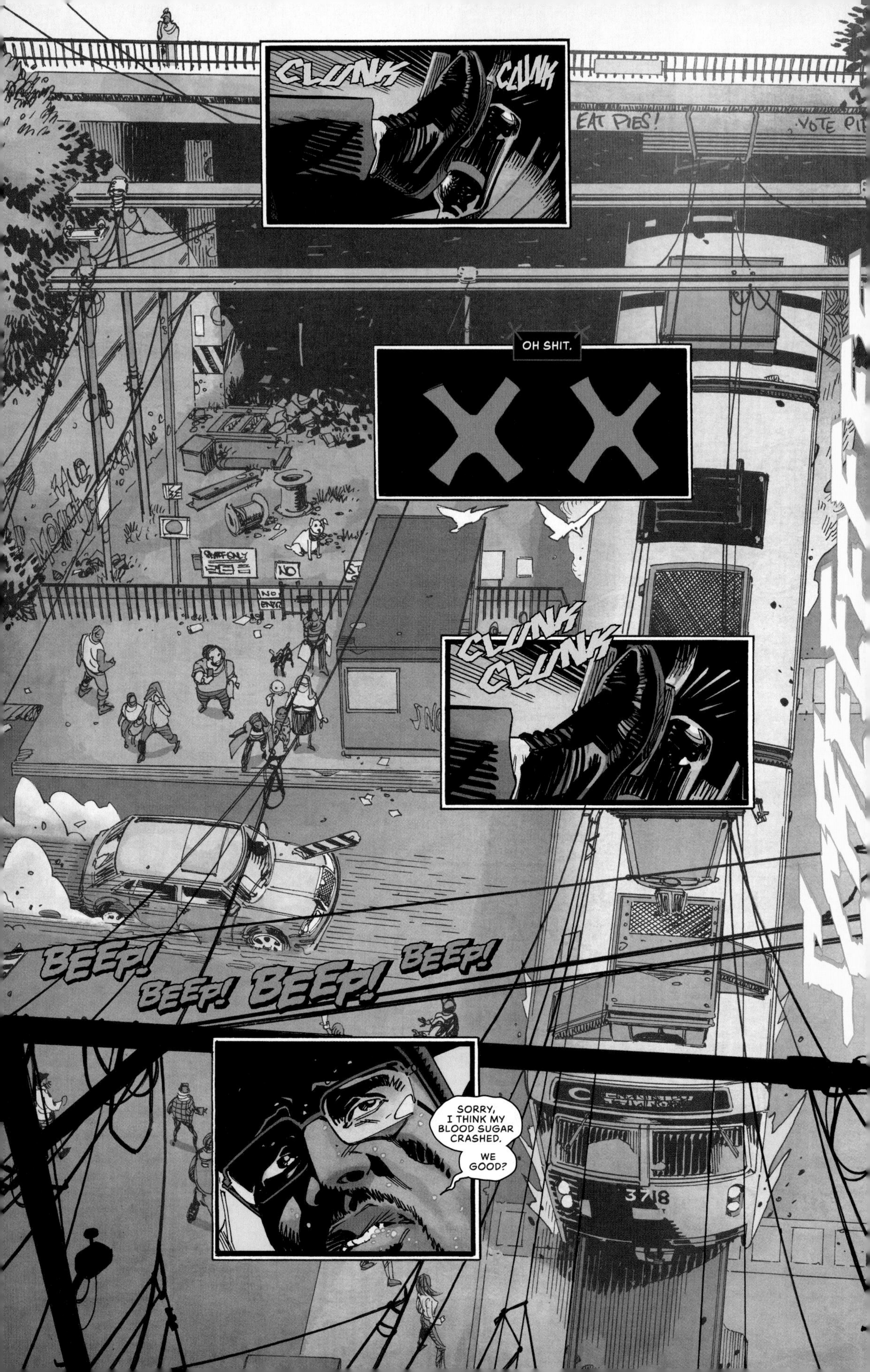
CLUNK
CLUNK
EAT PIES!
OH SHIT.
CLUNK
CLUNK
BEEP!
BEEP!
BEEP!
BEEP!
SORRY, I THINK MY BLOOD SUGAR CRASHED.
WE GOOD?
3718

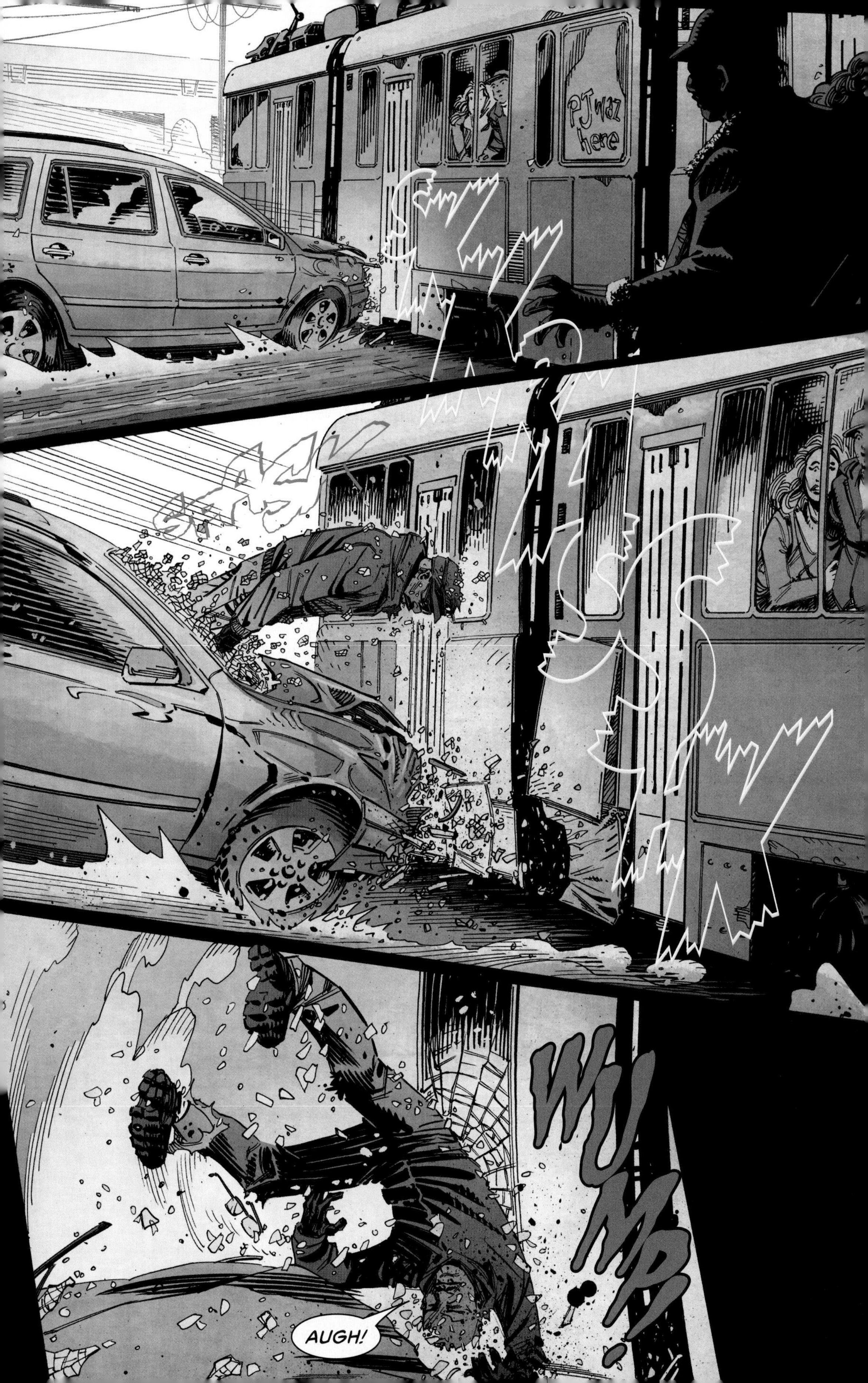
PJ waz here
WUMP!
AUGH!

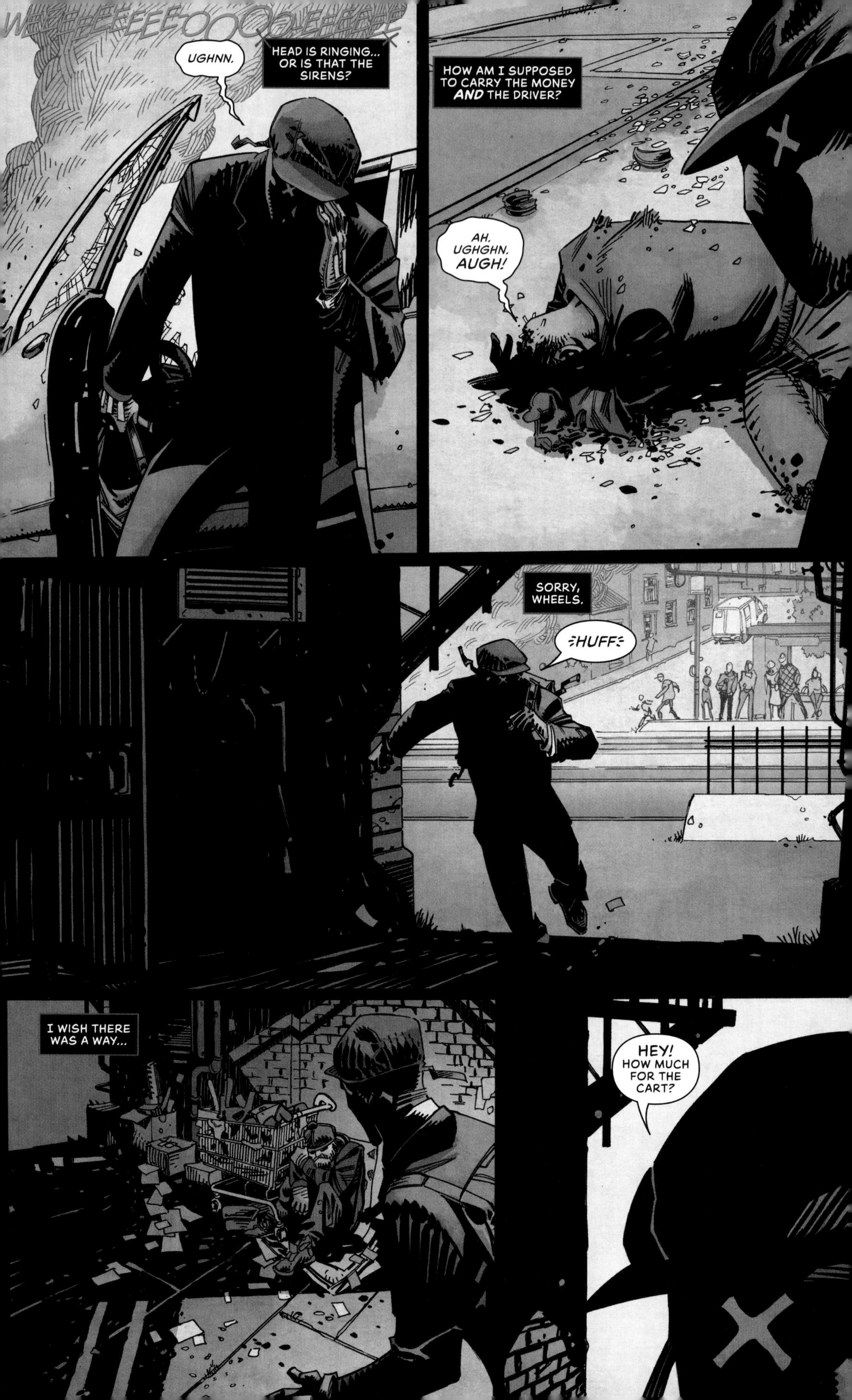
UGHNN.
HEAD IS RINGING... OR IS THAT THE SIRENS?
HOW AM I SUPPOSED TO CARRY THE MONEY AND THE DRIVER?
AH. UGHGHN. AUGH!
SORRY, WHEELS.
HUFF
I WISH THERE WAS A WAY...
HEY! HOW MUCH FOR THE CART?

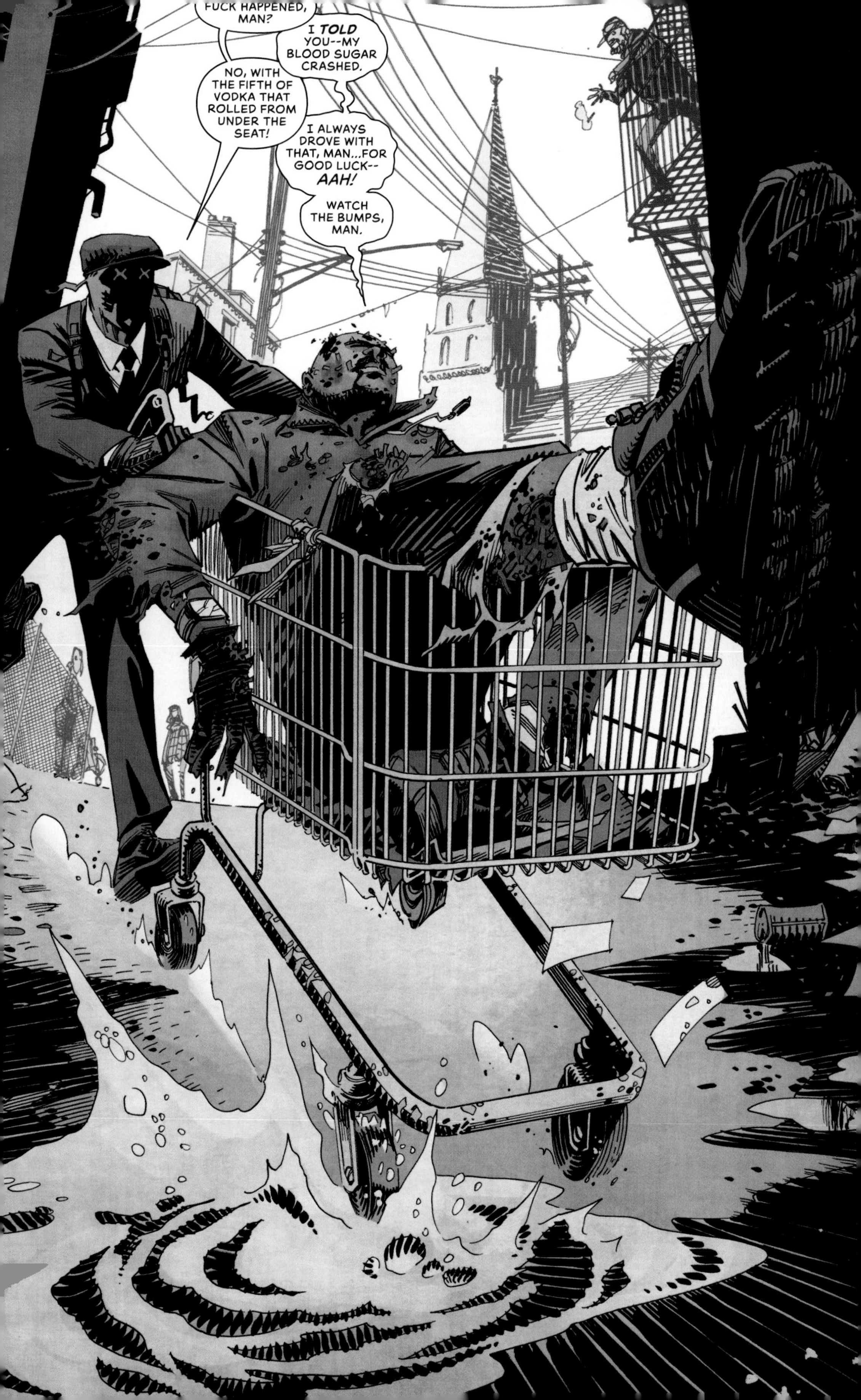
FUCK HAPPENED, MAN?
I TOLD YOU--MY BLOOD SUGAR CRASHED.
NO, WITH THE FIFTH OF VODKA THAT ROLLED FROM UNDER THE SEAT!
I ALWAYS DROVE WITH THAT, MAN...FOR GOOD LUCK-- AAH!
WATCH THE BUMPS, MAN.

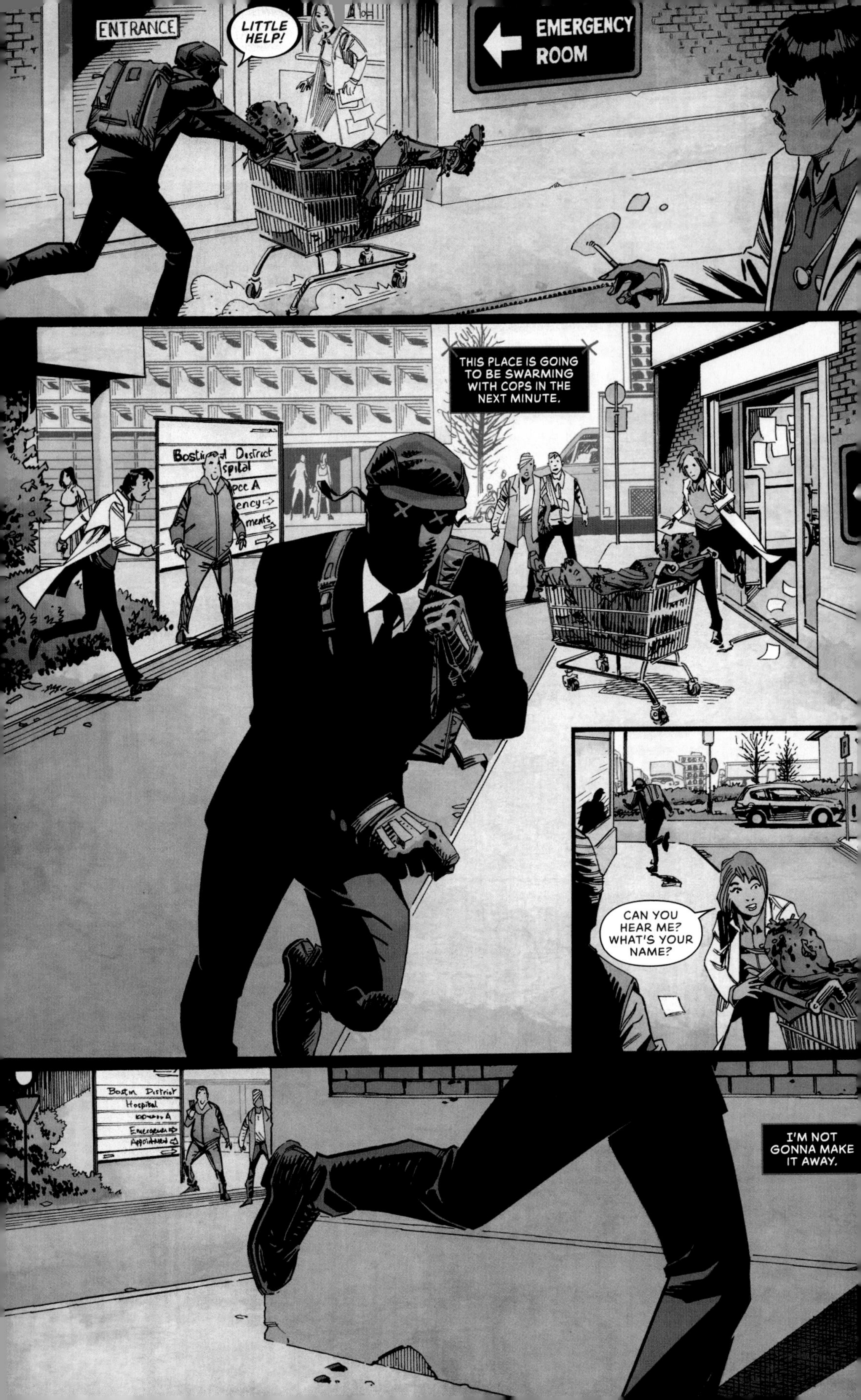
ENTRANCE
LITTLE HELP!
EMERGENCY ROOM
THIS PLACE IS GOING TO BE SWARMING WITH COPS IN THE NEXT MINUTE.
CAN YOU HEAR ME? WHAT'S YOUR NAME?
I'M NOT GONNA MAKE IT AWAY.

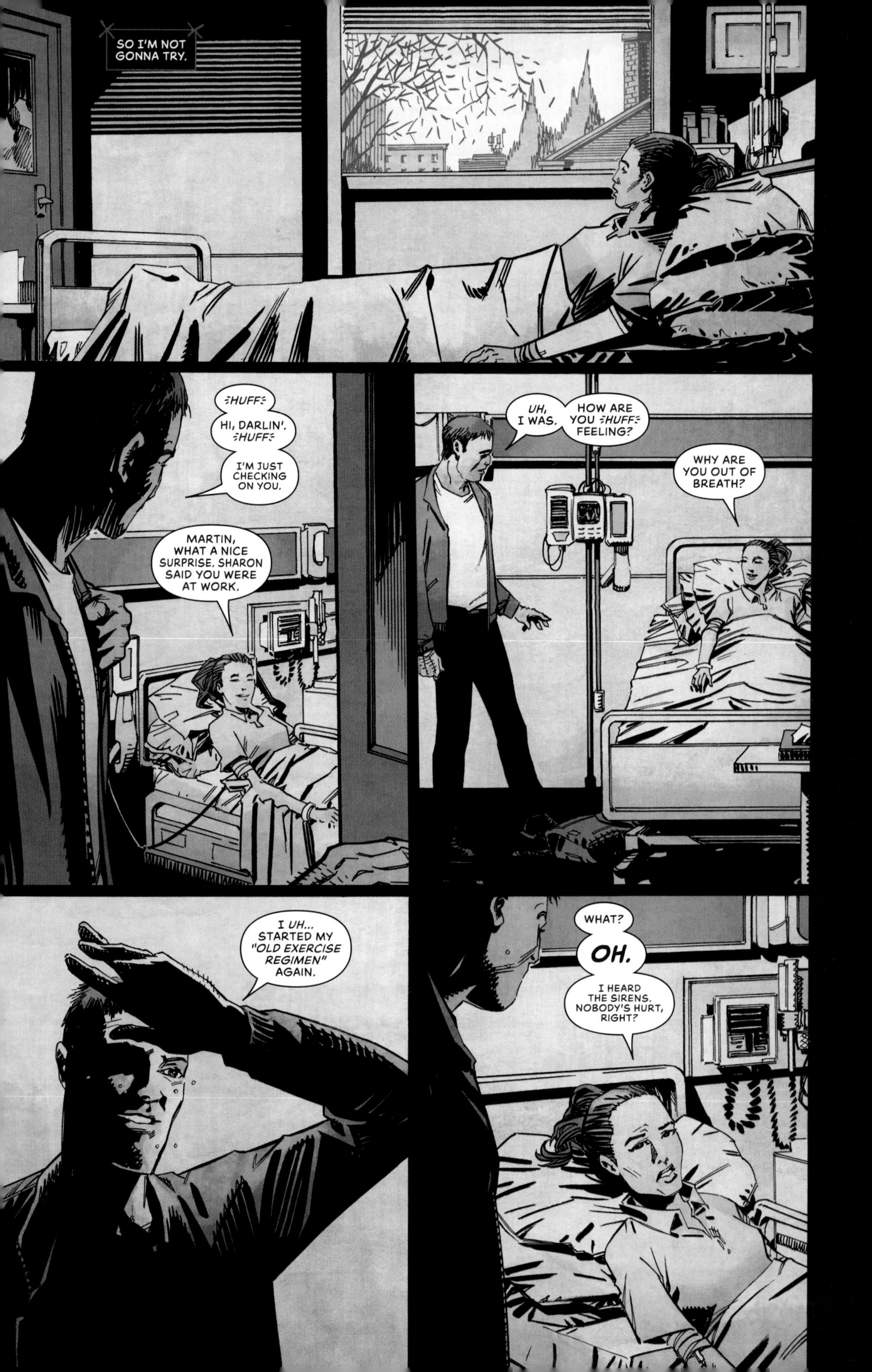
SO I'M NOT GONNA TRY.
HUFF
HI, DARLIN'. HUFF
I'M JUST CHECKING ON YOU.
MARTIN, WHAT A NICE SURPRISE. SHARON SAID YOU WERE AT WORK.
UH, I WAS.
HOW ARE YOU HUFF FEELING?
WHY ARE YOU OUT OF BREATH?
I UH... STARTED MY "OLD EXERCISE REGIMEN" AGAIN.
WHAT?
OH.
I HEARD THE SIRENS. NOBODY'S HURT, RIGHT?

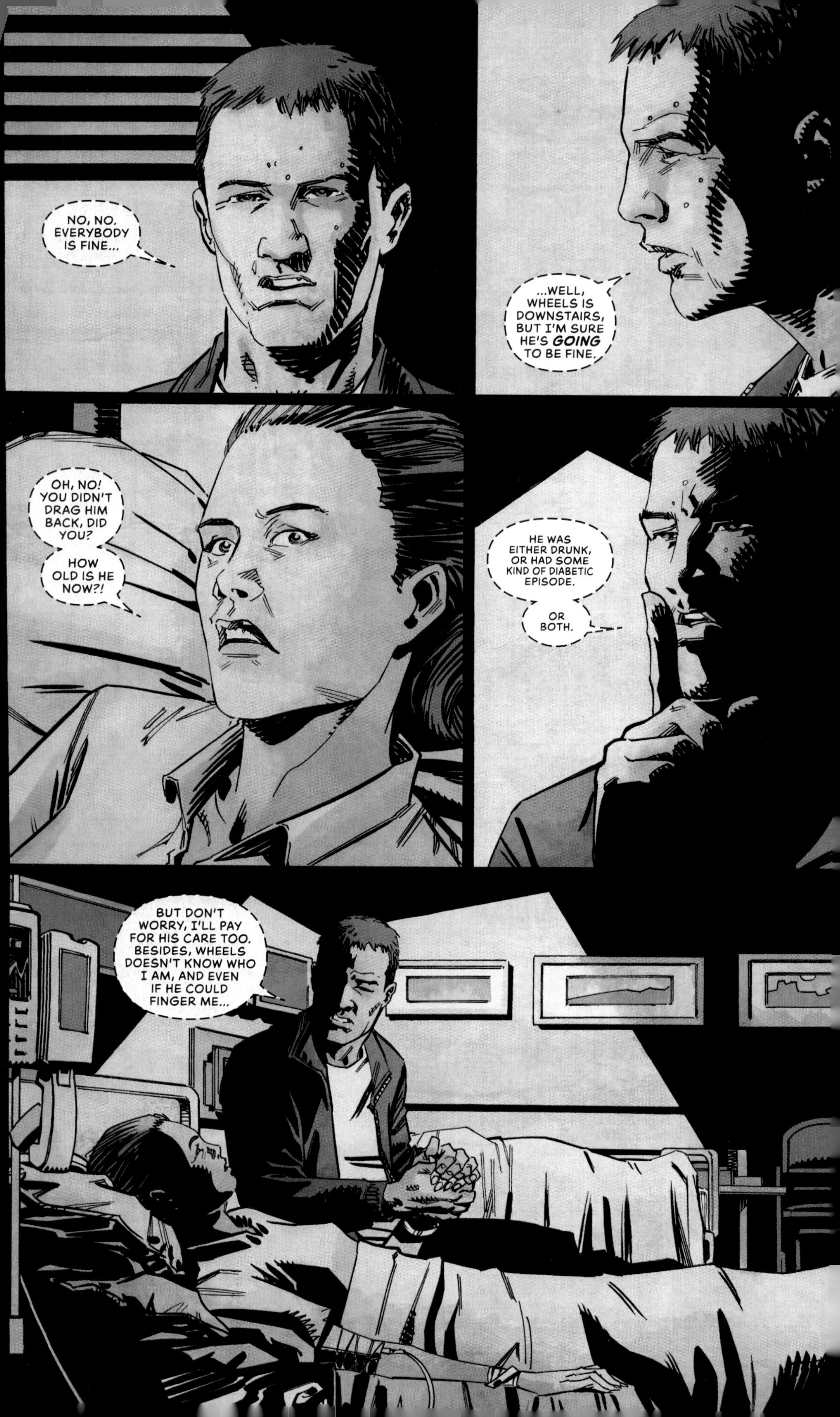
NO, NO. EVERYBODY IS FINE...
...WELL, WHEELS IS DOWNSTAIRS, BUT I'M SURE HE'S **GOING** TO BE FINE.
OH, NO! YOU DIDN'T DRAG HIM BACK, DID YOU?
HOW OLD IS HE NOW?!
HE WAS EITHER DRUNK, OR HAD SOME KIND OF DIABETIC EPISODE.
OR BOTH.
BUT DON'T WORRY, I'LL PAY FOR HIS CARE TOO. BESIDES, WHEELS DOESN'T KNOW WHO I AM, AND EVEN IF HE COULD FINGER ME...

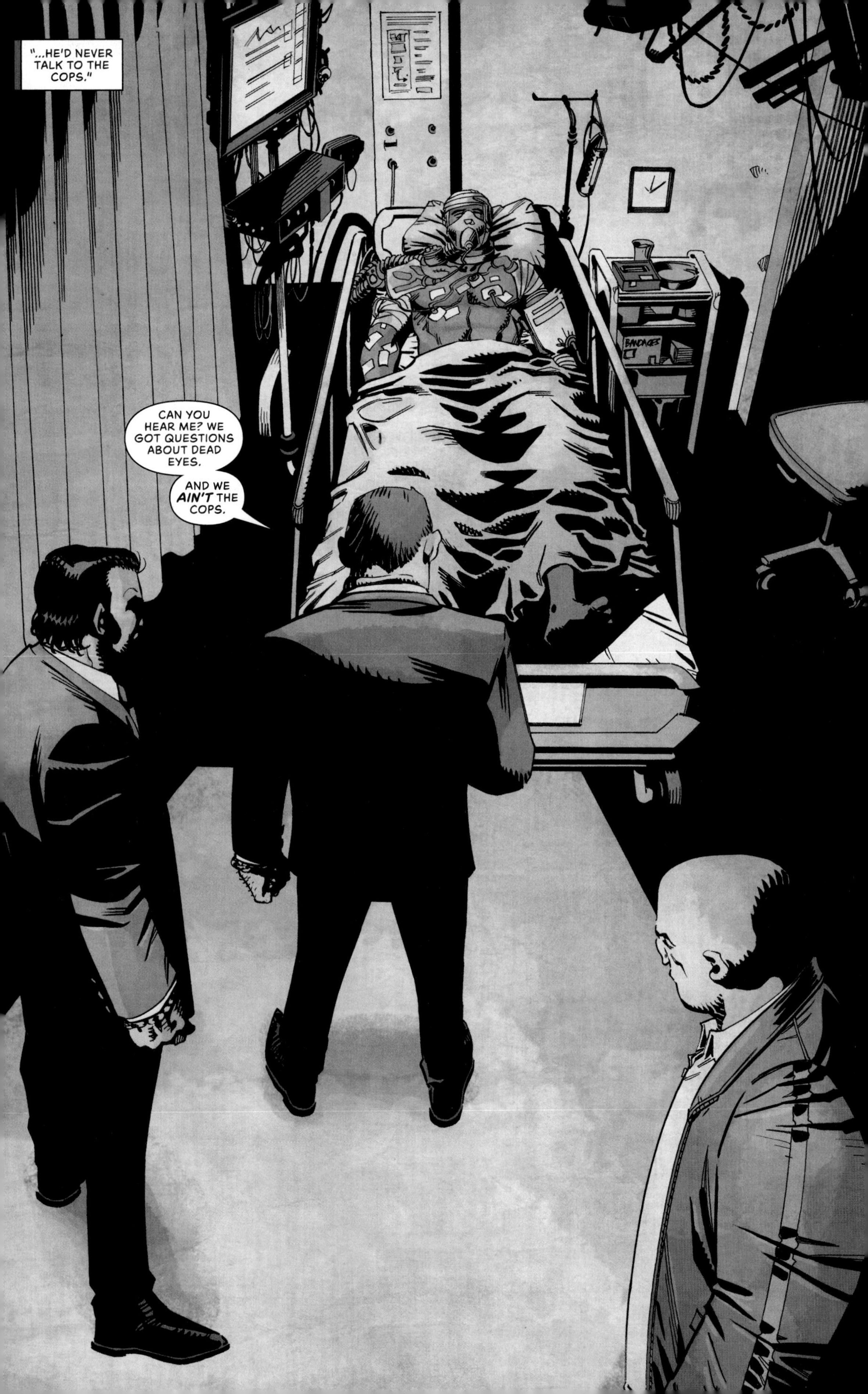
"...HE'D NEVER TALK TO THE COPS."
CAN YOU HEAR ME? WE GOT QUESTIONS ABOUT DEAD EYES.
AND WE *AIN'T* THE COPS.
BANDAGES

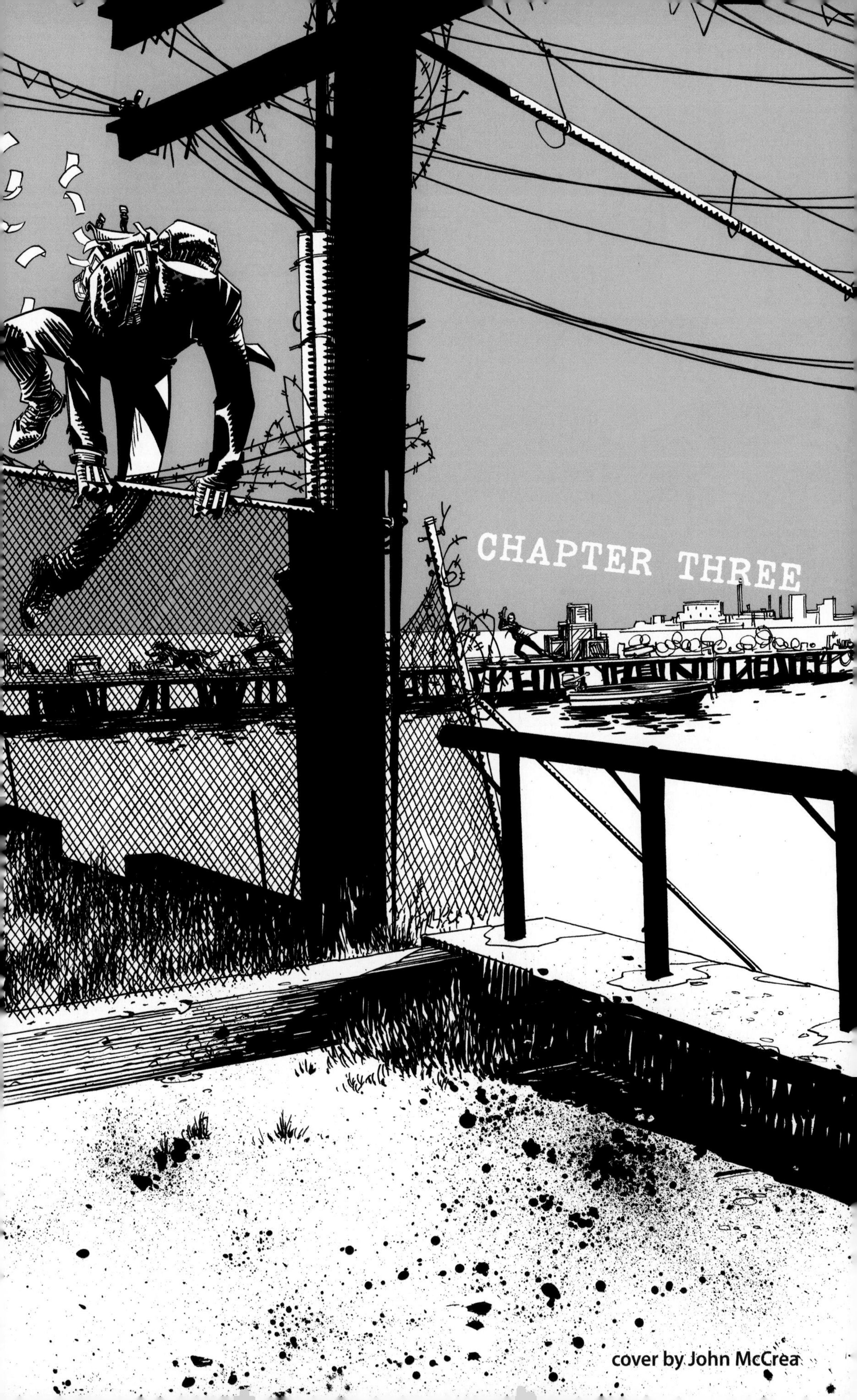
CHAPTER THREE

cover by John McCrea

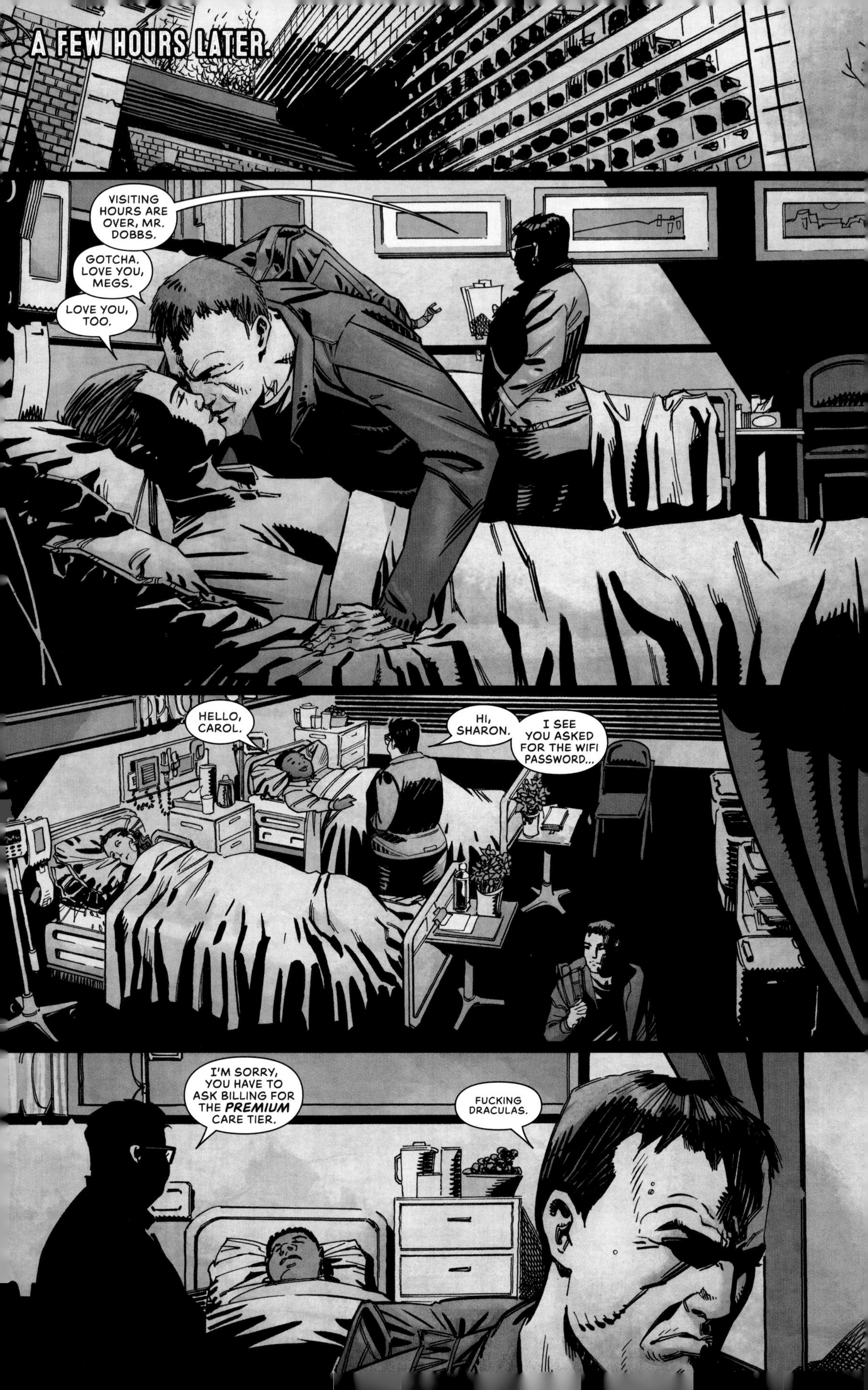
A FEW HOURS LATER.
VISITING HOURS ARE OVER, MR. DOBBS.
GOTCHA. LOVE YOU, MEGS.
LOVE YOU, TOO.
HELLO, CAROL.
HI, SHARON.
I SEE YOU ASKED FOR THE WIFI PASSWORD...
I'M SORRY, YOU HAVE TO ASK BILLING FOR THE PREMIUM CARE TIER.
FUCKING DRACULAS.

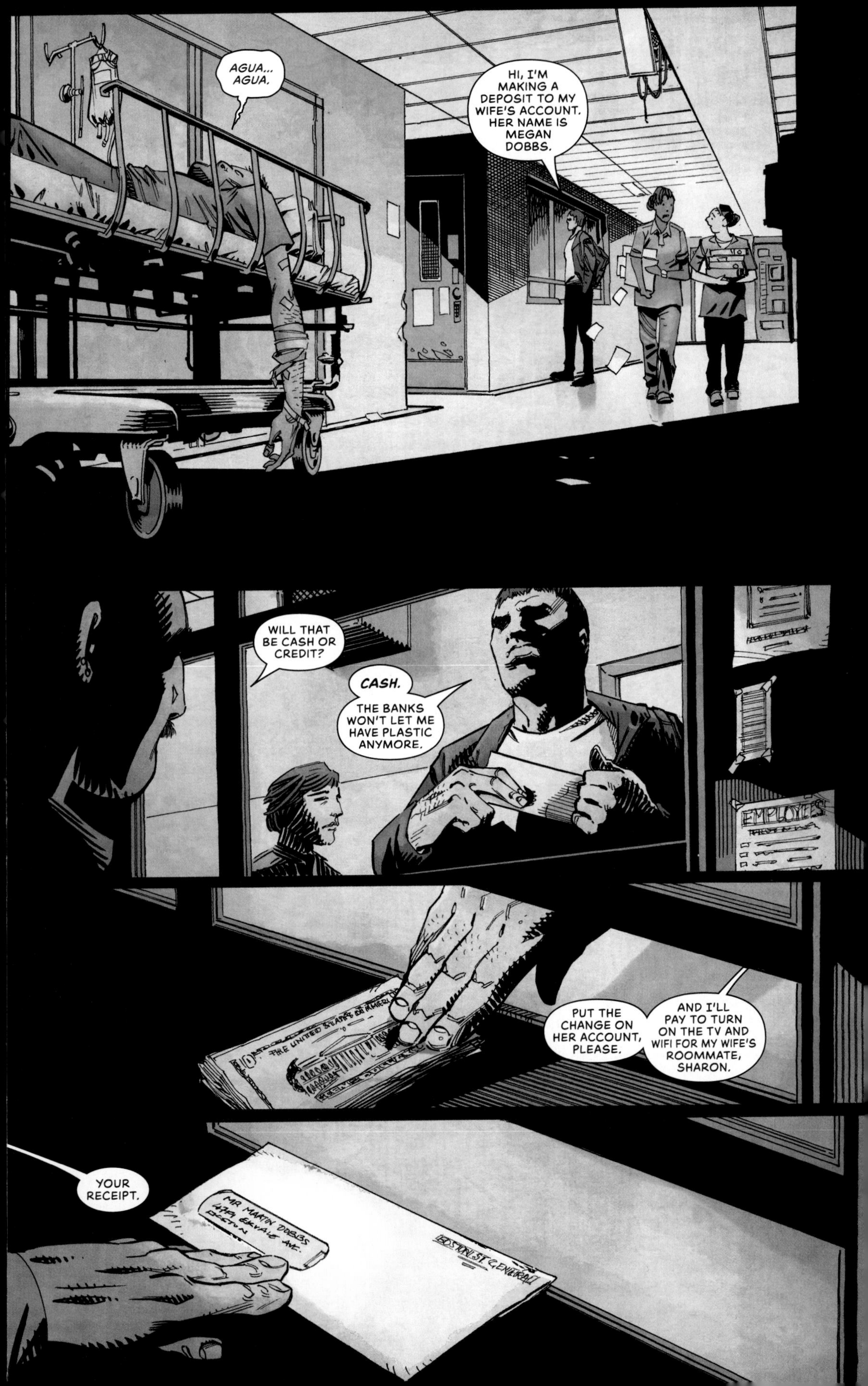
AGUA... AGUA.
HI, I'M MAKING A DEPOSIT TO MY WIFE'S ACCOUNT. HER NAME IS MEGAN DOBBS.
WILL THAT BE CASH OR CREDIT?
CASH.
THE BANKS WON'T LET ME HAVE PLASTIC ANYMORE.
PUT THE CHANGE ON HER ACCOUNT, PLEASE.
AND I'LL PAY TO TURN ON THE TV AND WIFI FOR MY WIFE'S ROOMMATE, SHARON.
YOUR RECEIPT.
MR MARTIN DOBBS

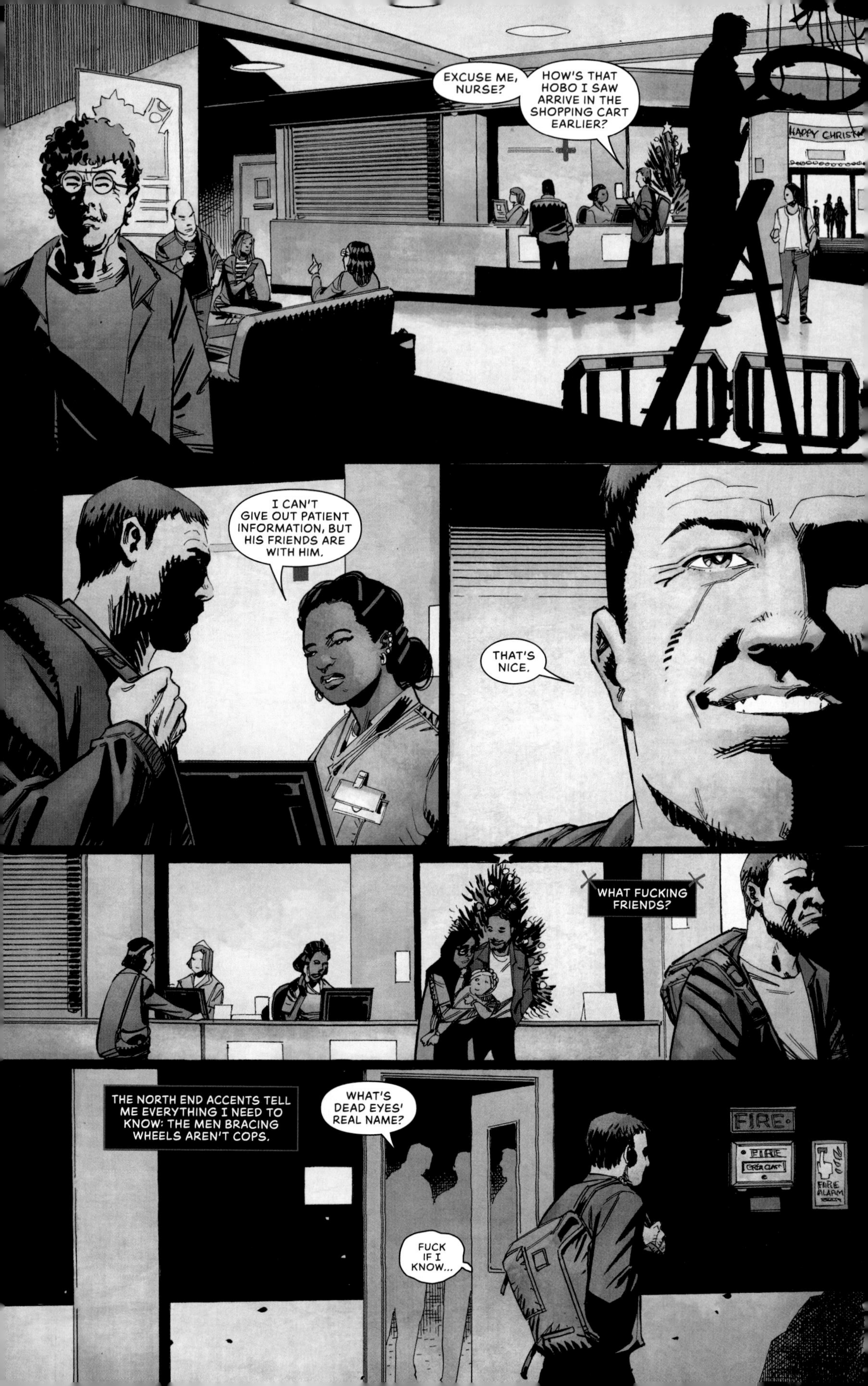
EXCUSE ME, NURSE?
HOW'S THAT HOBO I SAW ARRIVE IN THE SHOPPING CART EARLIER?
HAPPY CHRIST
I CAN'T GIVE OUT PATIENT INFORMATION, BUT HIS FRIENDS ARE WITH HIM.
THAT'S NICE.
WHAT FUCKING FRIENDS?
THE NORTH END ACCENTS TELL ME EVERYTHING I NEED TO KNOW: THE MEN BRACING WHEELS AREN'T COPS.
WHAT'S DEAD EYES' REAL NAME?
FUCK IF I KNOW...
FIRE
FIRE
FIRE ALARM

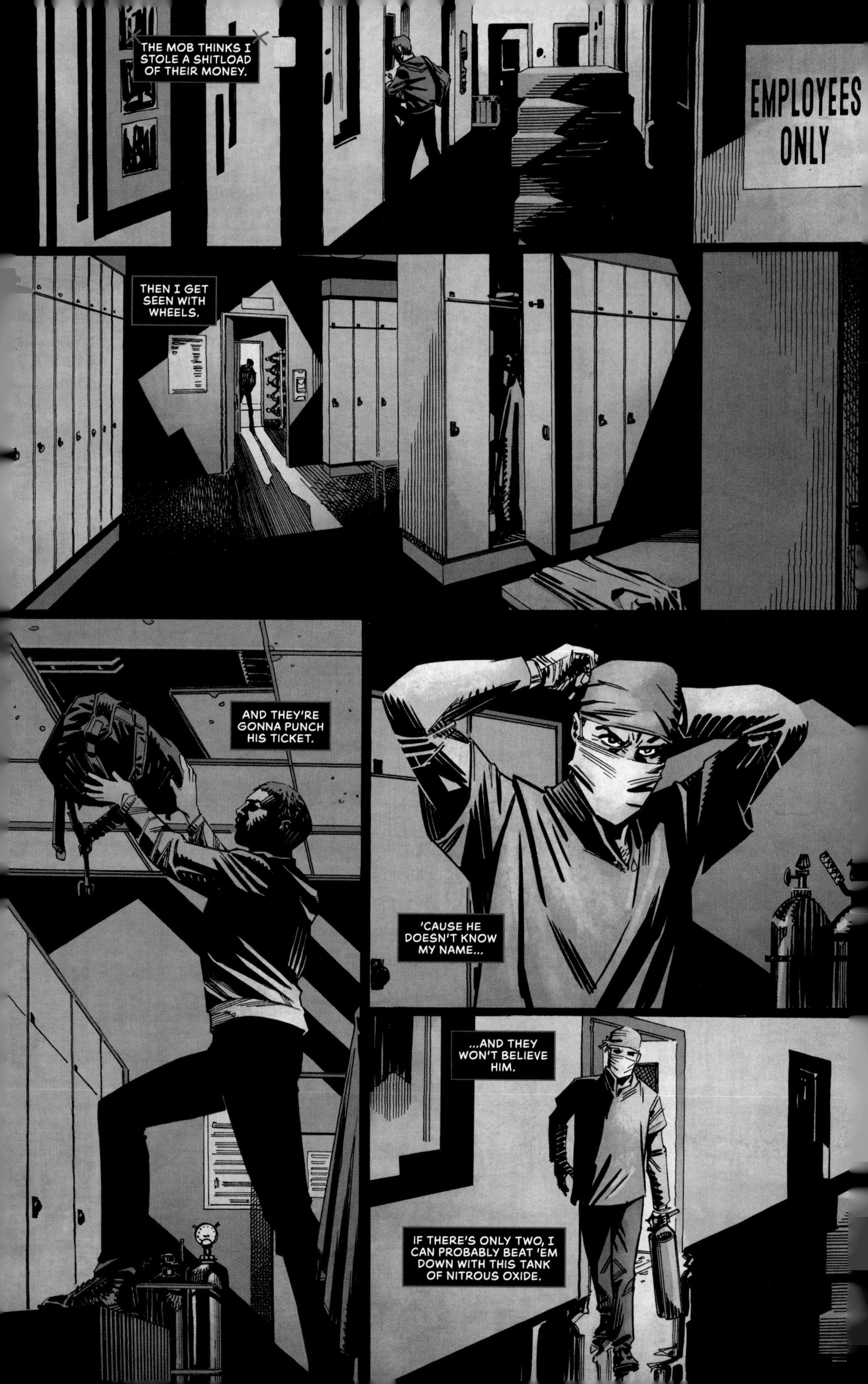
THE MOB THINKS I STOLE A SHITLOAD OF THEIR MONEY.
EMPLOYEES ONLY
THEN I GET SEEN WITH WHEELS.
AND THEY'RE GONNA PUNCH HIS TICKET.
'CAUSE HE DOESN'T KNOW MY NAME...
...AND THEY WON'T BELIEVE HIM.
IF THERE'S ONLY TWO, I CAN PROBABLY BEAT 'EM DOWN WITH THIS TANK OF NITROUS OXIDE.

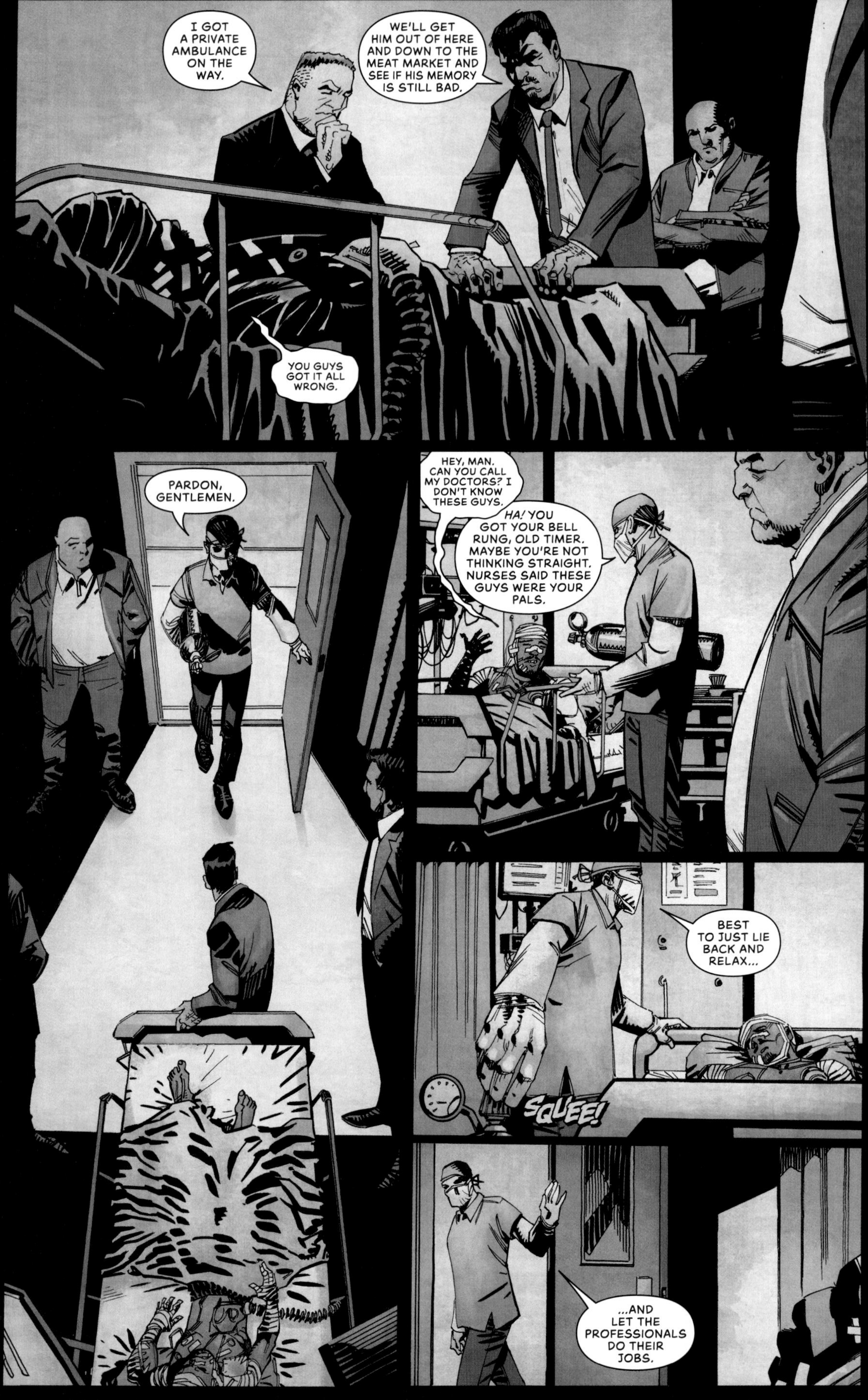
I GOT A PRIVATE AMBULANCE ON THE WAY.
WE'LL GET HIM OUT OF HERE AND DOWN TO THE MEAT MARKET AND SEE IF HIS MEMORY IS STILL BAD.
YOU GUYS GOT IT ALL WRONG.
PARDON, GENTLEMEN.
HEY, MAN. CAN YOU CALL MY DOCTORS? I DON'T KNOW THESE GUYS.
HA! YOU GOT YOUR BELL RUNG, OLD TIMER. MAYBE YOU'RE NOT THINKING STRAIGHT. NURSES SAID THESE GUYS WERE YOUR PALS.
BEST TO JUST LIE BACK AND RELAX...
SQUEE!
...AND LET THE PROFESSIONALS DO THEIR JOBS.

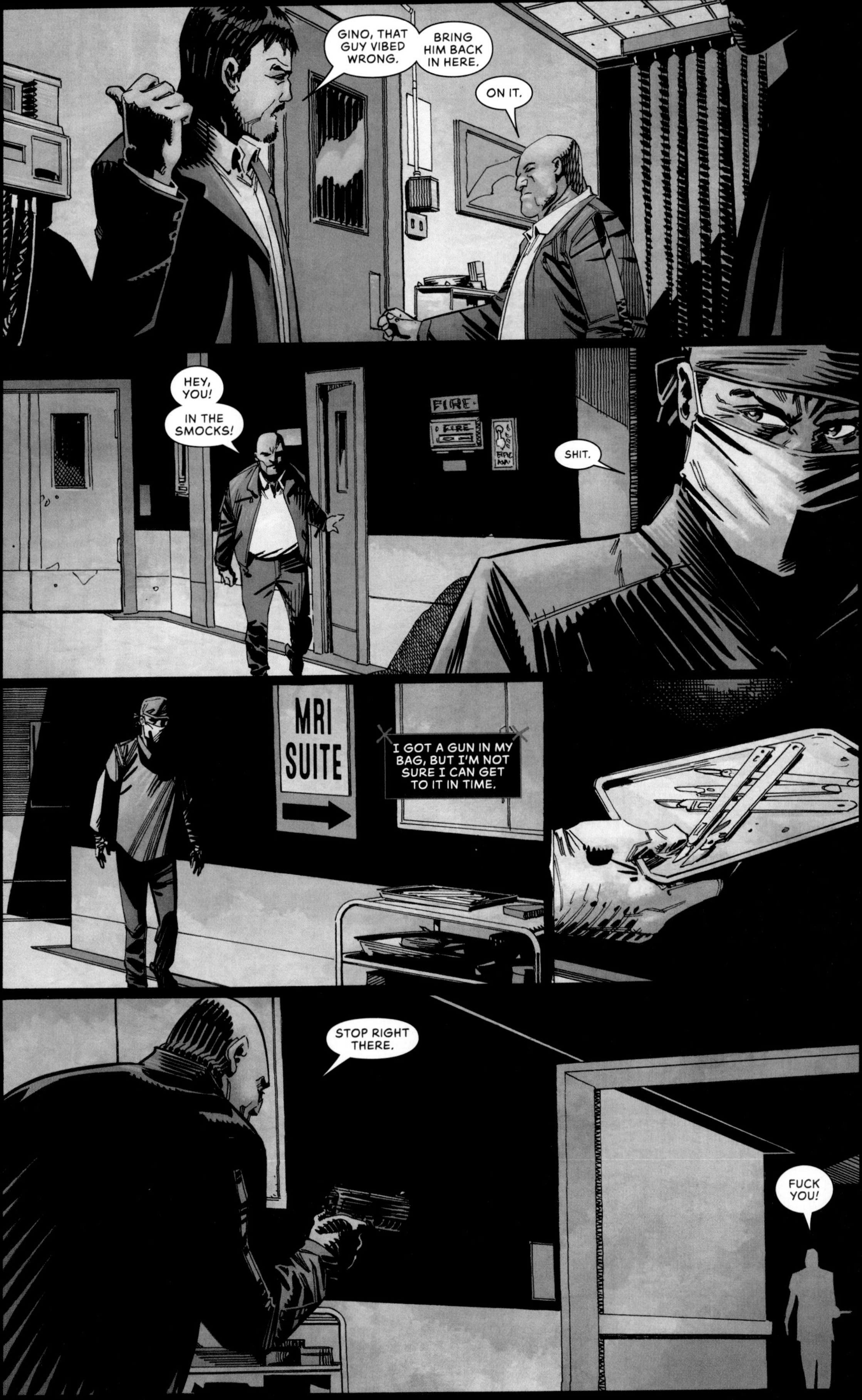
GINO, THAT GUY VIBED WRONG.
BRING HIM BACK IN HERE.
ON IT.
HEY, YOU!
IN THE SMOCKS!
FIRE
SHIT.
MRI SUITE
I GOT A GUN IN MY BAG, BUT I'M NOT SURE I CAN GET TO IT IN TIME.
STOP RIGHT THERE.
FUCK YOU!

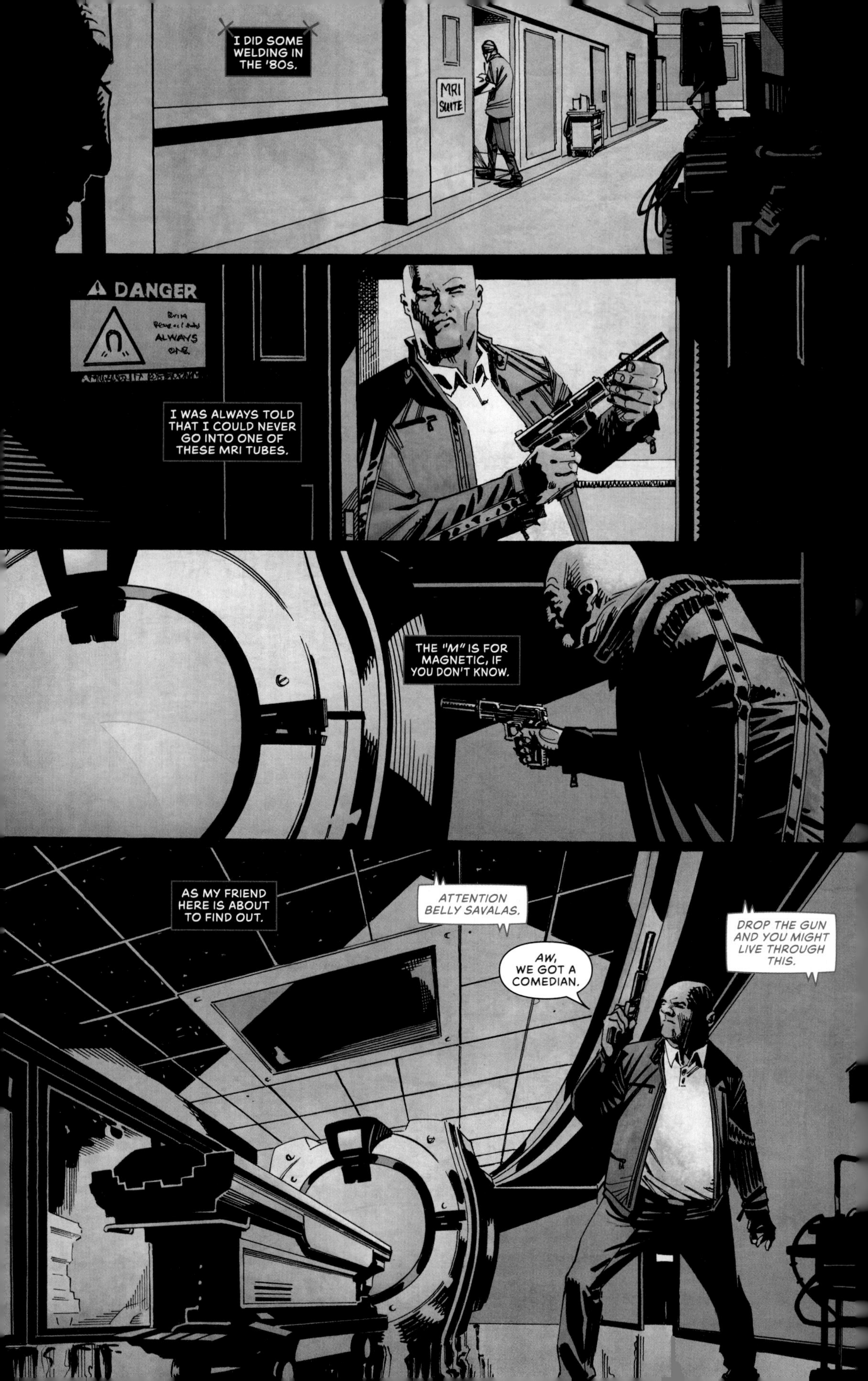

I DID SOME WELDING IN THE '80S.
MRI SUITE
DANGER
I WAS ALWAYS TOLD THAT I COULD NEVER GO INTO ONE OF THESE MRI TUBES.
THE "M" IS FOR MAGNETIC, IF YOU DON'T KNOW.
AS MY FRIEND HERE IS ABOUT TO FIND OUT.
ATTENTION BELLY SAVALAS.
AW, WE GOT A COMEDIAN.
DROP THE GUN AND YOU MIGHT LIVE THROUGH THIS.

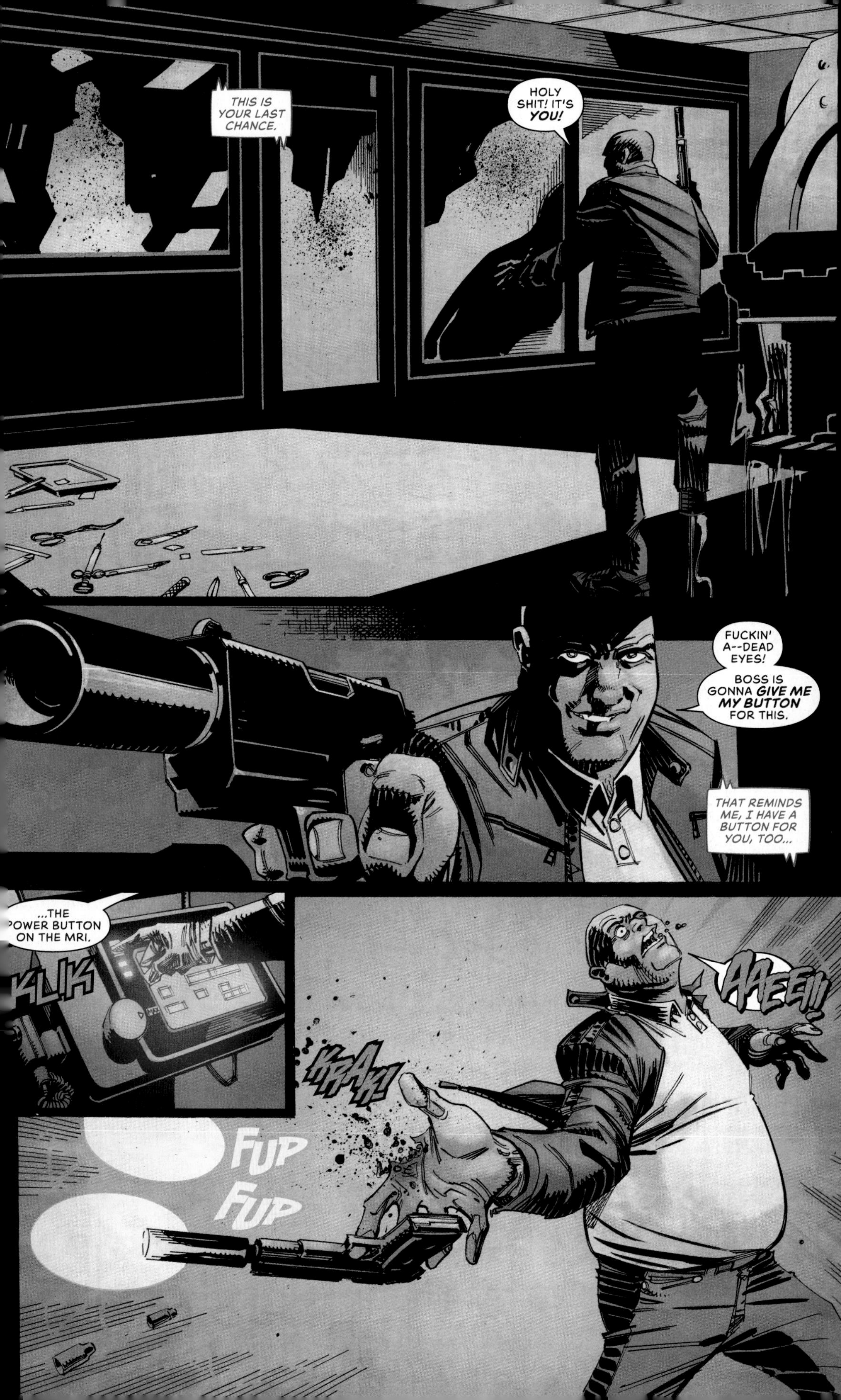

THIS IS YOUR LAST CHANCE.
HOLY SHIT! IT'S YOU!
FUCKIN' A--DEAD EYES!
BOSS IS GONNA GIVE ME MY BUTTON FOR THIS.
THAT REMINDS ME, I HAVE A BUTTON FOR YOU, TOO...
...THE POWER BUTTON ON THE MRI.
KLIK
AAEEII!
KRAK!
FUP
FUP

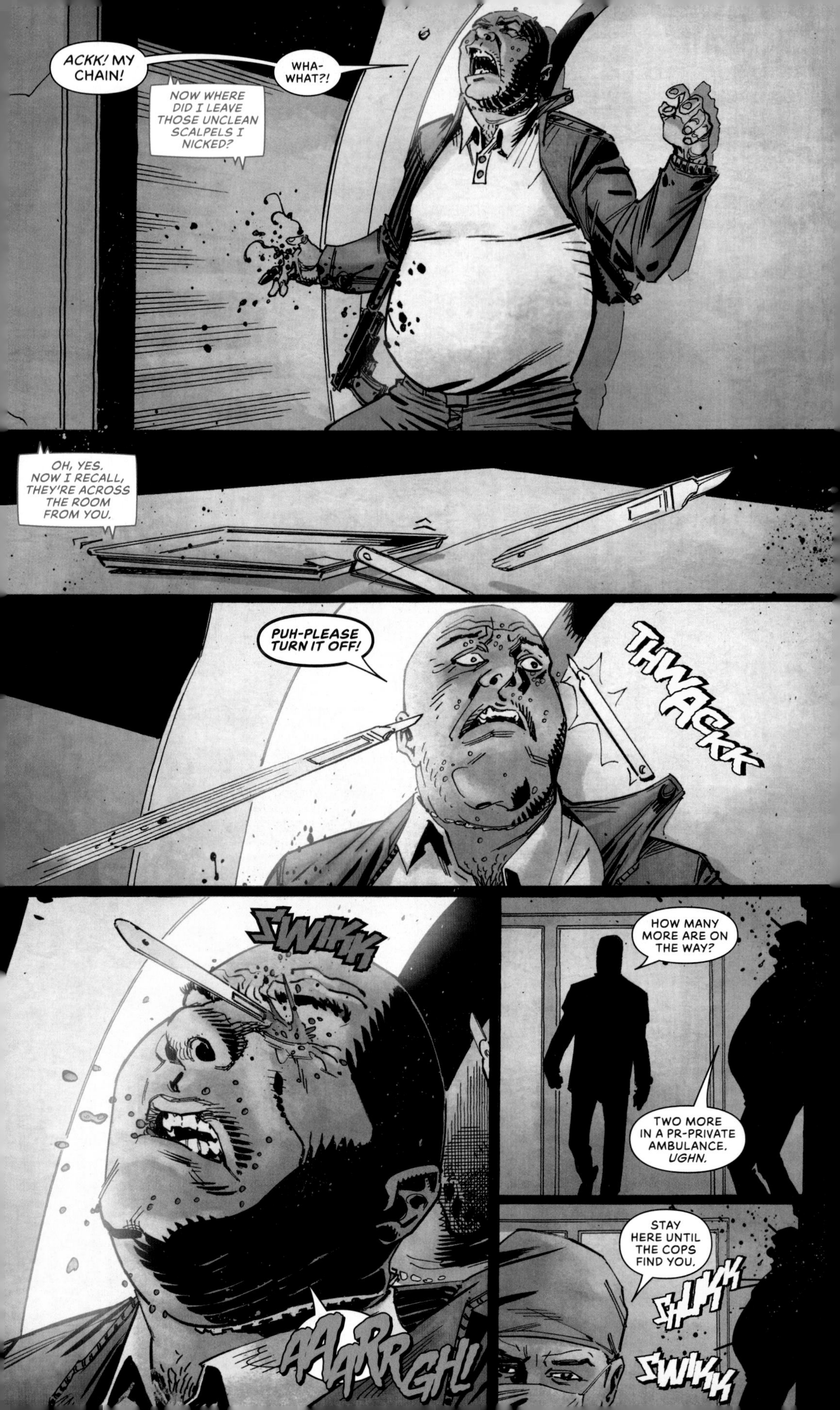
ACKK! MY CHAIN!
WHA-WHAT?!
NOW WHERE DID I LEAVE THOSE UNCLEAN SCALPELS I NICKED?
OH, YES. NOW I RECALL, THEY'RE ACROSS THE ROOM FROM YOU.
PUH-PLEASE TURN IT OFF!
THWACKK
SWIKK
AAARRGH!
HOW MANY MORE ARE ON THE WAY?
TWO MORE IN A PR-PRIVATE AMBULANCE. UGHN.
STAY HERE UNTIL THE COPS FIND YOU.
SHUKK
SWIKK

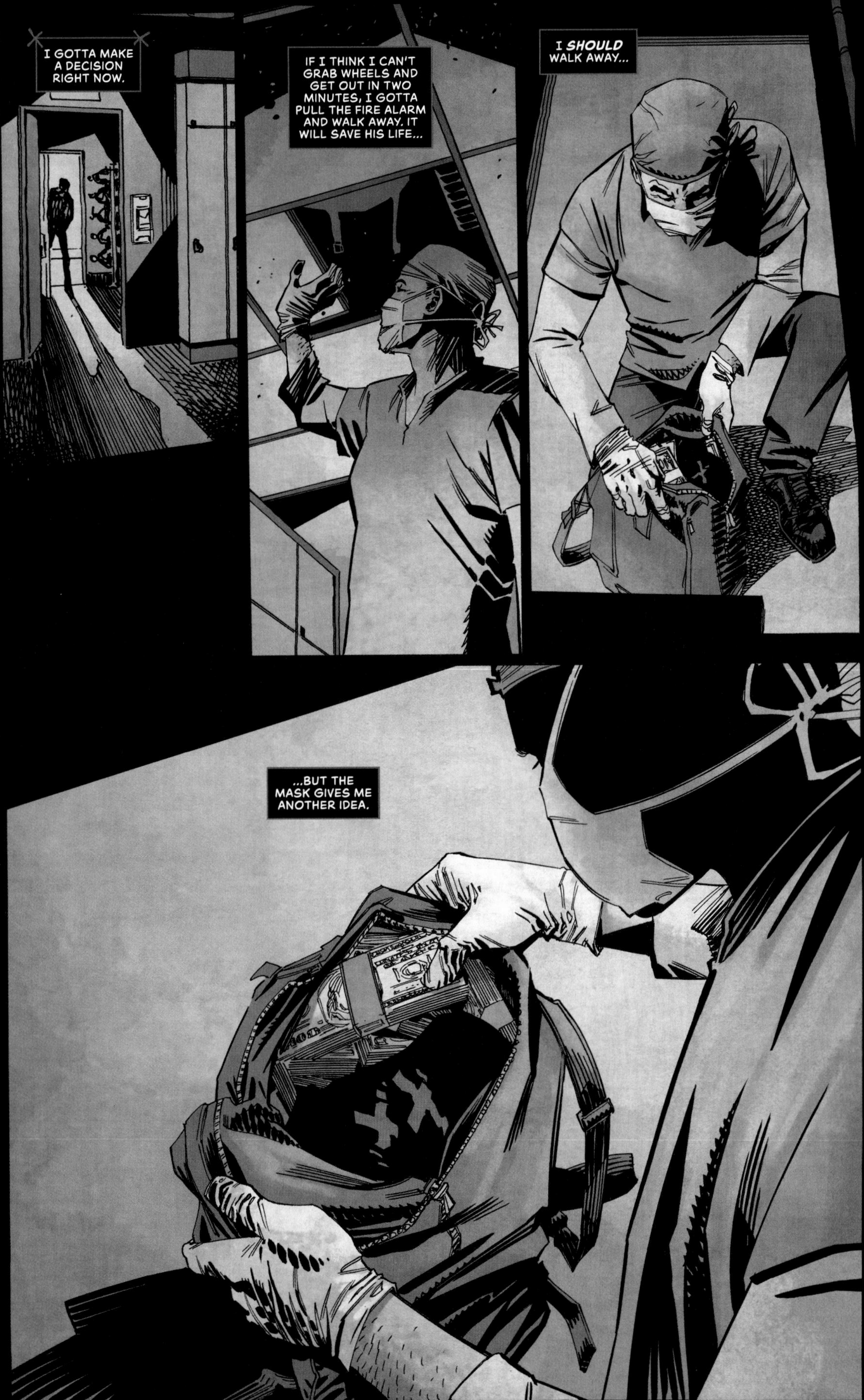
I GOTTA MAKE A DECISION RIGHT NOW.
IF I THINK I CAN'T GRAB WHEELS AND GET OUT IN TWO MINUTES, I GOTTA PULL THE FIRE ALARM AND WALK AWAY. IT WILL SAVE HIS LIFE...
I *SHOULD* WALK AWAY...
...BUT THE MASK GIVES ME ANOTHER IDEA.

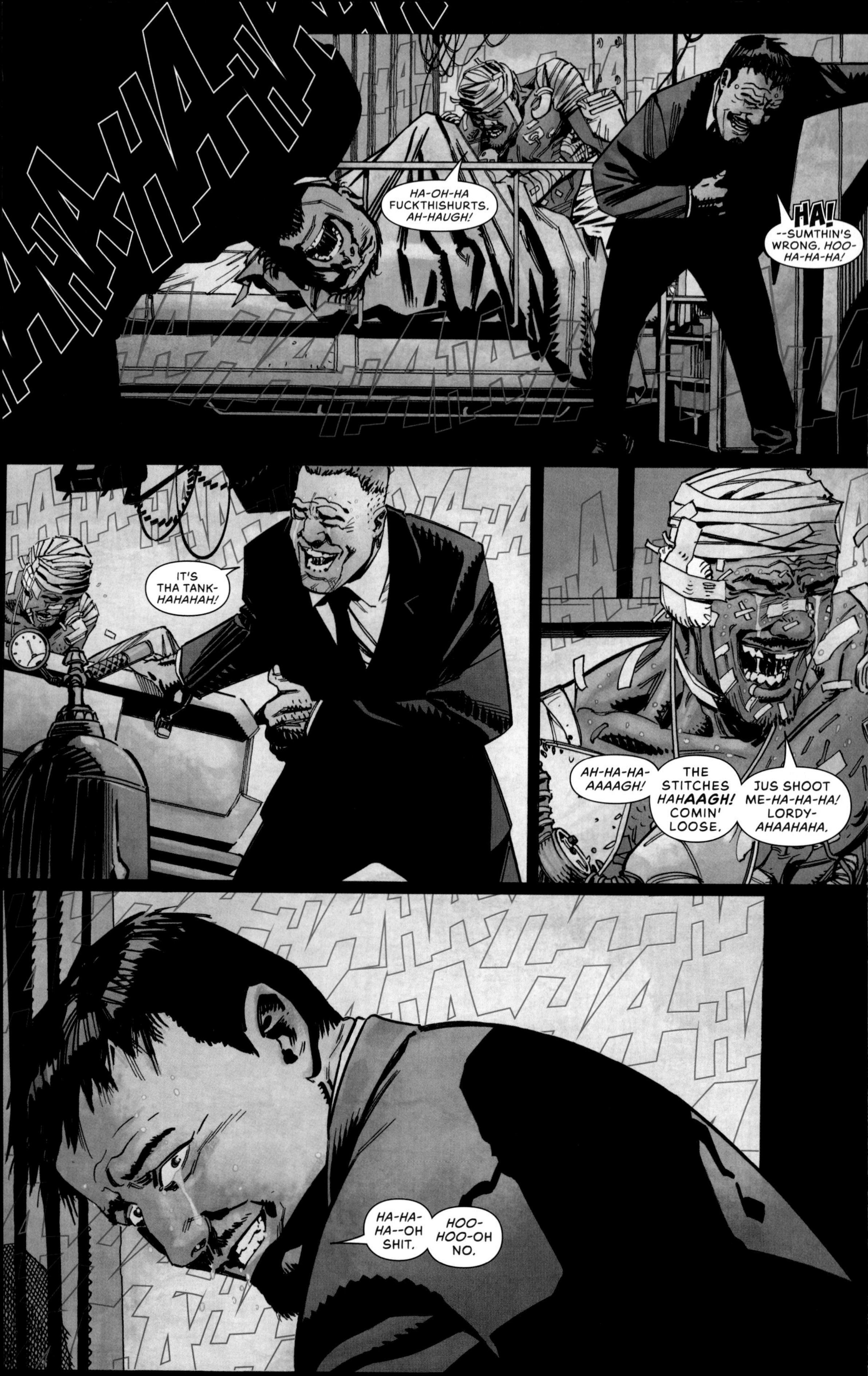
HA-OH-HA FUCKTHISHURTS, AH-HAUGH!
HA! --SUMTHIN'S WRONG, HOO-HA-HA-HA!
IT'S THA TANK- HAHAHAH!
AH-HA-HA-AAAAGH!
THE STITCHES HAHAAGH! COMIN' LOOSE.
JUS SHOOT ME-HA-HA-HA! LORDY- AHAAAHAHA.
HA-HA-HA--OH SHIT.
HOO-HOO-OH NO.

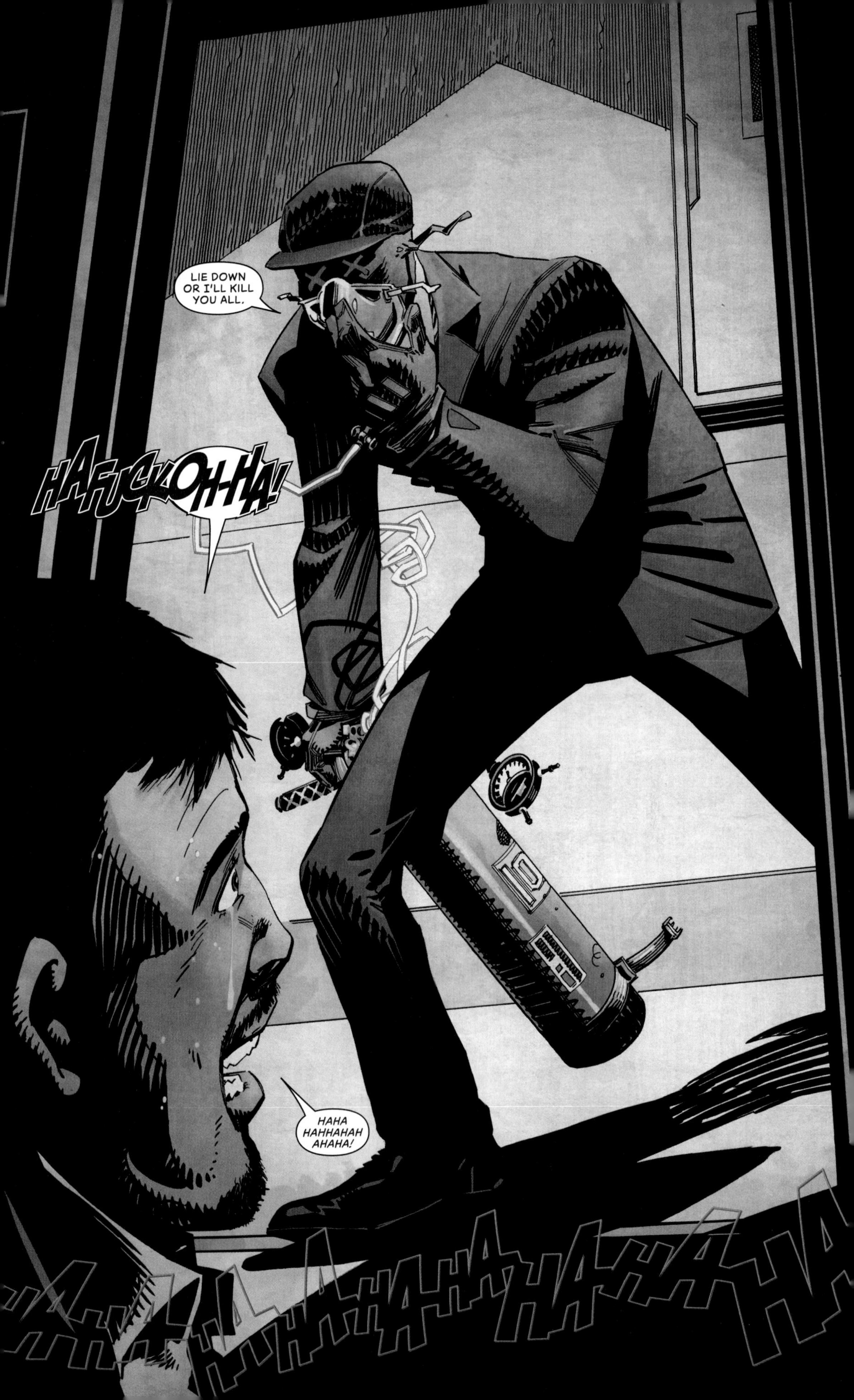
LIE DOWN OR I'LL KILL YOU ALL.
HAFUCKOH-HA!
HAHA HAHHAHAH AHAHA!
AHAHAHAHAHAHAHAHA

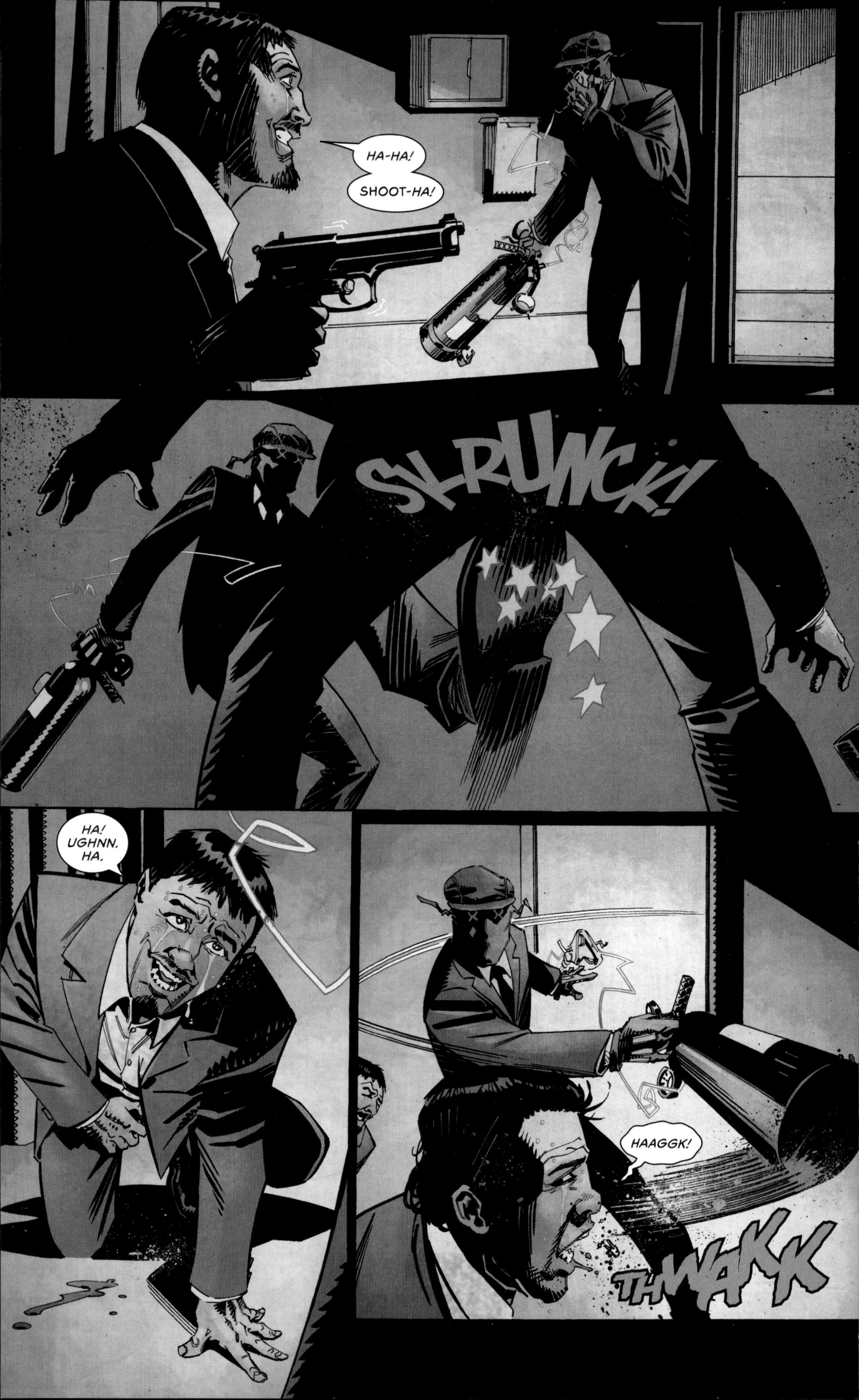
HA-HA!
SHOOT-HA!
SKRUNCK!
HA! UGHNN, HA,
HAAGGK!
THWAKK

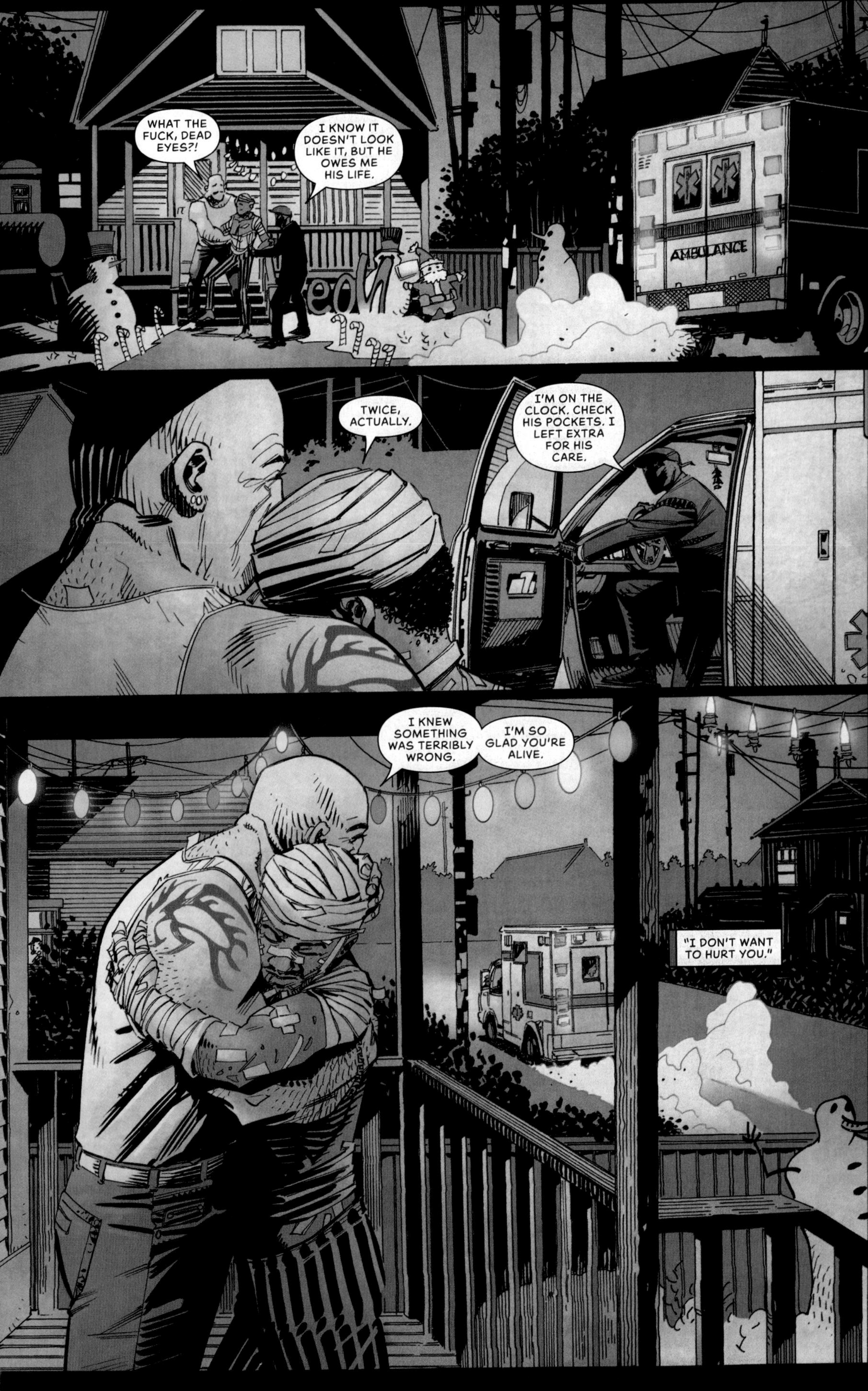
WHAT THE FUCK, DEAD EYES?!
I KNOW IT DOESN'T LOOK LIKE IT, BUT HE OWES ME HIS LIFE.
AMBULANCE
TWICE, ACTUALLY.
I'M ON THE CLOCK. CHECK HIS POCKETS. I LEFT EXTRA FOR HIS CARE.
I KNEW SOMETHING WAS TERRIBLY WRONG.
I'M SO GLAD YOU'RE ALIVE.
"I DON'T WANT TO HURT YOU."

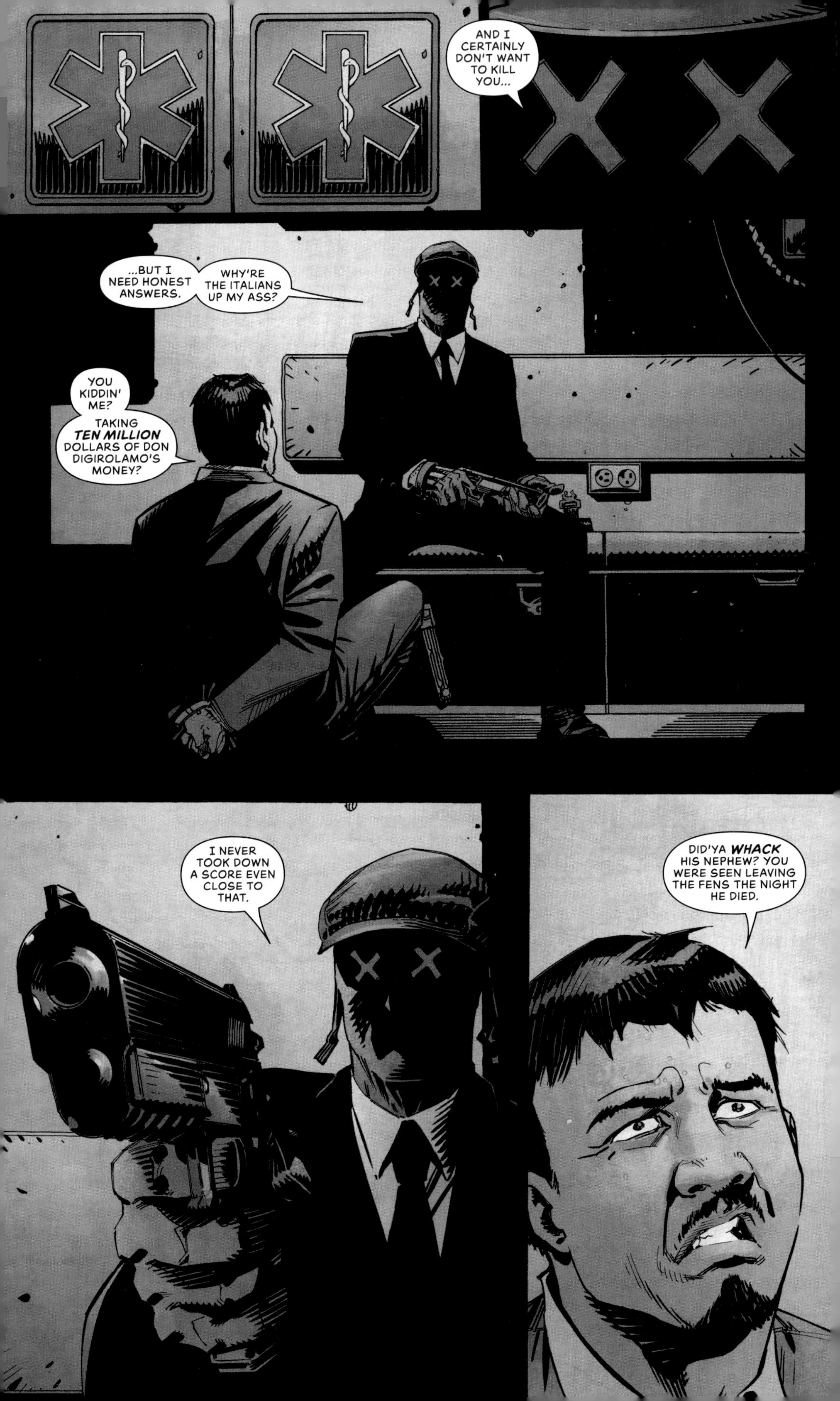
AND I CERTAINLY DON'T WANT TO KILL YOU...
...BUT I NEED HONEST ANSWERS.
WHY'RE THE ITALIANS UP MY ASS?
YOU KIDDIN' ME?
TAKING **TEN MILLION** DOLLARS OF DON DIGIROLAMO'S MONEY?
I NEVER TOOK DOWN A SCORE EVEN CLOSE TO THAT.
DID'YA **WHACK** HIS NEPHEW? YOU WERE SEEN LEAVING THE FENS THE NIGHT HE DIED.

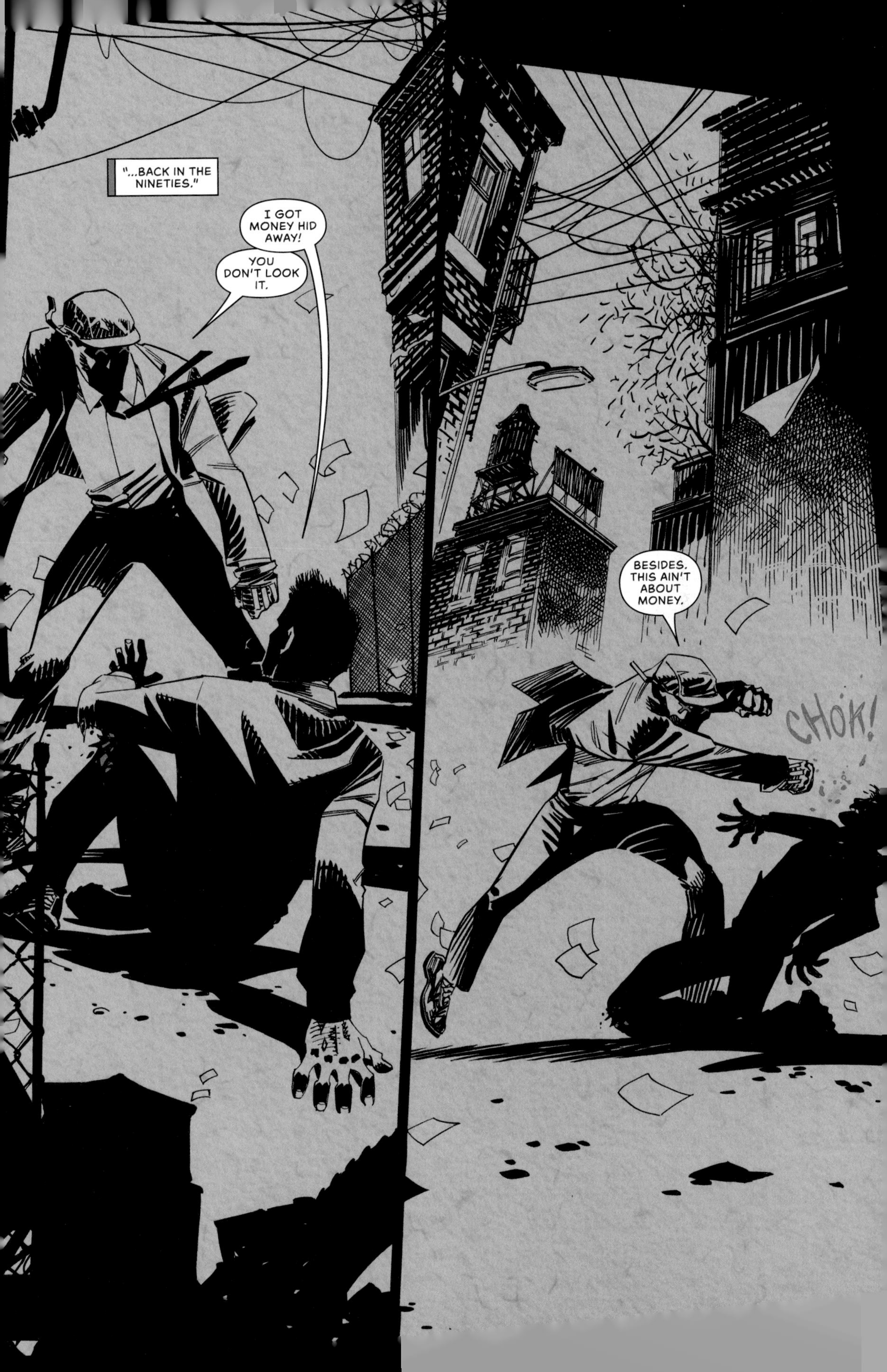
"...BACK IN THE NINETIES."
I GOT MONEY HID AWAY!
YOU DON'T LOOK IT.
BESIDES, THIS AIN'T ABOUT MONEY.
CHOK!

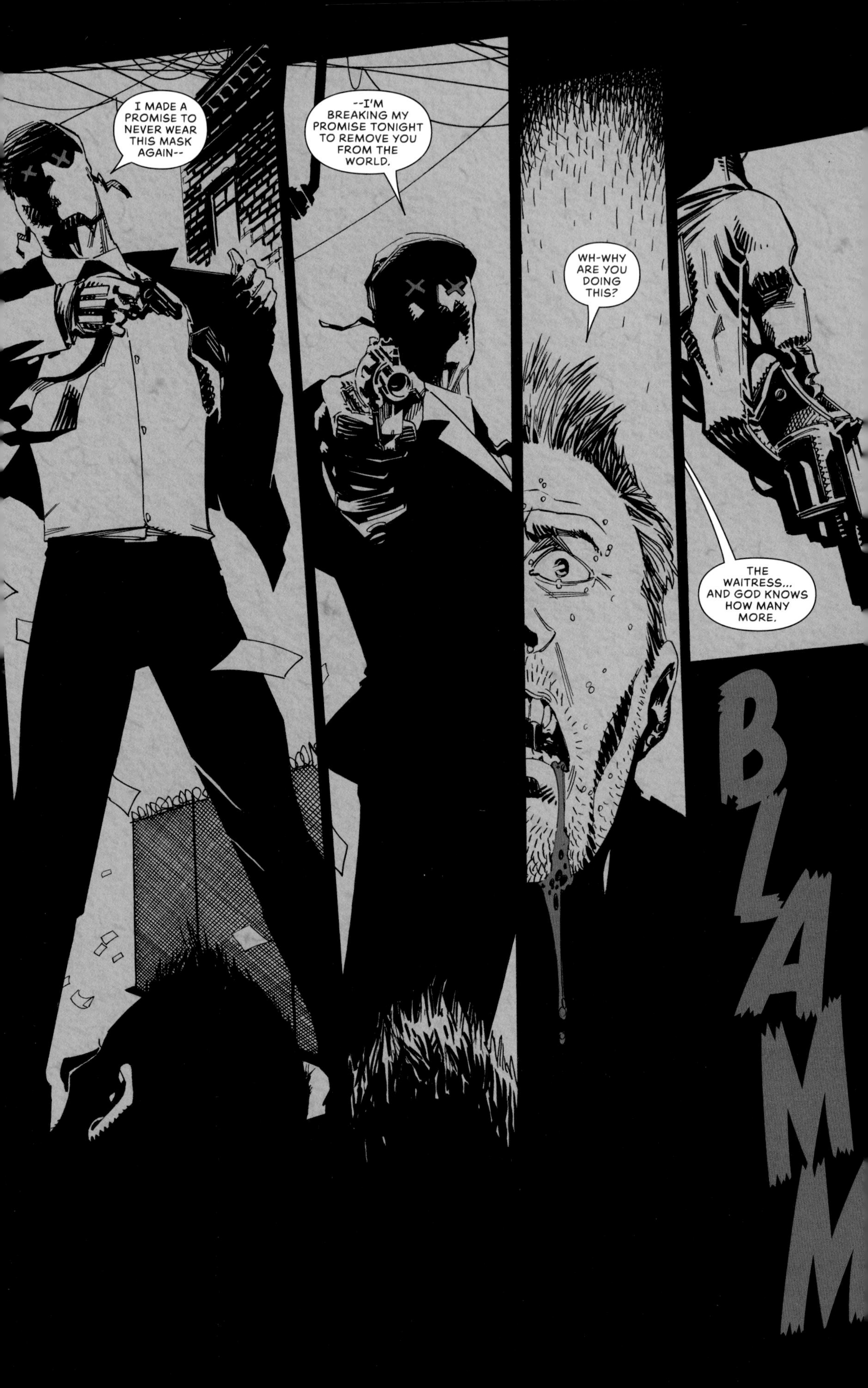
I MADE A PROMISE TO NEVER WEAR THIS MASK AGAIN--
--I'M BREAKING MY PROMISE TONIGHT TO REMOVE YOU FROM THE WORLD.
WH-WHY ARE YOU DOING THIS?
THE WAITRESS... AND GOD KNOWS HOW MANY MORE.
BLAMM

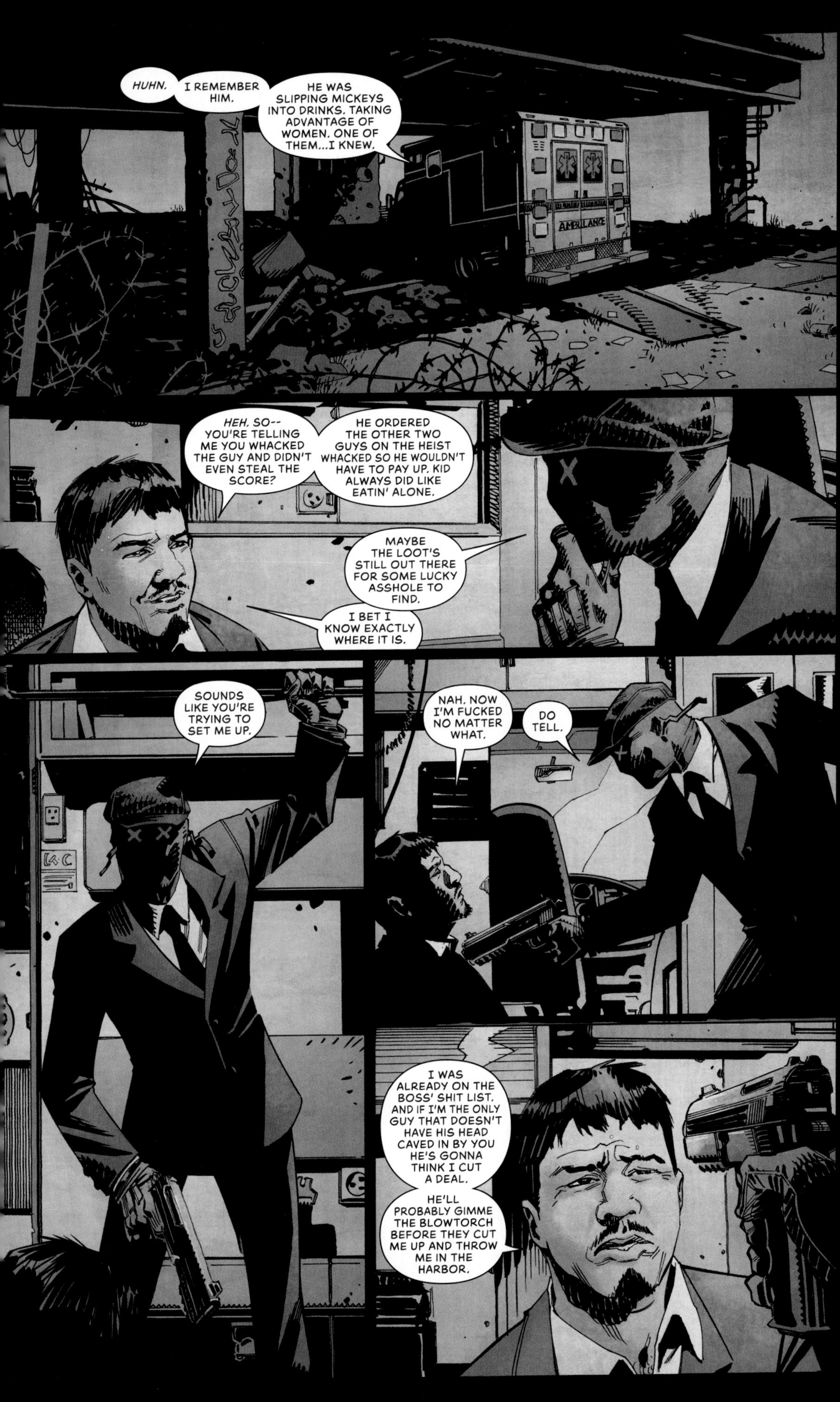
HUHN.
I REMEMBER HIM.
HE WAS SLIPPING MICKEYS INTO DRINKS. TAKING ADVANTAGE OF WOMEN. ONE OF THEM...I KNEW.
AMBULANCE
HEH. SO-- YOU'RE TELLING ME YOU WHACKED THE GUY AND DIDN'T EVEN STEAL THE SCORE?
HE ORDERED THE OTHER TWO GUYS ON THE HEIST WHACKED SO HE WOULDN'T HAVE TO PAY UP. KID ALWAYS DID LIKE EATIN' ALONE.
MAYBE THE LOOT'S STILL OUT THERE FOR SOME LUCKY ASSHOLE TO FIND.
I BET I KNOW EXACTLY WHERE IT IS.
SOUNDS LIKE YOU'RE TRYING TO SET ME UP.
NAH. NOW I'M FUCKED NO MATTER WHAT.
DO TELL.
I WAS ALREADY ON THE BOSS' SHIT LIST. AND IF I'M THE ONLY GUY THAT DOESN'T HAVE HIS HEAD CAVED IN BY YOU HE'S GONNA THINK I CUT A DEAL.
HE'LL PROBABLY GIMME THE BLOWTORCH BEFORE THEY CUT ME UP AND THROW ME IN THE HARBOR.

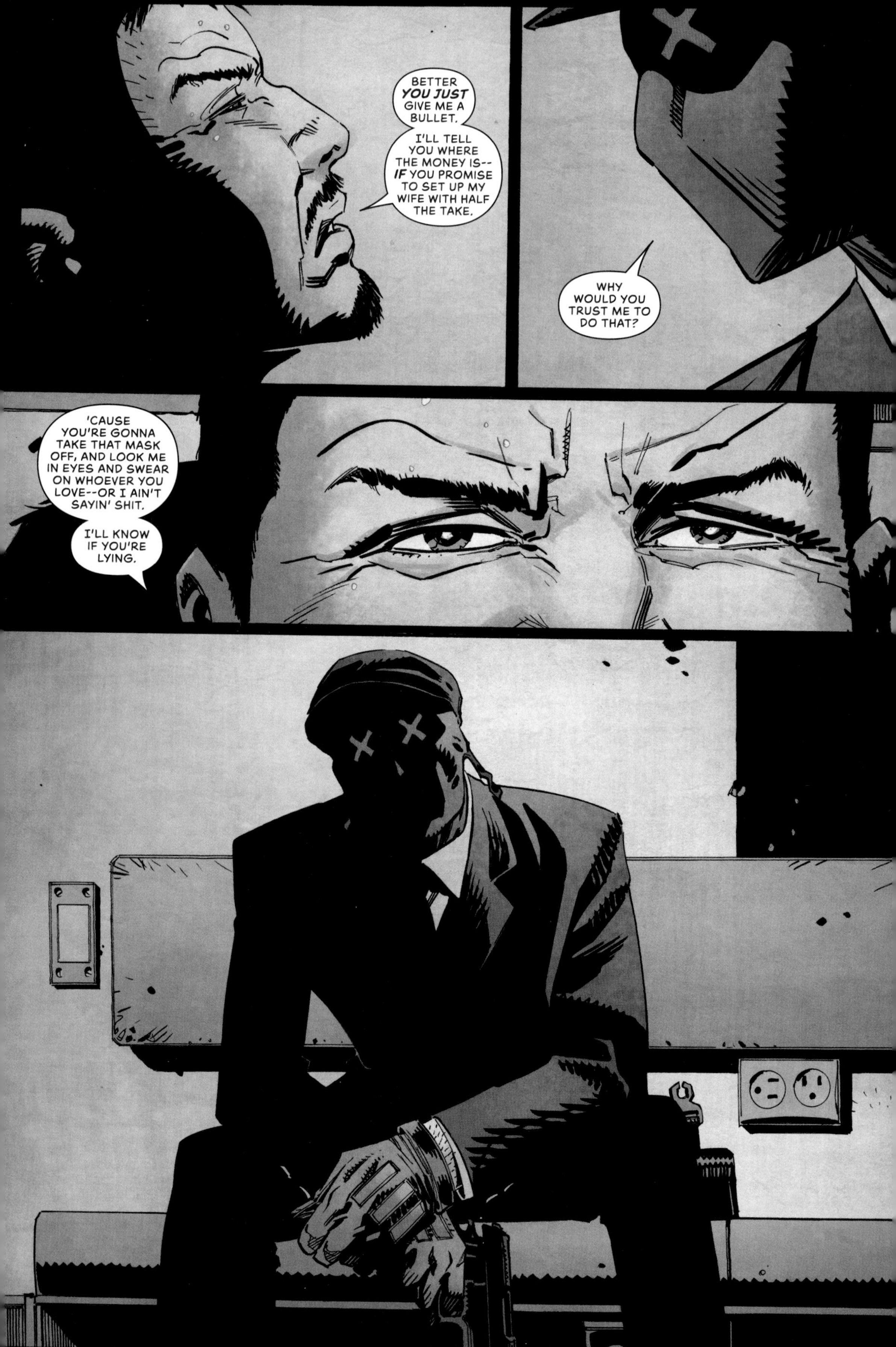
BETTER *YOU JUST* GIVE ME A BULLET.
I'LL TELL YOU WHERE THE MONEY IS-- *IF* YOU PROMISE TO SET UP MY WIFE WITH HALF THE TAKE.
WHY WOULD YOU TRUST ME TO DO THAT?
'CAUSE YOU'RE GONNA TAKE THAT MASK OFF, AND LOOK ME IN EYES AND SWEAR ON WHOEVER YOU LOVE--OR I AIN'T SAYIN' SHIT.
I'LL KNOW IF YOU'RE LYING.

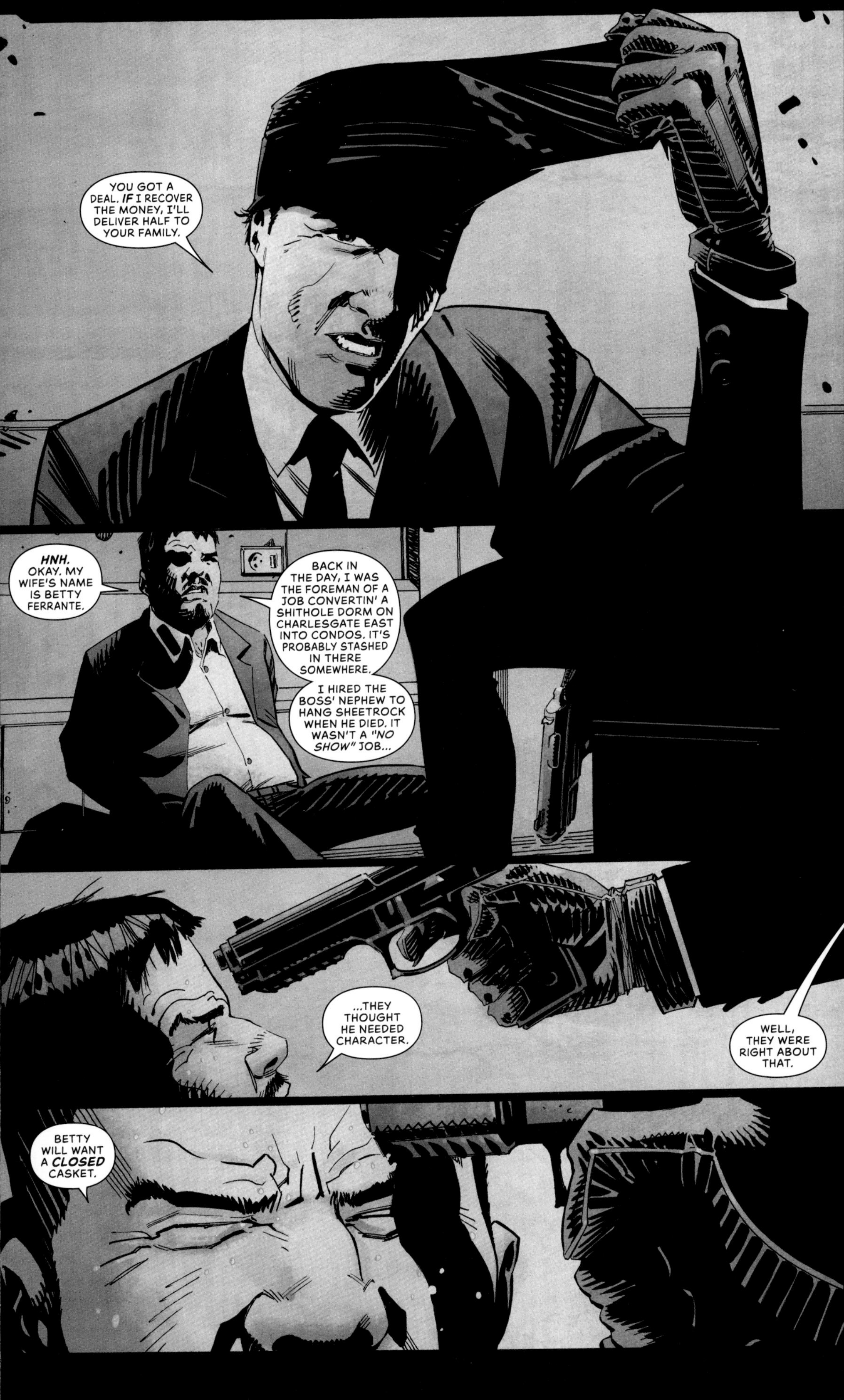
YOU GOT A DEAL. *IF* I RECOVER THE MONEY, I'LL DELIVER HALF TO YOUR FAMILY.
HNH. OKAY. MY WIFE'S NAME IS BETTY FERRANTE.
BACK IN THE DAY, I WAS THE FOREMAN OF A JOB CONVERTIN' A SHITHOLE DORM ON CHARLESGATE EAST INTO CONDOS. IT'S PROBABLY STASHED IN THERE SOMEWHERE.
I HIRED THE BOSS' NEPHEW TO HANG SHEETROCK WHEN HE DIED. IT WASN'T A *"NO SHOW"* JOB...
...THEY THOUGHT HE NEEDED CHARACTER.
WELL, THEY WERE RIGHT ABOUT THAT.
BETTY WILL WANT A *CLOSED* CASKET.

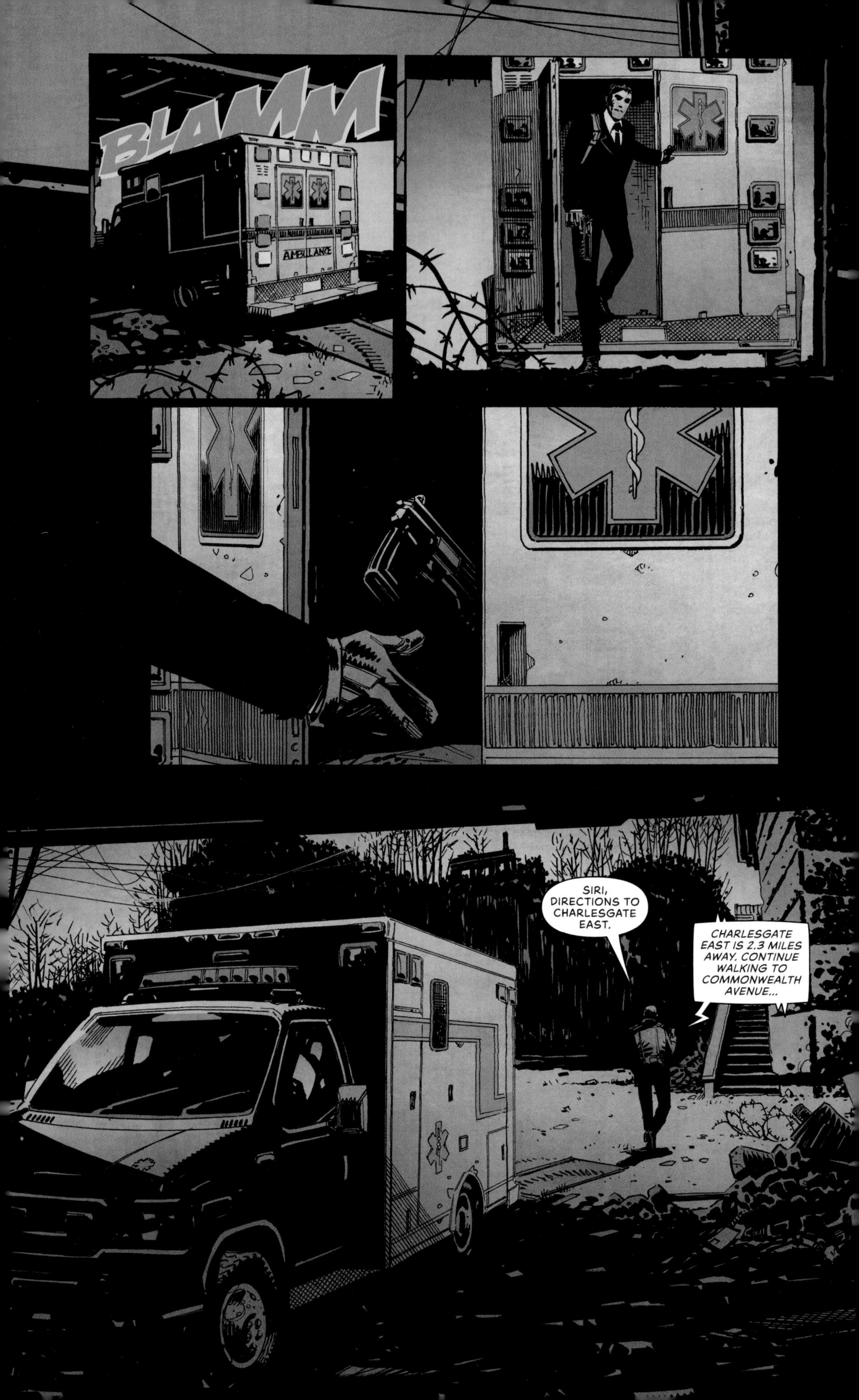
BLAMM
AMBULANCE
SIRI, DIRECTIONS TO CHARLESGATE EAST.
CHARLESGATE EAST IS 2.3 MILES AWAY. CONTINUE WALKING TO COMMONWEALTH AVENUE...

CHAPTER FOUR

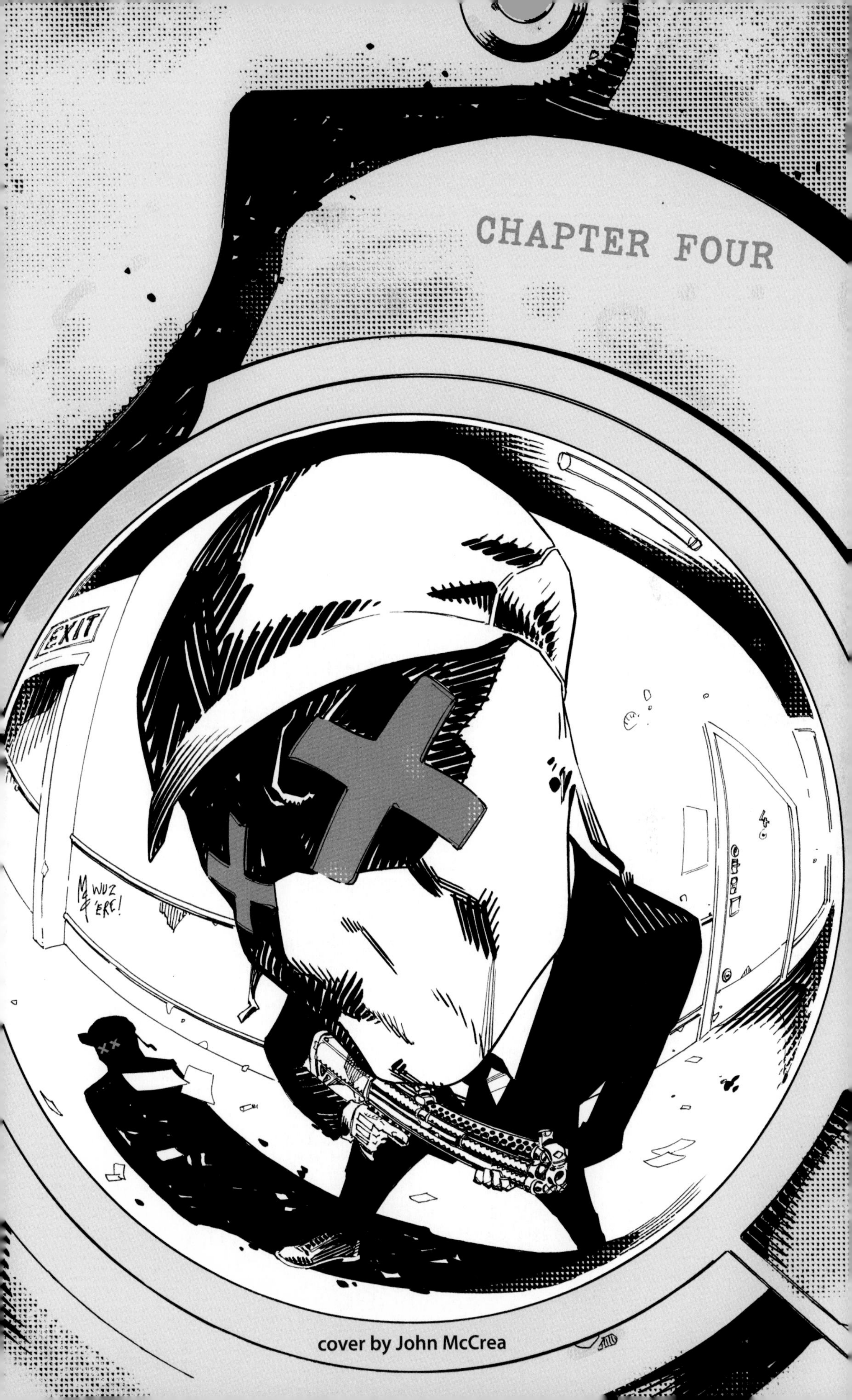
EXIT

cover by John McCrea

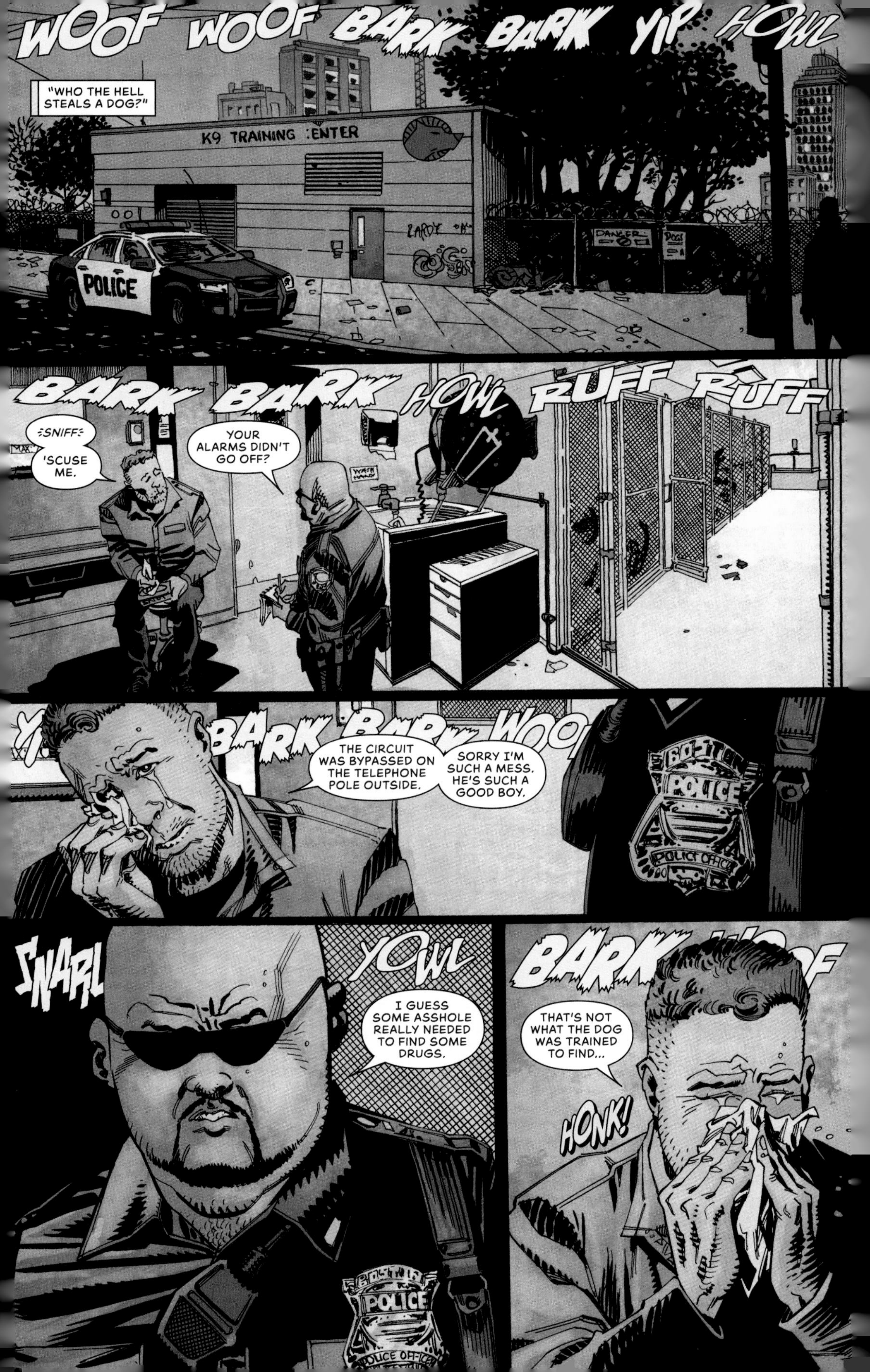
WOOF WOOF BARK BARK YIP HOWL
"WHO THE HELL STEALS A DOG?"
K9 TRAINING :ENTER
POLICE
BARK BARK HOWL RUFF RUFF
SNIFF
'SCUSE ME.
YOUR ALARMS DIDN'T GO OFF?
BARK BARK WOOF
THE CIRCUIT WAS BYPASSED ON THE TELEPHONE POLE OUTSIDE.
SORRY I'M SUCH A MESS. HE'S SUCH A GOOD BOY.
POLICE
SNARL
YOWL
I GUESS SOME ASSHOLE REALLY NEEDED TO FIND SOME DRUGS.
BARK
THAT'S NOT WHAT THE DOG WAS TRAINED TO FIND...
HONK!
POLICE

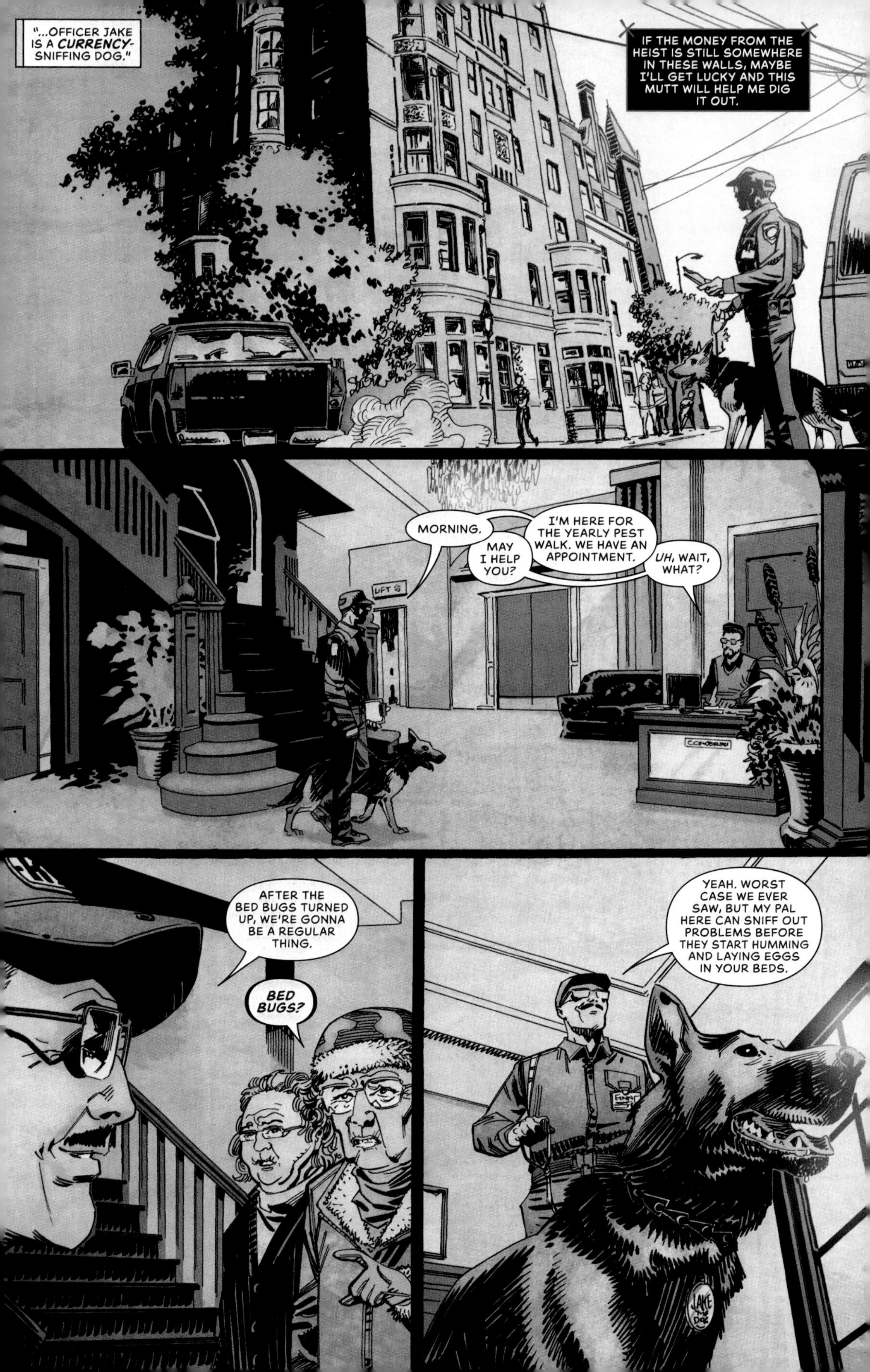
"...OFFICER JAKE IS A *CURRENCY*-SNIFFING DOG."
IF THE MONEY FROM THE HEIST IS STILL SOMEWHERE IN THESE WALLS, MAYBE I'LL GET LUCKY AND THIS MUTT WILL HELP ME DIG IT OUT.
LIFT
MORNING.
MAY I HELP YOU?
I'M HERE FOR THE YEARLY PEST WALK. WE HAVE AN APPOINTMENT.
UH, WAIT, WHAT?
AFTER THE BED BUGS TURNED UP, WE'RE GONNA BE A REGULAR THING.
BED BUGS?
YEAH. WORST CASE WE EVER SAW, BUT MY PAL HERE CAN SNIFF OUT PROBLEMS BEFORE THEY START HUMMING AND LAYING EGGS IN YOUR BEDS.
JAKE

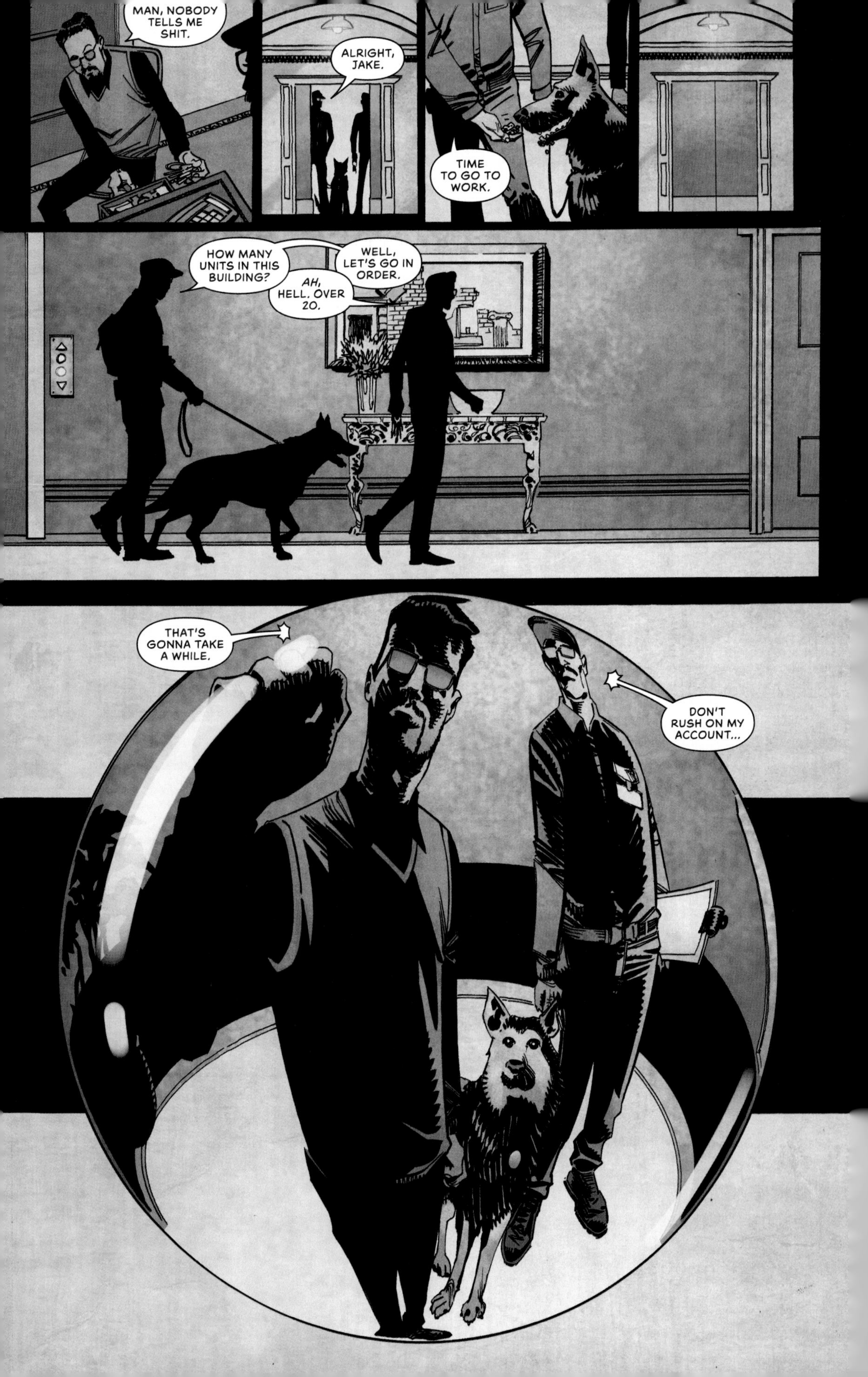
MAN, NOBODY TELLS ME SHIT.
ALRIGHT, JAKE.
TIME TO GO TO WORK.
HOW MANY UNITS IN THIS BUILDING?
WELL, LET'S GO IN ORDER.
AH, HELL. OVER 20.
THAT'S GONNA TAKE A WHILE.
DON'T RUSH ON MY ACCOUNT...

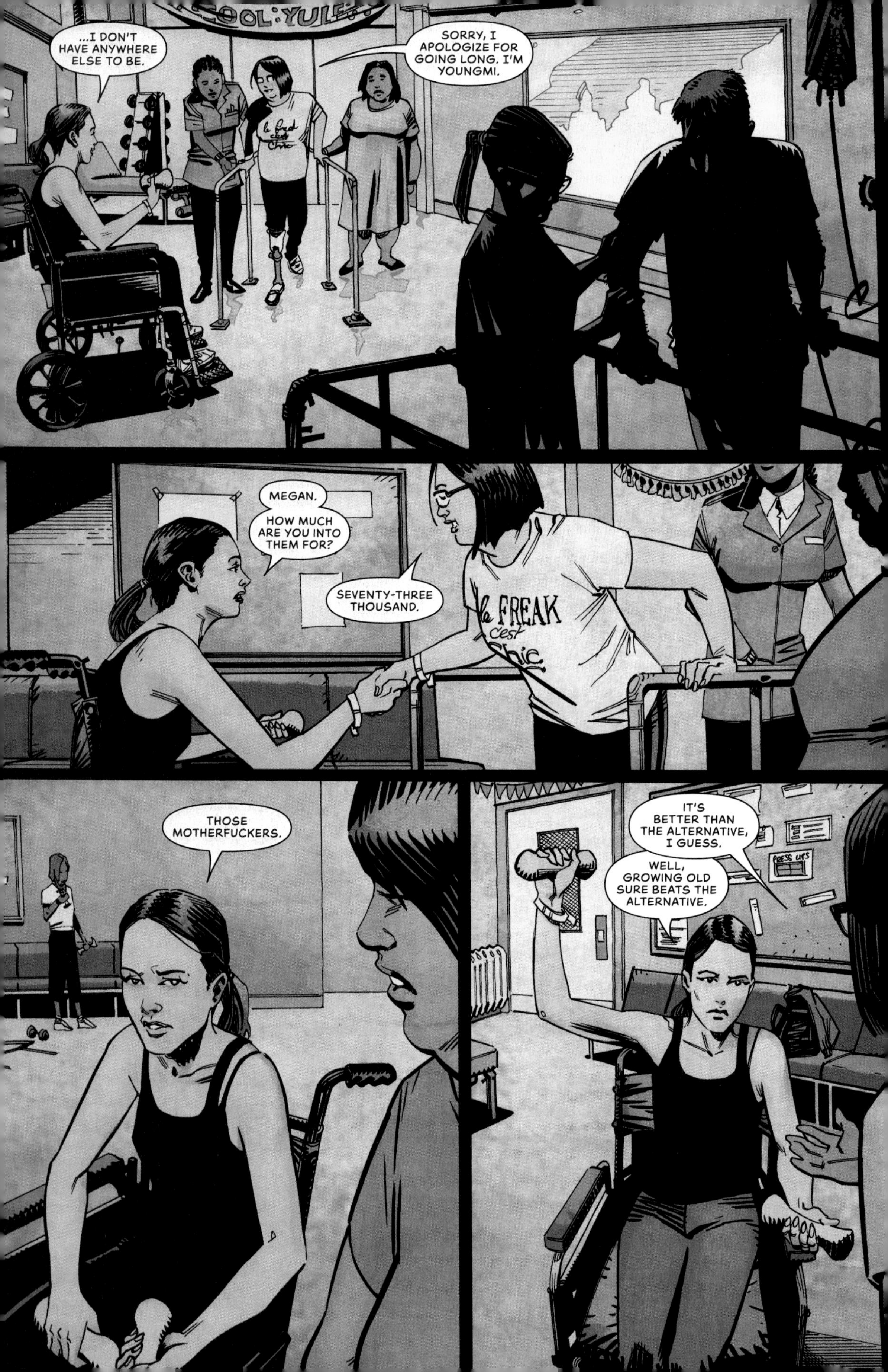
...I DON'T HAVE ANYWHERE ELSE TO BE.
SORRY, I APOLOGIZE FOR GOING LONG. I'M YOUNGMI.
MEGAN.
HOW MUCH ARE YOU INTO THEM FOR?
SEVENTY-THREE THOUSAND.
THOSE MOTHERFUCKERS.
IT'S BETTER THAN THE ALTERNATIVE, I GUESS.
WELL, GROWING OLD SURE BEATS THE ALTERNATIVE.

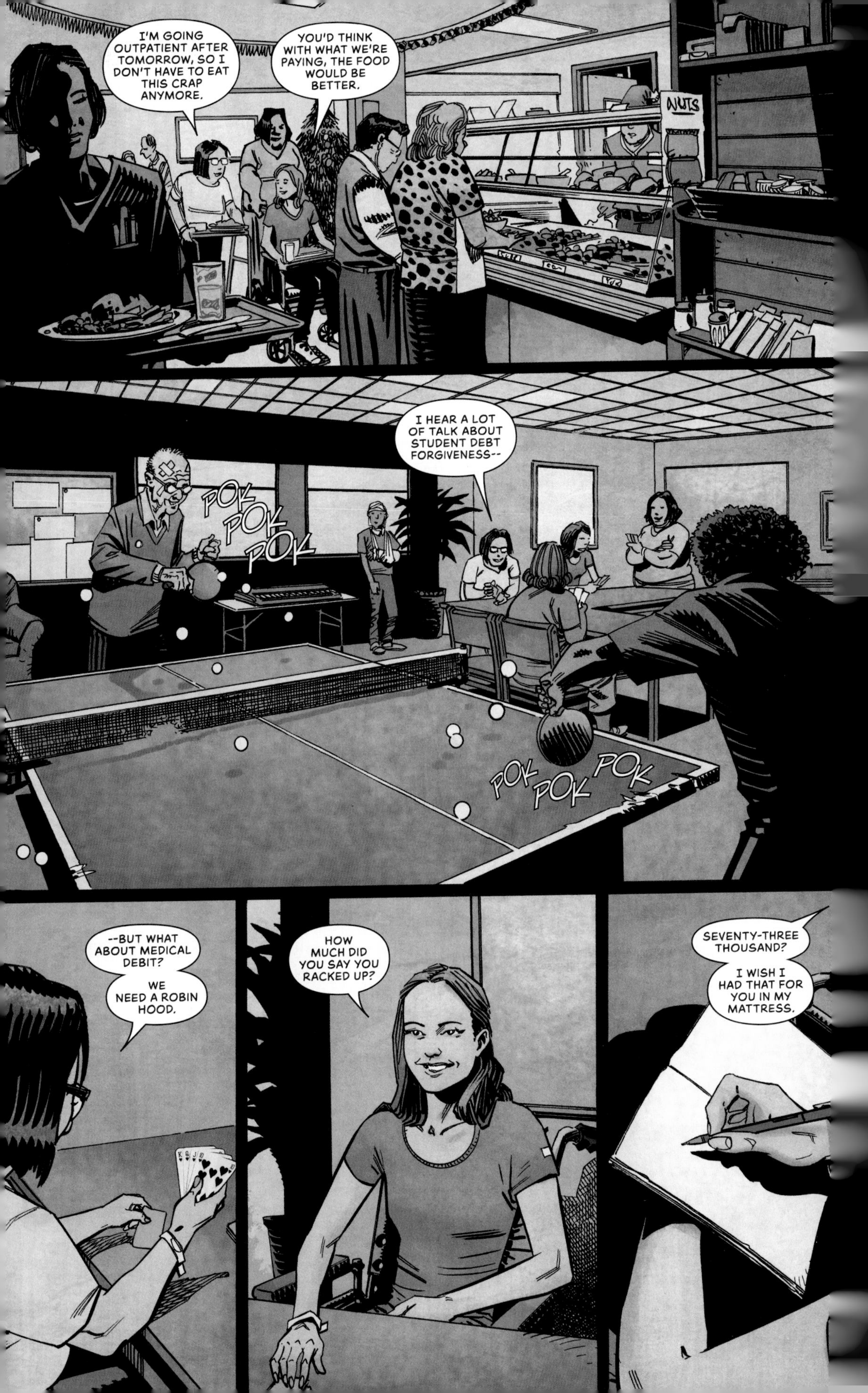
I'M GOING OUTPATIENT AFTER TOMORROW, SO I DON'T HAVE TO EAT THIS CRAP ANYMORE.
YOU'D THINK WITH WHAT WE'RE PAYING, THE FOOD WOULD BE BETTER.
NUTS
I HEAR A LOT OF TALK ABOUT STUDENT DEBT FORGIVENESS--
POK POK POK
POK POK POK
--BUT WHAT ABOUT MEDICAL DEBIT?
WE NEED A ROBIN HOOD.
HOW MUCH DID YOU SAY YOU RACKED UP?
SEVENTY-THREE THOUSAND?
I WISH I HAD THAT FOR YOU IN MY MATTRESS.

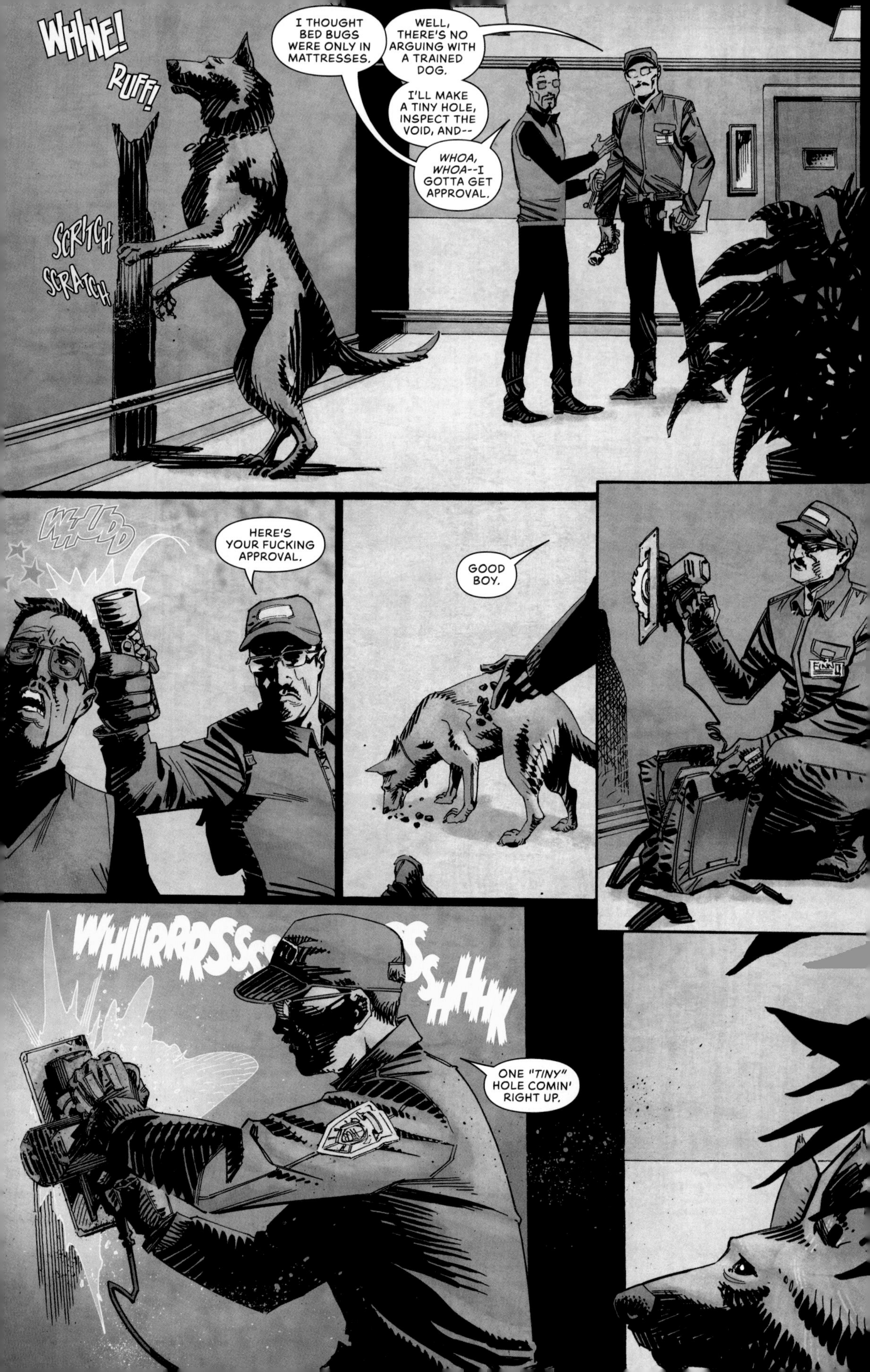
WHINE!
RUFF!
SCRITCH
SCRATCH
I THOUGHT BED BUGS WERE ONLY IN MATTRESSES.
WELL, THERE'S NO ARGUING WITH A TRAINED DOG.
I'LL MAKE A TINY HOLE, INSPECT THE VOID, AND--
WHOA, WHOA--I GOTTA GET APPROVAL.
HERE'S YOUR FUCKING APPROVAL.
GOOD BOY.
WHIIRRRSSS
SSHHHK
ONE *"TINY"* HOLE COMIN' RIGHT UP.

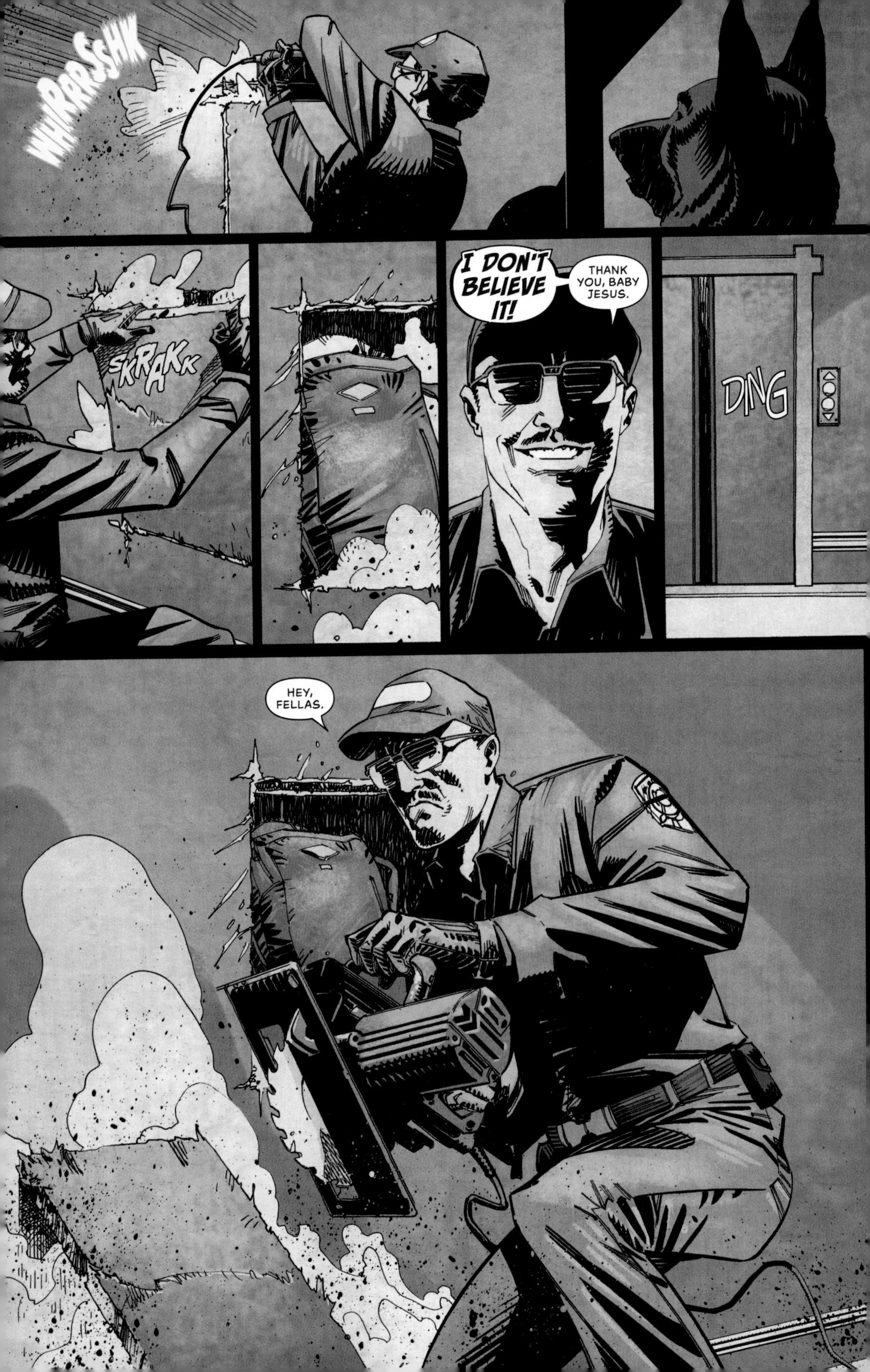
WHRRRSSHK
SKRAKK
I DON'T BELIEVE IT!
THANK YOU, BABY JESUS.
DING
HEY, FELLAS.

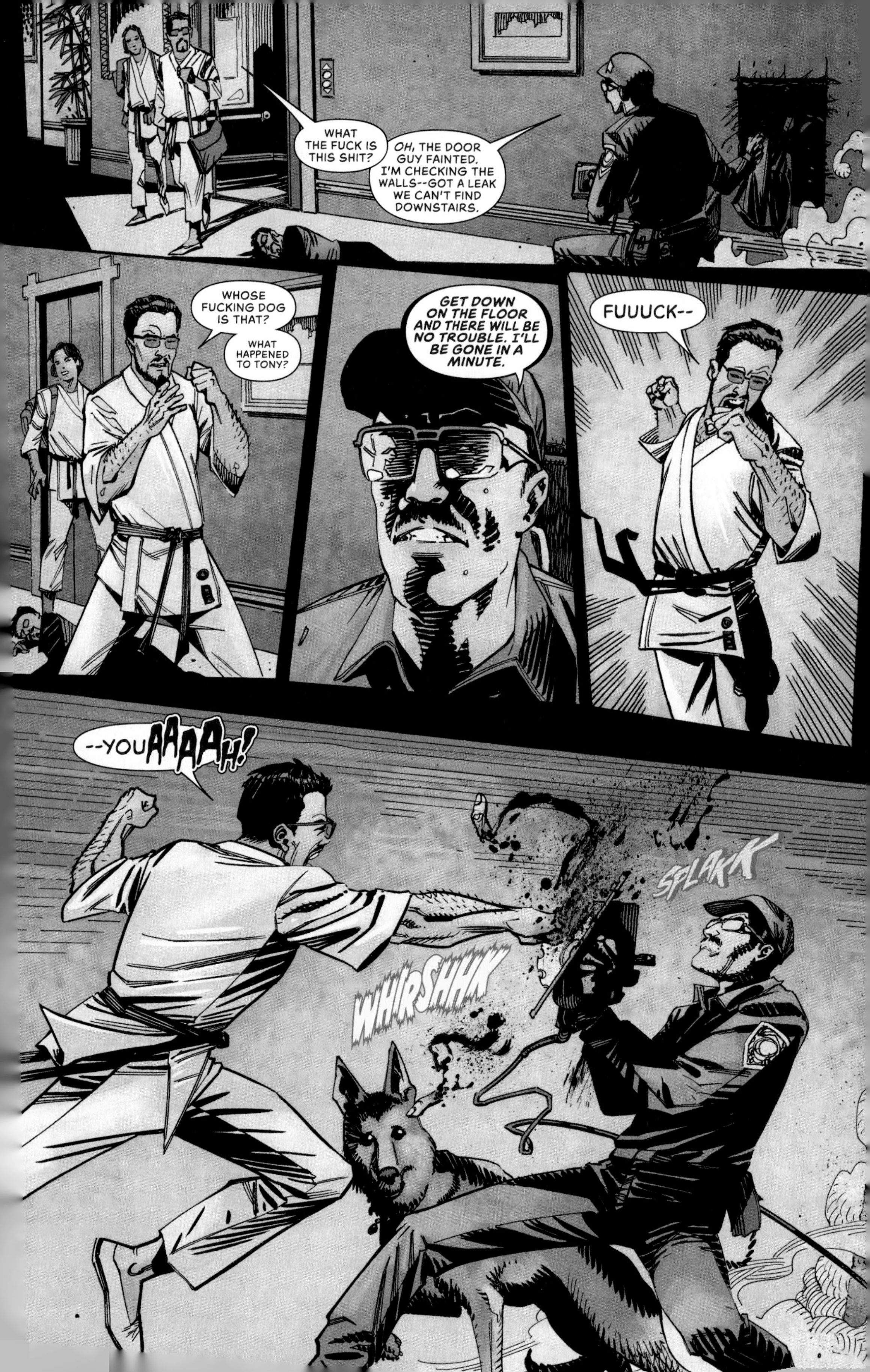
WHAT THE FUCK IS THIS SHIT?
OH, THE DOOR GUY FAINTED. I'M CHECKING THE WALLS--GOT A LEAK WE CAN'T FIND DOWNSTAIRS.
WHOSE FUCKING DOG IS THAT?
WHAT HAPPENED TO TONY?
GET DOWN ON THE FLOOR AND THERE WILL BE NO TROUBLE. I'LL BE GONE IN A MINUTE.
FUUUCK--
--YOUAAAAH!
SPLAKK
WHIRSHHK

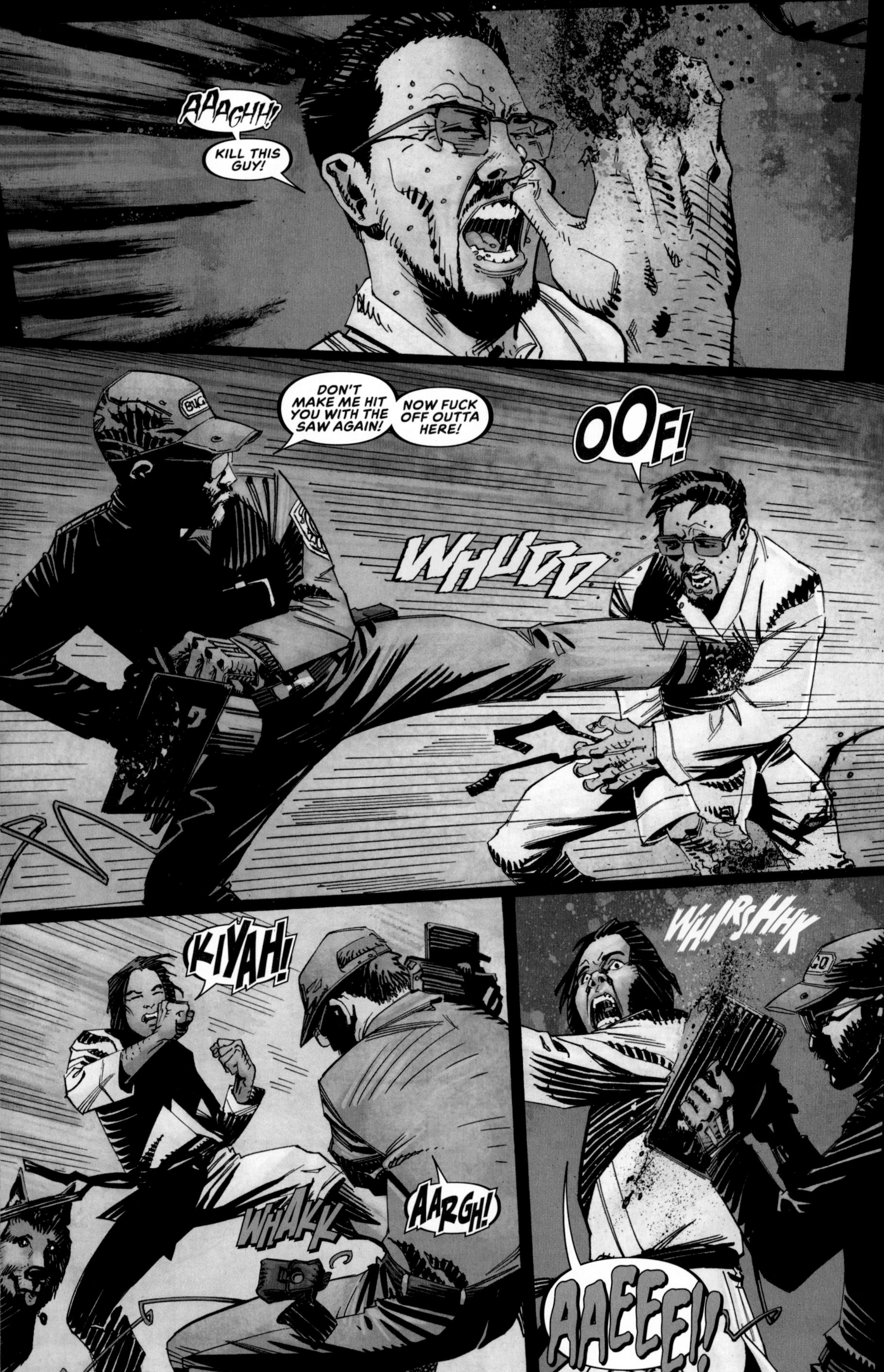
AAAGHH!
KILL THIS GUY!
BUG
DON'T MAKE ME HIT YOU WITH THE SAW AGAIN!
NOW FUCK OFF OUTTA HERE!
OOF!
WHUDD
KIYAH!
WHAKK
AARGH!
WHIRSHHK
AAEEEI!

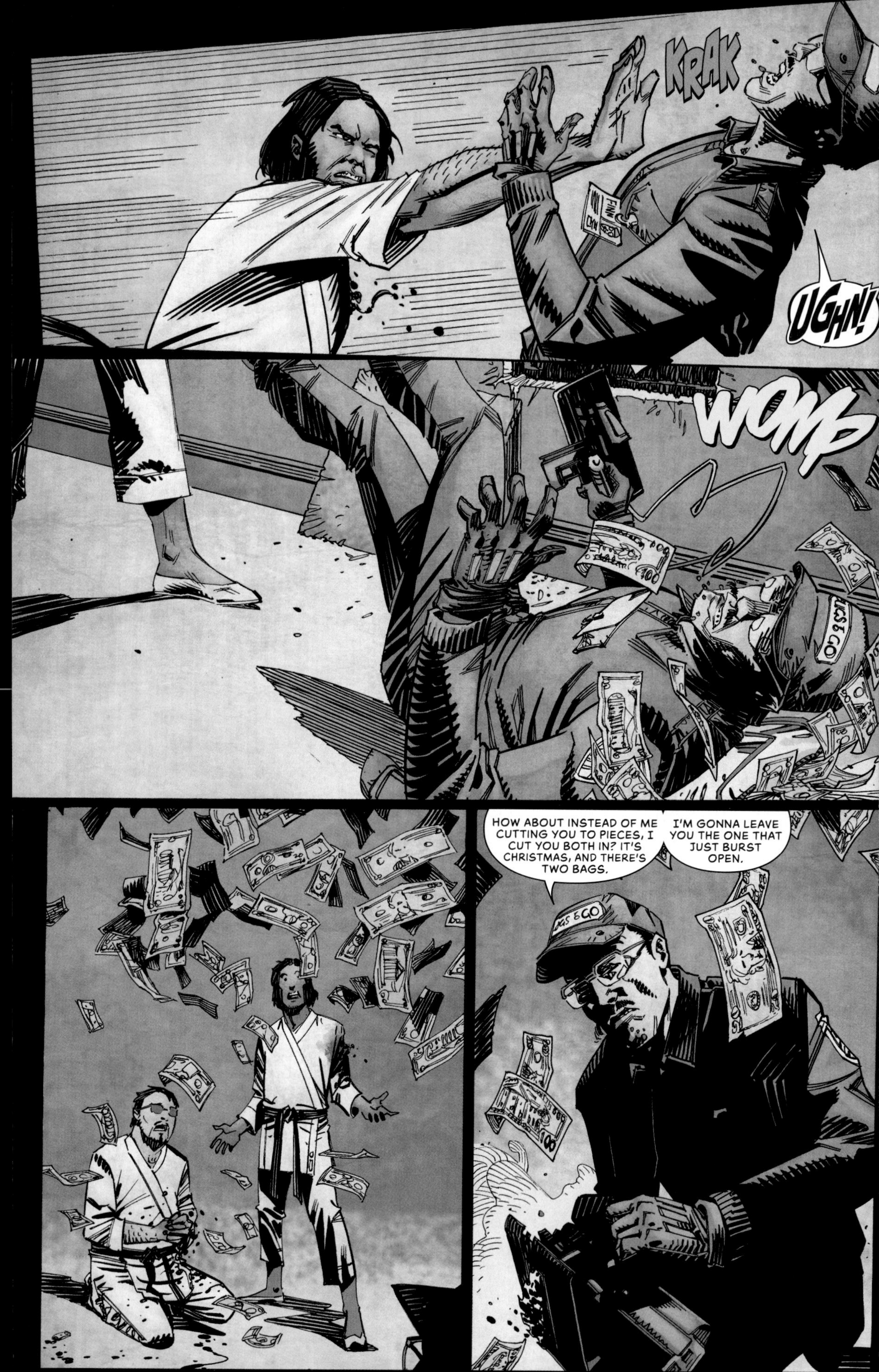
KRAK
UGHN!
WOMP
HOW ABOUT INSTEAD OF ME CUTTING YOU TO PIECES, I CUT YOU BOTH IN? IT'S CHRISTMAS, AND THERE'S TWO BAGS.
I'M GONNA LEAVE YOU THE ONE THAT JUST BURST OPEN.

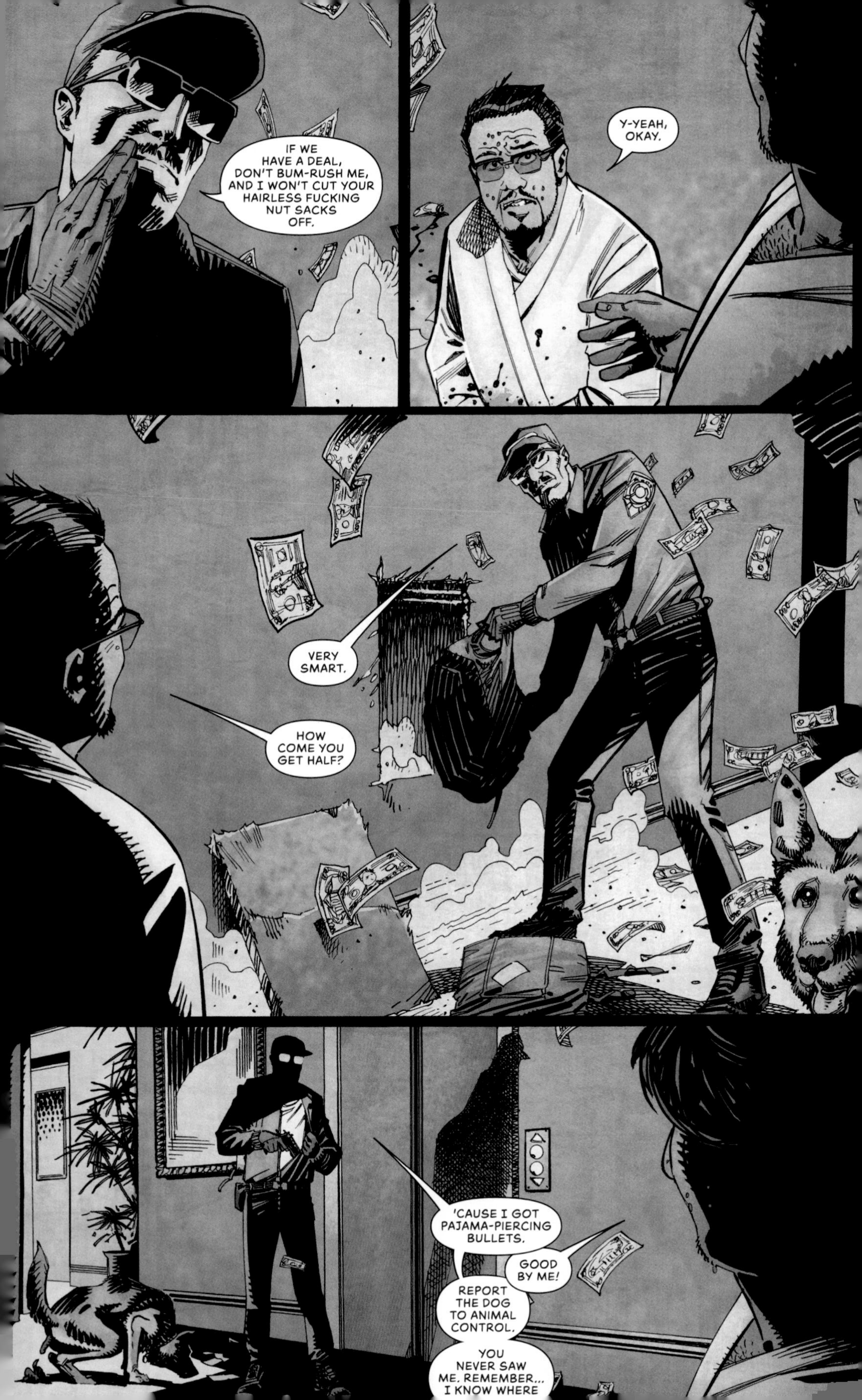
IF WE HAVE A DEAL, DON'T BUM-RUSH ME, AND I WON'T CUT YOUR HAIRLESS FUCKING NUT SACKS OFF.
Y-YEAH, OKAY.
VERY SMART.
HOW COME YOU GET HALF?
'CAUSE I GOT PAJAMA-PIERCING BULLETS.
GOOD BY ME!
REPORT THE DOG TO ANIMAL CONTROL.
YOU NEVER SAW ME. REMEMBER... I KNOW WHERE

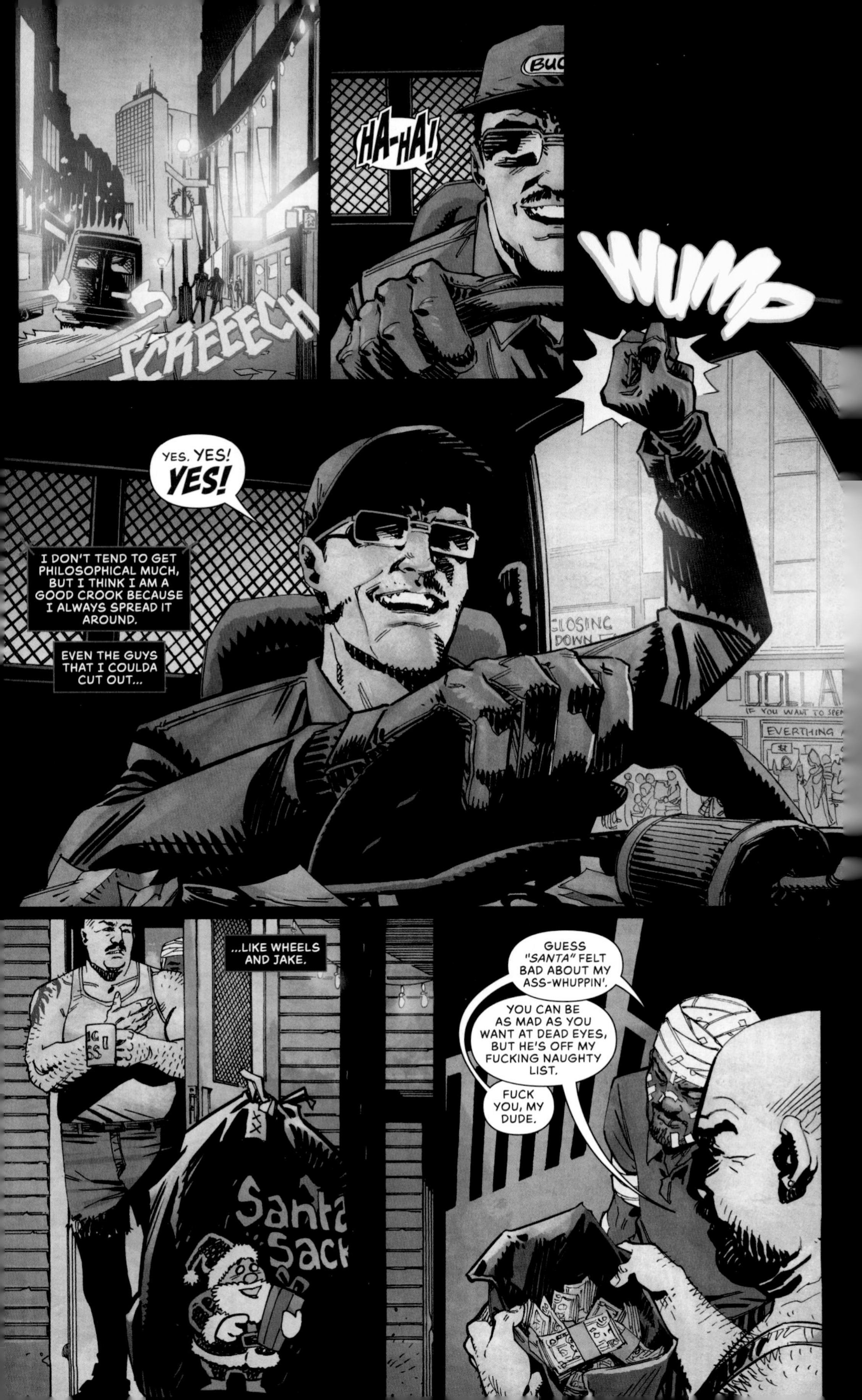
SCREEECH
HA-HA!
WUMP
YES. YES! YES!
I DON'T TEND TO GET PHILOSOPHICAL MUCH, BUT I THINK I AM A GOOD CROOK BECAUSE I ALWAYS SPREAD IT AROUND.
EVEN THE GUYS THAT I COULDA CUT OUT...
CLOSING DOWN
EVERTHING
...LIKE WHEELS AND JAKE.
Santa Sack
GUESS "SANTA" FELT BAD ABOUT MY ASS-WHUPPIN'.
YOU CAN BE AS MAD AS YOU WANT AT DEAD EYES, BUT HE'S OFF MY FUCKING NAUGHTY LIST.
FUCK YOU, MY DUDE.

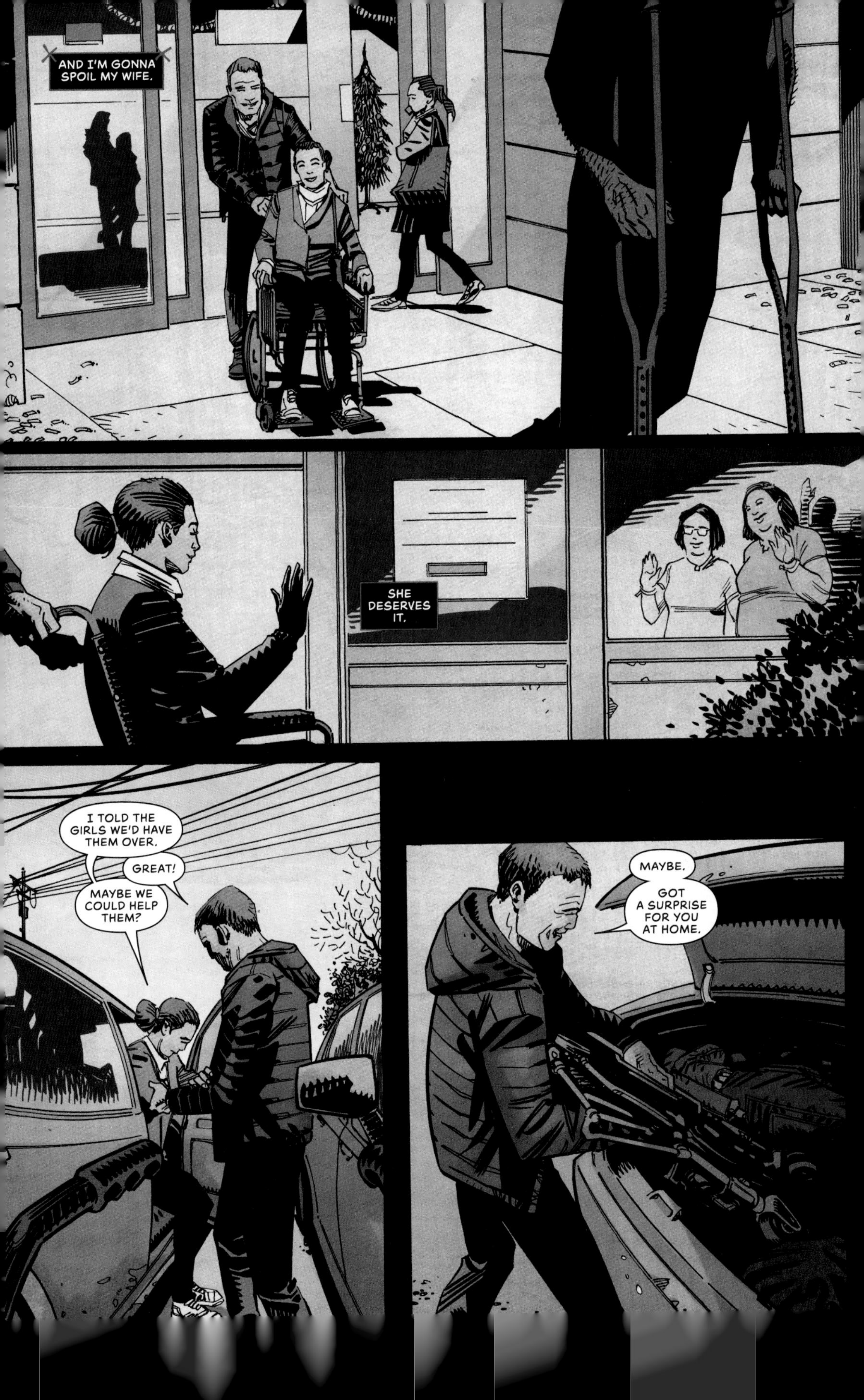
AND I'M GONNA SPOIL MY WIFE.
SHE DESERVES IT.
I TOLD THE GIRLS WE'D HAVE THEM OVER.
GREAT!
MAYBE WE COULD HELP THEM?
MAYBE.
GOT A SURPRISE FOR YOU AT HOME.

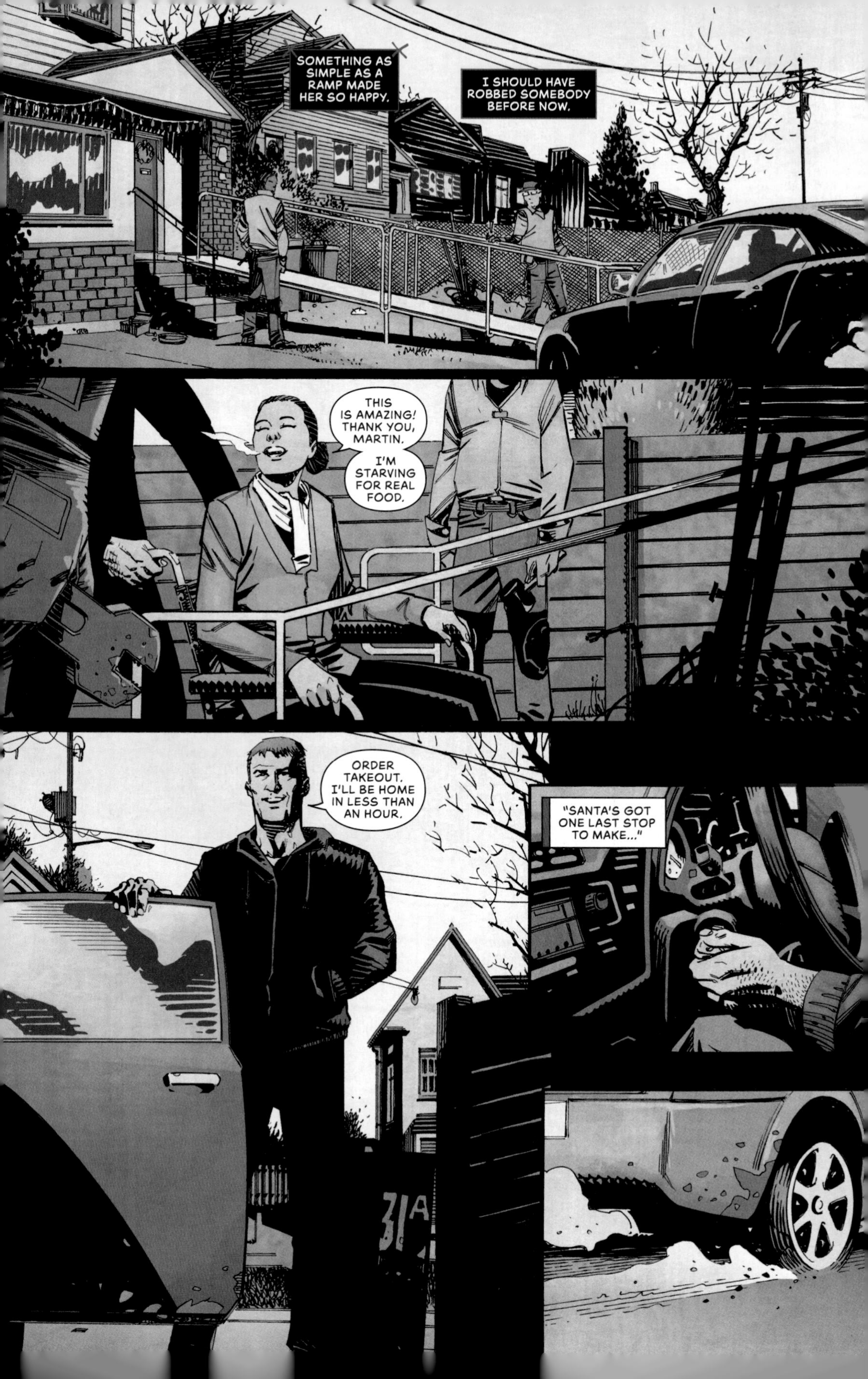
SOMETHING AS SIMPLE AS A RAMP MADE HER SO HAPPY.
I SHOULD HAVE ROBBED SOMEBODY BEFORE NOW.
THIS IS AMAZING! THANK YOU, MARTIN.
I'M STARVING FOR REAL FOOD.
ORDER TAKEOUT. I'LL BE HOME IN LESS THAN AN HOUR.
"SANTA'S GOT ONE LAST STOP TO MAKE..."
31A

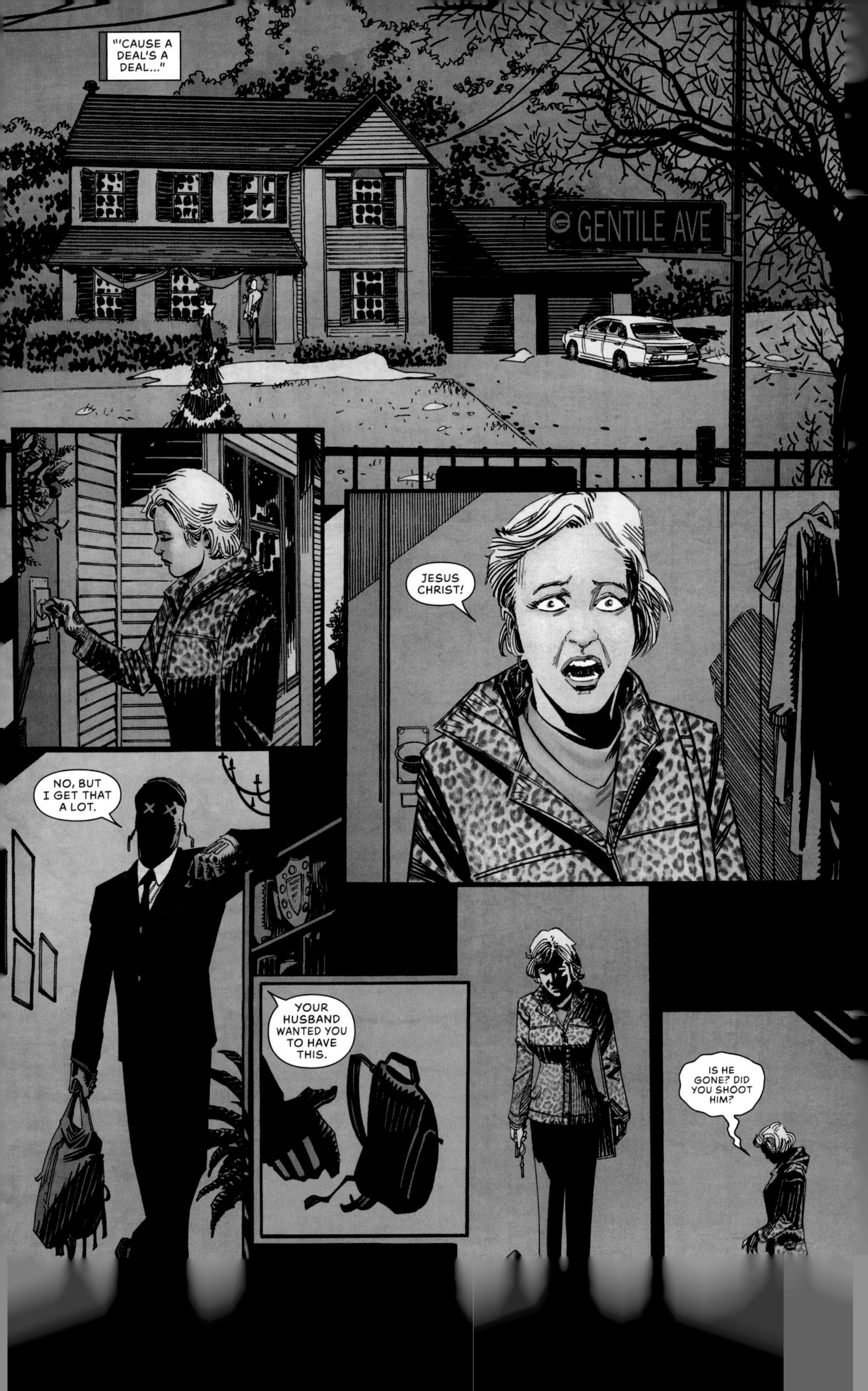
"'CAUSE A DEAL'S A DEAL..."
GENTILE AVE
JESUS CHRIST!
NO, BUT I GET THAT A LOT.
YOUR HUSBAND WANTED YOU TO HAVE THIS.
IS HE GONE? DID YOU SHOOT HIM?

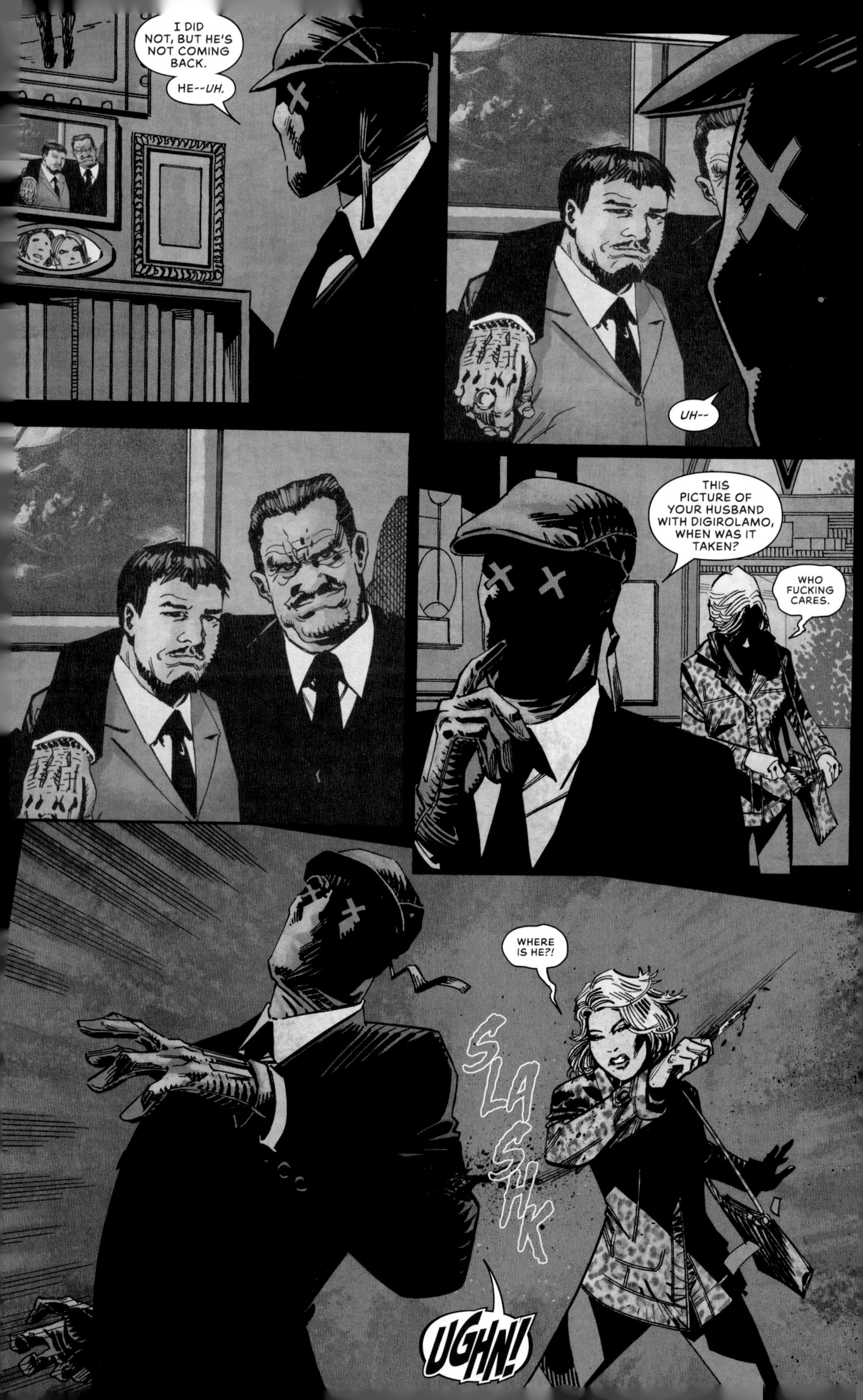
I DID NOT, BUT HE'S NOT COMING BACK.
HE--UH.
UH--
THIS PICTURE OF YOUR HUSBAND WITH DIGIROLAMO, WHEN WAS IT TAKEN?
WHO FUCKING CARES.
WHERE IS HE?!
SLASHK
UGHN!

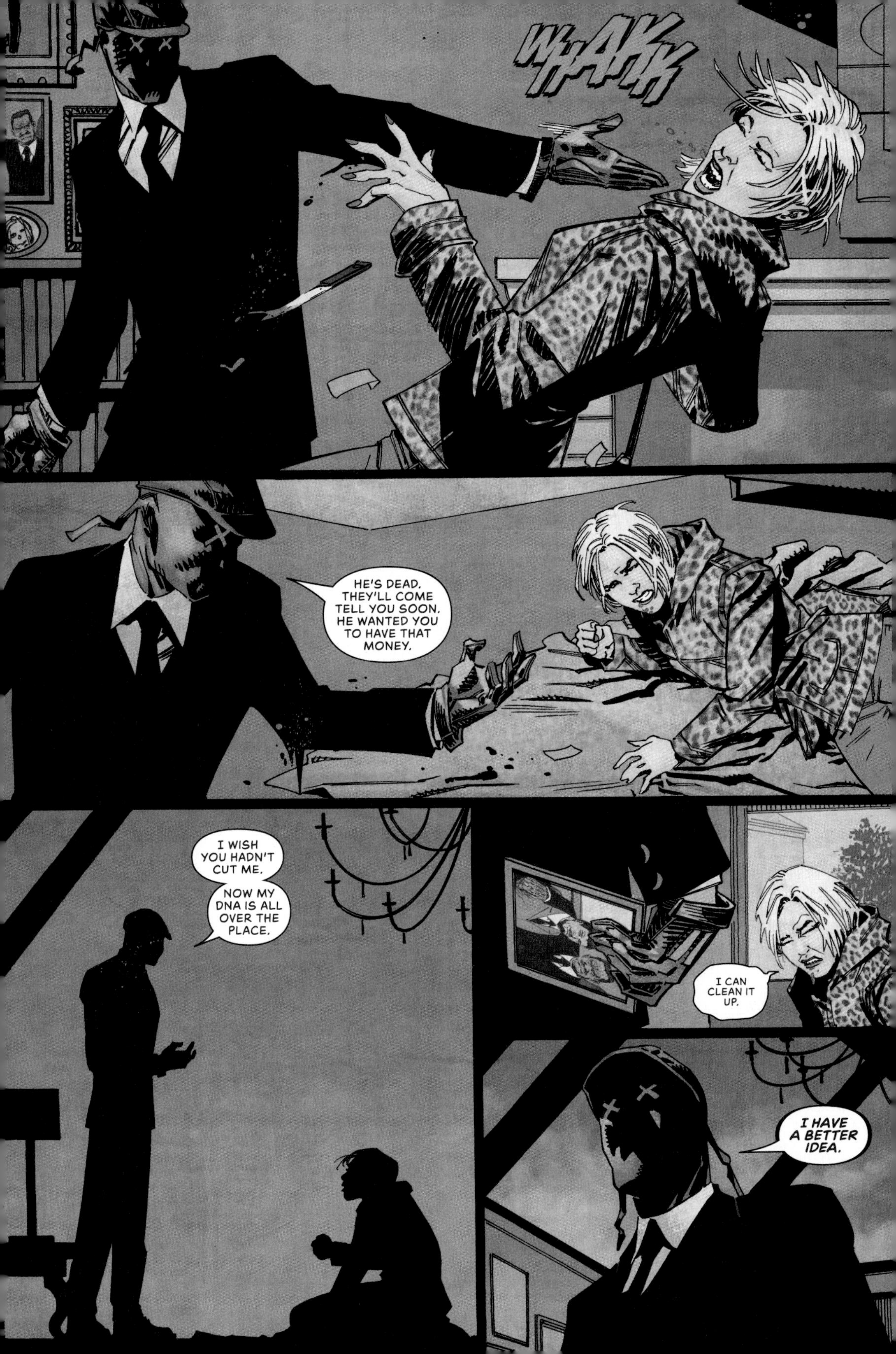
WHAK
HE'S DEAD. THEY'LL COME TELL YOU SOON. HE WANTED YOU TO HAVE THAT MONEY.
I WISH YOU HADN'T CUT ME.
NOW MY DNA IS ALL OVER THE PLACE.
I CAN CLEAN IT UP.
I HAVE A BETTER IDEA.

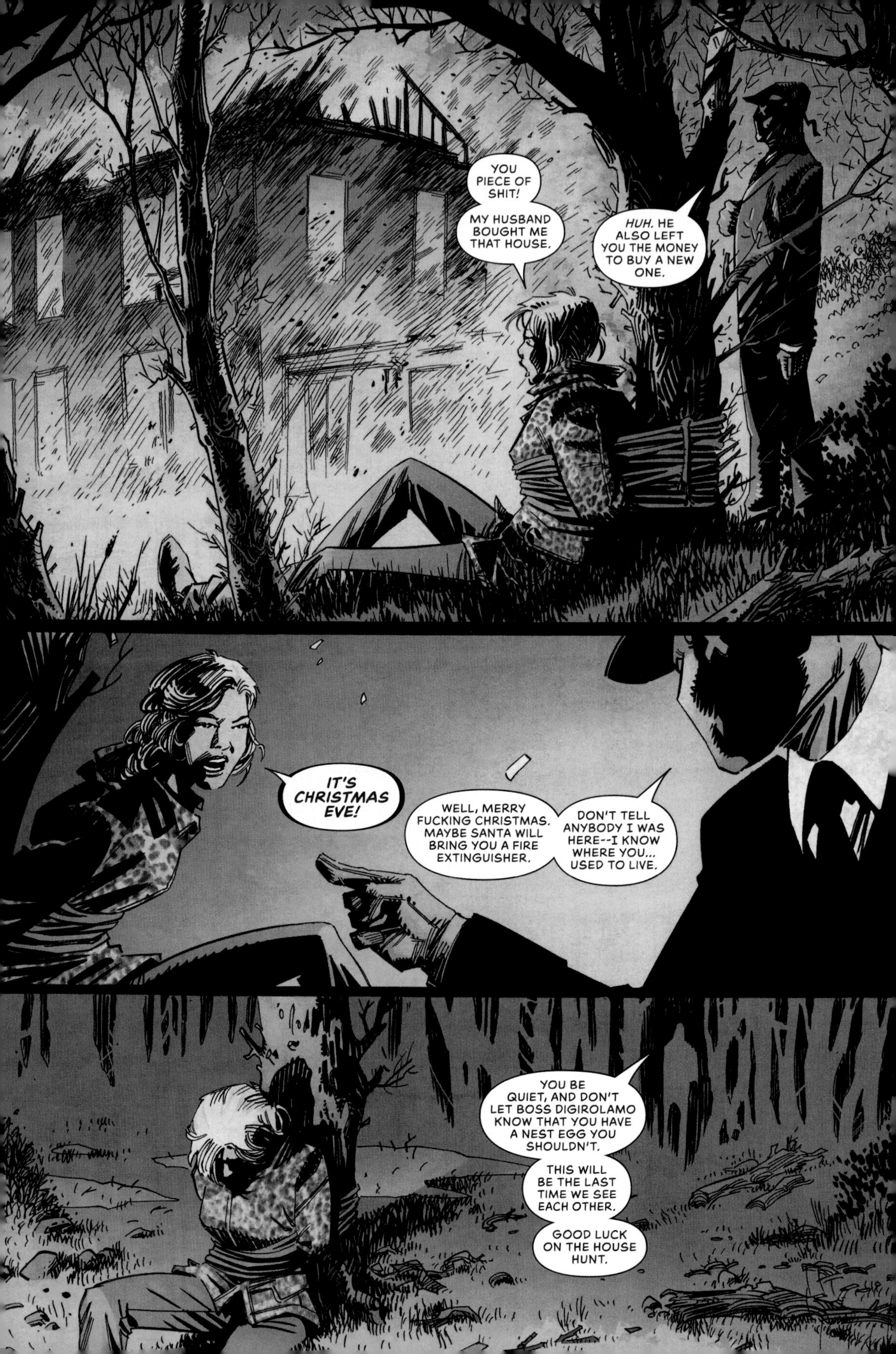
YOU PIECE OF SHIT!
MY HUSBAND BOUGHT ME THAT HOUSE.
HUH. HE ALSO LEFT YOU THE MONEY TO BUY A NEW ONE.
IT'S CHRISTMAS EVE!
WELL, MERRY FUCKING CHRISTMAS. MAYBE SANTA WILL BRING YOU A FIRE EXTINGUISHER.
DON'T TELL ANYBODY I WAS HERE--I KNOW WHERE YOU... USED TO LIVE.
YOU BE QUIET, AND DON'T LET BOSS DIGIROLAMO KNOW THAT YOU HAVE A NEST EGG YOU SHOULDN'T.
THIS WILL BE THE LAST TIME WE SEE EACH OTHER.
GOOD LUCK ON THE HOUSE HUNT.

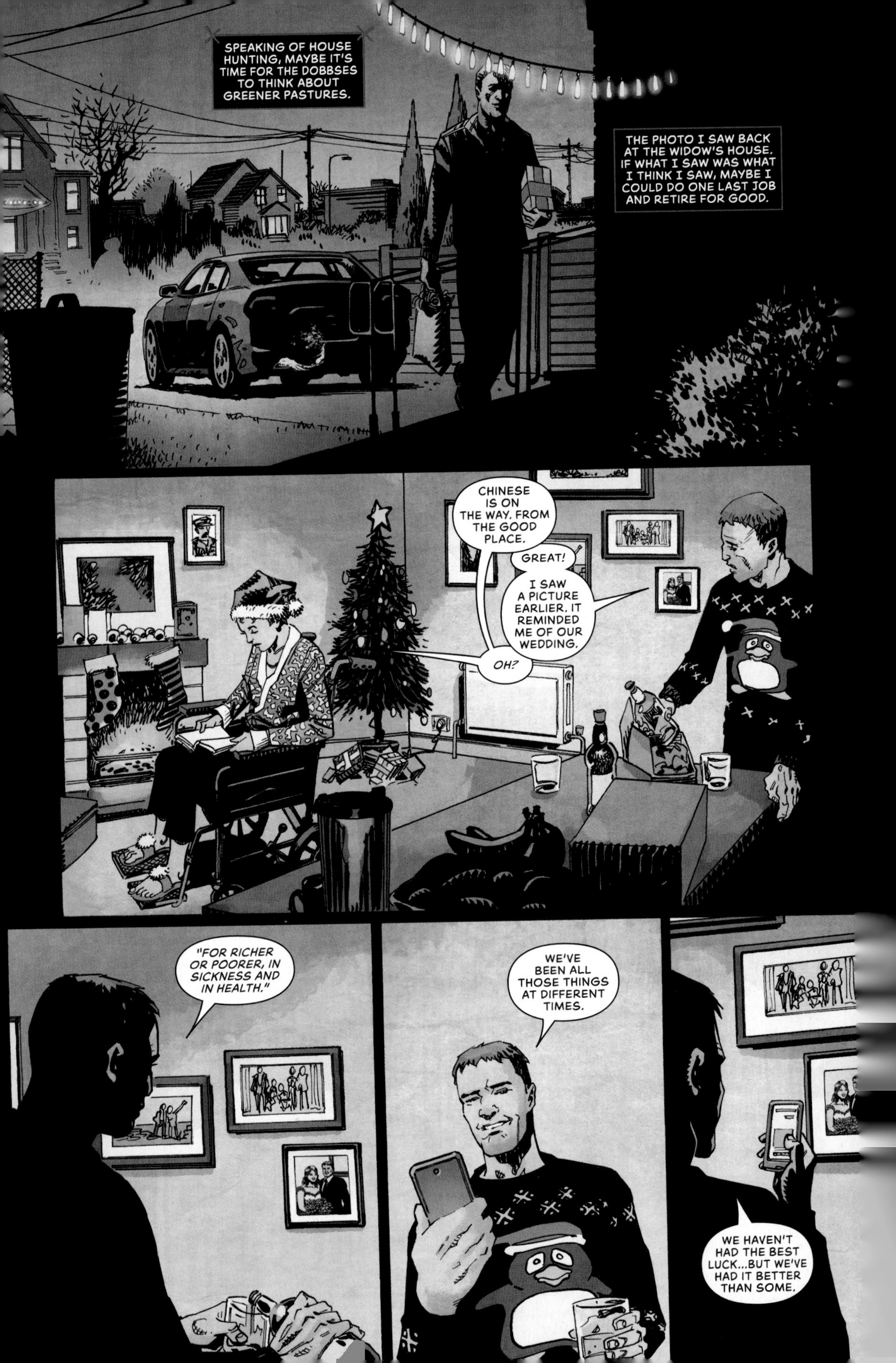
SPEAKING OF HOUSE HUNTING, MAYBE IT'S TIME FOR THE DOBBSES TO THINK ABOUT GREENER PASTURES.
THE PHOTO I SAW BACK AT THE WIDOW'S HOUSE. IF WHAT I SAW WAS WHAT I THINK I SAW, MAYBE I COULD DO ONE LAST JOB AND RETIRE FOR GOOD.
CHINESE IS ON THE WAY. FROM THE GOOD PLACE.
GREAT!
I SAW A PICTURE EARLIER. IT REMINDED ME OF OUR WEDDING.
OH?
"FOR RICHER OR POORER, IN SICKNESS AND IN HEALTH."
WE'VE BEEN ALL THOSE THINGS AT DIFFERENT TIMES.
WE HAVEN'T HAD THE BEST LUCK...BUT WE'VE HAD IT BETTER THAN SOME.

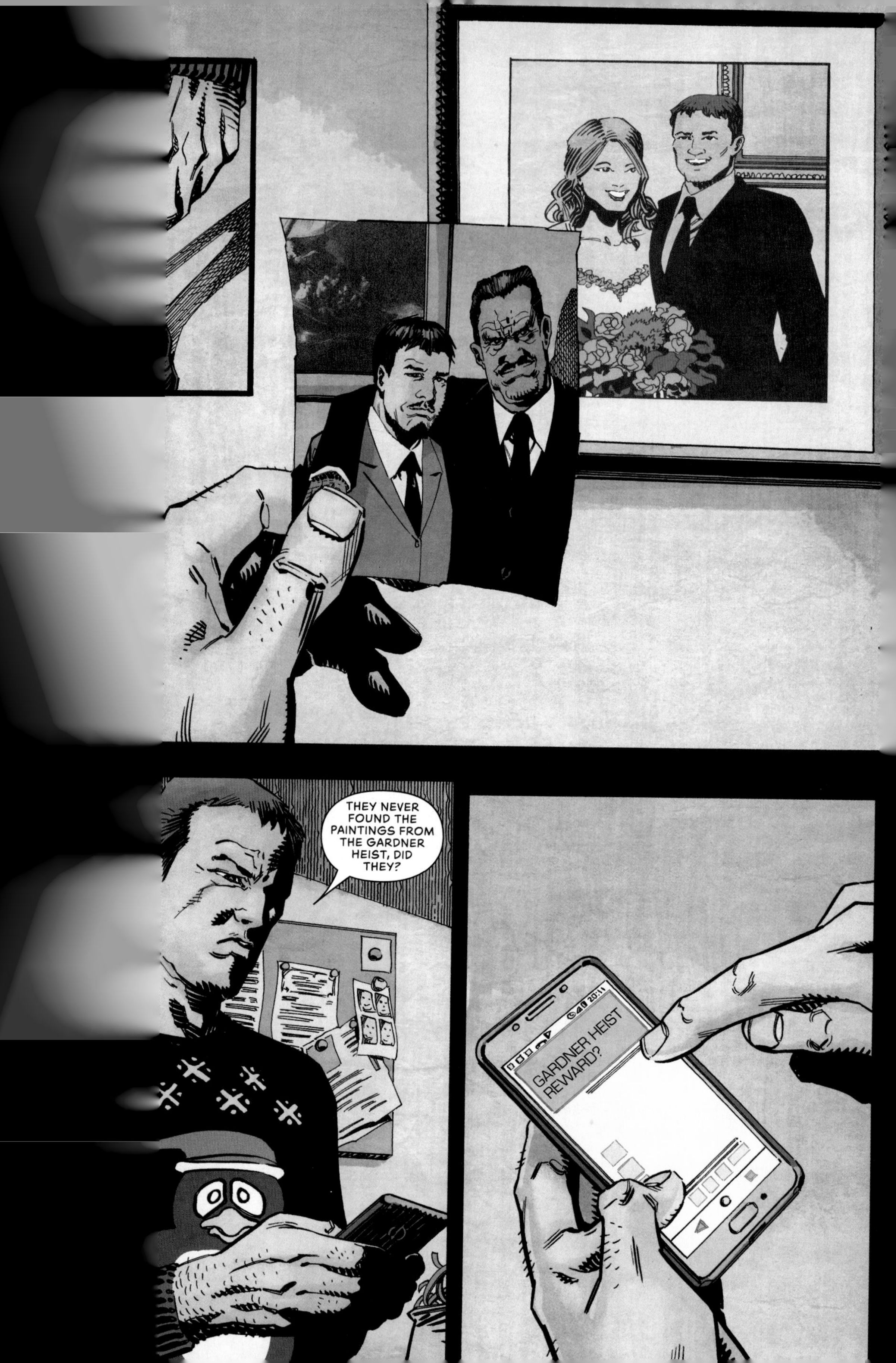
THEY NEVER FOUND THE PAINTINGS FROM THE GARDNER HEIST, DID THEY?
GARDNER HEIST REWARD?

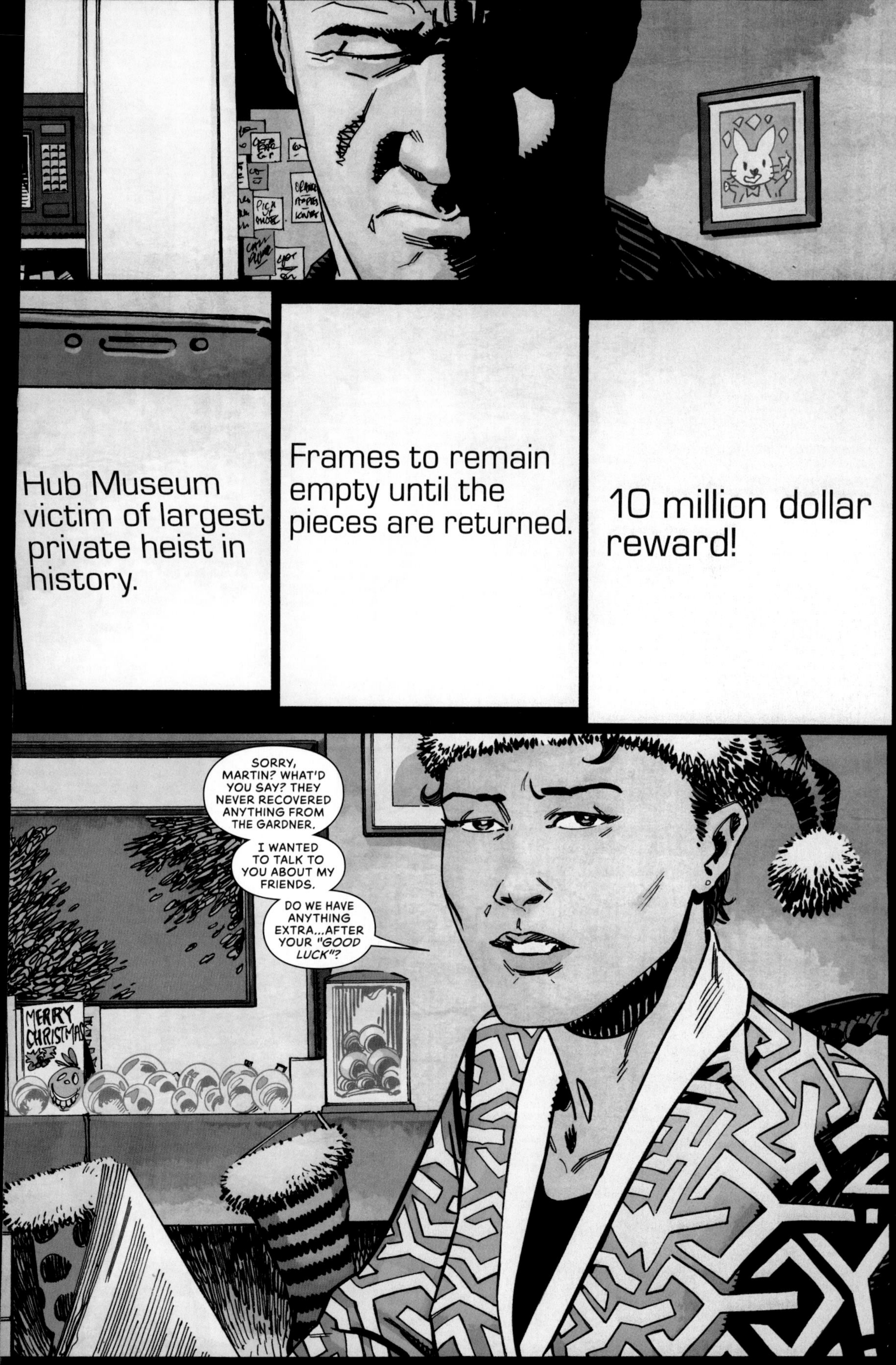
Hub Museum victim of largest private heist in history.
Frames to remain empty until the pieces are returned.
10 million dollar reward!
SORRY, MARTIN? WHAT'D YOU SAY? THEY NEVER RECOVERED ANYTHING FROM THE GARDNER.
I WANTED TO TALK TO YOU ABOUT MY FRIENDS.
DO WE HAVE ANYTHING EXTRA...AFTER YOUR "GOOD LUCK"?
MERRY CHRISTMAS

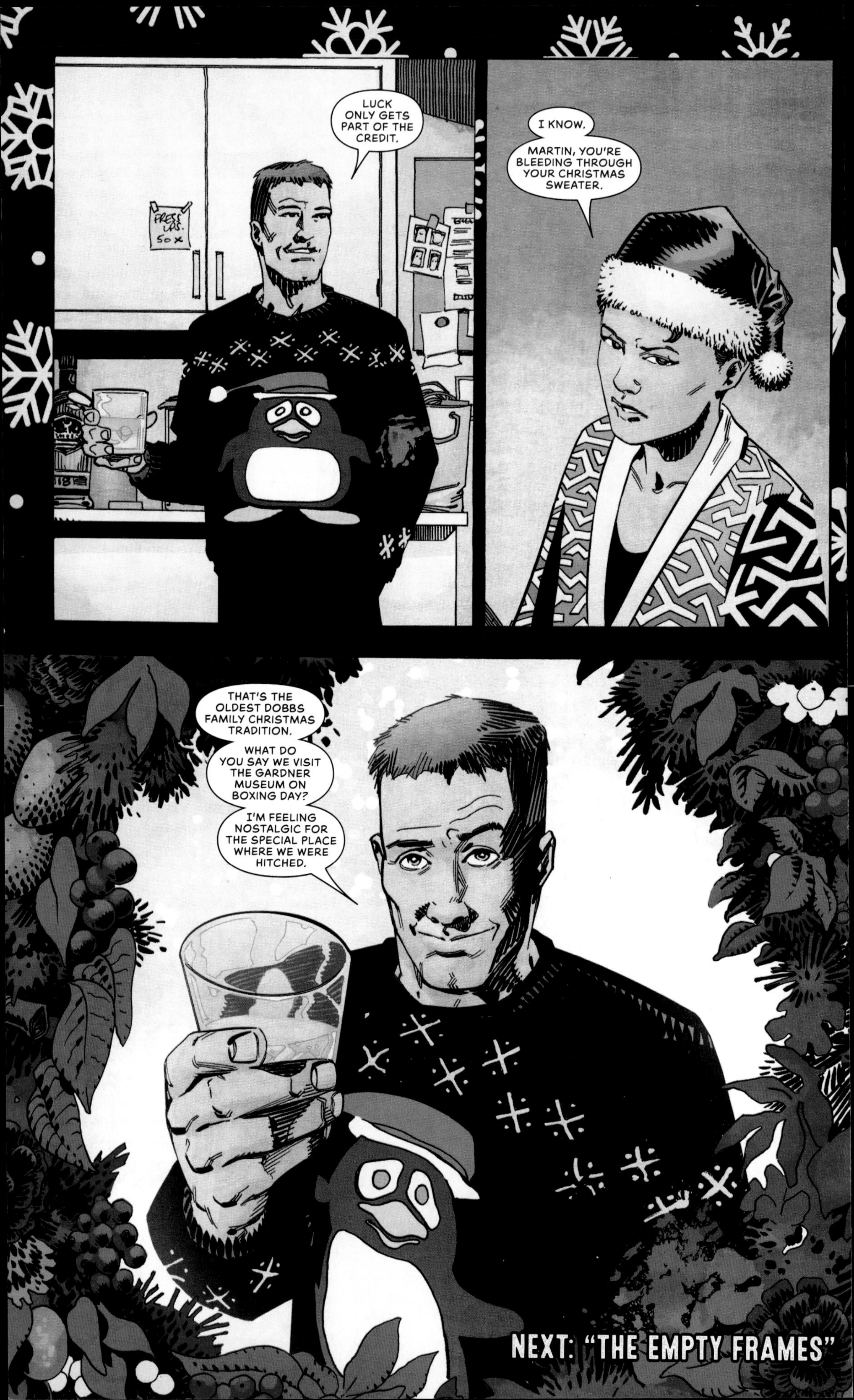

LUCK ONLY GETS PART OF THE CREDIT.
I KNOW.
MARTIN, YOU'RE BLEEDING THROUGH YOUR CHRISTMAS SWEATER.
THAT'S THE OLDEST DOBBS FAMILY CHRISTMAS TRADITION.
WHAT DO YOU SAY WE VISIT THE GARDNER MUSEUM ON BOXING DAY?
I'M FEELING NOSTALGIC FOR THE SPECIAL PLACE WHERE WE WERE HITCHED.
NEXT: "THE EMPTY FRAMES"

THE PROCESS

by John McCrea

I spent a lot of time redrawing panels (and whole pages) I wasn't happy with. Here are a few first tries that didn't meet the DEAD EYES standard...

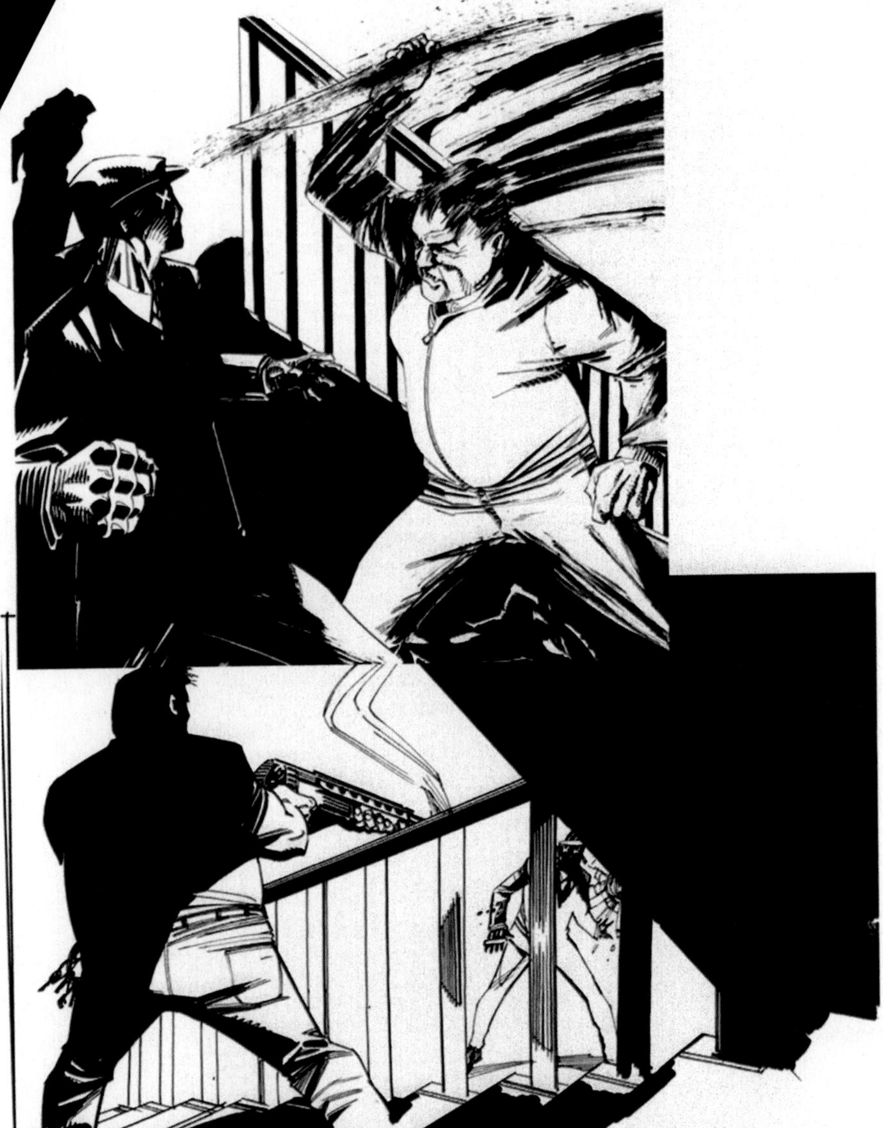

Figuring out the panel in my sketchbook—this is DEAD EYES' first big fight and I wanted it just right. I went through a lot of iterations to get the main panel on this page just as I saw it in the old mind's eye...

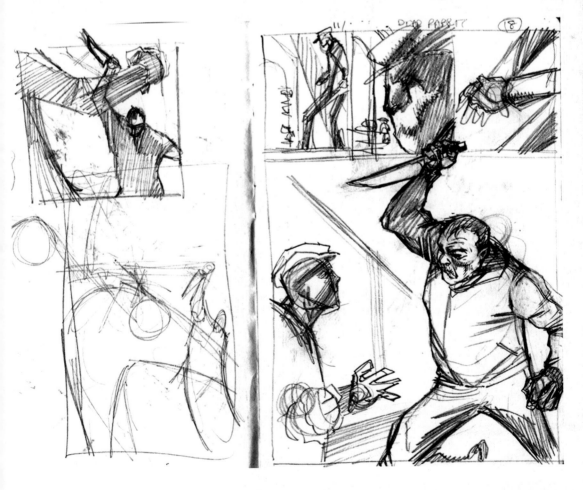

done as a mood board...

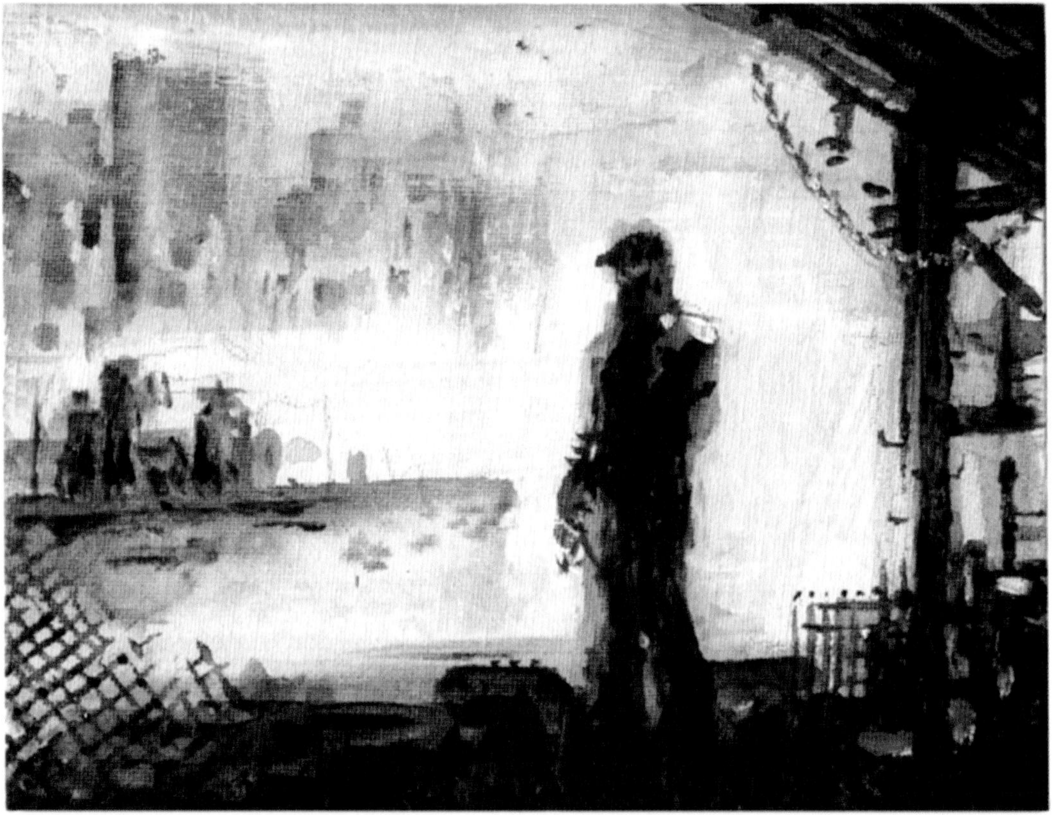

Early design work—my method was to chuck everything at it, throw away all the stuff that didn't work, and hope that I was left with a cool-looking character. The best characters are instantly recognizable with just the silhouette and one emblem—with DE it's the red crosses against that shadowed figure.

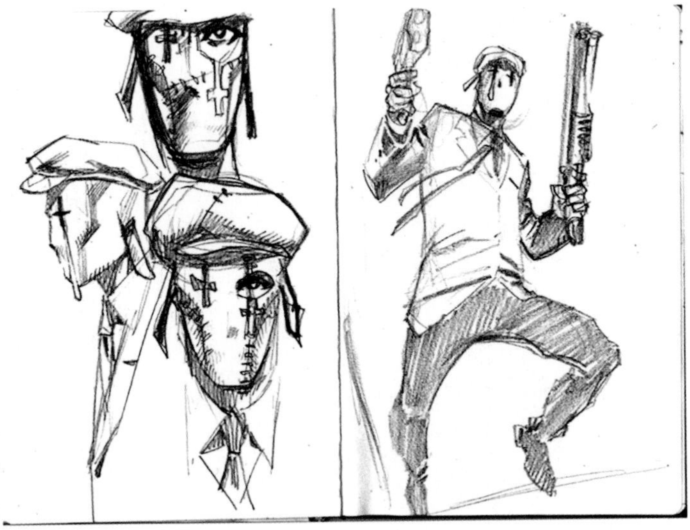

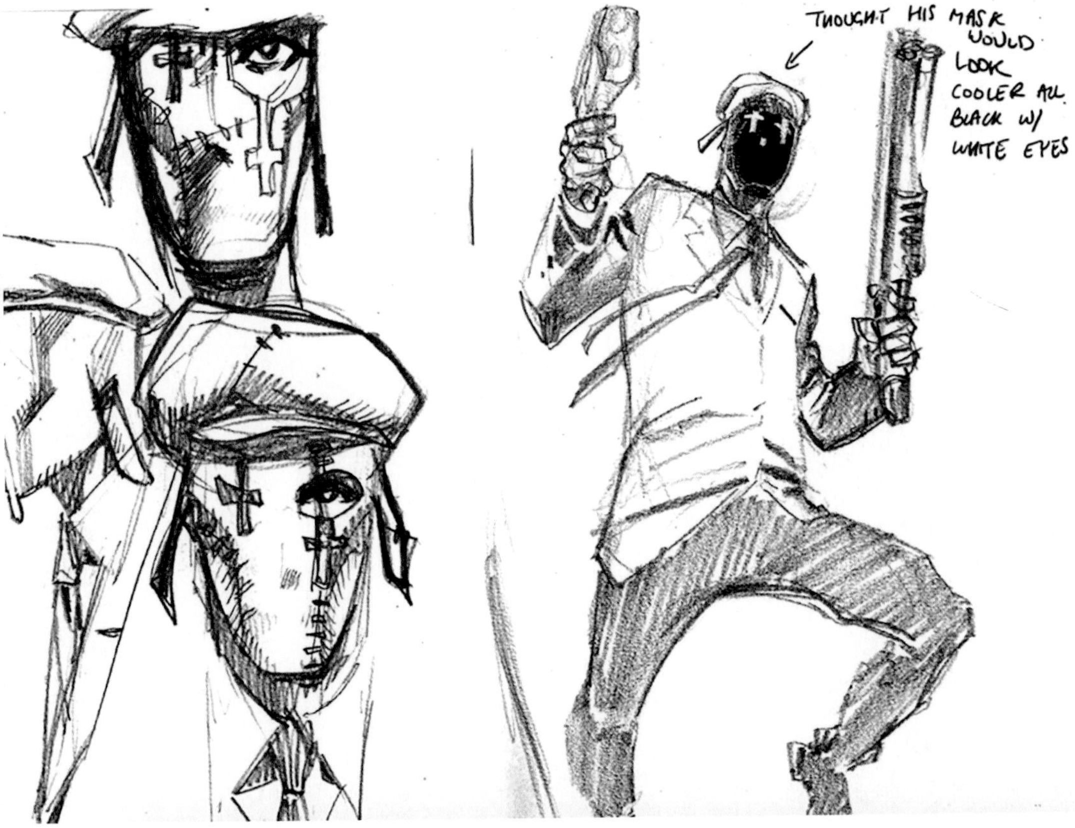
THOUGHT HIS MASK WOULD LOOK COOLER ALL BLACK W/ WHITE EYES

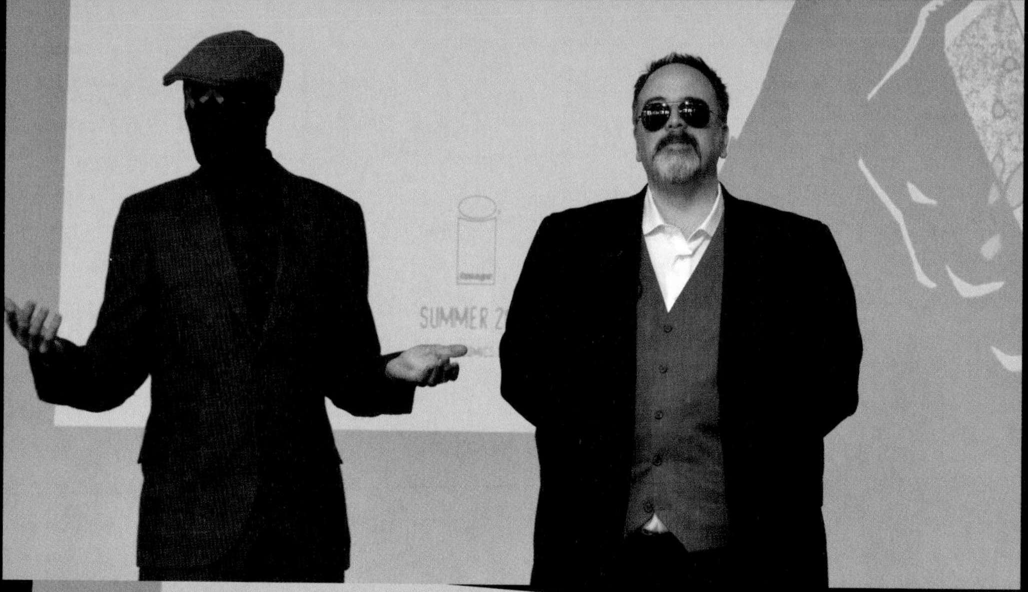

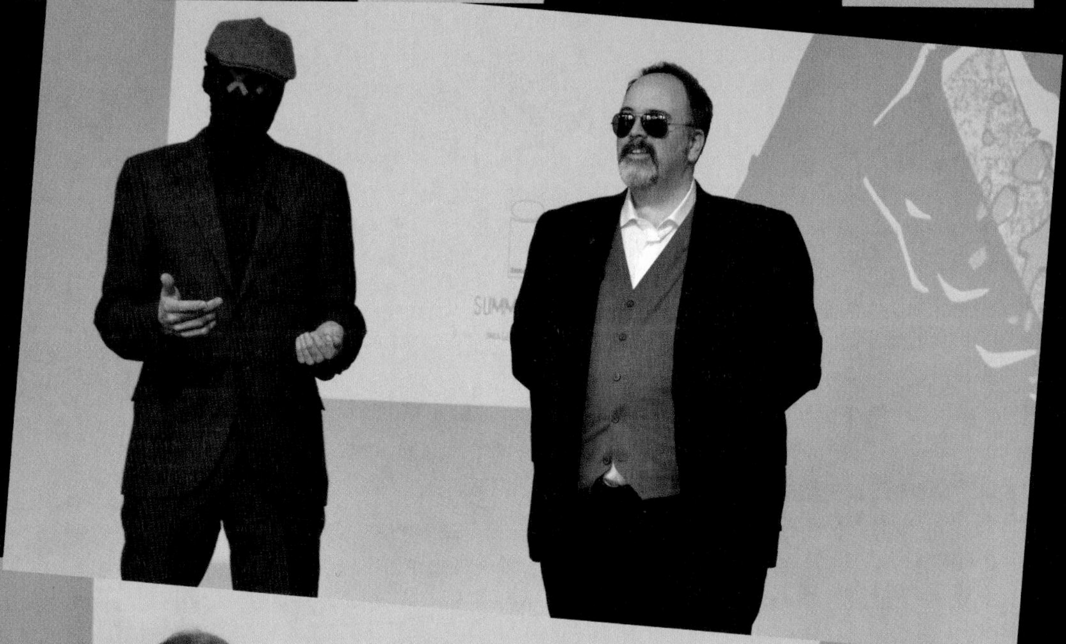

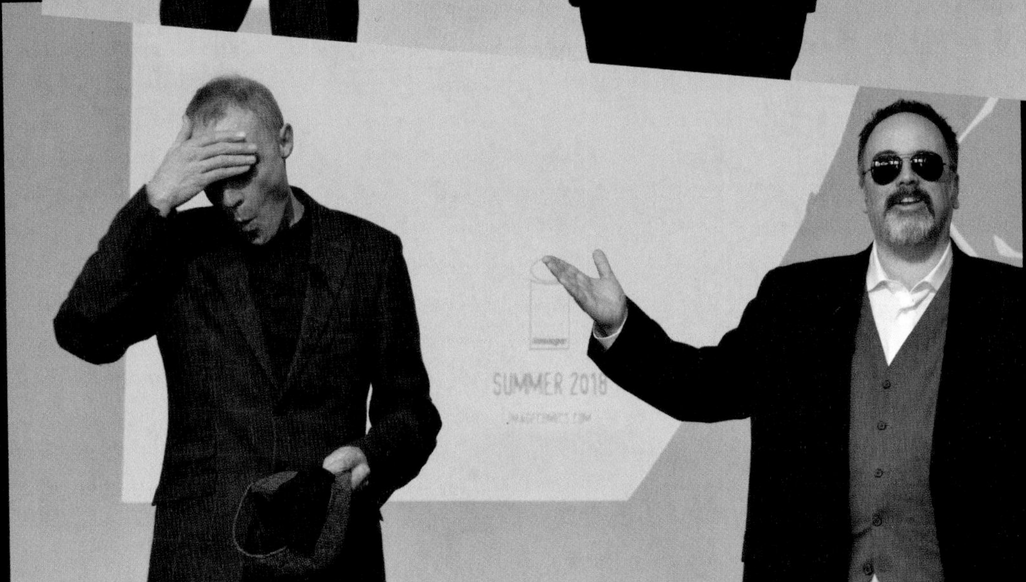
SUMMER 2018

JOHN

GERRY

DEAD EYES mask by Lizzy Jordan

photos by Deanna Phelps

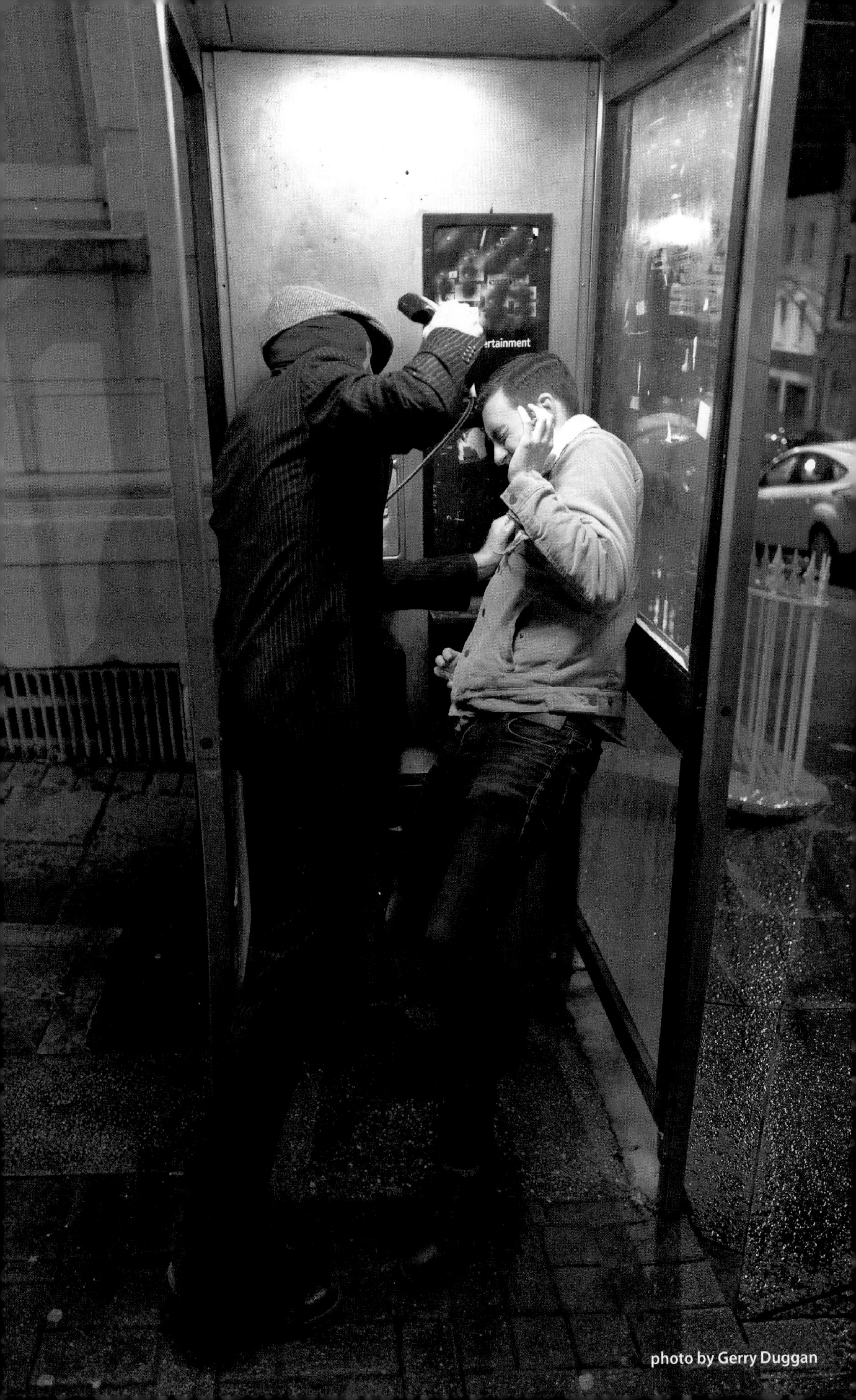
ertainment

photo by Gerry Duggan

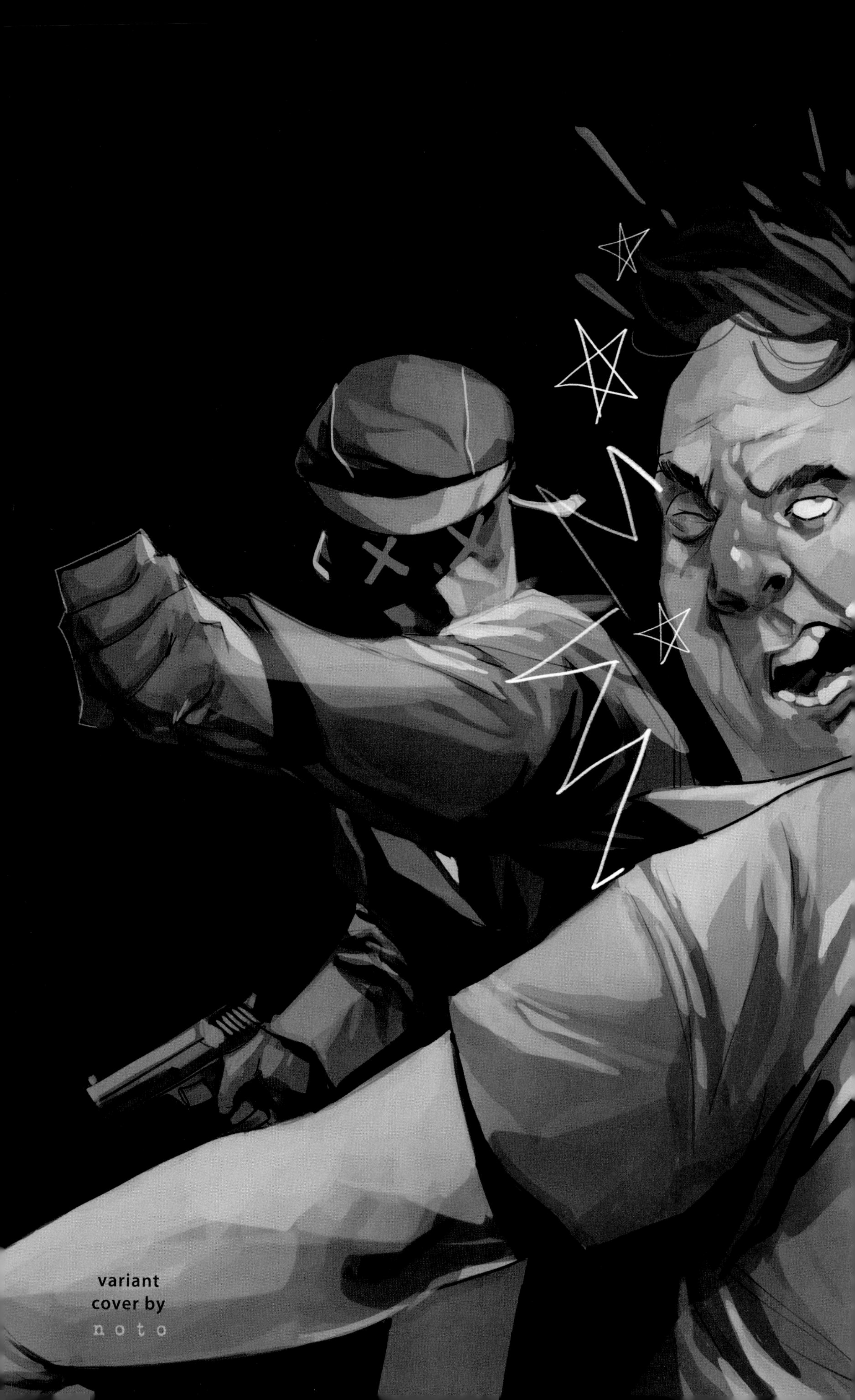

variant
cover by
noto

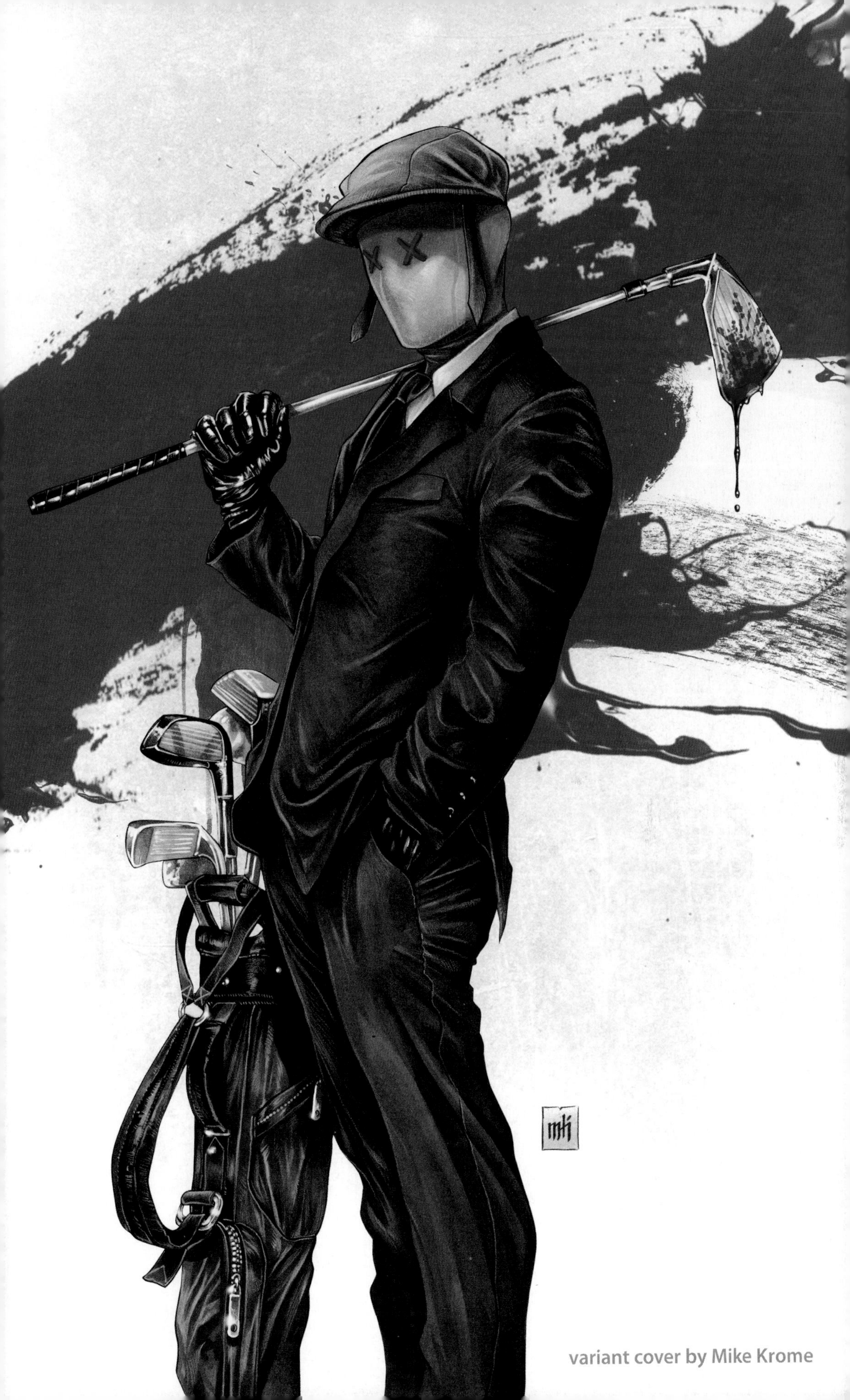

variant cover by Mike Krome

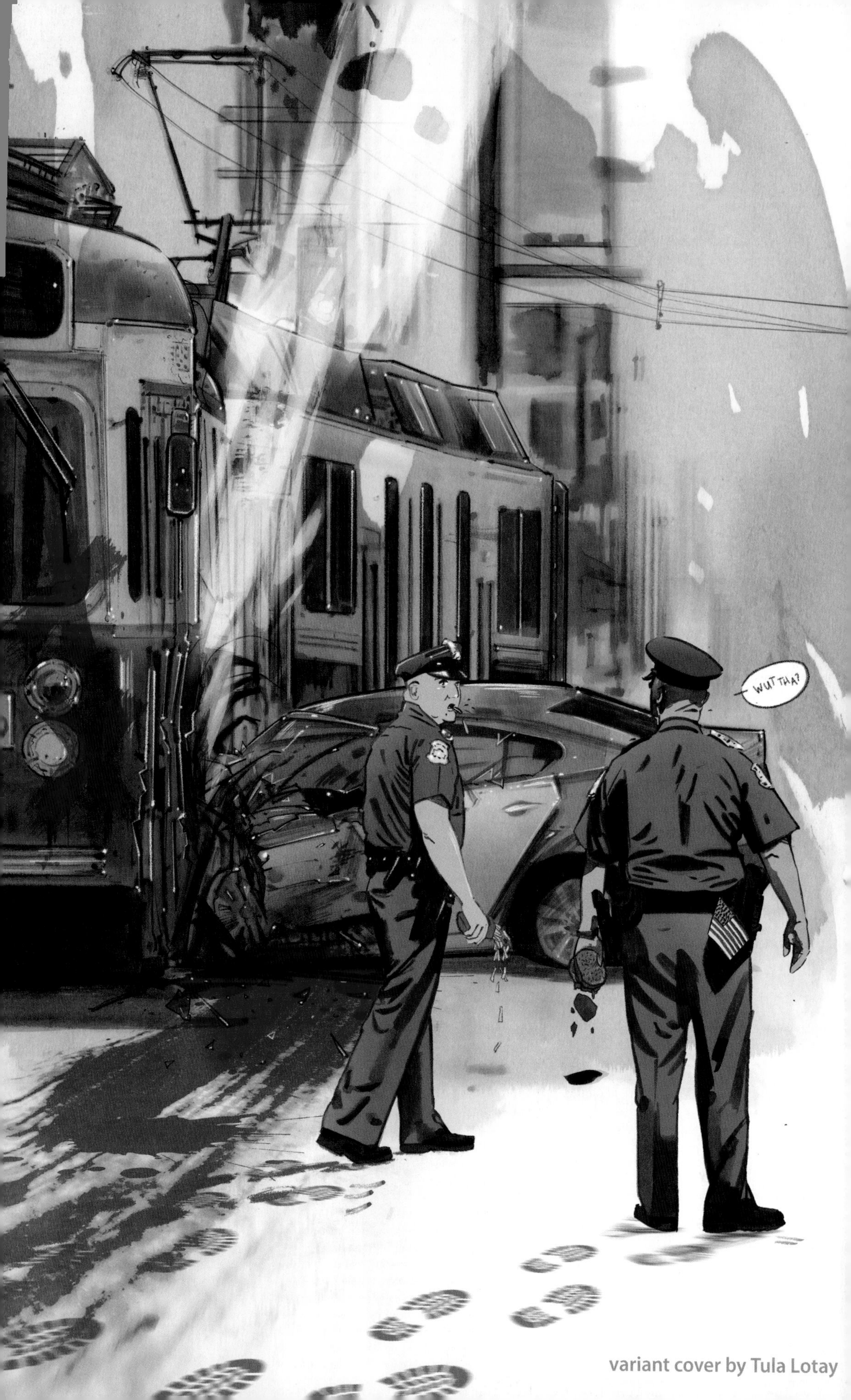
WUT THA?

variant cover by Tula Lotay

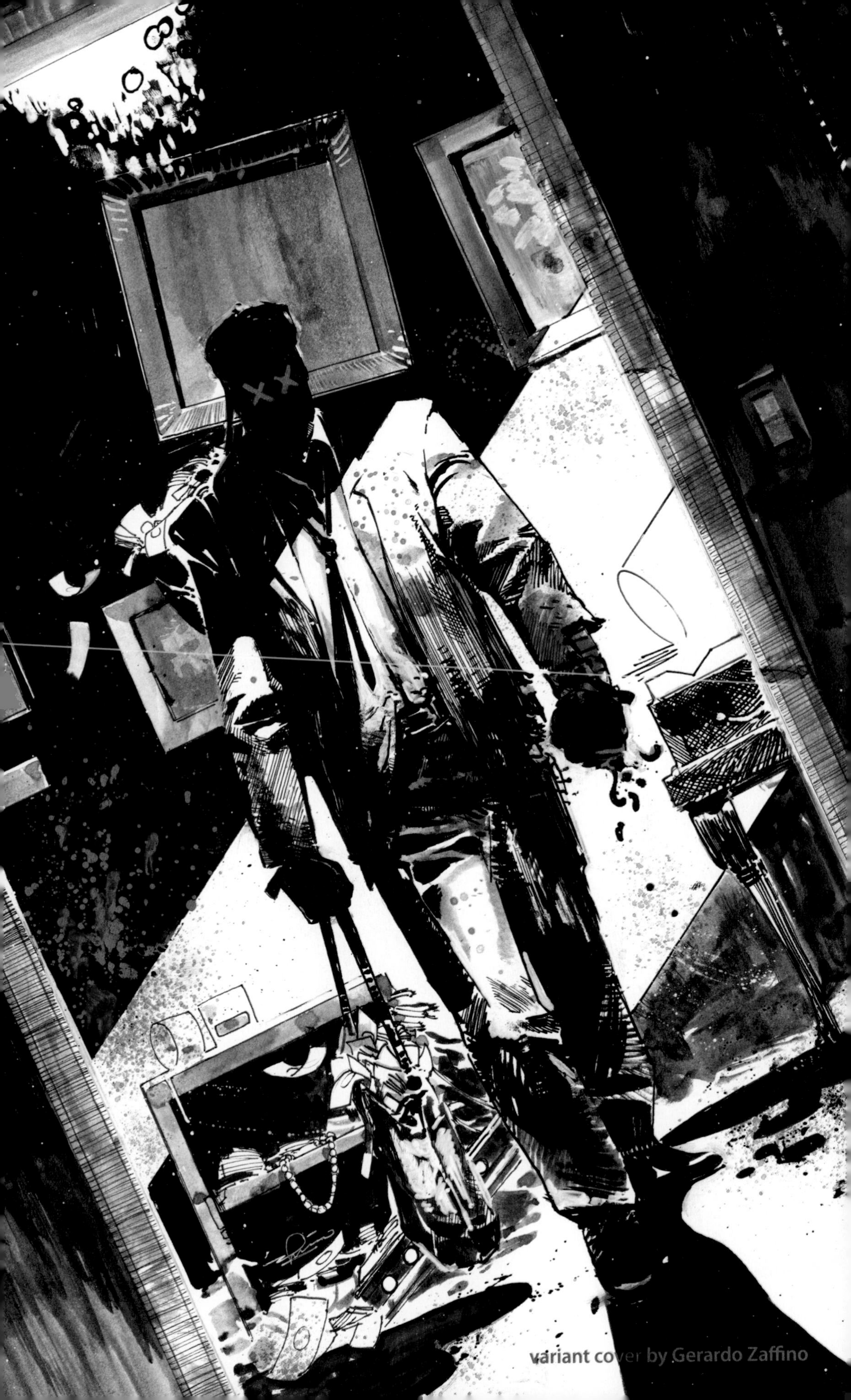

variant cover by Gerardo Zaffino

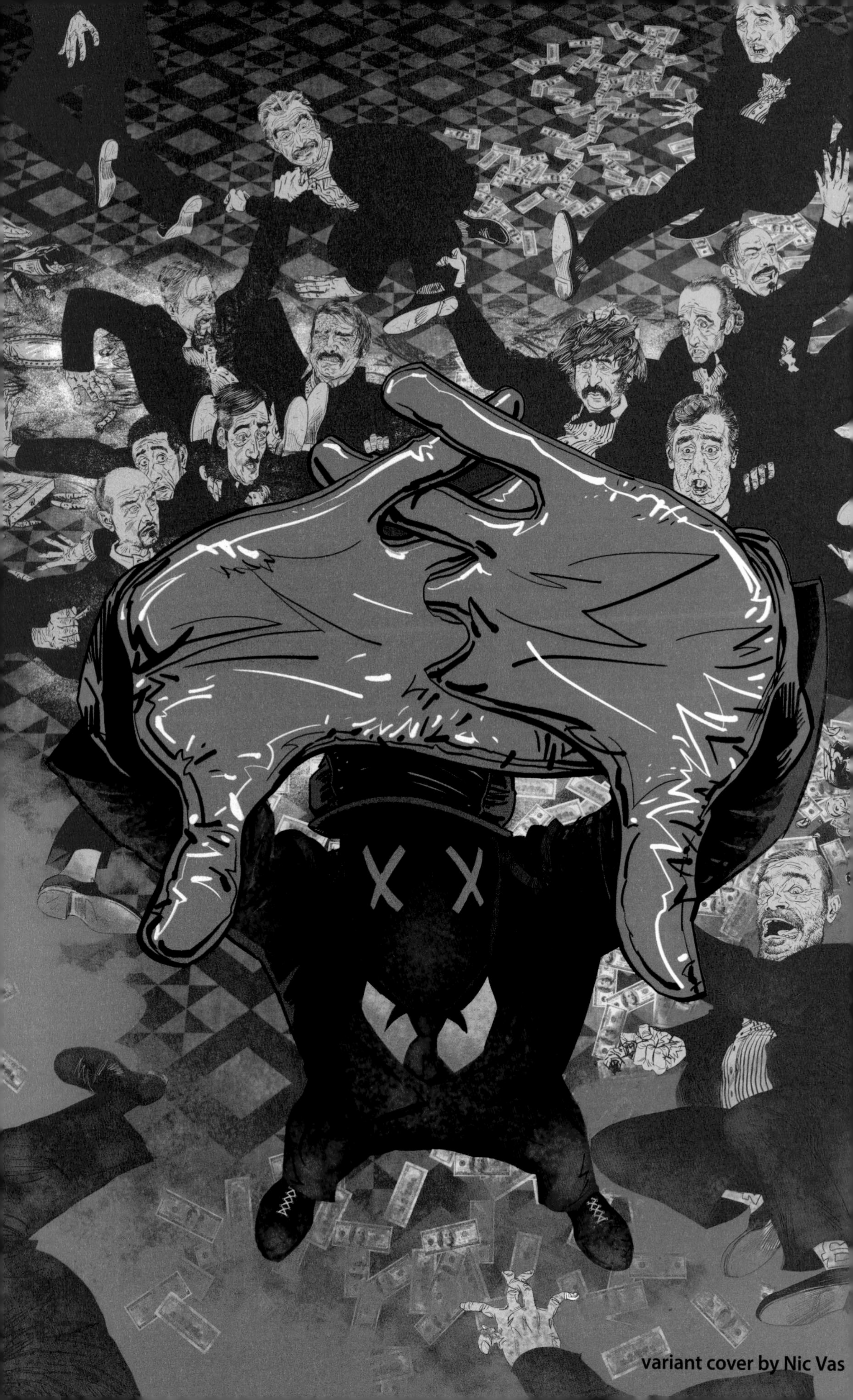

variant cover by Nic Vas

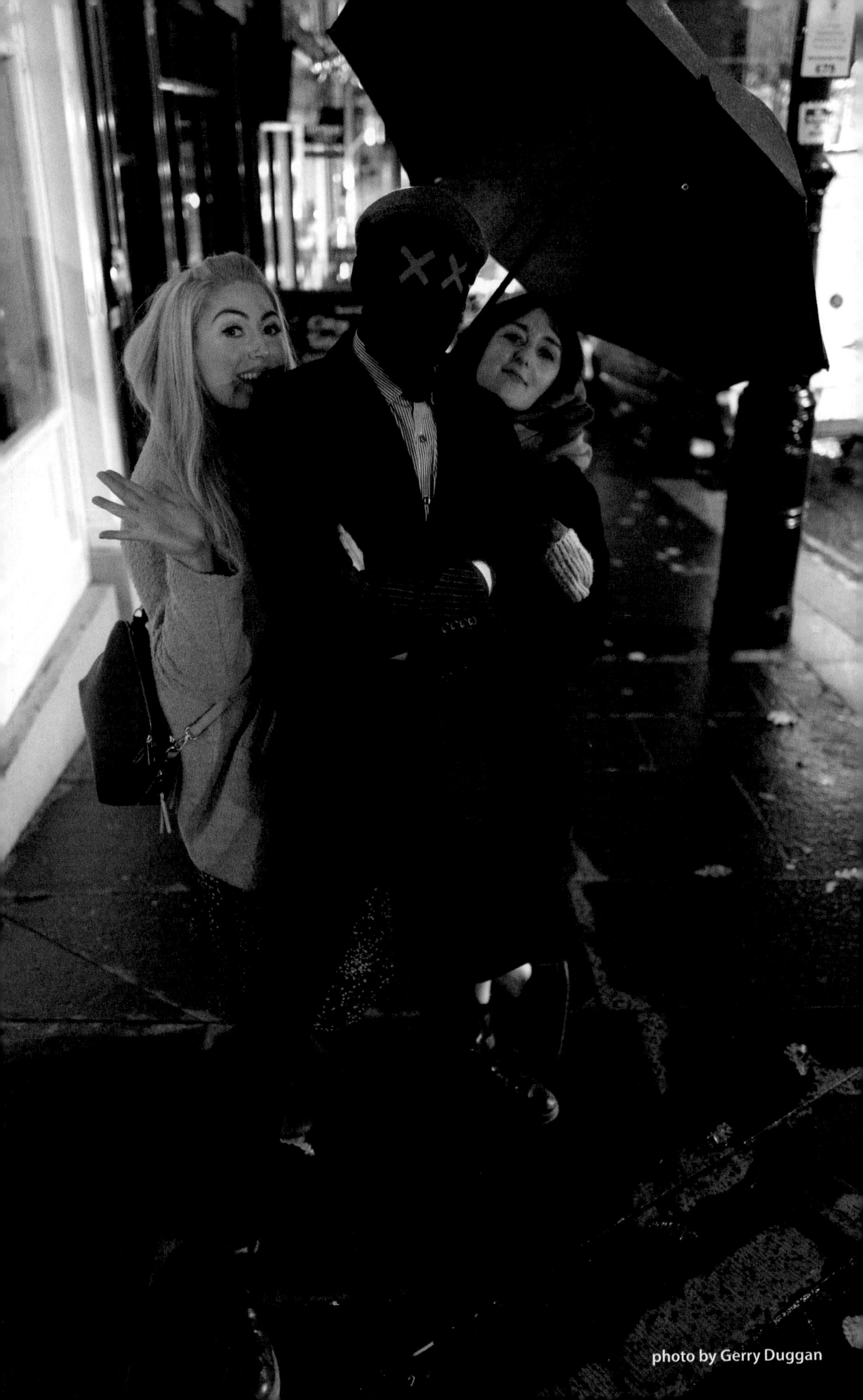

photo by Gerry Duggan